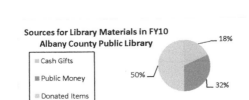

Sources for Library Materials in FY10
Albany County Public Library

- Cash Gifts
- Public Money
- Donated Items

18%
32%
50%

BETRAYER

DAW Titles by C.J. CHERRYH

THE FOREIGNER UNIVERSE

FOREIGNER
INVADER
INHERITOR

PRECURSOR
DEFENDER
EXPLORER

DESTROYER
PRETENDER
DELIVERER

CONSPIRATOR
DECEIVER
BETRAYER

THE ALLIANCE-UNION UNIVERSE
REGENESIS
DOWNBELOW STATION
THE DEEP BEYOND Omnibus:
Serpent's Reach | Cuckoo's Egg
ALLIANCE SPACE Omnibus:
Merchanter's Luck | 40,000 in Gehenna
AT THE EDGE OF SPACE Omnibus:
Brothers of Earth | Hunter of Worlds
THE FADED SUN Omnibus:
Kesrith | Shon'jir | Kutath

THE CHANUR NOVELS
THE CHANUR SAGA Omnibus:
The Pride Of Chanur | Chanur's Venture | The Kif Strike Back
CHANUR'S ENDGAME Omnibus:
Chanur's Homecoming | Chanur's Legacy

THE MORGAINE CYCLE
THE MORGAINE SAGA Omnibus:
Gate of Ivrel | Well of Shiuan | Fires of Azeroth
EXILE'S GATE

OTHER WORKS:
THE DREAMING TREE Omnibus:
The Tree of Swords and Jewels | The Dreamstone
ALTERNATE REALITIES Omnibus:
Port Eternity | Wave Without a Shore | Voyager in Night
THE COLLECTED SHORT FICTION OF C.J. CHERRYH
ANGEL WITH THE SWORD

C. J. CHERRYH
BETRAYER

DAW BOOKS, INC.

DONALD A. WOLLHEIM, FOUNDER

375 Hudson Street, New York, NY 10014

ELIZABETH R. WOLLHEIM
SHEILA E. GILBERT
PUBLISHERS

http://www.dawbooks.com

First Printing, April 2011.

1   2   3   4   5   6   7   8   9   10

DAW TRADEMARK REGISTERED
U.S. PAT. AND TM. OFF. AND FOREIGN COUNTRIES
—MARCA REGISTRADA
HECHO EN U.S.A.

PRINTED IN THE U.S.A.

To Joan and Buzz:
good neighbors, good friends.

Prologue

It was boring sitting by a sick person. But Cajeiri sat. And wondered if bullets counted as being sick.

He remembered the ship and his associates up in the heavens, and he wondered if Lord Geigi would keep his promise and help him find out if his letters ever got to the space station.

He remembered his two lost bodyguards and wondered how they were—if they were even alive.

He remembered Barb-daja, who had hair like nand' Bren's, like sunlight, and whom Great-grandmother thought a silly person. But Barb-daja had been very brave, in her odd way. And she didn't deserve to be kidnapped. He had been, once, but he was clever, and the kidnappers had had no luck at all. Barb was not as tough, and she had no way at all to talk to anybody who asked her questions. She could just say "Bren" and "Toby," and then somebody might figure out what she was saying, and that would not be good.

He thought about his mother and father, off in Shejidan. They were going to have another baby. But he was not going to let that baby be better than he was.

He hardly knew his father and mother. They had given him to Great-grandmother, and he had gone off to space to grow up, well, as grown up as he was, and they hardly knew him, either. So he had to prove to them that he was the best and the smartest and the quickest. He would prove that to everybody, when he got a chance.

Mostly, right now, though, he had to keep his promises. And he had given nand' Bren a promise. And even Great-grandmother had to respect it.

He sat. And sat. And even did his homework and read the book on protocols, which was so dull that sitting was exciting.

He waited. Which was all he could do, day and night. He slept, his bodyguard slept by turns, and they just waited.

1

There was a sleek red and black bus parked out on the lamp-lit drive, outside this magnificent administrative palace in the heart of Tanaja, in the Taisigin Marid. That bus held a number of the Assassins' Guild, armed with guns and explosives, and it held itself as a private fortress, surrounded by local forces—who as yet had not moved against it.

In the relative peace and quiet dark of the upstairs suite in the palace, in the baroque bedroom with its four-poster that Bren Cameron occupied, thick velvet draperies masked its lack of windows. It was black as the depths of a cave. And there was no way to tell the time except by his pocket watch on the side table, the lighted display of which said it was just before dawn.

At least there had been no gunfire, no alarms from his body-guard, or they would have notified him. The peace had officially lasted through the night. Tensions might be a little less now that nerves had had time to settle.

For which he was sincerely grateful.

Getting out of bed—still in the dark—was its own trial. A large bruise had spread across his chest, and he knew he had to put the compression wrap back on and, worse, put on that damned bulletproof vest again. He'd almost rather be shot without it, but the risk of that actually happening was still far too high.

He was human, an official in the service of the atevi, who owned most of this planet. He was, in the course of that service, on the southern coast, a guest in the house of the enemy, with no assurances that hospitality would continue.

He had come to negotiate with the lord of the Taisigin Marid, a district virtually at war with the Western Association, the aishidi'tat, which he had come to represent—if one counted the aiji-dowager, the grandmother of Tabini-aiji, as officially equivalent to Tabini-aiji himself . . . and Ilisidi clearly counted it that way. Ilisidi, the aiji-dowager, had considered it a good moment to make a radical move and had told him to take that shiny red and black bus and get over here, where *no* official of the aishidi'tat had ever set foot. His mission was to talk to Machigi, who had never actually seen a human, and persuade him *not* to go on expanding his power to the west.

The whole Marid district, the Taisigi, Senji, Dojisigi, Sungeni, and Dausigi clans, who were supposed to be part of the aishidi'tat, had never been tightly joined to it. They had conducted assassinations on the west coast for years, and recently they had sponsored an attack on Bren's own coastal estate at Najida and on his person at neighboring Targai—hence the painful bruise.

Thus far Machigi, lord of the Taisigin Marid, the master of this house, this city, this district, had been willing to talk to him. But he had no assurances that mood would last. Machigi was a young autocrat who ruled a fractious, faction-ridden clan in a local association that had always gone its own way, and nothing was guaranteed.

But Machigi was also in a bit of a bind with his neighbors to the north, the Dojisigi and the Senji, who were making a bid for power, which was why the aiji-dowager had thought it a smart move to send one Bren Cameron to conduct more or less clandestine talks with Machigi.

Bren set his feet on the floor and went in quest of the light switch in this windowless room. Knocked into a table he belatedly remembered.

Found the door.

Found the light switch.

He had left his two valets across the tenuous border at Targai. He could call servants from Machigi's household, but he
opted not to do that; he didn't want Machigi's people inside
this suite of rooms any oftener or any longer than absolutely
necessary.

Lights went on, brutally bright. He squinted, went in search
of clothes, and was very glad someone—in his exhaustion yesterday he could not remember who, but definitely one of his
four bodyguards—had at least opened his baggage last night and
hung his wardrobe to shed its wrinkles.

Investigation of the top bureau drawer proved someone had
put his linens, his gun, and his shaving kit where he liked to
have them. Probably Tano. Or Jago.

He hoped his bodyguards, next door to this room, were finally getting a little sleep. He had no wish to disturb them at
this hour asking where his socks had gone.

He had fallen asleep last night without his evening bath . . .
a scandal in itself. A hot bath this morning was unutterably
attractive—and there existed that uncommon luxury for atevi
guest quarters, a private bath and private accommodation down
the inner hall of their suite, instead of down a common hallway and shared with every resident on this floor. There was a
servant's access in the same inner hall; his staff had fixed that
door, so that was not a security issue.

So he could feel safe in that hall, and a bath was beyond
attractive—it was diplomatically necessary. Humans smelled
odd to atevi, especially after a day or two—vice versa, too, but
he was a minority of one here, in a place that had never seen a
human. So that was item one on his list, in an uncertain day.
Light from the bedroom gave him light enough in the hall to
get to the bath and turn that light on.

The bath provided a curious little one-person tub, quite unlike the communal bathing facilities in every great atevi house
he had yet visited, and more like, at least in principle, what he

would expect on his native island of Mospheira. It was atevi-scale, large for a human, a quickly filled little step-down tub—one stepped onto the seat and then down into the tub, then threw the lever to block the drain, threw another to admit hot water, which came out steaming, and then threw a third to mix in cold water just in time to save one's toes from scalding.

He settled down as the water rose around his ankles. He let the bath climb fairly rapidly to his chin—a foot short of the top of the atevi-scale tub. The water steamed pleasantly in the cool air, and he shut off the flow and leaned his head back and shut his eyes.

The heat embraced the sore ribs and eased the pain. He could stay here, oh, indefinitely.

But he had left his bed because the thoughts that had started to circle through his head had not been conducive to rest.

And now back those thoughts came, the moment he shut his eyes.

It was not quite accurate to say he was the first human to visit Tanaja. In fact, he was, by an undetermined number of hours, the second. Barb, his ex-lover and currently his brother Toby's partner, had shown up in his suite last night.

Barb had been kidnapped from Najida, where Toby still was.

Barb, by the grace of his host, had arrived here apparently unharmed.

She had arrived that way. She'd hit the floor hard last night. His bodyguard, specifically Tano, had had to stop her from a move that could have gotten them all shot—Machigi's guards were on a hair trigger and were unused to emotional outbursts from excitable humans—and one hoped she was not concussed.

Barb had taken her situation pretty well, considering. She might not understand everything that was going on, but she had understood she was not in a friendly place and had shut up. She wasn't conversant in the language. She'd been unable to communicate with anyone to any extent; and being Barb, she'd be vastly upset until she could talk to someone.

He had acquired, besides Barb, Veijico, a very young member of the Assassins' Guild, who didn't belong to him . . . in any number of senses. Veijico's assigned lord was Tabini-aiji's son Cajeiri, aged eight, who was back at Najida, presumably safe, presumably well, in the care of his great-grandmother, the aiji-dowager.

Which was where Veijico ought to be. But when Barb had been kidnapped, Veijico and her partner Lucasi had taken off in hot pursuit of the kidnappers—and Veijico had gotten herself caught by Machigi's forces, right along with Barb.

Complicating matters—as if matters wanted more complication—Veijico's equally young partner, Lucasi, another Guild Assassin, was armed and missing somewhere out in the wide rolling hills beyond Tanaja.

And one could only hope the kid didn't shoot anybody in Taisigi territory while the diplomatic mission was in progress. Bren's best current hope was that Lord Machigi's men would be able to intercept the young man without getting shot or shooting him—which might not be easy, given Lucasi's state of mind—or that Lucasi, in a sudden burst of mature judgement, would realize he was in over his head and take himself back to the safety of Targai, where he could get help and advice from senior Guild.

But rely on youthful ambition to do that sensible thing?

It hadn't prevailed so far.

And now he had two houseguests cluttering up his diplomatic initiative.

Their host, Lord Machigi, might or might not have been responsible for kidnapping Barb in the first place. Machigi had very generously handed over Barb *and* Veijico when he arrived. But that was no promise of good will. Lord Machigi was certainly responsible for a good deal else, including assassinations and a widespread scheme to dominate the whole west coast.

And Bren Cameron, paidhi-aiji, translator and negotiator, was supposed to turn this all around.

What gave just a little leverage to the plan was, as the aiji-dowager suspected, the very strong possibility that Lord Machigi had *not* kidnapped Barb, had *not* installed a deadly mine on a public highway in Najida district, and was *not* behind the latest assassination attempt on him at Targai.

In fact, Lord Machigi had had his own problems—notably his neighbors, the Senji and the Dojisigi. Machigi was a young lord who had sprung onto the scene relatively recently, pushing the usurper, Murini of the Kadagidi, to power in Shejidan—and maintaining his power when Murini went down. All through that period he had refused to be respectful of the more senior lords of the Marid, who had just assassinated his predecessor; and now, far from assuming a quiet posture after Murini's demise, Machigi had made independent moves to expand his territory to the long-desired West.

One had no idea how much of the ensuing mayhem in the southwestern corner of the continent was all Machigi's action and how much was his neighbors' trying to get ahead of the energetic young warlord they had unwittingly put in power.

It was highly likely that Guild had mined a public road and kidnapped a minor who was a civilian, two very illegal acts, according to the rules of the Assassins' Guild, acts that would get both the perpetrators and the lord they served outlawed. The Guild leadership back in Shejidan was proposing to outlaw Machigi and any Guildsman who served him—a very bad situation for Machigi—on the assumption Machigi had ordered it.

It was one thing for a lord to be Filed upon by someone in particular, like a rival; that meant a small number of the filer's Assassins might go out with Guild-granted license to take him out.

It was quite another for a lord to have himself and all his bodyguard as well as the perpetrators of the offense outlawed by the Guild; that meant that any and every Guildsman alive, of any house whatsoever, was directed to execute the offenders *and* the lord who had directed them—on a priority above any other assignment in their local district.

The aiji-dowager, on the other hand, had judged Machigi had *not* been responsible for either act. She was trying to get the Guild action stopped, no mean feat, so that her emissary, namely Bren Cameron, could talk to Machigi.

In point of fact, the actions at Najida were as obvious as a bloody handprint left on somebody's front door—too damned obvious, too clumsy, and too many violations all at once, a score of handprints laid all over Machigi's operations in the West. Somebody had gone overboard in his attempts to get Machigi in hot water.

And who would both be that reckless of the welfare of the public on the west coast and be likely to profit from Machigi's demise?

There was a short list, comprising the four other lords of the Marid, particularly the two in the north: Senji and Dojisigi.

But even *that* was not the scariest prospect. The disjointed character of the several attacks argued for a lack of central authority, several groups operating at once.

Letting the Guild Council proceed with a declaration of outlawry might have solved the Machigi problem quite nicely—and permanently—except that one of the two likeliest lords behind the trouble would immediately move into the power vacuum, filling the space Machigi had created in the cosmos.

And of those two, neither would be strong enough to keep any sort of peace, even inside the Marid. One would quickly assassinate the other, successors would rise up, the south would split from the north—again. The whole region would be in ferment—again. And whoever was temporarily in command of the Marid might attack the west coast, trying to snatch the power that Machigi had almost had; or he or she might just start a general war with everybody in reach, including, possibly, Tabini-aiji and the rest of the continent.

The whole matter trembled on the edge of chaos, right at a

time when the continent was just settling down from the last Marid-sponsored event.

Peace was the least likely outcome once the five clans of the Marid spiraled into a power struggle.

As it had recently, reaching even into the midlands of the aishidi'tat and causing death and upset right into the capital.

So here he sat, Bren Cameron, paidhi-aiji, up to his neck in hot water again . . . on a diplomatic mission without precise instructions, in a spur-of-the-moment move . . . because the aiji-dowager had seen things about to go to hell and proposed to save Machigi, of all people on the planet, from imminent outlawry and assassination.

Would Machigi be grateful if she succeeded?

Machigi was suspicious of gifts from outside. Who wouldn't be?

But Machigi was curious. Curiosity drove the young warlord, perhaps even more than ambition. And he had never seen a human. Those were two things Bren had on his side.

And besides the company of an unofficial sister-in-law ex-lover, a stray junior Guildswoman with a death wish, and a busload of much more senior Guild armed with explosives out in the driveway—none of which he counted as assets—he had his own aishid with him, his four-person senior Guild bodyguard, experienced in delicate situations, and *that* was the best asset he held. His bodyguard were still armed and still in contact with that busload of the aiji's finest outside; and both those facts were reassuring about Machigi's mood of the moment.

His bodyguard had gotten him in here safely. They had made all the right moves. They had talked their way in. They had kept the situation from blowing up, despite a Filing of Intent by Tabini-aiji against Machigi personally.

He hoped that everybody was getting a little deserved rest at this hour.

Not quite so, however. He heard a footstep in the hall, in

this back end of the suite where no stray household servant of Machigi's should come at this early hour. He froze. Listened.

It cost him a few seconds of doubt, wondering if perhaps he should get out of the tub or, conversely, sink under the surface and pretend not to be here.

A glimmer of gold eyes appeared with a substantial shadow in that doorway, in just the hint of features: Banichi, senior of his bodyguards, wearing his black uniform pants and nothing more. Black-skinned, gold-eyed like all atevi, and head and shoulders taller than a tall human, he filled whatever space he was in.

"One is very sorry to have waked you, 'Nichi-ji," Bren said. "Go back to bed. One is just soaking in the heat."

"Breakfast will arrive within the hour," Banichi said. "We have just had a notification from staff. One might advise you eat last night's bread this morning, Bren-ji, if you have any concern for its safety."

"One takes it then that Lord Machigi does not expect me for breakfast?"

Banichi walked entirely into the bath and stopped, arms folded, a looming shadow. "One rather believes the lord may be consulting with his advisors this morning," Banichi said quietly. It was a dead certainty the place was bugged and that every word they spoke was being listened to and parsed for hidden meaning. He had been too long in atevi politics to have any doubt of that at all.

Would their host take offense about his staff's caution with the breakfast? Hardly an uncommon worry in an atevi household—and it was no secret at all that humans reacted adversely to the alkaloids atevi quite relished in a sauce. Thus far the local kitchen had been quite careful not to poison him, and one was certain staff had talked to staff and reminded Machigi's people of the problem.

But who knew which cook was on duty at this hour?

Still—a hot breakfast—tea. He really wanted hot tea.

And, alas, no meeting. Machigi was, as Banichi surmised, very likely doing business of some kind this morning. One only hoped his host was not preparing to eliminate the bus from the driveway.

But that, like all other aggressive acts, such as doing in his guest, would have been safer done last night, in the dark.

"We do need to make our several phone calls," Bren said. "As soon as it is some decent hour, and when I have contact, I shall hope to get clearance from Lord Machigi."

"Yes," Banichi said, and that was all. Excluding any meeting with Machigi himself, there were two very urgent items of business on their day's agenda.

First on the list was calling someone who could get those Guild deliberations officially suspended before the Assassins' Guild laid down a formal declaration of outlawry on paper; that would require *another* meeting to rescind, and meanwhile Machigi would be in imminent danger.

Second was calling on Tabini-aiji, head of the aishidi'tat, the Western Association, to rescind his own Filing of Intent with the same Guild, and table the current assassination order *he* had out against Lord Machigi, binding on any one of the men on that bus in the driveway. The two items were unrelated. The Guild Council action was because of infractions of Guild rules, of which Machigi might actually be innocent. Tabini's Filing was in general annoyance with Machigi's existence and a reasonable conviction that Machigi had been behind various assassinations and attempted assassinations, of which he probably was *not* innocent.

As far as communication with Tabini's local agents to be patient—the Guild on the bus had been under Banichi's orders, as senior of the paidhi-aiji's bodyguard. The need to restrain those very dangerous agents from upsetting the situation was why the paidhi-aiji had set out on the bus in the first place. His presence had put Banichi in command of the aiji's men, the paidhi-aiji being a court official—yesterday.

Now, however, with him and his bodyguard off that bus and up here, command had reverted to the seniormost of Tabini's people, and that could be no secret. Tabini's officer was a sensible man, but the situation out there in the driveway remained a very delicate one. The wrong move, the wrong information, somebody's assumption, or just some suspicious movement of, say, the gardener or a delivery truck near that bus—and the whole district could blow up.

District, hell. They could have a continent-wide war on their hands if he didn't get those two phone calls through fairly soon, and he had counted on being able to talk directly to Machigi about that problem this morning.

So Machigi's failure to invite him to breakfast had become a complication in his day. They had to get permission via Machigi's staff and hope somebody was willing to go high enough to get a yes.

Beyond that—beyond that—the paidhi had some urgent thinking to do . . . involving how far to go with Machigi and how much to promise to keep Machigi interested in talking.

He had had Machigi's attention yesterday. But Machigi was a young man. His interest could collapse without notice. Advisors could get to him and persuade him the dowager's proposals were not in his interest.

And then they all were in trouble.

"Help, here, 'Nichi-ji, before you go." Getting into the sunken bath was easy with bruised ribs. Getting out . . .

He lifted a hand, and Banichi came over to the tub and gave him the leverage he needed. Against atevi stature, he was only the size of an eight-year-old, a light and easy lift up to footing on the seat of the tub, and safely back up onto the ridged tiles that gave sure footing around the edge of the bath. There was a large towel on the rack; Banichi offered it, and Bren gratefully wrapped himself in it, trying not to shiver, since shivering hurt.

"One has to shave," he said to Banichi, rubbing his chin. Atevi didn't have that problem, and he had always felt he did that operation with a surer hand than his valets. "And I can dress myself, Nichi-ji. I can manage quite well with everything except the queue."

"I shall be back to assist, Bren-ji, in about that time."

Banichi left him, to go see about their business. Bren shaved, using the sink, then walked back to his room and dressed, slowly and carefully, in clothes that could, indeed, have used the services of a valet . . . but they were all right, under difficult circumstances.

He found his pain pills in his personal kit and popped two, dry. He was in less pain than yesterday evening, but that had been a high-water mark of discomfort.

Dressed to the waist, he wrapped the compression tape around his chest, which afforded a curious combination of pain and relief, protecting him against shocks or an injudicious stretch. He was just trying to fasten the bandage when Banichi showed up and quietly finished the job.

"Boots,'" he said, " 'Nichi-ji, if you will help me with that. Bending hurts."

"Yes," Banichi said, and helped him sit down on the bench, then knelt down and helped him on with the boots. Banichi, big, broad-shouldered even for an ateva, went on playing valet and brought him the shirt hanging foremost of the three he had. Banichi helped him on with that while protecting it from his damp hair with a towel about the shoulders.

"I am worse than a child," Bren said. "I take far more tending."

"Your bodyguard has great and personal sympathy," Banichi said, running a comb through his damp hair, preparatory to braiding it. "The ribs, one expects, will be sore for a number of days."

"It was a stupid act," he said, "on my part. One can only apologize for it."

Banichi deftly parted his hair for the queue and began the braid tactfully without comment. Banichi finished it in a matter of moments, and tied it with the ribbon waiting on the bureau, a fresh one, the white of neutrality, the paidhi's color. That white ribbon, more than guns, more than reinforcements, was the major protection they had—for what it was worth in this place, where he clearly represented the hated north to a lot of citizens of the Marid.

Banichi helped him stand up, then provided the bulletproof vest, brocade on the outside, and with one notable breach in its integrity. It looked to close from the front, but it didn't; it overlapped at the side. It was stiff, it was hot, and while it did not weigh much, it got heavier, over the hours.

At least, once fastened, its close embrace provided support for abused muscles—or would, until the muscles grew tired of being supported and restricted. The pain wasn't as bad as it had been last night. No misery could be as bad as it had been last night.

He put on his lighter coat with Banichi's help. And Jago came in—Banichi's partner, only a little shorter than Banichi—in black tee and uniform pants.

"We are all awake, Bren-ji," she said, meaning Tano and Algini as well. "Breakfast will arrive soon."

"Excellent," he said. "I shall do very well, now, for myself, Nichi-ji. Thank you."

Jago was Bren's lover, when they were not under hostile observation. She had slept last night in Banichi's room, and she appeared immaculate as usual despite the lack of her uniform jacket. Armed? Yes. Always.

Even the paidhi carried a pistol at times. At the moment it still resided in his dresser drawer, where one of his bodyguard had placed it. Weapons about the person of Guild were universally expected—but a concealed pistol in the pocket of a member of Tabini-aiji's court—that could make Machigi's security justifiably nervous.

So he left it there today and trusted his staff—little good he could do anyway in his condition. He took the left-hand door of his bedroom, which opened onto the sitting room, an elegant room of light greens and pale furniture. It was a very comfortable arrangement, with a fireplace, chairs, a table, a couch—

And two sleeping figures occupied that couch, one black-on-black, Guild-uniformed, leaning on the left arm of the couch; on the right arm, another, pale-skinned, with a mop of blonde curls, sleeping in a russet gown.

Young Veijico, to her credit, was not that far asleep. She lifted her head immediately as the door opened and got up fast, despite a rough couple of days.

Not as hard a couple of days as Barb had had. Barb was asleep, a matter of some worry as she had taken that nasty crack on the head last night.

"Nandi," Veijico said in a low voice—caught, in plain fact, drowsing, when she had been assigned to keep Barb awake as long as seemed needful. "One has not been negligent. The lady stayed awake into the early morning."

Veijico was in a difficult position with him and with his bodyguard. True, she had doggedly tracked Barb and a handful of kidnappers—kidnappers who now were dead, thanks to her. It would have been *extremely* significant to world peace had Veijico had the least clue for him as to what clan the men belonged to. But she hadn't.

Had she recognized their accents? No, she hadn't heard them. Barb had. Unfortunately, Barb couldn't tell a Padi Valley aristocrat's accent from a Marid fisherman's.

Had Veijico any clue as to whether the men she had shot were Guild at all?

Yes, but she didn't recognize any of them. Had she seen them up close? Well, no. They'd fallen, and pretty soon after that, they'd been captured by more Guild.

There were a lot of points in which Veijico had performed both extraordinarily bravely and a great number in which she had created some serious problems. Veijico was on very thin ice with Jago in particular—who did not approve much of Barb, either.

But the latter was on personal issues.

Barb had stirred at the sound of voices and muzzily opened her eyes and sat up, raking a hand through her curls. She looked scared for a second, and then her eyes lit on Bren. There were little sun lines around those eyes—there hadn't been when Barb had fancied herself his fiancee. She had married someone else. Then divorced. Now she was his brother's sailing partner—grown wind-worn and tanned; and Bren felt an uncommon tenderness toward her, considering the predicament, which was *not* wholly her fault, and the sore skull, which was. But Barb seemed to accept it was her fault, and she hadn't complained.

"How's the head?" Bren asked her in Mosphei', the human language.

Barb felt her skull, and winced. "Miserable headache," she said.

"I'm not surprised at that." He came and perched aslant on the farther arm of the couch, the one Veijico had left. "There's a bath down the hall, all our own. A little tub. I recommend it."

Barb was always slow waking up. Suddenly she blinked, and looked at Veijico, across the room, and at Banichi and Jago, and at him. "Are we all right?" she asked.

"Still all right. I promise you. Go wash up. Are you all right to walk?"

She nodded, winced, and levered herself stiffly to her feet. Veijico looked uncertain what to do at that point, whether to go with her.

"You may wait here, nadi," Bren said. "The lady will manage."

Barb walked toward the door, managed, in passing, to lay a hand on his arm, which he was sure nobody—particularly Jago—missed. A human gesture. But human gesture that it was, Barb wasn't just *any* human, and Jago's view of that little gesture was not benevolent: Jago knew Barb, oh, too well. There was past history. A lot of it.

He didn't forget that history, either, though he viewed Barb with more tolerance than previously—so much so that he could interpret that touch as a thank you, not possessive, not even consciously done. She'd been brave, she'd been sensible throughout—

Well, except when the shooting had started back at Najida. She'd run up the sidewalk, by all reports, probably screaming at the top of her lungs, which had landed her very conspicuous blonde self in the hands of atevi kidnappers . . .

. . . who might or might not have been Taisigi clan—the clan of their current host.

God, he wished Veijico, who'd been tracking them, had some knowledge of Marid clans, enough to know the origins of the men she'd shot.

At least she'd had the sense to surrender Barb on the spot and wait for negotiations.

Which was his job. The sun was up, beginning to shine beyond the heavy curtains of windows that didn't overlook anything close or useful—and after the miracle of their surviving getting in here, and recovering Barb and Veijico, now came his business: actually getting them all out of here alive.

He very much wanted his morning tea, a hot drink, a space of quiet contemplation. He wanted a place to sit and not have to be in charge of things for at least an hour while he got his wits together and imagined what on earth he could scrape up to negotiate a meaningful cease-fire with this young lord.

"Might we have tea while we wait for breakfast?" he asked Banichi and Jago. "Did we drink it all last night?"

"There is a supply, nandi," Veijico piped up. "And a heating plate."

A tea caddy and service for nine stood on the buffet. So they had a heating plate somewhere. That was, among amenities their host had provided, a very welcome one.

"Then a pot of tea, if you please, nadi." Veijico, for her past sins, had not yet ascended to "nadi-ji" in his book. But with Barb safe and ambulatory this morning, and in spite of her answering out of turn, Veijico was rising a bit in his esteem.

Veijico rose still further in his good graces when she brought him the hot tea and several pieces of toast without saying a word. Bren had found a seat in a straight chair at a small side table, and Jago had brought him an occasional pillow for his back, which, with the tea and momentary quiet in the room, set him up very well.

He had time for serious thoughts over one entire cup before Barb came back from the bath, scrubbed and with her hair a little damp and wearing the russet gown—the clothing she had worn the night she was kidnapped.

"Cup of tea?" he asked politely, and Barb sat down in the opposite chair, across the little table, moving slowly and carefully.

"So when are we going home?" Barb asked.

Home. That was a curious way to put it. But, then, Barb and Toby's only home, their boat, was in harbor at his estate.

He poured her a cup of tea himself and offered it, with a saucer and a piece of dry toast. "It's not that simple, I'm afraid. I've been assigned a diplomatic job to do here that is going to take a few days. If I can get you sent home, I will, but otherwise, just settle in, stay inside the suite, and be patient. The dowager has given me a problem to solve."

Barb held the cup in both hands to drink. It was large and it was warm, and she sat in the atevi-scale chair with her feet off the ground. She had two sips, eyes downcast. Then: "I haven't even a change of clothes."

"Best here that you wear exactly what you're wearing." Atevi dress was far less apt to excite comment. "We can ask staff to try to find you a change. Child's sizes will work."

"I haven't my makeup!"

"Next time you're kidnapped, try to pack."

"Don't joke, Bren!" *There* were the tears, just under the surface. "I look like absolute *hell.*"

He'd gotten wary of saying things to Barb. No, you don't look like hell, was the automatic reassurance, but he'd had enough trouble disengaging Barb after their several-year relationship.

And of all people on earth he could have shared close quarters with, Barb wasn't his choice of roommates.

Of all people on earth he could have underfoot during a life-and-death diplomatic mission, Barb wouldn't be his choice, either: not Barb and her emotional reactions—and not the aggressive inexperience of the young Guildswoman who'd turned up with her.

"Were you at all able to speak to anybody?" he asked her. Barb understood far more Ragi than she spoke. "There were no Mosphei' speakers among them, were there?"

"No," Barb said, and her lip trembled. She held the atevi-scale teacup in both hands, elbows on the table, and took a steadying sip. "I tried to talk to them, and they hit me."

"The kidnappers? Or the people here?"

"The kidnappers."

"So the locals have treated you fairly well?"

"Fairly well, I guess," Barb said. "But they wouldn't listen, either."

"What did you try to tell them?"

"I'm not too fluent."

"Well, but what did you want them to know?"

"I tried to say I was from Najida, and I mentioned your name and the aiji-dowager. I hoped they'd phone you."

Interesting point. Barb had drawn a mental difference between her kidnappers and where she was now. It might not be a real difference; but somewhere in Barb's subconscious, it might signify that she had, in fact, seen a difference.

But he didn't bet their lives that nobody on Machigi's staff had a few words of Mosphei', either, and the room was undoubtedly bugged. So it was worth being careful and steering Barb away from certain topics.

"Well, but by then we were out trying to find you. Did you stop at any house, even a shed, a fueling station?"

"We just drove. Forever."

"Didn't stop at a fuel station."

Shake of her head, gold curls moving. And a wince. "Ow. No. We didn't."

So they'd come prepared, maybe with a double tank. "Did you hear any names?"

"I couldn't hear much. I was in the back of the truck, and this man—he didn't talk. Just sat there with a gun in his hands."

"Rifle?"

A nod.

"Guild uniforms?"

A nod.

It confirmed Veijico's story. The truck had been moving incredibly slowly, but it was still moderately impressive that Veijico *had* managed to intercept it afoot. It was much more impressive that she'd taken them out.

He was certain that the truck had been trying to draw attention to itself and get a reaction, wanting to be tracked into Taisigi clan territory. What they might not have anticipated was the desperation and outright rule-breaking lunacy of one young Guildswoman tracking them. They'd have expected her to follow Guild procedure: contact authority and track them until they chose to lose her.

Their mistake.

And the behavior added points to the dowager's theory that it wasn't Machigi who'd ordered that kidnapping. Machigi had been a bit more subtle than that.

The Taisigi had reportedly closed in immediately after Veijico had shot the kidnappers, so they had been watching, too. Guild were not prone to emotional reactions or personal retribution. But there was a limit to that professionalism, if Veijico had just shot down a number of their partners.

The fact was they had *not* shot Veijico, roughed her up, or even questioned her closely. They had handled her as someone attached to Barb and kept her *with* Barb, proper treatment for a high-ranking prisoner, one assumed by her situation and her species to be a prize worth taking home.

It was a jigsaw puzzle of pieces that *could* fit together, if one assumed someone was setting up the Taisigi and also assumed that Machigi had had time to hear about it, investigate it, and set his people in place.

His people still hadn't stopped that truck themselves. Possibly they'd spotted Veijico, who was staying hidden from the truck, but maybe they hadn't seen her at all and had been surprised by her attack on the kidnappers.

Possibly Machigi, if innocent of the kidnapping, as he maintained, had had a report from his own observers at Najida as to what had happened and where the kidnappers were going . . . an incident that, more than any argument the aiji-dowager's representative might pose, might have already convinced Machigi that he had a problem, that his neighbors were setting him up.

Interesting notion, all considered.

"What are you thinking?" Barb asked.

"I'm thinking it's a dead certainty we're bugged, and it's not impossible there's someone hereabouts who can understand some Mosphei'. There's a lot of that going around lately. But there's a lot more that doesn't add up in what happened. We thought you'd been taken to a place called Targai. That's Lord Geigi's clan residence, though he's not been there in years. So Geigi and I went there to ask questions, and the clan lord at Targai turned out to be a problem. Tried to shoot us, in fact. Geigi ended up taking over his clan lordship. He's over there now, trying to put his clan association back together, and he's not happy to be there."

"Why not happy?"

"He doesn't want to be lord of Maschi clan. He's got enough to do being lord of Sarini Province, and he absolutely intends to go back to the space station and live up there safe from all of this. But that's where he is." He'd said what he'd said for the benefit of anyone eavesdropping. If they understood. And afterward he drew a breath.

Mistake. He winced.

"You're hurt," Barb observed.

"Oh, bruises. Nothing much." Quick diversion to Barb's favorite topic: Barb. "Your head's far worse. Nasty crack you took. Tano's very sorry. You just mustn't emote around armed security. Mustn't. You could have been shot."

"Tano knows me! Did he think I'd assassinate you?"

"It wasn't Tano who'd have shot you. The lord's men in the hall might have, thinking you were coming after me. I was under their lord's protection, and you were about to touch me. That's the way it works. Just don't touch people. And keep a calm face, no matter what."

Bowed head. "I was doing pretty good up to that point."

"You really must have been," he said honestly, and he saw that Tano and Algini had come through the hall door.

Banichi and Jago went over to them. For a moment there was a low conversation with a notable absence of handsigns. His bodyguard evidently *wanted* their eavesdroppers to have no trouble with whatever they were saying to each other.

Jago came over to him, then, and quietly refreshed Bren's cup and Barb's. "One may report some progress with staff, nandi," she said—the singular address, along with a turned shoulder, pointedly though quietly ignoring Barb. "We have sent word through the lord's staff that we wish to make two phone calls in Lord Machigi's best interest. We have received permission. Tano and Algini will be going to a house security area to make the calls. We are to make them ourselves, under observation, with a written text."

"Are we to call Shejidan to reach the Guild?"

"No. They have agreed to our contacting Cenedi at Najida."

"Tell Cenedi this: that we have spoken at length with Lord Machigi and are favorably impressed. Say that he had already recovered both Barb-daja and Veijico from the kidnappers and released them to me as an act of good will, besides agreeing to look for Lucasi. Machigi, we are convinced, is not the agency behind the recent attacks in Najida, and possibly he was not involved with other actions that have been attributed to him. We are establishing proof of this and hope to present it soon."

Jago nodded, a little bow, and went over to the others.

"What's going on?" Barb asked.

"We've gotten permission, we hope, to phone home to Najida. We've added, if we can get it in, that we've recovered you and Veijico. I can't promise we'll get that concession. Local security will be very worried about prearranged signals and verbal code. Things are going to be somewhat tense around here until the lord gets word certain proceedings have been canceled."

"Can you get a message from me to Toby?"

To his brother. Toby had been wounded in the kidnapping incident—and he'd assured Barb that Toby was all right. He wished he were entirely sure that was the case. "No. We can't. We may not even get the permission to talk about you at all. Excuse me." He set his cup down and got up and went over to his bodyguard, seeing that Algini and Tano were about to go out the door.

"Take care, nadiin-ji," he said to them, wishing at the same time he were going with them. Glad as he was to have recovered Barb and Veijico, he just was not getting his thoughts together with them in the room. He needed somewhere else. He needed a buffer between himself and Barb's questions, and most of all needed a buffer against her asking him questions about Toby while he was trying to keep his nerves together and think.

Tano and Algini left on their mission. He didn't go back to the couch. He tried turning his back on the whole room, standing by the fireside, trying to compose a mental list of things he needed to keep in mind. His computer was back home. He didn't have its resources.

Barb, to her credit, took his signal; she sat still and sipped her tea and didn't talk to him for at least the next five minutes.

He was framing a course of logical argument, an approach to negotiations with Machigi, what he could imply, what he could offer in the way of inducements—

A knock at the door announced some arrival.

Thoughts flew in a dozen directions. Tano and Algini wouldn't be back this soon. His heart rate kicked up a notch. Barb sat there looking frightened, while Jago's hand rested very near her sidearm and Banichi stood similarly poised, on the other corner of the room.

It proved to be nothing more than house staff bringing their belated breakfast, a rather large breakfast on a rolling cart, and they were clearly bent on serving it.

It smelled good. A lot better than last night's toast.

"Just leave it, please, nadiin-ji," he said, and that had to be that, courteously. The servants would assume what they liked and report him as rude. But they were *not* going to linger in the room, big-eared and listening.

"Veijico," Jago said with a meaningful glance, and Veijico took a plate and took a little of every dish, plus a cup of tea, and sat down and began to eat.

Barb looked confused.

"Veijico tries it first," Bren said. "We'll wait about half an hour."

"I'm starving," Barb said.

He felt like saying, peevishly, Suit yourself, but he didn't. He didn't say anything, discovering himself in an uncharacteristically short temper. He just turned and went back to the fireplace.

Barb followed him. "Are you upset?"

He really, truly didn't want to argue right now; and he wasn't in a good mood. But he said, patiently, "I'm thinking. I have to present a case to our host, and I haven't composed it yet, and there's nowhere to work but here. I'll eat when I'm done. It's all right. I'll just stare into space for about an hour. Please."

She looked a little put out. Barb was good at that. She didn't understand any activity that didn't involve discussing the matter. But at least she took a broad hint and went away under her small dark cloud.

And he'd known her long enough he could accept that she'd take quiet offense, and be upset, and want to know intimately everything that was going on. He'd known her long enough and well enough to accept her reactions with a total failure to give a damn, except for Toby's sake.

Getting her back to Toby and getting both of them on their boat, out of atevi waters and back to safety at Port Jackson, where he could be sure they weren't a target . . . even that had to be put on a lesser priority. All personal questions did. Toby mattered in these equations only because he was, among other things, an agent of the Mospheiran government and knew things that might be of interest to certain people on this side of the straits. Barb knew an uncomfortable lot—but couldn't speak but half a dozen words of Ragi.

But the only way now to keep that knowledge out of play was to ignore it, stop worrying about Toby—and hope Barb never dropped the wrong name near a hidden microphone. He couldn't even tell her what names not to drop.

He stood, he thought through things Lord Machigi might ask him, and what he could answer—he asked himself what he could possibly offer as inducements for better relations with a young warlord bent on conquest as a means of keeping his several clans in line. Machigi had been practicing the old Momentum theory of leadership: start a war, keep everyone facing the enemy—and avoid discussing domestic problems for another decade.

Most long-term successful leaders of the Marid had adopted that policy in one form or another.

So how could he get anything different out of Machigi? How to be sure he caught Machigi's lasting interest?

Trade him something really good short-term?

What did a young warlord want that a diplomat could give him?

What was Machigi going to want that the aiji-dowager could give him?

They had talked vaguely yesterday about the space station, but that was far, far from something Machigi could actually realize—let alone explain to the peasant fishermen and the city ship owners and merchants who were the majority of Machigi's district. Fishermen and merchants were his constituency, the people who kept him in power, despite the ambitions of certain high-level local influences that might want to replace him. Machigi's hold on *them* was his popularity with the trades—and with the subclans. But it was a precarious hold, and let Machigi present some proposal that was too far from the interests of fishermen and merchants, and he could lose that popularity.

Tell them they were all going to be prosperous up in space? Or as a result of others going into space?

They weren't going to understand that. They wouldn't believe the Ragi would give them an equal chance at anything.

Tell them they were going to give up on conquering the west coast and accept an alliance with the hated north?

That wasn't going to be an easy sell, either.

Then there was the old quarrel with the west coast Edi, an ethnic group who had been moved onto that coast many, many decades ago, at the very founding of the aishidi'tat. The Marid had been claiming the west coast—and the Ragi, the ruling clan of the aishidi'tat, had high-handedly moved Edi refugees in and given the west coast to them—fierce fighters and absolutely determined on their own independence. The Edi themselves were allied to the Gan, another displaced ethnic group to the north, who would involve themselves inside the hour if things blew up. And the Edi in particular had been the target of Marid reprisals, and there was exceedingly bad blood there.

Tell these fishermen and merchants the Edi, already entrenched in Najida Peninsula, were going to gain a lordship in the aishidi'tat and be voting, thanks to the other part of the aiji-dowager's personal agenda? The whole Marid was going to have a fit when they found that out.

What in hell could he offer Machigi to induce him to let *that* slide by unchallenged?

What was in Machigi's interest?

Power.

Survival.

Pleasing those fishermen.

Underlying issues. Poverty, perpetual poverty in most of the Marid, poverty locked to traditionalism and a general low level of literacy.

An educational system based on apprenticeship, which didn't include more than one needed to know to buy and sell or to fish and maintain a boat.

Bloodfeuds two centuries and more old. In some places on the continent the network of allies and shared bloodfeuds was the cement that held communities together.

The whole district, with its internal wars and feuds, had lagged half a century behind the technology of the rest of the aishidi'tat. The district had phones, they had electrification— but not everybody in the country did. Their fairly modern freighters got their fuel from refineries to the north, and the whole region stayed dependent on the north for that resource, while hating them for it.

They had rail, a straight but antique line from the west coast of the Marid to Shejidan, running through Senji and ending at Tanaja. Everything else, absolutely everything else, moved by boat, among clans situated around a common sea.

The dowager, too, came from a staunchly traditionalist region. Over on the east coast wooden boats still went out to fish. Not every great house and not every village in the East had electricity, to this day, and the dowager's own house had it only as an afterthought—but in that case, it was stubborn traditionalism.

In some ways the dowager's East had a great number of values in common with the Marid.

In some Eastern districts, by choice, technological development lagged. Distrust of the western Ragi Guilds meant minimal rail and air service, though that was increasing.

Damn, yes, there were lot of similar points.

Get the Marid, the most dedicatedly hostile district in the aishidi'tat, to refrain from ancestral feuds and talk to the aiji-dowager?

He had to be crazy. But there *were* points in common.

Machigi would never agree with the West. But being approached by the East?

There was a shred of hope in that idea.

2

It was at least half an hour before Tano and Algini came back from the phone business, looking unruffled and fairly pleased.

"Lord Machigi himself listened in, Bren-ji," Tano said. "So we were plainly informed. We asked permission to call Cenedi with your message. We further asked to report that Barb-daja and Veijico are found. That was granted, with a written text to read from. So we did. We expressed to Cenedi-nadi your personal doubt that Lord Machigi's orders were behind the kidnappings and the illicit explosives and that you wish him to request a suspension of Guild proceedings against Lord Machigi. Cenedi-nadi agreed and we terminated the call on that basis. We also, under the same arrangement, called the head of Tabini-aiji's security in Shejidan and informed him first that we are here in Tanaja and that negotiations with Lord Machigi are proceeding at the personal urging of the aiji-dowager and under her auspices. We asked him to relay to Tabini-aiji that you request his personal Filing against Lord Machigi be voided on the same grounds. We are assured that message will be conveyed. Both messages have answers pending, and Lord Machigi's staff will notify us once the answers arrive."

"Well done," Bren said with a deep sigh. "Very well done, nadiin-ji. Breakfast is here, should you wish." As if they hadn't noticed. Banichi and Jago had just taken up plates, and Barb had declared she would venture it, Veijico having finished her breakfast half an hour ago without dying.

"Yes," the pair said in near unison, and headed for the buffet.

He had a little fresh toast, himself. He was by now not quite in good appetite, whether from the compression bandage, subliminal pain, or the fact that the job was far from finished with just two phone calls. He had now to produce results with Machigi, personally, and even toast with orangelle preserve did not sit well on his stomach.

Indeed, before he had quite finished his breakfast tea, there came yet another knock at the door. A servant advised the pai-dhi that Lord Machigi would receive him in half an hour.

So he would get to see Lord Machigi today.

That was good.

He was still forming his notions of what to say.

That wasn't.

Well, but he had enough bread on his stomach to cushion the pain pills. He had two thoughts that lay in a straight line. He supposed he could be ready.

Damn, he'd so desperately needed time and resources; and Barb and Toby and Veijico and the missing kid, Lucasi, all kept nagging at his mind.

But they were all side issues. They had to be. If he couldn't work his way through the minefield of Marid relations with the rest of the aishidi'tat in the next hour, at least in some tentative way, they could die, all of them, first strike in a general war.

And he wouldn't bet he knew how Machigi's mind worked, not by a long shot.

Well, but he'd wanted a chance to talk to him. He had it.

He went to his bedroom in the few moments left, and sat down for a few private moments, at least, trying to get his domestic worries out of his mental circuits.

He stayed there until a knock on the door announced and Jago's entry advised him Machigi's escort had shown up.

"Nandi," Jago said, all formality now.

"Yes," he said, and went out to the sitting room, where Banichi and the others waited. The outer door stood open, and two of the local guard were waiting for him. He didn't look at Barb.

And Barb, who wouldn't have understood above three words of anything anybody was saying, plaintively asked where he was going.

"Business conference," he said, still not looking at her, not wanting to make her the focus of a scene in front of the guards, and walked out, Banichi and Jago in close company with him.

Machigi elected to receive his guest in a large sitting room, this time with his Minister of Affairs, Gediri, present, along with two other persons, one a plump, bespectacled, middle-aged woman, the other a grim fellow of like age with part of an ear missing. The woman was, Machigi said, Adien, his Minister of Trade and Transport, and the half-eared man was Masitho, his Minister of Information.

There were, necessarily, bows and acknowledgements. Banichi and Jago had taken their places at the door, with eight others of the Guild. Bren personally bet that two of them—besides the two attending Machigi, ones he recognized from the last meeting—were attached to the Minister of Information: they had Masitho's kind of look, suspicious and hungry, and not an encouraging sort of attendance in the meeting. Banichi and Jago, though armed like the rest, were seriously outnumbered.

But Bren put on a moderately pleasant, noncommittal expression, bowed, and sat down. He was, he knew, in no position to dictate the agenda for the meeting. He still had to read Machigi, and read him carefully, so he was quite content for now to let Machigi take things in his own direction, without trying to steer him at all. It was a good guess that Machigi likely knew even less, psychologically speaking, about him as a human than he knew about Machigi as atevi.

But it was also a fairly good guess that Machigi had been brought up to want every human on the planet dead, and not to give a damn about human ways and mores. This whole region tended to that opinion.

Machigi was the youngest of the present company, by no few years. He was reputed to have great intelligence and ruthlessness—a young man whose enemies had great reason to worry and whose advisors, however powerful, had better not exceed his patience.

That was certainly the personal impression he gave. He was a handsome fellow—dark gold eyes gave his face a somber cast, making it hard to see what he was thinking. An old scar slanted across his chin. That had been no minor injury.

There was the customary round of tea, a little pleasantness— of a sort.

"We understand you are injured, nandi," Machigi said. "If you have need of a physician or medicines, please advise my staff."

"Your graciousness is appreciated, nandi." In fact, it was the last thing he wanted to advertise. Nor did he want to take drugs provided by Machigi's staff.

"Nothing is broken, one hopes."

"Bruised, only, nandi. I thank you for your courtesy." They had likely gathered their information from the bugs upstairs, not a surprise. They might suspect he was on painkillers and therefore at some disadvantage. "It slows me a little, but not excessively." He took a chance and added: "Your erstwhile neighbor, for some reason, saw fit to attempt my life. One is obliged to report, nandi, that Lord Pairuti is no longer your neighbor."

Brows lifted. Machigi took a final sip of tea and set his cup aside. "Indeed. So Lord Geigi of Kajiminda has now claimed the lordship?

"For the moment, nandi, Lord Geigi is indeed in charge. I understand he wishes to settle the responsibility on some other individual . . ." Bren set his own cup aside and said, deliberately, "But Lord Geigi is lately embarrassingly short of relatives."

There was about one heartbeat of deathly silence. Then

Lord Machigi laughed, a silent laugh that began to be a grin, giving that grim face an astonishingly boyish look . . . considering they were talking about murder.

"Is he, now?" Machigi asked. "And what does one suppose he will do about it?"

Geigi's one marriage had not been a success, either in the production of an heir nor in personal relations with his Marid wife. Geigi's late sister had ruled Kajiminda in Geigi's absence. Her untimely demise had promoted her fool of a son, Baiji, to lordship at Kajiminda. And the assassination and Baiji's lordship were both plausibly Machigi's doing—or the plan of one of the advisors in this room.

"One thinks it likely Lord Geigi will appoint an interim lord at Targai and then go back to space. He has a very comfortable residence there."

"Of what people will he appoint a successor at Targai?" Machigi asked, and he was not laughing.

"If one had to guess, likely Peijithi clan, nandi." That was the subclan of the Maschi, inland folk, not, as might be a great concern to Machigi, the coastal Edi people, neighbors to Geigi's personal estate at Kajiminda—who were moving into a position of authority there, a fact that Machigi might or might not know. "But I have a certain knowledge of Lord Geigi. One is very certain he will discourage any border disputes from his side. It is the aiji's policy; it is the aiji-dowager's policy, and it is certainly my own wish as another of your neighbors."

"Ah," Machigi said, as if he had forgotten something and only just remembered it—which one didn't at all believe. "We have had a response from Shejidan this morning." A pause, deliberate, judging effect. Bren kept his face absolutely under control and managed, he hoped, to look confident.

"One trusts it was a favorable answer, nandi," he said.

"We are informed Tabini-aiji's Filing against us is rescinded," Machigi said. "We are still awaiting word on the other Guild matter."

"One hopes that may have as favorable an outcome, nandi."

"Do you think that it will?" Machigi asked.

"One has no reason to believe it will not, nandi." The other Guild matter: outlawry. It was clearly the one Machigi should be most worried about and, involving the whole machinery of the Guild, the one hardest to get stopped. "You have the dowager's statement of her own position. Tabini-aiji tends to listen to her. And the Guild will take this move of his into account, one is sure."

"You are sure of a great many things."

"Of a few central things, nandi, among them the purpose of the aiji-dowager in sending me here. And the likelihood that you are not necessarily our adversary."

Machigi leaned back in his chair. "You have had a long and close relationship with the aiji-dowager."

"Yes, nandi."

"Yet you serve the aiji, her grandson."

"Quarrels between them are far fewer than reported."

"Has she possibly sent you here without consultation with her grandson?"

Interesting question. "One has no way to know. You say he *has* rescinded the Filing. He may be considering her position in making that decision."

"Guesswork?"

"One surmises he is to some extent aware of these negotiations—now, if not earlier. I was at Targai, engaged with Geigi in attempting to settle that problem, when the aiji-dowager directed me to come here. I have had no advisement as to what contact she had with her grandson." He made a snap decision, to turn the question-and-answer in his own direction. "But I have also had a long and close relationship with Tabini-aiji, nandi. The relationship between the Marid and Tabini-aiji has been uneven, to say the least. But may one . . . advance an observation in regard to the aiji's view of these events, nandi?'

"We shall be interested. Do so."

"Tabini-aiji is an innovator. If there seems to be advantage in doing a thing, he will consider it, even if it goes against precedent and previous policy and even if some consider it outrageous. The world as a whole is still dealing with the advent of new humans in the heavens. The human enclave on Mospheira is now flooded with change sent down from the station during my absence from the world, to counter Murini's rule on the mainland. These two situations could rapidly upset the technological balance. This concerns me. It concerns him. We also now know there are strangers in the heavens who are not human or atevi. Those strangers have promised they *will* someday come here to visit us, partly to test the representations made to them. This brings us a problem, since we cannot prevent them from coming, and *they* have enemies about whom we know far less than we wish."

This brought frowns all around.

"We hope to steer around this difficulty, nandi. But Tabini-aiji does *not* wish to have humans making the sole decisions up on the station when this visit in the heavens take place. He has kept and increased atevi authority in space. Lord Geigi is a part of that establishment, hence the aiji's urgent wish to have Geigi's business on earth settled and Geigi returned to his post in the heavens."

"What concern is this to us?" the grim man asked.

"A matter of understanding the other side's position, nandi. Tabini-aiji has been accused of shifting too often. But his adaptability in the face of change may turn out to be a very great asset to all atevi. Including you, Lord Machigi." Getting the exchange back to him and Machigi was essential. "You also have a reputation for flexibility, beyond any other lord of the Marid. What the dowager has heard of you encourages her belief that you may be another such individual as her grandson. She thinks you more valuable to the Marid than any other lord, and far too valuable to have at odds with her."

"Shall we be flattered by that?"

Right off the edge of the cliff. Live or die. "She extends an offer of negotiation and, in my belief, association with her, nandi. That is no flattery. She is eminently practical. You lead the Marid Association. Others may claim that position, but they have done nothing creative in their entire administrations. The aiji-dowager does not see any advantage to her or to the aishidi'tat in your fall from power, which would only bring chaos to the Marid."

Machigi leaned back in his chair and swept an uneasy glance toward his advisors. "So Tabini-aiji has formed designs on the Marid? This is no news at all."

"The aiji-dowager has no territorial ambitions here. And this is her offer, not Tabini-aiji's."

"Which can lead to a Ragi navy in our ports," the scarred man muttered. The central district was dominated by Tabini's Ragi clan; in effect, the aishidi'tat's core was Ragi clan. "Ask the human, aiji-ma, how long until the Ragi show up for a good-will tour, to survey our defenses?"

Machigi made a move of his hand, tossing the question to Bren.

Bren drew a breath. The Marid lords being legendary sea-farers, the sea had always mattered to them—emotionally—and one did not think the sea would ever cease to matter. "Again, nandi, the aiji-dowager does not command a navy. Nor is she, in fact, Ragi."

A silence followed that parry. The aiji-dowager was often thought of in one breath with the Ragi. But in fact she was not. She was Eastern. Foreign.

"Then what is the benefit of such an alliance?" the woman asked. "Where is any advantage to us in dealing with her? What have we possibly to do with the East?"

There was the question. And Bren had thought about it—with absolutely no instruction from the dowager, no brief, no preparation, and no possible consultation with the dowager. He flatly made it up out of whole cloth, *hoping* to come up with something that would involve no weakening of the Ragi position, no concessions on the west coast, and would actually pose some benefit to both sides.

It started with the word most valued by the Marid and proceeded to a word favoring one of their two factions.

"Ships, nandiin. Development of an eastern market, to the dowager's benefit and yours."

"What moves by sea," the scarred man asked, "that the aishidi'tat does not move by rail? This is no offer."

"Rail does not touch the east of the East. The aiji-dowager has gathered power and influence over a very wide area of that half of the continent. It is a rural, traditional population, particularly along the coast, which has seafaring villages, like the Marid. Unlike the Marid, however, having no land within reach, the East has never developed a shipping industry. The East has never trusted the Guilds. It views rail as a Ragi-run institution, which reaches to the center of the East, but not to the coast, and there is only one line. Getting rail through the mountains has been slow and full of politics. So trade flows, but not enough. The dowager has no desire to change the traditional ways of her people; but she does not intend the people of the eastern coast to continue in the relative poverty that afflicts that district. The development of fisheries and villages up and down that coast would be of great interest to her, but Easterners are not, traditionally, adventurous seafarers. The harbors there are small. There are coasters that go up and down to small ports, but nothing launches out to the wide sea. The area is mostly fisherfolk and cottage industry and has no wish to industrialize. It is, in short, much like the Marid itself." Everything he was saying now was true, top to bottom, and for at least the duration, they were all listening: adrenaline flowed. It was the thinnest tissue of a construction, and an adverse word could shred it. He had to say the right things, head off objections as they popped into very foreign heads. "The aiji-dowager has no territorial ambitions on this side of the continent. You have your position on the south coast, halfway between the ports of the West, and the undeveloped areas of the East. You have deepwater ships the East lacks. I mention these areas of common interest first, as the starting point. Ultimately, the dowager's associations on the orbiting station could bring new offers to the negotiating table. But let us deal with ships and ports. These are not ephemera she offers: this is a lasting relationship between the East and the Taisigin Marid, and she is *not* offering it to any other lord of the Marid."

Silence followed. Glances slid one way and the other among the taciturn ministers. The last had been risky, but it seemed a damned good shot.

Machigi lifted a hand, commanding attention.

"Well," Machigi said, "attractive as these new ports may be, the question facing us is the intention of the aishidi'tat to dictate to the Marid."

"Indeed," Bren said. "Through association with the aiji-dowager, your relations with the aiji in Shejidan could greatly improve. You would have an advocate."

"Tabini-aiji is Ragi born and bred, greedy, and bent on taking the south. She is his grandmother."

The old feud, the Ragi with the South, the old resentment. The whole argument could shipwreck on that rock.

"Traditions are both a brake and a compass; but the engine—the engine of the aishidi'tat, nandi, is a leader who can effect change and who *will* listen if you have proposals, particularly if you have the aiji-dowager's support going in. Traditionalists in the north will always temper Tabini-aiji's desire for change—but if any association is going to survive into a changing future, the leader of that association has to have the freedom to move. *The dowager* is such a leader. *You* are such a leader. You, nandi, can step straight into a very profitable association *without* the untidy process of a war. And she, through her personal connections, can entirely alter your relationship with the north in a favorable direction. *That* is the dowager's proposal. Look to the East. *There* is where you can change everything."

Machigi tilted his head, considering that statement, and it might have pleased him, or amused him. He had that slight expression—which slowly evolved into a brief smile.

"You are *good*, paidhi."

"One hopes to be helpful to both sides, nandi. The aishidi'tat and the Marid have spent too much of their wealth and invention on wars."

Machigi swept a sober look about at his ministers. "We have things to consider, do we not, nandiin-ji?"

There was not a word from the ministers, no lively give and take. No acceptance. But no rejection.

Was there ordinarily that sort of session with this man? Bren asked himself. Was it the presence of an enemy that restrained them—or was it the habit of restraint with a touchy young autocrat?

He gathered no clue from them at all. Machigi gave a flick of his hand on the chair arm, and the ministers all rose and bowed and left, collecting the majority of the guards as they went.

Bren didn't stare after them. He watched Machigi, and Machigi watched him, while their two sets of bodyguards stood watching over both of them.

"Well," Machigi said, "well, shall we take a walk together, nand' paidhi?"

Machigi got up. Bren did. And Machigi led the way to the large doors at the far end of the room. Machigi's guards moved to open them. Banichi and Jago shifted to stay close to Bren, and out of the line of Machigi's guards.

The doors let in a widening seam of light, and the room beyond proved to be a hall of windows with a view of the harbor—a pleasant room, with small, green leather chairs, with large and ancient maps on the other three walls. Fishing boats were evident in that panoramic view. So was a larger freighter, moving slowly beyond the smaller boats, and the horizon beyond the city wharves was all water.

"A magnificent view, nandi," Bren said.

"This is the heart of the Marid," Machigi said. "This is *our* sea. *This*, with our ships, is our power. Of the five clans of the Marid, only the Taisigi and the Senji have any extensively useful land inward. But you know this, being what you are."

"You have grain fields, nandi, and the Senji have their hunting range and their orchards."

"Well-learned, are you?" Machigi turned from the windows and faced him with a curious tilt to his head. "Hearing that Ragi accent come from your mouth continually amazes me. You have the size and the voice of a young child—one hardly means to offend you, nand' paidhi, but I have constantly to assure my eyes that you *are* the one speaking."

One might justifiably be offended, but it was rarely the paidhi's prerogative to be offended. Bren simply bowed in acknowledgment of the honesty and smiled slightly. "I have often wondered how I appear to others."

"You have a reputation, paidhi, for great tenacity, among other things. Tenacity and audacity. Commendable qualities, up to a point."

"I hope to uphold that reputation, up to a point, nandi."

"You have asked very little of our hospitality except that I recover a stray Guildsman of yours, which unfortunately we have not yet done. Possibly he is not in Taisigi territory."

"Possibly he is not. But he would move slowly. He was injured."

"Baji-naji. You and your household seem to have had a hard few days, nand' paidhi."

"It has been an interesting trip, nandi."

"So Pairuti is fallen. And Lord Geigi claims the clan lordship of the Maschi—to pass it on to an out-clansman, perhaps—or not. And now the dowager wishes to make common cause with me because she admires my character. You will understand that I take all this news with a little skepticism."

"If we go to negotiations, nandi, it will be my job to present your position to the dowager as energetically as I present hers to you. Admittedly, this venture was set in motion without extensive preparation. I have no documents for you, I have no absolute assurance that the dowager will agree with every detailed point of what I have proposed to you—" *God help me*, he thought. *First I have to explain to her what they are. What did she* expect *me to do, approach this man with* no *offers in hand?* "But I shall argue earnestly for it, nandi. I believe it represents a fair exchange of positions, no one parting with anything at all. Your collective needs and assets fit with the dowager's like key and lock."

"In what matters do you think she will balk, nandi? Be more specific." Machigi sank into a chair, offering the one opposite, before the immense windows. Light fell on them and reflected off the polished table between them. "We have just had the retraction of the Filing, which I assure you never greatly troubled me. When has the aiji *not* wanted me dead?"

"Well, *now* would be a just answer. He does not *now* wish you dead, nandi. That is some improvement in relations in just the last few hours we have talked."

Machigi rested his chin on his fist. "Spell out for me the things the dowager proposes—and those things you think she will not grant."

"The message instructing me to come here was delivered while I was in transit, nandi, so as aforesaid, one has not had the opportunity to consult with her. However," he added quickly, lest Machigi's patience run out, "I can state certain things with some assurance. First, a stable Marid is essential to peace in the aishidi'tat. Second, she believes that membership in the aishidi'tat is beneficial to her district." That produced a frown, and he added rapidly: "The aishidi'tat is not perceived as beneficial to the Marid, but it can become so. One can even surmise, nandi, that the character of the Marid Association itself might change, *if* the relationship between Tanaja and Shejidan were suddenly stable, and *if* it had a fortunate third participant, in the East. If the Marid once and for all defines its long-term interests in ways that bring about a stable, peaceful, and profitable association with the aiji-dowager, the aishidi'tat would have to take those interests into account."

"And if these interests include rule over the west coast?"

"The Marid has no great land-based establishment to the West and never has had. I argue it would be of no great value to you, compared to the offer on the table."

"Disputable."

"Yet you were only *claiming* the West when the Edi arrived. While all your wealth and prosperity, as you have shown me in the harbor outside this window, is the sea and its shipping. The greater quarrels with the west coast have always been disputes principally over rights of shipping and trade. What do you care about the land?"

"A great deal, considering the aishidi'tat in its wisdom moved in a batch of wreckers and pirates onto the coast!"

"Honestly, one cannot but commiserate with the Marid on that grievance. Several decisions were taken under pressures of that time, one of which was to settle the Edi and the Gan peoples, without direct representation, into the middle of two troubled districts. You may have heard, nandi, that the Edi situation is currently being addressed." He did not anticipate that the granting of a lordship to the Edi would be met with any joy in the Marid, but as well lay that card on the table from the start. "One might anticipate the Gan will make their own requests."

Machigi frowned, but he did not look startled. That told him something.

"The Edi situation is one major change," Bren continued, "bound to force other changes—including political ones—on all the people of the coast. But if this change comes, the Edi and the Gan will become signatory to the aishidi'tat, and the Edi will be constrained by the law. If the law is violated, and

Marid ships are interfered with—there will be repercussions *within the law*, and you will be compensated and protected. This is a firm principle of the administration in Shejidan. The Edi have been outsiders both to the law and to the aishidi'tat, and there has been very little the aiji in Shejidan could do about piracy without further destabilizing the coast. If the coast *is* stable, and the Edi become insiders, then there will indeed be recourses, and someone will be answerable."

The frown persisted. "So the pirates become part of the aishidi'tat. Is that a recommendation for the aishidi'tat? And the Marid is to get *nothing* by standing by and allowing this to happen?"

The paidhi-aiji was considerably out on a limb. And making extravagant promises that could only be unmade by Tabini totally repudiating him and his office and leaving him to face whatever mess he'd created.

He said, quietly, "Again, I plead the lack of advance consultation, nandi. But what I personally would support, in every possible way and with all the influence of my domestic office, is, first, the safety of Marid ships to move in all waters. And second, as I have mentioned, the training of Marid personnel for work on the space station. Increased trade. The development of a major airport and rail access here in the Marid for commercial traffic. Besides the development of *east* coast harbors, which is the dowager's particular gain. The Marid can gain the advantages that, in my own opinion, it should have enjoyed long since—advantages that would have prevented much of the past bitterness and made the lives of its people the better for it. Your predecessors and Tabini-aiji have had their differences, which were set in motion by unfortunate decisions two hundred years ago. One respectfully suggests the disputes of two hundred years ago are no longer profitable to either side. That they are, in fact, even inimical to both sides' best interests— and even if they are embedded in popular sentiment, popular sentiment is very rapidly affected by profit and prosperity."

"But you do not speak for Tabini in offering this."

"For the aiji-dowager. Who does not *offer* you anything in the West. Only in the East." A deep breath. A gathering of panicked, skittering thoughts. "I assure you, nandi, I have asked myself, from the moment I received the dowager's orders—why now? And I have reached two conclusions: first, she saw a moment of opportunity; and second, she is greatly vexed by certain decisions involving the formation of the aishidi'tat that *she* did not get the chance to overturn. She had wielded the power on her son's death. You may recall she came very close to *being* aiji in Shejidan. Ragi interests stepped in to hand the office to her Ragi grandson."

Machigi's face changed somewhat in the course of that. It was not a communicative face, but one could surmise that Machigi, being quite young, had *not* been that in touch with history.

The Ragi dominance over the aishidi'tat, however, was right at the core of resentments in Machigi's local universe.

Ilisidi had been double-crossed by Ragi connivance? True. And it set Ilisidi and the Marid curiously on the same side of the fence in that regard. He watched Machigi weighing that bit of history, which was perhaps new to his thinking.

"An interesting perspective," Machigi commented finally. He did not stop frowning.

And meanwhile the paidhi-aiji had had the most uncomfortable feeling in the pit of his stomach regarding what he had just said—that it could be *exactly* the aiji-dowager's game, and not only in the Marid.

Power. Ilisidi had come within an ace of being aiji *twice* in her life, once after the death of her husband, Tabini's grandfather, and again at the death of her son, Tabini's father. She had come so close, in fact, that suspicion had attached to her in those two deaths—not to mention to Tabini, in the latter instance. Atevi suspected foul play by default, in any change in parties in power—

But in that case, suspicion had perhaps been justified. And maybe she was getting back to old business. Kingmaking, in this case, spotting a likely candidate and making a move to bring him under her influence.

Machigi was capable of utter ruthlessness. Give him more power, and the difficulty was going to be in keeping Machigi in his bottle. In the same way Ilisidi had always been dangerous . . . so was this young man.

But Ilisidi had been around a long, long time. And Machigi *was* young. The potential in that relationship was frightening. And Machigi had better count his change in the transaction.

The silence went on a few more heartbeats. Then Machigi shifted in his chair, folded his hands across his middle, and gave a very guarded smile.

"You come up with all this structure of air and wishes, all because the dowager concludes some of my neighbors in the Marid would like to see me dead."

"If you were dead, nandi, it would even disadvantage your neighbors, though they may not see it that way now. The Marid needs a strong, single leader or it falls apart in internal conflict. But it is quite clear to me, and I think to the dowager, and perhaps to her grandson, that chaos in this region at this time would in no wise benefit them."

"So we are now favored as trusted allies?"

"If there were no Marid, nandi, there would be worse problems for the aishidi'tat. Humans have a saying: Nature abhors a vacuum. Peace first. Then profit. With freedom of the seas— and space—there *will* be profit."

Machigi lifted a hand in a throwaway gesture. "Of course. And my own relations with the western coast? Lord Geigi in particular will not be my ally."

That was fairly direct.

"His sister's death is the most grievous matter. Are we unjust to suspect it?"

"Not unjust."

"May one be even more blunt, nandi, and ask, in fact, about the kidnapping of an Edi child and the mining of the Kajiminda road—whether, despite your not having been responsible, you were knowledgable?"

"Would it actually matter to the aiji-dowager, paidhi-aiji?"

"Frankly, no, nandi. If we achieve peace, that question becomes irrelevant—unless the answer is no."

Machigi's eyes had flickered through the convolutions of that statement—until the last. Then the grim smile came back.

"The answer *is* no," Machigi said. "We were surprised at the news. We are attempting to discover who did plan it, and Tabini-aiji will not have to trouble himself to deal with it."

One yes, one no. The odds Machigi was dealing in the truth—rose.

"May one then relay to the dowager that she was entirely right?"

"Let her worry," Machigi said. "When you next speak to her, you officially speak under our man'chi. Is that not your duty?"

Speak under our man'chi. Hell! Speak as Machigi's representative? He'd promised it—but that wasn't entirely what Machigi meant.

The shift of man'chi Machigi invoked was the old way. There'd been an institution among atevi a long time ago, before the aishidi'tat . . . a way of settling things, a specialized negotiator. The white ribbon had gotten to mean the paidhi-aiji, the human interpreter's unique badge of office, over the last couple of centuries. And he'd represented both sides of the *human-atevi* divide . . . until it just wasn't that divided, nowadays.

But he did wear the white ribbon. He'd been sent into the house of an enemy—and Machigi, out of a district that hadn't, over all, ever adopted Ragi ways, any more than Ilisidi's East had ever done, had just called him on it.

He'd probably, he thought, turned a shade of white.

"One is honored by your suggestion," he said, trying to appear unruffled, and told himself it was actually encouraging that Machigi was willing to consider him in the mediator's role . . . a role in which he had some protection—as long as Machigi was willing to play by the ancient book, and so long as the negotiations didn't collapse.

Mortality among ancient negotiators had been tolerably high as one party or other decided to terminate the negotiations— and terminate the negotiator, who now knew too much—all in one stroke. Ancient rulers had used to saddle spare relatives and very old courtiers with that duty.

And of *all* lords he could ever represent, Machigi of the Taisigin Marid was not at the top of his preferences.

"It is not a forgotten custom in the Marid."

"So—yes. If you have that confidence in me, nandi, send me to Najida, and I shall state your positions to the dowager and come back again with precise offers."

Machigi pursed his lips slightly. "Not yet. Not yet, nand' paidhi. Your continued presence is, one trusts, no great inconvenience to anyone at this moment."

Well, he was still stuck. But they were still being polite. He assumed a pleasant expression and inclined his head in calm acceptance. "I am willing," he said, and decided to go for all else he could get. "And in no hurry. Though continued phone contact with Najida would be a decided convenience. Most particularly, I would wish to send the bus back to Targai. It is very cramped quarters for them and cannot be pleasant."

"We have offered local accommodation for those aboard."

Of course Machigi had. "Indeed," Bren said, "but they are the aiji's and not directly under my command while I am separate from them. I am, quite frankly, interested in preventing any misunderstanding out there. I would like to send everyone back except myself and my personal guard. One has utmost confidence in your hospitality—and I hope not to wreck these negotiations on a missed communication. Let us clear the area of all persons who might make a mistake."

Machigi smiled, and this time a little of it did reach the eyes. "We both understand."

"Understand me, nandi, that I am quite serious in my representations to you. You have an opportunity that has not existed for the last two hundred years."

"Since we were robbed of the west coast, in fact."

"What advantage, nandi, to hold the west coast at continual warfare with the center and the West *and* the station aloft— when you have a fair offer of access to the East, the untrammeled freedom of the seas, *and* a presence on the station? There is every advantage in that agreement. There is *nothing* held back from you."

"Except the west coast."

"It is *small* compared to the scope you can have elsewhere."

"Little profit to me in exposing myself to assassination by your allies."

"We can, nandi, get past the infelicitous history of relations, even recent ones, even the matter between you and Lord Geigi, if we may be specific. We have his nephew Baiji in custody. You have no further use for him, one assumes, but the dowager has—in terms of the bloodline he carries and in terms of her concern for Lord Geigi. So it would be convenient for Lord Geigi officially to forget Baiji's indiscretions, which is the course one is sure he will take. He is a practical man. Besides, Lord Geigi's primary interest is in returning to the station."

"Out of reach and unassailable. But not incapable of Filing with the Guild."

"His man'chi is to Tabini-aiji, and he has a strong association with the aiji-dowager and with me. He will place those interests foremost. I know him very well, nandi, and I am sure that he will decline to pursue a feud that undermines a peaceful settlement on this coast, not out of weakness but because he is a practical man."

The hand lifted. Machigi leaned his jaw against his fist. "Go on, paidhi. Give me more of your specifics. How would you perform this wonder?"

"First among necessities, nandi, a series of moves to stabilize the situation here with the negotiations: I have stated what I would ask—freedom to communicate. Simultaneously, I would ask the dowager's support for your continuance as lord of Taisigi clan; the dowager and the aiji in Shejidan have already made encouraging moves in that regard, in canceling one Guild action against you and working to derail the other. And, felicitous third, I would secure from you a formal agreement of association with the aiji-dowager."

"All these airy promises do nothing for us."

"They do a great deal, nandi. I can fairly confidently predict that Tabini-aiji would restrain any move that might unbalance your negotiations with the aiji-dowager, once underway. Agreement with her would be a good arrangement for both sides, necessarily, understand, removing any approval from the *legislature* from the equation."

That got a little flicker of Machigi's eyes.

Bren continued: "*Tabini-aiji* is the one that directly controls atevi access to the station. The relationship between yourself and the aiji-dowager would urge his agreement to your access there—again, nothing the legislature has to approve. He can do it with the stroke of a pen. Certain things can be done to build confidence on both sides."

Machigi lifted a brow, a surprisingly boyish look.

"You have a piratical bent, yourself, paidhi-aiji."

"The path with fewest rocks, nandi, is the fastest. And while the matter will be discussed in the legislature—nothing prevents that—the flow of trade will ease that debate. We prevent conflict—"

"Meaning I would agree not to assassinate Lord Geigi and he would agree not to assassinate me."

"Nothing to excite comment. The less news that comes out of the arrangement at first, the faster we can move. Speed will alarm certain elements—on your side and the dowager's, quite likely. But if we lose momentum on this, one can foresee there will be altogether too many participants in the decisions, and things will fly off in all directions. Controlled change is the purpose of my office, nandi. Nothing too fast or too slow and having everything in order and agreed before the news gets out is the best policy."

"So," Machigi said, chin on hand. "If we were to proceed on this course you name, what would be your first desire? Not that I shall grant it, understand, but let us see where you would start."

"I have already started, nandi, by being sure the Guild does not blame you for the outrages in Najida. It remains for you to deal with your internal enemies."

"So we do the bloody work for you—and weaken our own territory."

"Within the Marid, nandi, you will have a far surer sense where to apply force—and justice. You are the authority here in the Marid. That is agreed."

A slow smile came to Machigi's face, and this time it seemed less cold.

"We shall see, nand' paidhi. You will continue to be my guest, you and your aishid. Should you desire to dismiss the bus inconveniently blocking the public driveway and send Tabini's agents elsewhere, they will have safe passage, so long as they do not get off the bus inside Taisigi land. You will have free access to phones at any hour. And you may have any material comfort and convenience you may wish. Cease to concern yourself about poisons. If we quarrel, you will know it well before suppertime. My cook has been strongly cautioned."

"One is gratified to know so, nandi. And may one ask one additional favor? Might I send my brother's wife and the young Guildswoman back to Najida on the same bus?"

A wave of Machigi's hand. "Do as you please in that regard."

"One is personally grateful, nandi," he said, and he meant

it. "And maps. I shall need access to continental maps. I need place names."

"So. Go, give those orders, see the lady and her bodyguard off, and do as you please today. I wish my drive unobstructed and my land free of the aiji's men. Request your maps of staff, make your notes. And then we shall talk again, nand' paidi."

That, and the gesture, added up to dismissal. Now he had to get up. He tensed muscles and made the try. Twice. The second time he made it.

And Banichi and Jago, across the room, had both broken impassivity but stopped themselves from any untoward move.

"You should allow my physician to attend that."

"Bruises. Only bruises, nandi. Thank you, but my aishid's attendance suffices."

"As you choose," Machigi said with a wave of his hand. "Send and dispose, use the phones, ask staff for any comfort or service. Be at ease in my hospitality, nandi."

"Nandi," he responded, with a parting bow, and walked toward the door. Banichi and Jago joined him, and he didn't look back.

3

It was silence all the way back to the suite—Banichi and Jago were observing strictest formality, and they went escorted by two of Machigi's bodyguard, despite Machigi's assurances of freedom.

They reached the rooms, closed the door behind them, and Bren let go a carefully held breath, as much breath as he had with the bandages and the heavy vest.

Barb was on her feet to meet him. So was everybody else. But nobody spoke.

"Is there any objection," Bren asked Banichi and Jago then, "to taking advantage of the permissions granted?"

A slight hesitation. "No," Banichi said. "There is no objection."

Jago had reservations, perhaps—she had that look—but none tat she advanced, considering everything they said was under surveillance. She nodded agreement once, emphatically.

His aishid, the four of them, would be the ones to die along with him—if he was wrong in his approach, or if the negotiations blew up in some reversal of intention. He apparently had the chance to get everybody else out of the Marid . . . assuming there was no deception involved.

There could well be. He couldn't know if he was dooming everybody on that bus.

But if that was the case, he and his bodyguard were fairly well doomed, too, in the long run.

They were given a chance to communicate with Najida—knowing everything they said would be recorded.

But Machigi had encouraged the notion that the dowager was not that wrong in her assumptions. He had signaled willingness to consider the dowager's offer—at least in theory. One could not take it for an absolute. It was, however, better than the alternative.

"Barb," he said, "whatever you've got to pack, pack."

"We're leaving?" Barb exclaimed.

"You're leaving. I have work to do. Veijico." He changed to Ragi. "You will go with Barb-daja down to the bus and go back to Targai, then on to Najida."

"Yes," Veijico said, just that.

"Bren," Barb protested, "are you going to be all right here?"

"I think so," he said. "I'm not kidding, Barb. Right now, I want you to get together whatever you came with and go, this minute. Veijico, too. We've got a chance to get you out. Toby needs you. I promised I'd get you back."

Barb spread her hands. "This is what I've got to pack," she said shakily. "I'm ready."

"Then advise staff, Tano-ji," Bren said. "One has no idea whether they will let us go down to see them off, but let us get this moving. We shall send Tabini's men back to Targai, and then the bus will pick up my domestic staff at Targai and take them and Barb-daja and Veijico on to Najida. Set that in motion, nadiin-ji, and whatever we need to do, do it."

"Nandi," Tano said, acknowledging the order, and Algini went past them to the hall outside, presumably to talk with the staff stationed to guard them.

Bren decided a chair would be welcome, that one near the fire.

But Barb intercepted him, linking her arm through his, hugging it tight. "Bren, are you *sure* you're going to be safe?"

He gave a little laugh. "I don't think you could protect me if I weren't. But you can get back to Toby. Once they tell you it's safe to sail, you and Toby take that boat and get the hell back to Jackson." That was their home port, over across the strait. "Tell him I love him."

"Don't be giving me goodbye messages!" Barb turned around and was about to grab him around the ribs, but he fended her off at arms' length, and she held onto his arms. "Bren!"

"Shhsh." He took a firm grip on hers and shook her gently. "Shhsh. We'll be fine. The reason I want you and Toby off the continent right now has less to do with what's happening here in Tanaja than what's likely to happen if this negotiation goes well. People opposed to it, some in this district, some maybe even up north, are likely to strike at any target they can find, and I don't want them to find you and Toby available. You're tolerably safe in Najida, but I don't want you to get stuck on this side of the straits during a prolonged situation. All right? We're talking about convenience."

"You're lying through your teeth."

"Now, that's unkind, Barb. I'm not. I'm telling you quite a bit of the truth, and I want you to convey it when you get back to Toby. You just take care of him. He's doing all right, but he'll do a lot better when you get there. Hear me?"

A nod, damp-eyed.

"Good," he said, and set her back, with a look toward Tano.

"We are clear to proceed, Bren-ji," Tano said. "The staff has received a confirmation from their lord's guard. We have informed house staff that two persons will be coming downstairs to the bus, and house guard has confirmed the bus is free to leave. Guild will come to the door and escort the lady downstairs."

He was not encouraged to go downstairs to see the bus off. He was not surprised at that. If he had become an asset in Machigi's hands, Machigi was not going to wave temptation past armed personnel with man'chi to Tabini. It was not reasonable in his own mind that Tabini's guard might assassinate him, but Machigi could know no such thing.

"Veijico," he said.

"Nandi?" Instant, earnest attention—a vastly different young woman than before this situation.

"I have requested the Taisigi to look for your brother, nadi. If I can secure his safe return, I shall do so."

A bow, a more than perfunctory bow. "Nandi." And not a word else.

A knock came at the door, and it opened. Servants were there, along with uniformed Guild. Things were moving uncommonly fast.

"Barb," he said, "this will be your escort. Veijico will translate and speak for you. Let her. You take care. Understood?"

He was afraid for a second that Barb was going to throw her arms around him. But she came and put her hands on either side of his face and just looked at him.

"Bren, please be careful!"

"I'm the soul of caution. Give everybody my regards. And get moving. They won't wait around."

He was unprepared for Barb to kiss him. She did, a quick kiss, and let go and went toward the door. Veijico moved with her.

Barb looked back once, in the doorway. Then she left, and Jago shut the door.

It was, on the one hand, a relief. On the other—

He couldn't worry about it. He couldn't let his mind go down that track.

And a man like Machigi—

Was damned hard to read. He'd gained some freedom: Machigi was undoubtedly watching him, wondering what he would do with it, and he couldn't misstep.

It was also likely Machigi would tweak the situation to see how he reacted. But hopefully whatever Machigi did wouldn't involve the bus. The situation in the driveway couldn't go on for days and days—food and water, among other things, were limited—and for Barb and Veijico—

Barb was no asset in an emotional situation. Not with atevi involved. She'd just proved that. He had around him now only those who *were* assets . . . those he least wanted to endanger, but that was the choice he had. He'd given Banichi orders to get out if he couldn't salvage the situation. It was the most he could do for his bodyguard.

Except worry. And he couldn't afford to give way to that, either.

They had just dismissed the one member of their party most likely to create an inadvertent situation with armed guards—that was Barb—and the young hothead most likely to try to be a hero—a word difficult even to express in Ragi, but Veijico's inexperience had gotten them into this situation in the first place.

They'd also, in Veijico, dismissed their food taster.

Well, but that bus would get them to safety.

Which was a major load off his mind.

Machigi had promised him maps. He could look at the east coast, figure the possible assets, and make proposals. He could make phone calls . . . one of which could let him know the bus had gotten to safety.

He heaved a sigh, which encountered the solid restriction of the vest.

And he quietly unbuttoned his coat and shed it into Tano's hands, then reached under his arm to unfasten the vest.

"Bren-ji," Jago chided him.

"Just for here," he said. "Only here."

Jago helped him off with it, and Tano had gone to his room and come back with one of his ordinary coats, an informal one of plain blue cloth. He put that light garment on with a sigh of relief. It was cooler, it was lighter, it left him only the compression bandage, and that relief went a long way toward clearing his head. The painkiller still had him a little under its influence—God, he hadn't wanted to deal with Machigi with that in his system, but without it—he wasn't worth that much either.

Had Algini come back in? He'd lost track. It stuck in his somewhat muzzy head that Algini hadn't come back inside the suite.

"Tea, Bren-ji?" Tano asked, and there was that chair by the fire and the little side table.

"Yes," he said. "For all of us. Thank you, Tano-ji."

Tano didn't act as if anything was amiss. Maybe Algini had gone back to the rooms down the inside hall.

He sat down, a little light-headed, and Jago fixed a pillow for his back. It was a situation of fair comfort, and Tano quietly made sufficient tea for the lot of them. The door opened without a knock, and Algini came back into the room, from the outside door. He spoke to Banichi, then left again.

Maybe seeing to the bus's departure. But nobody was saying anything. The business worried him—but there were listeners. He said nothing, just took the teacup when Tano brought it to him . . . and wished he knew what was going on.

Maybe nothing. He let Tano and Banichi and Jago relax for a bit in the peace of a round of tea and contemplation. He tried to think peaceful thoughts. Tried to think about the maps he needed and whether to ask for them brought here, or whether he should request to go to the sunny map room or whatever library existed here—every stately home had a library.

Algini stayed gone.

He set his cup down. So did the others.

"Since we are allowed phone contact," he said, "if we can arrange a call to the dowager, nadiin-ji, that would probably be a good start. I also need maps of the region, of the west coast, and detailed maps of the East, including the coasts. If they can bring them here, excellent. If I have to go to the maps, that will be fine, too."

"Yes," Jago said, and she got up and went to the door to talk to whatever servants were stationed with the guards.

"I have a report to give to the dowager," Bren said to Banichi and Tano in the meanwhile. "Tano-ji, Banichi may have told you that Lord Machigi has taken the position that I am his mediator as well as the dowager's—" He used the ancient word for the office, with all it implied. "So I shall eventually be conveying his position, so far as I know it, as his representative. As yet, I have no idea exactly what that position is, except that he has said that the dowager is generally correct in her perceptions."

Tano nodded—and probably already knew everything he had just said, unless the local Guild had been interfering with his aishid's communications. He was stating things for their eavesdroppers, putting the slant on things he wanted. And he smiled somewhat grimly. "They will monitor what we say. Which is expected. And since our purpose here is exactly what we said it was, we have no reason to object. We can do very little until Lord Machigi tells us what he concludes, but I also have to advise the dowager what proposals I have made, so at least we can be accurate about her position. I have some hope this negotiation will work. There is absolutely nothing gained for anybody by another war. And a lot to be gained for the Taisigi in particular if we can work this out."

Solemn nods. They knew exactly what he was doing.

And they knew their own business, which was to keep the situation as quiet as possible as long as possible, give no information away, and hope that even if every assumption the dowager had made was wrong, he could still talk sense to Machigi.

The lord of the Taisigi, he told himself, was young but not stupid.

That was the best asset they had.

Jago came back in and closed the door. "They will bring a phone, nandi," she said. "And the maps, with writing materials."

"Excellent," he said.

Algini also—finally!—came back into the room, from the hall, and cast a look at Tano, then came and picked up Bren's teacup; when he set it down again, it weighted a piece of paper. A note.

That ticked up the heart rate a bit. Bren quietly picked up the note and read it.

Certain Guild disappeared from Shejidan in Murini's fall. Most of these, outlawed by Guild decree, entered service in the Marid, from which they trusted they would not be extradited to face Guild inquiry. Not all such are reliably in Guild uniform, and some may have falsified identities. My own presence here is known. Your mission here directly threatens the lives of these outlaws, since if Lord Machigi associates with the dowager, their sanctuary is threatened. Lord Machigi's bodyguard is aware and is taking measures as of this hour.

Measures. When the Guild said that—there was bloodshed.

So there were high-level fugitives, then, the very highest— Guild members who, two years ago, had carried out the overthrow of Tabini-aiji and the murder of no few of Tabini's staff, on behalf of the usurper Murini.

The Guild in Shejidan had cleaned house after Tabini's return. Some of the people responsible for the coup had been killed. Others had run for it—mostly south, even those with no southern connections.

Outlaws. Desperate, skilled Assassins.

Machigi himself might be in increasing danger.

Should I have sent the bus off? he wondered. Here they sat, his four bodyguards isolated and out of touch with the Guild, and now with Machigi's bodyguard evidently engaging in a purge of individuals who, until his arrival, might have assumed they had a permanent safe haven here.

Certainly the renegades would bear him no good will at all. Persons who employed them wouldn't, either.

And . . . *my own presence here* . . . was downright chilling. Whoever knew what Algini was, or had been, in the Guild, was *not* the average Guild member. They were individuals possibly with very high-level skills, and were already proven to bear a very chancy man'chi to anything at all. There were a dozen atevi words for people who betrayed a service. On the one hand, they had the disposition to govern—to be aijiin. On the other—and a paper-thin distance removed from that—they had the disposition to be a problem to society.

The Guild itself was a focus for man'chi: in a sense it was a clan of its own.

But it had fractured during Murini's takeover. It had become fragmented.

And now some of its problems were aiming at him *and* potentially at Machigi himself . . . with ambitions and intentions of its own.

That was not a comfortable thought. And now Machigi's guard had found out and presumably had told Algini what Algini had just reported to him.

Nobody from Machigi's bodyguard wanted to come here right now and explain things to the rest of them. Algini had gone outside to talk to—whoever he had talked to, and he had stayed out long enough to worry him.

Second point—Algini had written it out, not said it aloud, so it was something to be kept even from those elements of Machigi's guard that were monitoring their conversations.

That was very worrisome.

Maybe the servants were equally suspect.

The cook they had to trust?

Damn.

Damn.

And damn.

Bloody damn it. He hadn't expected local politics to come to a head this fast even with him stirring the pot.

But it was predictable, wasn't it? He had come here in a pain-killered fog, upset the political situation with his brain just a little too closely focused on the good Machigi could become to the situation, and now Machigi himself had become a target.

Depend on it, Machigi's potential enemies would have long since moved agents in on him, watching . . . that went on in every noble house in the aishidi'tat. In whatever houses there had ever been marriages and associations with other houses, staff traveled, staff joined other houses, settled in—and functioned as an information network. If the lords were getting along nicely, it was two-way. Or information moved only one way if things had gone to hell.

Staff spied. That was a given. A sensible lord dismissed servants who were suspected of dual loyalties, but sometimes the most astute judge of man'chi made a mistake.

And cell phones, hell. Members of the legislature in Shejidan had been tying themselves in knots over whether to import cell phone technology from the human enclave, sure that there were benefits to be had. *He* had been trying to think of a dozen arguments against it going into public use, but atevi great houses didn't need cell phones. Their problem was keeping information *inside,* not making it one step easier to disseminate. There was always the information you knew but politely weren't supposed to know, so you didn't act as if you knew; and there was the information your associate knew, and you knew he knew, and it was good he know, for the sake of trust, but it was just too hot for you ever to mention to him personally. Servants told other servants, who told the lords and movers, who then didn't have to *officially* know.

Which saved a lot of lawsuits and Guild actions, not to mention personal stress.

Machigi didn't *officially* know who was gunning for him at the moment, but very likely his staff was busy sussing out who it was. And if Machigi's staff was faithfully in *his* man'chi, they would be telling him all they dared, all they could, all they guessed . . . because *their* whole interest would be Machigi's survival, no matter what.

The paidhi didn't *officially* know that he wasn't safe under this roof, nor had Machigi officially told him—quite the opposite, actually—but nearly simultaneously Machigi's staff had told *his* staff the paidhi was in danger, which was actually encouragingly good behavior on the part of his host's household

Did Machigi know?

Possibly he had found out at about the same time Algini had handed him that note.

Jut after Machigi's staff had let him send Barb, Veijico, and that bus off cross-country.

And there wasn't a damned thing he could do now.

The fact that the paidhi had initiated that request to get the bus out of here could, in the way of atevi subterfuges, make Machigi wonder how much the paidhi had specifically known.

But if you went on wondering who knew what in atevi politics, you could tie yourself in knots. It had been logical for him to want to clear the decks. He had asked. Machigi had agreed. More, Machigi's *staff* had agreed. He just had to sweat it out for the next few hours.

Letting house staff come and go in the apartment unsupervised right now wasn't a great idea.

"And the phone?" he asked after his moment of silence.

"We shall arrange it with staff, Bren-ji," Tano said, and added: "One assumes Cenedi may wish to receive the call—officially speaking."

"One would expect that," Bren said, "and I gathered our host has no objection to our speaking to him." Cenedi, Ilisidi's chief bodyguard, would at least listen in on any conversation—and might insist on taking the call himself to preserve the dowager's distance from the situation.

"A moment, Bren-ji," Tano said, and got up and went out to the hall.

"We shall be relying on our host's hospitality," Bren said, "since we have sent Veijico away. I hope we shall manage to have some teacakes on hand today. That would be welcome. But use your own discretion, absolutely."

"Your staff has necessarily become very well-read in recipes," Banichi said with some humor. "Tano in particular is very good at detecting substances you would rather not eat. And we have a list we routinely clear with kitchens, where we have the opportunity. Shall we officially pass it to Lord Machigi's staff?"

It was nice little list of spices that *would* reliably poison a human, some fairly subtly. "Do so, at your discretion," he said. It wasn't as if spies over the years couldn't have found it out. And advising staff meant there was a record, so if something did turn up, they at least had grounds for complaint.

In a very short time Tano came back in carrying the promised phone, which he plugged in beneath a small table just inside the room . . . where it would reside permanently, one hoped.

And it was time to use that phone and try to give Machigi some solid ammunition in arguments with his advisors. Bren reached for the chair arm and levered himself up. Jago got up and slipped her hand under his good arm.

"At your pace," she said, and without the weight of the vest, movement was far easier and less painful, he was glad to know. He stood on his feet and straightened with a deep, almost unrestricted sigh.

Tano meanwhile had begun the process of connecting to Najida, which had to have clearances from the local operator, who had to consult security, who apparently immediately gave the go-ahead. Machigi's household interface was thus far very good.

So, one was certain, was security's finger on that line. The question was now—how many sides of the household were listening.

Tano made contact with Najida. A junior servant answered the phone at his estate and requested the dowager's attention—a request that would ordinarily go through the major d', Ramaso, and then through the dowager's chief bodyguard, Cenedi, about as fast as it took a junior servant to traverse the main hall at a near run.

But the dowager's own chief of security, in charge of the house, had pounced right on an incoming long-distance call. "Cenedi-nadi," Tano said with no delay at all, "the paidhi-aiji wishes to speak to the aiji-dowager."

Now footsteps were involved; and Tano had time to pass the handset to Bren.

He listened. Evidently Ilisidi was going to talk to him with no intermediary. That was a little unexpected—indicating Ilisidi had uncharacteristically *wanted* this call. He heard the pickup on the other end.

"Nandi?" he said, a choice of address which itself ought to alert the dowager that something was odd.

"Nand' paidhi." Ilisidi said quietly.

"Nand' dowager, my respects. Lord Machigi has chosen to view my office as that of a mediator, in the ancient sense. I have acquiesced to this view and I have made certain proposals to him in your name." *God*, had he! Machigi had appropriated him somewhat *after* he had done that, but the precise sequence was neither here nor there in the current. "I ask you hear all my proposals to Lord Machigi in that light, nand' dowager."

There was a small silence after that warning—a small silence that weighed very heavily and made him wonder whether Ilisidi might now break off contact, at least temporarily. Or hand him on to Cenedi, to be dealt with at a lower official level.

But she said, calmly and formally: *"We shall hear you, nand' paidhi."*

He found he'd held his breath. He took another. "This is the situation, nand' dowager. Lord Machigi's interests are first of all linked to the Marid itself, which in his view has not prospered equally with other regions of the aishidi'tat. I have informed him that your district presents advantages in association and that you are approaching him with that in mind. He has asked further. I have pointed out to him the undeveloped fisheries and markets of the extreme East Coast, and his advantage of deepwater ships and shipping, which the Taisigin and their associates have in abundance; and I have proposed, as your representative, nand' dowager, that you would hear suggestions for trade and development in that district of the East, using Marid shipping. He, speaking for the Taisigin Marid, maintains that the Marid was dealt with unfairly from the outset of the aishidi'tat, in the dismissal of Marid claims to the west coast and in the settlement of the Mospheiran peoples in that district without consultation with the Marid. This action, he feels, is the origin of the ongoing disputes between the aishidi'tat and the Marid as a member state. This remains a sore point, but the east coast is not without interest to Lord Machigi. And . . ." Another breath. The next point was major. "One has also mentioned access to the space station, *after* the establishment of good relations. This would seem to be a logical step, in due course."

"Go on, nandi."

She had not hung up, or passed him to Cenedi—so perhaps Ilisidi was at least not outraged. He had taken wild, desperate chances.

But she had sent him without consultation. Had trusted him to use his knowledge creatively.

"I have proposed, nand' dowager, that if you entered association with the Tasigin Marid, it might begin a pattern of remedy, first undertaking agreements for development of east coast harbors and shipping, to your benefit and to the benefit of the Marid as a whole. Second, I have officially informed Lord Machigi that you are bringing the Edi and the Gan into the aishidi'tat. I have maintained that the law of the aishidi'tat, once binding the Edi and the Gan, will assure the safety of Marid shipping on the west coast. And, felicitous third—" God, was there felicity at all in a structure of tissue and tape? "Nand' dowager, I am about to propose that Lord Machigi seek more frequent rail and air links between Shejidan and the Marid, to carry the goods of the East up to Shejidan, once they arrive in Marid ports. This would provide economic benefits to the region, enable goods from the Eastern trade to flow up to Shejidan from Tanaja, while maintaining the traditions and culture of the Marid. The traditionalism of the Taisigin Marid is a close match with the sentiments of the east coast.

It seems essential to bring a prosperity that will not damage that culture."

There. He had gotten it all out, in decent order, sounding saner than it was. And if the dowager now called him a lunatic and burst the bubble, he was in a great deal of trouble.

Another silence followed. *"We will take all these matters under advisement, nand' paidhi."*

He hardly expected instant agreement. He said, one last clarification, one plea for a crumb of progress: "The premise of personal association, nand' dowager, between yourself and Lord Machigi underlies the initial section of the proposal. One would hope that exploring that, at least, is not out of reach."

"We have counterproposals," Ilisidi said crisply. *"We can restrain the aishidi'tat and the Guild from proceeding against the Marid. When he can claim the same from his side, he will hold sufficient power, and we shall then be favorably disposed toward these proposals."*

Fly to the moon, that was. Control the Marid. *Nobody* could control the Marid. A thousand years of history had said *nobody* could control the Marid.

But in principal, she hadn't disagreed. She hadn't come back with the microfocused specific he'd hoped for. She'd offered Machigi a sweeping counterproposal.

Become the head of the Marid.

Then talk.

He felt numb all the way to his fingertips.

But he represented Machigi. He had to *represent* Machigi's interests.

"May one infer, nand' dowager, that you will persuade your grandson to view Lord Machigi's moves as self-defense?"

Silence for a moment.

Dared one remotely suspect she was getting all the aishidi'tat's enemies down to one vulnerable neck?

No. It wouldn't work like that. Machigi might dominate the

others, but every district would still have its lord. Kill him, and the whole structure went back to chaos.

"We have stated our position," Ilisidi said. "What happens within the Marid will not greatly concern us, until it has issue."

Us. Who was *us?* And what was she up to? He'd honestly *tried* to structure a peace deal. She hadn't repudiated what he'd done—she'd just made a counterproposal.

She'd promised the Edi a lordship and a seat in the legislature. She'd declared Machigi should take over the Marid. Not a shred of reference to her grandson. Had he somehow gotten *ahead* of her next step? Ilisidi was finally, after half a century, making a serious bid to dictate a solution to the old issues that had dogged the aishidi'tat from its founding—things *she* had backed God knew how long ago.

"And how do you fare, nand' paidhi?"

Give me information, that was. He didn't dare mistake it for sentiment.

"We are in Tanaja, comfortably housed in very fine hospitality. You will soon have a direct report of that, nand' dowager. Lord Machigi found Barb-daja on Taisigi land, along with Veijico-nadi, and delivered both persons to my care in good health. I have just sent my bus back to Targai with them aboard, as well as the Guildsmen your grandson sent with me. I have asked the two be transported on from Targai to Najida, possibly arriving at your door late this evening."

"One is very glad to hear so, nand' paidhi."

That, at least, was warmer. "We have also had confirmed, nand' dowager, that the aiji your son has rescinded the Filing against our host. This is welcome news in this quarter. Is there news on the other matter?"

"The Guild Council, within this last hour, has tabled their discussion of outlawry, at our request. You may deliver that information to your host."

Thank God. And thank Ilisidi. "I shall, aiji-ma." Damn. He

couldn't blame that *aiji-ma* on the pain pills. It was so automatic. He hadn't the hard-wiring to feel it, at least not in the
same way.

And since Taisigi agents were recording every word, he
couldn't mend it. The information had been relayed, in effect,
and the dowager certainly knew that.

"For the rest, nandi," he said, resuming his more objective
stance, "we hope our access to phones will remain open." He
dared not report what else they knew, that his bodyguard was
evidently in direct communication with Machigi's bodyguard
on issues only the respective bodyguards knew.

And there was one thing he ached to know. Toby's welfare.
But it had no place in official business.

"Tell Lord Machigi," Ilisidi said, *"that we shall be interested in his response to our small notions."*

"I shall tell him so, nand' dowager."

"We have had word your brother is making good progress."

That was a personal kindness. A signal. She was not upset.

"One is *very* glad to hear so, nand' dowager."

But, given the constraints of his position, he compromised
himself if he expressed personal gratitude.

The dowager surely understood that. She said, coldly, *"Keep
us informed, paidhi-aiji."* And hung up.

Well, it was a performance. And both sides would have heard
it.

He had shamelessly complimented his host. He had indicated to the dowager and to Cenedi that they were not exactly
free . . . that they had lost their armed escort, they were down
to their own resources, but were not panicked . . .

And he had, he hoped, conveyed that it was not time yet to
call Tabini and admit that the paidhi-aiji was being held hostage in Tanaja. Toby was getting better. He was beyond glad
about that news.

And he had managed to advise the dowager that the bus
should arrive and with whom. If it didn't—well, *she* would

have no doubt they had a problem, whether or not he ever had a chance to know it.

The legislature had declined to make her aiji in her departed husband's stead—partly because her proposals about the west coast had scared hell out of them . . .

So it was round two.

Or round three . . . she'd outlived her son and was down to her grandson.

And for one reason and another, her great-grandson had now spent more time in her hands than in Tabini's.

Now she was kingmaking in the Marid.

Now he began to understand it. She'd been watching Machigi. She'd been calculating.

And she'd made her move.

Hadn't Tabini warned him, when he'd first sent him off into Ilisidi's domain—beware of my grandmother?

He felt just a little light-headed, and stood there a moment quietly and deliberately redistributing blood where it belonged.

He had great confidence in Ilisidi. He knew her. He understood her impatience with war and waste . . . and her utter contempt for special interests that had gotten their fingers into the legislative process. He knew her resources, and he had known he had to work within what she had, not what she could obtain.

So his creative lies on her behalf were not off the map. He'd stayed within possibility, and she was going to back him.

Whether or not she ultimately intended to follow through with the alliance in any way, shape, or form, or whether her aim was to create the possibility and paralyze the Marid in internal conflict—he was still alive. So were his people. There was a good chance the bus really was going to get through.

And even if all she currently intended was to create a mess in the Marid to ensure a time of tranquility on the west coast, she was an opportunist: if he presented something she wanted, she would listen.

So there was nothing for him to do now but sit down with a

cup of tea and think through just what else he had to propose to Machigi. Once Machigi had heard the report of that conversation, with all the understanding another ateva could bring to the issues, he was going to have questions, objections, and points to raise.

And did Ilisidi know about the situation with the renegade Guild?

What Algini had learned from Machigi's bodyguard was ominous, and there was no way he could have told Ilisidi what they had learned. That would have blown everything. But the Marid situation was possibly more worrisome than Ilisidi knew; possibly more than Tabini knew . . .

The entity that *might* know was the Guild leadership itself, who might or might not want to share that knowledge with members not under its administrative roof.

Maybe there was a reason the Guild had leaped at the chance to outlaw Machigi. And he had put himself in the middle of that situation.

Well, he had gotten it stopped.

But was the epicenter of the renegade problem here, in Tanaja, or was overthrowing Machigi the aim of renegades based elsewhere?

That left the Senji or the Dojisigi, or both, as the base of renegade operations.

The Farai, a subclan of the Senji, with strong ties to the Dojisigi, had snuggled close to Tabini, tried to establish residency in the Bujavid in Shejidan, right next to Tabini's apartment, on the strength of an ancestral claim to that residence. It was one thing if it was ordinary Marid mischief afoot.

But if it was not the Marid itself pulling the strings . . . if it was an operation aimed at letting renegade Guild into the Bujavid . . .

God.

They could have a problem. They could have a *serious* problem.

He needed to do his job here and get back to Najida where he could get contact not only with Ilisidi but also with Tabini, on an urgent basis. He had to hope Machigi could be persuaded, and could become useful in solving the renegade Guild problem from inside the Marid.

He had no references. He had none of his accustomed, familiar maps. He had what he had in his head. And he had what maps Machigi would be willing to provide, of whatever vintage or accuracy.

"Nadiin-ji," he said to his bodyguard, "I shall sit down and take a few notes until the maps arrive."

4

The *bus* was coming in. Everybody in Najida had known for sure the bus was coming since afternoon, when it had dropped off people at Targai and picked up people and set out for Najida.

The bus coming back meant a lot of things.

It meant everybody must be all right, but things were still dangerous: Cajeiri had that figured. Great-grandmother almost never showed worry, but house staff did: they were in a dither.

And Great-grandmother had been just a little sharp with him at lunch, when he had come up to get lunch for nand' Toby. He had asked if he should tell nand' Toby that Barb-daja was coming back.

"Never promise what you cannot personally swear to, Great-grandson!" Great-grandmother had snapped at him. "Think!"

Well, he *had* thought, had he not? That was why he had asked, and it was not fair of mani to have spoken sharply to him. He was only infelicitous eight, and he made a few mistakes, but he was making far fewer lately.

Still mani had chided him.

Mani was worried about nand' Bren, and worried about the whole situation. That was what he picked up.

But if she was *that* worried, why had she sent nand' Bren and Banichi and all over there in the first place?

He saw no sense in what mani was doing. Lord Machigi was the same Lord Machigi who had caused holes to be shot in the woodwork at Najida and who was responsible, Cajeiri was still relatively certain, for doing in Lord Geigi's sister and corrupting Baiji, who was still locked in Najida's basement, just down the hall from where he took care of nand' Toby.

But on mani's orders, nand' Bren was a guest of this lord, along with his bodyguard, and they were all in danger. Nand' Bren had phoned to say he was all right, but that did not make anybody less worried about him.

So Great-grandmother, who had ordered him to go there, and who was being nervous, also thought things could still go wrong.

Machigi's people might have attacked nand' Bren's bus and all those Guild aboard before it even got out of Taisigi land. That had been the first concern when they knew nand' Bren had sent the bus back.

But it had gotten safely to Targai, over in Maschi clan territory, and Targai had phoned and said it was coming on to Najida.

With Barb-daja and Veijico.

And now it had really, truly almost gotten here with nobody shooting at it.

So Cajeiri felt more and more anticipation—and still a little dread, because nobody had said whether Barb-daja was entirely all right, that was one thing.

But the other passenger—

Veijico.

Veijico was *his* problem. Vejico and her brother had deserted *his* aishid, run off into the night, drawing nand' Toby into an ambush and getting nand' Toby shot and Barb-daja kidnapped.

And then she had run off, following Barb-daja, maybe to undo what she had done, but to no great good, and they *still* had not found Lucasi, who was lost somewhere in really dangerous territory and maybe dead.

He would be sorry if Lucasi should turn out to be dead.

But the two of them going off like that and causing all the

trouble they had caused was behavior he, being their lord, even at infelicitous eight, had to say something stern about. They had broken Guild regulations. Cenedi was mad at them. Everybody was.

More, what he felt about them was complicated, because he was glad Veijico was alive, but he was not sure he wanted Veijico and her brother back in his household at all, and there was nobody, with everything else going on, who had time to tell him what to say or do if he wanted her to go back to Shejidan. Those two had been nothing but trouble since his father had assigned them to him, and they had been constantly rude to Antaro and Jegari, who were only apprentice Guild, but who were in their way.

Antaro and Jegari had volunteered to be his bodyguards from when he had come back to the earth, and they had been in very serious situations and had people shooting at them and always protected him. Antaro and Jegari had risked their lives keeping him safe—and were still with him, did what he wanted, and would throw themselves between him and a bullet, he had no question, while Veijico and Lucasi had gone off and left him.

But there ought to be value in them, all the same—because Veijico and Lucasi had been assigned to him by his father—*real* Guild, not just apprentices—because Najida was a dangerous place.

They had sounded all right at first. They had promised him all sorts of things they could do, including hurrying Antaro and Jegari through their courses and teaching them, personally.

But Veijico and Lucasi had taken serious exception to his still having Antaro and Jegari as number one partnership in the household.

That was where all the trouble had started—well, plus the fact that Veijico and Lucasi really were very smart, and thought they knew everything about everything, and had even gotten pert with senior Guild—which told him they were not as smart as they thought they were.

They had offended Cenedi, who had been extraordinarily patient with them, and that was just stupid on their part.

And they gave orders to nand' Bren's household staff as if they owned the estate.

They had *not* gotten into the household network, which they had been supposed to do to keep him informed: Cenedi had refused to give them access, since they had been contrary with Cenedi.

They had run out of the house without orders and let Toby and Barb go with them.

And then, when things had gone totally wrong, they had run off without telling Cenedi or him where they were going.

So they had made a mess of things. And Lucasi could be dead.

He had to admit he had not managed them well. And they *were* his staff, even if he had had no choice in having them. He hated failing at something.

He supposed, in the first place, he should have expected they would resent Antaro and Jegari, and maybe he *should* have done something different about organizing his staff.

But why? Was he to demote Antaro and Jegari just to suit two newcomers, when he had never even asked to have them in his household in the first place? That was just not fair. He had promised Antaro and Jegari they would be first. How could he break a promise like that?

Maybe they had had feelings about being assigned out in the country, too, when they thought they were so good.

Maybe they had come in a little mad in the first place because they were being assigned to a child, even if he *was* his father's heir. Well, that was understandable. He was not very glorious, yet, compared to being assigned to his father's household in Shejidan.

And to top all, after acting as if they were so knowledgeable, they had lost track of him between the upstairs and the downstairs of the house, panicked, and then let nand' Toby and Barb-daja go out of the house hunting him, with disastrous results.

That part had *not* been his fault. He had disappeared downstairs to teach them a lesson about ignoring him, and *they* had turned it into a total disaster. It was absolutely *their* fault, not his.

Mostly.

And all of that had led to nand' Bren getting sent into the Taisigin Marid, in Tanaja, under the roof of Machigi, who was the person who had been trying to kill all of them ever since they had gotten here.

He was mad at Veijico. He made up his mind he was entitled to be mad at her.

And he did not know what he was going to say to Veijico when he saw her, but he was already determined she had better not say anything pert to him to start with. And she had better not blame *him* for what had happened. And she had better be respectful.

He had just as soon not see her at all if he had a choice. But because of Barb-daja coming back, he was very anxious to be early on the scene when that bus came in. He stationed Antaro in the upper hall to advise him when it was about to arrive. *He* had to stay close with nand' Toby, and he could not leave him with just staff. Nand' Toby could speak a few words of Ragi, but he made mistakes, and some of the staff had strong rural accents, which made it worse.

And he had to be very sure nand' Toby did not hear any rumors, especially if it was bad news, because he already had mani's instruction on that point.

At least nand' Toby, though tall for a human, was about his size, and Cajeiri *could* help him—ship-speak was almost Mosphei', and he, better than anyone in the house, could make nand' Toby understand him.

So he was *essential* if nand' Toby got upset, and he had promised nand' Bren.

What nand' Toby wanted to do today, unfortunately, was get up and walk. Nand' Toby said the bed made his back hurt, and he was tired of lying there.

So he just helped nand' Toby walk up and down the hall, with him on one side and Jegari on the other. They made three trips the length of the hall, nand' Toby seeming a little steadier as they went. He wanted most of all to keep nand' Toby busy and keep him from asking questions.

This morning nand' Toby had asked him very plainly, "Have you heard from Bren?"

And at that time it had been an easy answer: "No, nandi, not yet."

This afternoon it would not be an easy answer, and once they had gotten nand' Toby back to his room and back to sit on the edge of his bed, he asked again, "Nothing from Bren yet, is there?"

Lying was wrong, most of the time. But telling the truth right now went against mani's orders. It was clear that nand' Toby was tracking things very sharply, and starting to think about things, and maybe he had heard somebody talking out in the hall this morning.

Barb-daja, when she came, could tell nand' Toby the truth about where nand' Bren was—it was all but impossible she would not tell him—but first she had to get here safely, which would calm nand' Toby a lot.

So he lied again and said, "No, nandi, not yet."

"I'm getting worried, here. Don't they have phones over— wherever he is? Isn't his bodyguard communicating with Cenedi? What's going on?"

"I'm sure the Guild is communicating, nandi. But I don't know what they say, and my bodyguard doesn't know." He had never regretted being fluent in ship-speak, until now. He said, miserably, "They don't tell me everything."

Toby looked him in the eyes. Toby's eyes were brown as earth, and honest. Like nand' Bren's. "I forget how young you are sometimes. You're as tall as I am."

"Almost," Cajeiri agreed, wishing word would come so he could get out of this conversation. He knew nand' Toby was going to find out he had lied. It was all going to come out, and nand' Toby was going to be his enemy forever.

And then footsteps came running down the hall, light footsteps that raced straight to nand' Toby's door. A knock, and Antaro opened the door herself and said, "Nandi!"

"Just a minute," he said to nand' Toby, and he got up and went outside with Antaro and shut the door.

"The bus is up at the crossroads," she said in a low voice, breathing hard. "They are coming, nandi."

"Is Barb-daja all right?"

A slight bow. "One has not heard, nandi. They are not talking with the bus because of security."

He put his head into the room, said, "I'll be right back!" and then shut the door, leaving nand' Toby only with Jegari. He headed down the hall with Antaro, keeping up with her long strides—Antaro, like Jegari, was in her late teens and at least a head taller than he was. They were Taibeni, from the woods, hunters, even if the Guild would not let them have weapons as a matter of course. They were protection: they knew how to move; and they were apprentice Guild, at least.

The two of them climbed the stairs fast and came up onto the main floor, which was not bare stone and concrete like the basement. Upstairs was all polished wood paneling, stone pavings, and a glorious stained glass window—except the window was all dark, now, covered in boards outside, the way every window in the house was kept shuttered. The whole house had a feeling of being wrapped in blankets, darkened, made into a stronghold. The lights upstairs were always on, day and night, and servants were always somewhere about—in this case, gathering in the hall, waiting.

Mani had her suite in mid-hall. Cenedi came out of that door. And the security station was set up in the library, which was even closer to the big double doors that led outside: Nawari and

Casari came out of there, and joined Cenedi. Ramaso, nand' Bren's majordomo at Najida, came and stood on the other side of the hall from Cenedi, with several of the staff. The servants all had heard the news, just about as fast.

If one was still a little short of fortunate nine, and wise about it, one situated oneself at the intersection of the dining room hall and the main hall and kept very quiet and out of the way.

One hoped Jegari could keep nand' Toby in bed downstairs. Jegari was at least bigger than Toby.

The crossroads with the main road was not that far from the house, and the bus would not be wasting any time, he was sure. Cenedi was just keeping the house doors shut because having them open even for a moment had been dangerous lately, and the bus was big and noisy and could draw fire if there happened to be snipers out there. The several of Great-grandmother's body-guard who were posted on the roof would take care of enemies if any showed themselves, but Cenedi was still being careful.

"One hears the engine," Antaro said, and it was true: he could hear it too, and so must everybody else. Cajeiri took a deep breath and composed himself not to fidget. He straightened his cuffs and tried to look as proper as possible, given he had been working and did not have on one of his better coats. Antaro had a wisp of hair loose from her queue, but he did not point that out to her, either. Antaro had been working hard and had an excuse.

Outside, the bus rumbled up until the sound echoed off the portico roof, and it came to a stop right outside the doors.

Then Cenedi signaled to open those doors, Ramaso passed the order with a move of his hand, and two servants unlocked them and threw the bar back.

The bus was out there, an amazing apparition, its shiny red sides dusty but looking undamaged and without bullet holes.

Everybody crowded toward the door. Cajeiri took the chance and got a view, but he did not tempt mani's wrath by going outside.

And then the bus doors opened, and first down the steps came Barb-daja, her bright curls loose and bobbing. She was wearing the same red-brown atevi-style gown, looking very bedraggled, but heading for the house doors on her own and in a hurry.

She came inside. Her face looked different, paler than usual, exhausted and a little desperate as she looked around the gathering in the hall.

Her eyes lit on him and locked. On *him*, not Cenedi—and she went straight to him and took him by the arms—startling him *and* Antaro. "Nandi. Where's Toby? Is Toby all right?"

"Yes, Barb-daja," he said in ship-speak. *Him.* Who was the only one here who really *could* understand her. Her eyes were watering. She looked older and so, so desperate. "But my great-grandmother will want to see you first," he warned her. It was not politely put, but she absolutely had to call on Great-grandmother or be rude, no matter how desperate she was, and Barb-daja was sometimes rude, and he did not want her to have trouble from it.

Except now she looked as if she might collapse in the middle of the floor. She was a tiny person, even to him, and her eyes kept darting about, looking, he suddenly realized, for nand' Toby among the bystanders. And she had hold of him, which was not good manners in front of the servants, but Barb-daja probably had forgotten that. "Cenedi-nadi," Cajeiri said to Great-grandmother's chief of security, "does my great-grandmother wish to speak to Barb-daja right away?"

Cenedi nodded politely. "She will wish to do so. Ask the lady, nandi, about nand' Bren."

"How is nand' Bren, nandi?" Cajeiri asked in greatest courtesy.

"He was fine. Well, he wasn't. He was shot. Only he had the vest on." Barb-daja's eyes poured wet trails down her face and her voice shook, but she was trying to be helpful and proper. "His guard is with him. They all seem all right. Bren's talking to Machigi—he's talked to him quite a lot. We were having—we were having to live in his apartment, all crowded in. And the other guards were all stuck on the bus, and that was getting pretty bad down there. But Bren sent everybody back to Targai. And Lord Geigi said—" Lord Geigi was very fluent in ship-speak. "Lord Geigi—I talked to him while they were topping off the bus. He said Toby was going to be all right. He said everything was all right at Targai, too, and he gave me a letter—"

She pulled it out of her sleeve, a flattened roll of paper instead of a little message cylinder. Her hand shook as she offered it, and Cenedi promptly took it.

"Do you think Bren's all right where he is?" Barb-daja asked. "His bodyguard—they're carrying their guns and they have a nice suite, all to themselves. Geigi said—Geigi put us on the bus. Bren's people at Targai wanted to stay and wait for him, or something about that, but Geigi insisted they come back here. So they came back with us."

Some of nand' Bren's domestic staff had gone to Targai with him, staying there when nand' Bren had gone out in the bus looking for Barb. And now they had come back with the bus. Cenedi was going to want to talk to them about the situation at Targai.

And Barb was going to have to talk to mani, and then he was going to be relieved of his duty with nand' Toby.

And then *he* was going to have to figure out what to do with Veijico, who had come in and was standing very quietly near the door.

But he supposed Cenedi would want to talk to her first. There were a lot of people on that bus who had been in a position to know things that Cenedi would want to know— and Veijico would be one of them. She might be in a lot of trouble, but she was also Guild, and she would have kept her eyes open. She had been with Bren in Tanaja, and he was sure she would give a clearer report than Barb-daja.

So all of a sudden there was all kinds of information, but none of it was in his reach, except the very welcome report that nand' Bren was not being held in a basement and that his bodyguard was still armed.

And nand' Toby was going to be hearing the coming and going and asking questions Jegari could not understand, let alone answer.

He was thinking that when Great-grandmother's door opened just down the hall. One of Great-grandmother's young men came out, and then, with another of her young men in close attendance, Great-grandmother herself came out to meet Barb-daja. It was a very great courtesy to Barb-daja—but it was mostly, Cajeiri thought, because Great-grandmother wanted news faster than it was coming, even with Guild talking to Guild, short-range. Once Great-grandmother was sure that Barb really had shown up on the bus, Great-grandmother would want to know how she was and what she knew, and some of it would have flown right to her bodyguard and to her, but she wanted to see Barb-daja for herself.

Great-grandmother came down the hall, tap-tapping with her dreadful cane. She was dressed in black—she usually was—and with very little lace and very little jewelry today. She came right up to them, and Cajeiri said to Barb-daja, under his breath, "Bow. Bow *lower.*"

Barb-daja bowed. Great-grandmother, like Cenedi, understood a little ship-speak, but she was the last person who would ever admit it.

Great-grandmother politely bowed her head ever so slightly and flicked a glance at Cajeiri. "She seems healthy enough. We are glad to see that."

Great-grandmother wanted information, a lot of it, and fast. That was as direct a question as Barb-daja was likely to get, and Cajeiri had no idea how to make her understand that. Cenedi-nadi said:

"Nand' Bren seems at some liberty in the premises, aiji-ma.

One of your grandson's men has arrived on the bus to report. We have this young person." He meant Veijico. "And we have the paidhi's staff who have just come in from Targai. We will debrief everyone in order."

Great-grandmother frowned and stamped her cane on the stone floor. "We should do it in some hurry, since we have no knowledge on which to make decisions. Divide into teams and debrief everyone at once."

"Yes," Cenedi said. And Great-grandmother swept a stern glance right toward Cajeiri.

"Barb-daja will talk to nand' Toby. Take her there, young gentleman. *Stay* there and pay attention to what she says."

The Guild was talking to everybody else and getting information as fast as they could. And if Great-grandmother could take Barb-daja into her sitting-room and get everything she knew in good order, Great-grandmother would be doing that, but she was right: Barb-daja would tell everything to Toby.

So he had an important part in things. "Yes, mani-ma," he said with a quick little bow, and said, "Barb-daja, Great-grandmother says go downstairs. Nand' Toby wants to see you."

"*Toby,*" she said, and forgot to bow to Great-grandmother, then remembered and halfway did, and headed for the dining room hall at a near run.

She startled mani's guard—but not him. He bowed for both of them and started to follow her.

And happened to catch a look from Veijico, who was upset and let it show. The look was directed at *him.* Worried. Unhappy, maybe, that he had not really looked at her or made a fuss about her safe return.

Well, she had reason to be upset about that. But so did he, considering everything was her fault. He was responsible for her. More, Veijico was about to be in a lot of trouble with Cenedi, who was very senior Guild, and if there was a rule Veijico had missed breaking, as Jago would put it—one hardly knew what that was.

Definitely she hoped he might stand up for her. But she had hardly deserved it.

And Great-grandmother had just given him a direct order, and Barb-daja was already headed down the back stairs.

He went after Barb-daja, with Antaro close on his heels. He ran the steps to catch up and was with Barb-daja as she reached the basement hall.

She had no idea where she was going. "This way," he said and walked with her down to the corner and to nand' Toby's room. He opened the door himself, and Barb-daja shoved past him, intent on Toby, who, it turned out, was sleeping—the painkillers made sure he did a lot of that. Jegari got up, looking shocked.

Cajeiri signed it was all right and stood by the door watching and listening, as mani had told him to do.

"Toby?" Barb said, sitting on the bed and patting his face. "Toby?"

And Toby woke up and saw her. "Barb," he said, sounding confused and sleepy. Then: "Oh, my God. *Barb!*"

Barb-daja laughed in a funny way, and kissed him, and when she sat back, Toby took hold and brought her hand to his lips, which was sort of embarrassing. But mani said listen. "Barb," Toby said, really awake, now. "Barb, are you all right?"

"I'm fine." Barb starting crying and wiping her eyes with her fingers. "I was so *scared.*"

"Are you hurt?"

"No," she said, gulping air. "No. Veijico rescued me."

"Veijico."

"She shot them. And then both of us got caught by Machigi's people. And then Bren—Bren got us sent to him. He's there. With Lord Machigi."

There was no way to stop her. Now Toby knew.

"He's one of the bad guys," Barb said. "Isn't he?"

"A very bad guy," Toby said faintly. "What in hell is Bren doing there?"

"He's talking to Machigi. I don't know what all about. But his bodyguard is with him. They all have their guns. He seems to be getting along all right."

"God." Toby raked a hand through his hair, and propped his head up higher, to look at her. "In the Marid? Is he in the *Marid*?"

"In Tanaja."

"And you were *there*?"

"I was there."

Toby moved his hand and let his head fall back.

"I remember—" Toby said, staring at the ceiling. "I remember people on the walk, in the dark. You were up there—by the house . . ."

Nand' Toby's memory was not very good for that whole hour. He'd been shot, bleeding all over the walk, and when Barb-daja had run up the walk to get help, kidnappers had carried her off. Cajeiri knew that part all too well. He'd run into Veijico and her partner Lucasi at that point, and he told them—

He had *told* them to help Barb-daja.

He remembered that part now. It upset his stomach.

He had *told* them to go after her.

And Veijico and Lucasi had done exactly that. They had not been smart about it. They had gone off on their own without linking up with other Guild. They'd tracked the kidnappers clear out of Najida's territory, clear out of Sarini Province.

But they had done what he told them to do.

"I don't remember much," Barb was saying, sniffing and wiping her nose, "except these people. Guild. They were so strong—I couldn't do anything. We were running through brush, they carried me as if I were just nothing, and they got in a truck, like a workman's truck, and threw me in the back of it, and they just drove off down the road. I think—I think we went east. I'm not sure. At some point I know we did."

Nand' Toby moved to sit up, and Barb-daja moved to stop him.

"No, it's fine," nand' Toby said. "I'm doing pretty well now. Considering. I'm up walking some."

"Where were you hit?"

Nand' Toby put a hand toward his ribs, where he still had bandages, but no more tubes. "Not too sore. Stitches. Lot of bruises from falling down the damn steps. Bren—Bren went looking for you. And he promised me he'd bring you back. I didn't know he'd follow you clear to Tanaja."

"He's staying there. He says he has business. He's still negotiating with Machigi. I don't know what about."

"There's a long list. Damn. But he got you out."

"Me. Veijico. A whole busload of Tabini's people."

"In Tanaja?"

"They were. They came in with Bren."

That confused nand' Toby. "Tabini's people."

"I'm sure they were. They came back as far as Targai and Lord Geigi."

"He's *there*." Toby rubbed his forehead. "But Bren's in Tanaja. Since when?"

"A couple of days ago."

"How is he?"

"He's fine." A little wobble crept into Barb's voice. Toby looked at her from under his hand.

"*How* fine, Barb?"

"He's all right. He—he had a kind of an accident. Not in Tanaja. He's sore. But he's getting around all right. And he's working, he says."

"Working."

"It wasn't bad. It wasn't bad at all after I got there. They were taking good care of us." Her voice went thin. "But I didn't have my makeup. I just had what I'm wearing. I'm just a mess."

"Barb. You're beautiful. How did Bren get there? Did the aiji send him?"

"I don't know. He came with a busload of Guild, but they wouldn't get off the bus. They stayed parked in the driveway, out front of this house, or palace, or whatever that place is, and Bren's in a really nice suite, very fancy. Veijico and I stayed in the sitting room. Bren kind of needed his bed. He's pretty sore. And he was talking with Machigi, long sessions. I couldn't understand much of it. I hit my head." Barb put a hand on the back of her skull. "When I first saw him. It was my mistake, not his. And Bren was—Bren was, you know, the way he is when he's working. Dead serious. Focused. But I don't think he's scared. Just worried and working."

"Damn. Damn," Toby said, and in Ragi, with a glance in Cajeiri's direction. "Young gentleman?"

That was that. Nand' Toby knew Bren was in trouble and now nand' Toby had figured out they'd been lying to him. Cajeiri folded his arms and fervently wished he had somewhere else to be.

"Do *you* know what's going on?"

That was a very big question. A very scary question. But now, finally, he had to answer it and not make nand' Toby too mad at Great-grandmother while he was doing it.

"Great-grandmother sent him there," he said, "because the Guild was going to kill Machigi."

5

It was a quiet afternoon, at least—a small stack of atlases and a growing number of sheets of paper, with more sketched maps, sites of interest noted, and a rough list of points one wanted to make with Machigi.

Machigi might, personally, be a scoundrel and possibly a murderer. In the cold equations of diplomacy, it didn't matter—if greed could bring Machigi to link his self-interest to a program that would produce peace for the majority of innocent citizens.

Let a people get their personal economic interests linked to a program, and the whole Marid would want to grow in that direction, no matter the virtue or lack of it in their leader—who, if corrupt, could be pacified with profit and if fractious, could be removed in due time. Hell—if *neither* side was playing fair, all right, he could cope with that. Ilisidi had put him into this situation, she'd thrown him in here with no adequate instruction, and he was going to play his own side of it and *make* them deal, damned if he wouldn't.

Old enemies could become economic allies—even real and reliable allies. A bad history ceased to matter once trade was flowing and once the merchants that stood silently behind any government, providing the money, began to see their best interests meant preservation of that agreement. A leader who wanted to take unwilling merchants to war was taking on a real problem.

The paidhi-aiji made notes, more notes, and notes on notes. When he finally did get into his next face-to-face meeting with Machigi, he would have to function on memory. If he was going to carry his points and sell what he was offering, he had to have answers ready, not something he had to look up.

Most of all he had to be ready to be attacked by the advisors, and he had to be quick, polite, and convincing in his answers.

On the other side of the equation, he *wished* he knew more about the intricacies of interclan relations in the largest bay on the east coast. He knew there were problems in the district. They hadn't mattered because the district hadn't mattered greatly, even in the East. Let a previously impoverished area get prosperous however, and that would roil up more trouble within the Dowager's own territory.

But maybe it was better if he didn't know too . . .

Pop.

Boom. A vibration shuddered through the floor. A second boom shook it.

His bodyguard, sitting about the room, had heard the first sound. At the second, they calmly and quietly got up from their chairs. Banichi, on his feet, momentarily frowned, listening to something.

The paidhi-aiji did a lot better to stay in his chair and wait for a report or advisement from them. They were listening. They needed no questions from him.

And there was no other such sound, but the mind scampered over and around dire possibilities. Machigi might be a scoundrel, but Machigi being assassinated somewhere downstairs entrained a whole host of unpleasant possibilities.

Who would the successor naturally, if only publicly, blame for it?

Them.

And who could be the successor? Machigi was young and had no heirs, only a clutch of relatives, some of whom were in other ambitious clans. Civil war was likely.

Or if Machigi's guard had been responsible for those sounds from below—were they winning or losing?

Banichi, senior of his bodyguard, was the one who would be in contact with the situation, if any one of them was.

Jago came over quietly to his chair and said, "Best you go to your room, Bren-ji."

"Yes," he said, and got up and walked with her back into his bedroom.

Jago shut the door, brought him the damned vest and helped him put it on, then, bending, put her lips next to his ear. "You can stay here and be comfortable for now, Bren-ji. But if trouble enters, go down the hall to our room. There is a door wedge on the table next to the door. Use it."

He nodded, not saying a thing, not knowing who, now, could be monitoring what they said or how sensitive the pickup might be. He sat down on the side of the bed and stayed quiet, while Jago stood by the sitting room door.

It was a last ditch defense Jago was talking about. A door wedge was exactly that, one of several simple items his guard traveled with, a simple wedge designed to immobilize a door, so that anybody breaking in would not have easy access.

Barring the door in the next room could not keep him safe longer than a minute or so. Attackers wouldn't care about Machigi's woodwork.

But if intruders split up, some coming after him, it could give his bodyguard maybe that one more minute, in a floor plan that, with that inner hallway, roughly described a circle. They wouldn't all be in one place.

Jago stayed with him, standing. She was listening to something in the connection his bodyguard had with each other.

She said something, two monosyllables, the sort of coded communication Guild used for brevity. She perhaps got an answer back and kept listening intently.

So are we going to have intruders with explosives up here next? Bren wondered. He had his gun, right over there in the top bureau drawer. He was going to go over and get it if Jago in any wise indicated there was trouble coming. He'd fight *for* his bodyguard, as long as there were any of them with him. If it was just him left—probably, pretty surely, he thought, he would shoot someone to protect himself. He knew for damned certain he didn't want to become a Marid hostage, asking Tabini or the dowager to bargain to get him back.

He wasn't sure they *would* bargain anything to get him back. And they should not. Hell of a thing, to work for years to try to knit up the fractures in the aishidi'tat and possibly to end up a pawn in the hands of the people trying to take it apart.

If that was the case down there.

Guild renegades. It was not a pleasant prospect.

Jago turned, finally, still listening, but gave him a high sign—progress.

So she was getting good news from somewhere, and if Banichi was tapped in anywhere at all, it had to be to Machigi's guard, so if he was getting good news, it had to come from that source.

Good news, from his viewpoint, because it confirmed what Machigi's guard had told his guard. Truthfulness on Machigi's side was certainly good news.

It was good news, too, to think that Machigi's guard was still alive, still out there.

And it was good news because Machigi's bodyguard was concerned that his bodyguard didn't decide to take him and make a break for it. Machigi's guard could be sure they wouldn't join any other side inside the Marid, but they could certainly mess up any plan by bolting in mistrust.

Encouraging set of thoughts.

Not definitive, but encouraging.

Jago stayed on her feet, pacing a few steps now and again, listening and not talking at all. He kept silent, watching her for any clues whether she still liked what she was hearing or not. She was restless. She wanted to be out there. She wanted to be doing something. He knew Jago.

A fairly long time he watched that pacing.

Then Jago stopped moving.

Something was going on. He said nothing, just waited—a much longer time. Jago was staring at the other wall, at the sitting room door, as happened. And she didn't move a muscle, a suddenly rigid black statue, armed, on a hair trigger and heeding something he couldn't hear.

Are they coming up here? he wondered.

Are we about to defend this place?

I'd surrender to whatever happens if doing it could keep them alive.

If they were alive, I'd have options. I'd fight for them, all right. I'd fight for them my way, to do with any *other* Marid lord what I'd hoped to do with Machigi.

That could work.

If I can keep *them* alive, I can get us *all* out of this.

I should get up. Go out there. Tell Banichi we're not going to fight. Let me deal with whoever it is . . .

Jago shifted a foot suddenly, looked his way, meaning business. "Bren-ji. Go."

To the other room, she meant. Bar the door.

"Jago-ji, let me deal with them."

Fierce shake of her head.

He was getting up. It was a process, and Jago strode over and lifted under his arm. He protested. "I can deal with whoever—"

Lips next to his ear and a gentle simultaneous reorientation toward the other door. "Lord Machigi's guard is coming."

Lord Machigi's guard was coming.

Reinforcements? Or was Machigi attacking them? All of a sudden he *didn't* understand what was going on, and not understanding, he could offer no help at all to his bodyguard. He yielded to Jago's insistence and went out into the hall, down to their room, at a fast walk.

The table right by the door had a small array of odd objects he didn't recognize,and a gun: and the wedge. He picked the wedge up, shut the door, started to bend over . . .

With the vest, *that* was a problem. He dropped the wedge on the floor, managed to nudge it into place with his foot, picked up a secondary doorstop, a clever metal piece that fitted into the crack on the hinge side.

Then he took up the gun, which was rather large even for atevi hands, and took the safety off.

He wished they'd left one of their communications units with him. He was standing here holding the fort—but the people he cared about weren't in the fort in question, and everything he'd thought was going on, wasn't going the way he'd thought it would.

It was either fairly all right out there or going very damned bad.

And if he had to set off this cannon he was holding, the recoil was going to blow him across the room.

He waited. He heard the outer door open. No shots followed. That was good.

He waited a very long time.

And finally footsteps approached the door. If Guild was involved, they wouldn't rush a door dead center, and they'd expect a stop to be in place. They might blow the door out. And maybe him with it. He shifted over against the inside wall.

A knock, then.

"Bren-ji?"

Jago's voice, calm and ordinary. He lowered the heavy gun and let go the breath he'd held the last several seconds.

"Shall I open?" he asked.

"You may," she said, and with great relief he laid the gun on the table, pried out the top doorstop, and kicked the bottom one out of the way to unlock and open the door.

Jago looked entirely unruffled. "Tano and Algini have gone into the hall to speak with Machigi's men. They declare they have just taken care of the local problem. They say certain other suspects have left the city or are headed in that direction—not as good news as might be, but one can at least rest easier here."

So his bodyguard was talking directly with Machigi's security, who had taken out infiltrators. And maybe let others escape. Or not. Damn, he hated partial information.

"Of what man'chi were they?" he asked. "Do we have any clue, Jago-ji?"

Granted they could believe the information Machigi's guard was passing them.

Jago didn't sign him to silence. *She* was trusting it was now safe to talk. She said, "We have no information yet, but Tano and Algini will be asking for details."

"One would like to sit by the fire for a while." He began to walk with Jago down the hall, toward the sitting room. The thought of his comfortable chair and a cup of strong tea drew him.

And information. Whatever had just gone on—he needed to know. There was division in the Marid. Or someone was attempting to foment division. Whether one or more of the other clans was behind whatever had happened, or whether it was renegade Guild either independently or associated with one of—

Jago stopped in her tracks. He stopped, just short of the door to the sitting room. She was listening to something—and then she reached and opened the door for him.

He walked ahead. Banichi was there, standing by the outer door, listening to something, too.

He didn't ask. Things were going on. Tano and Algini were out there exposed to whatever politics might be afoot.

Could there be any issue between Machigi's intentions and his bodyguard? The bodyguard, granted they were both native and Guild, should have solid man'chi to their lord.

They might, however, disagree with their lord about what posed a threat and what didn't. They were capable of acting contrary to orders on that issue—God knew his own bodyguard would do it. He and Machigi were in a similar situation in that regard: there were two sets of bodyguards doing their own negotiating and, in the case of Machigi's, apparently deciding a certain interest in the household posed a threat, under the changed circumstances of the paidhi's talks with Machigi. So they had moved to take it out before it could so much as twitch in self-defense.

Machigi might find himself having to mop up the diplomatic consequences inside his own district.

Which could be an advantage, if Machigi's bodyguard had just, in the process, tipped the scales toward the dowager's proposal.

"Lord Machigi wishes to see you, nandi," Banichi said, breaking his silence, "in half an hour, in the map room."

Guild talked with Guild. Lords talked with lords. *He* had Machigi to deal with . . . the thought struck him—it was Tano and Algini out there talking to at least one of Machigi's bodyguard. Algini, who had been high-up Guild, under the previous Guildmaster.

The question was—and he likely would never know—exactly what Algini was now and whether Algini had done any negotiating on Guild matters that neither Machigi nor the paidhi-aiji knew about. Possibly Banichi and Jago didn't know that answer. Possibly even Tano didn't.

Damned right the Guild's ruling hierarchy up in Shejidan was concerned about what was going on down here. In one single day they'd gone from a debate on outlawing all of Machigi's Guild members to—

Maybe they were adopting a different position and were making their own offer.

Hell of a situation. He had come here representing the dowager.

By the terms on which Machigi was willing to talk, he was now representing Machigi.

And now half of his aishid was very likely representing the Assassins' Guild in what was a districtwide crisis.

"One doubts we will be discussing the maps or my proposals in this meeting," he said wryly, wishing he could stay safe in this apartment for, oh, the next few days. "But yes, Banichi-ji, one will be glad of the opportunity."

6

Nand' Toby ought not to be coming upstairs, but there was no reasonable way to stop him. And Barb-daja was with nand' Toby, helping him.

Cajeiri just climbed the steps behind them, with Antaro and Jegari in front of him, on the theory that the two of them could stop both of them falling backward.

Nand' Toby wanted to talk to Great-grandmother directly. And there were very few people Cajeiri thought might go up against mani to get an answer, but nand' Toby, while ordinarily very quiet and polite, had gotten himself dressed and declared he was going upstairs, and that was that. Barb-daja had wanted her cosmetics, which were down on the boat, and had gotten upset about it, but nand' Toby had talked her out of that.

So they all went upstairs. Nand' Toby was out of breath by the time they reached the upper hall, and Jegari unceremoniously took hold of his left arm—Barb-daja had his right arm—and made him stand still a moment.

It was a chance to get out in front of the expedition and maybe to keep mani from blaming him for nand' Toby being mad at her. "You wait there, Toby-nandi," Cajeiri said. "I'll find Cenedi."

Nand' Toby was too out of breath to argue. Cajeiri took that as agreement and hurried off with Antaro in close company, past two worried household servants and Ramaso-nadi. The whole household knew that nand' Toby was supposed to stay downstairs, and it was clear to anyone now that there was some sort of trouble keeping him there.

Cajeiri went straight to mani's door, since that was where one generally found Cenedi, and Antaro knocked before Cajeiri opened the door and went in.

Mani and Cenedi both were there, with Nawari, and they were talking to Veijico, who was sitting in a chair in front of them.

Mistake. He had walked in on something that was not going to put either mani or Cenedi in a good mood.

Great-grandmother turned her attention toward him, shifting her cane ominously to rest squarely on the floor. Cajeiri pulled a fast bow to his great-grandmother and a lesser bow to Cenedi, who was standing, looked sternly down at him.

"Mani-ma," he began, "nand' Toby has come upstairs. Barb-daja has told him nand' Bren is in the Marid. He has questions."

"He understands the Marid, does he," mani asked.

A third bow. Fast. It gave him time to get a breath. "One is sure he understands, mani-ma. He wishes to talk to you. One apologizes. He is very upset. One dared not restrain him. One is not certain . . ."

Thump! went the dreaded cane against the carpet. "Uncertainty gets no respect, Great-grandson. *That* is why he has come up here against your advice."

"Yes, mani. But—"

"But he is out the hall with his questions, is he?"

"Yes, mani, in the dining hall. I told him to wait."

"We shall speak to him." Mani thumped the cane more gently and gave a wave of her hand. Nawari had moved from near the wall to stand beside Cenedi. Veijico quietly got up from her chair and retreated to the edge of the room to stand. At a flick of mani's other hand, Nawari went to the door and opened it, while Veijico, who was probably glad not to be debriefing to Great-grandmother for a moment, tried her best to be furniture.

Nand' Toby and Barb-daja arrived, both very pale and very

frail-looking . . . so much so that mani instantly waved her hand and ordered Nawari to have the staff bring tea and cakes. And Veijico—

"You! Chairs for them! Be *useful!*"

Veijico moved in an instant, and meanwhile nand' Toby and Barb-daja both bowed very properly. Veijico had chairs under them as fast as possible, and they were able to sit down, nand' Toby first.

"Well!" mani said. "We shall have a nice cup of tea. And *you,* boy!"

"Mani!" Cajeiri said, immediately standing forward.

"Inform nand' Toby that we have heard from the paidhi-aiji, and he is faring very well, accommodated in lordly estate and courteously dealt with in Lord Machigi's house."

He translated that quickly. Nand' Toby already knew something about that, from Barb-daja.

"Thank you," Toby said in Ragi, with a little nod, and said flatly in Mosphei: "I want to know why she sent him there."

"They are grateful for the news, mani, and hope to understand."

"Pish! Let us anticipate their questions and do quick business, since the tea will arrive quickly. We are relatively confident Lord Machigi has become worried about his own survival and has found his neighbors plotting against him, thinking him young and in over his head in trouble with the aishidi'tat, all his plots having collapsed. The paidhi on his own initiative has extended an offer from us. Lord Machigi is considering it. Should Lord Machigi deal badly with the paidhi-aiji, he would not long survive our retaliation, and he knows it. And if he will not deal with us reasonably at all, it is not likely he will long survive his neighbors' actions, especially since we would then File with the Guild. Lord Machigi is a brilliant young man, attempting to counter what is going on in the north of the Marid, but his operation on the west coast has been infiltrated, and he is in danger on two fronts. If his precarious situation becomes known to his subclans, his position will be substantially weakened, and he will not see the summer."

Cajeiri drew a breath: mani grew very angry if anyone missed any of her spoken messages, but he did not know how to say all that in ship-speak. "Mani is answering fast before tea comes and nobody can talk. She's pretty sure nand' Bren is safe, because Lord Machigi is in bad trouble. His enemies in the Marid want to kill him because he's very smart and they're scared of him. The Guild was going to kill him, and Great-grandmother stopped that. And if he did anything to nand' Bren, Great-grandmother would kill him." He could not think of all the words he wanted. His ship-speak words were going away under pressure, even though he had been practicing with nand' Toby, and that upset him. "Lord Machigi's enemies have taken over what he's doing here at Najida. His Marid allies want him dead. So he's in trouble, and mani knows it. She sent nand' Bren there to get Machigi out of the trouble he's in, and then he'd better listen to her."

He got it all out, in scrambled order, but he must have said it fairly right. Nand' Toby listened, frowning a little, and slowly looked happier.

"One is very grateful, nand' dowager," nand' Toby said in passable Ragi. "One is grateful for your patience."

That made Great-grandmother happier. She set her hands on her cane and nodded back.

What mani had said made a sort of sense. And mani *was* getting phone calls from nand' Bren.

And Machigi had gone from attacking them to sending Barbdaja and Veijico back. So maybe the other lords in the Marid were starting to worry about Machigi.

When one played chess with Great-grandmother, one really had to watch everything on the board.

He thought of questions. He was suddenly absolutely bubbling over with questions.

But just then the servants brought tea in, and everybody had to be quiet a while.

7

Tano and Algini arrived back to the suite half a minute before Machigi's guards showed up at the door as an escort to the conference with Machigi.

So there was no time for Tano and Algini to indicate what they had discussed, either with whom, or where, but it seemed highly unlikely that the arrival close at their backs was coincidence. They were probably, Bren thought, the same individuals Tano and Algini had been talking to.

Banichi and Jago elected to go with him as his own escort, their usual divison of labor, both armed, the same as the aggregation of Machigi's guards around him—but they were outnumbered three to one.

Tano and Algini had given them no sign that things were going badly—at least that Bren had caught. More, Banichi and Jago had eased off indefinably—they didn't *feel* quite as tense as they had been on the last outing.

But Bren obediently wore the vest, considering what had just gone on in the building. Things inside Machigi's perimeters were not necessarily safe at the moment. And Banichi and Jago might have relaxed a little toward Machigi's guards, but not toward the premises. They were on alert as they went, watching everything.

There was no sign of damage in the halls—at least none in the pale, elaborately decorated stairways and corridors they walked. Whatever had gone on with the gunfire and the explosion, it had gone on in some deeper recess, probably in the service corridors, which were guaranteed to exist everywhere in an atevi structure. But there was not one other soul to be seen, not a servant, not a resident. *That* said something. The place seemed under lockdown, the servants entirely invisble . . . or keeping to their quarters.

There were black-uniformed Guild, however, abundant in the lower hall: twenty or thirty besides the four with them. The odds were getting impossible—if there was trouble.

Down that last stairway and into the hall. They were the object of universal attention.

There goes the meddling human who caused this mess, he could imagine these Guildsmen thinking. There goes the foreigner.

They passed between the magnificent pillars and through the open door of the audience hall. There was still no hint of any violence that had gone on—no hint except the extraordinary number of guards that quietly folded into the space behind them. The place was vacant. They walked across the reception hall and up to the doors of the map room, escorted by the original two of Machigi's Guild and Banichi and Jago, but two more guards stood at those doors. They opened and let him and his escort in. The others, one was glad to see, all stayed outside in the audience hall.

Machigi waited standing, a shadow against the white sky in the windows. Machigi turned toward them, and that light made him all silhouette, expressionless.

While the same light showed Machigi the paidhi's face, no question, an examination that would discover any weakness.

"Nand' paidhi," Machigi said by way of greeting, and Bren gave the requisite bow.

"Nandi," Bren said. "One rejoices to see you well." Even close up, he couldn't see how Machigi's face reacted, if at all. "One has spoken to the aiji-dowager on your behalf and received favorable replies."

It was pretty damned sure Machigi—and possibly the

whole Marid, given the goings-on in the household—was well-informed on that phone call.

But still there was no help from that blank, black shadow, not even the grace of a profile, just a silhouetted, head-on statue.

"The aiji-dowager," Machigi said, "has created us a great deal of trouble in sending you here."

Machigi might be featureless black. But an inner light shone brightly enough on the landscape: it was the challenge the aiji-dowager had deliberately posed to a young and fractious warlord in sending him here, and that phone call had made it clear to both sides.

Here, young fool. Here is the paidhi-aiji, my personal emissary.

Kill him, imprison him, or otherwise offend me, and you will not live out the year.

Admit him to your lands and treat him well, and you may, in time, find out why I sent him.

You know what crimes were done in the paidhi's district. You know that the aiji now has been handed all the excuse he needs to remove you. The Guild still has the paperwork necessary to outlaw you.

Your enemies were acting inside your perimeter and setting up trouble with your neighbors.

You were about to fall.

Yet . . . here is my emissary.

What will you do now, Lord Machigi?

He hadn't seen it in its entirety. He hadn't the hard-wiring to *feel* how it had played in alevi senses. Possibly everyone else had felt the undercurrents—from Banichi and Jago down to young Veijico, though in the latter case, he somewhat doubted it.

Machigi had begun to read his own situation, probably when the first advisement came in that the paidhi-aiji, in a bright red and black bus, the Ragi colors, had crossed the fuzzy but lethal boundary, accompanied by enough Guild to give the district hell if any weapon threatened that bus.

And Machigi would have just figured out that not all the forces operating in his district were under his command.

The dowager had read the situation, put two and two together after Barb's kidnapping, and figured that the second-to-last thing a ruler of the Marid would want at this juncture was Barb-daja being kidnapped—the last thing of all being Barb-daja noisily carried across his lands toward his capital in full view and witness of everybody.

Ergo—and bet that the dowager had been morally certain of it—Machigi had *not* ordered Barb's kidnapping.

Ergo, someone else had.

Ergo, that someone else would *not* be one of the paidhi's associates and not one of Tabini-aiji's, not one of the dowager's, not the Guild itself, and not one of any other lord of the western coast.

Ergo, the responsible party was somebody inside the Marid.

The perpetrators had run their trail of misdeeds right across Machigi's district, figuring on hot pursuit and maybe figuring that Machigi would attack that pursuit—thus getting Machigi to attack the dowager's forces. That would have set matters boiling!

They had committed an extravagance of illegal acts over on the coast, figuring Machigi would be blamed for them and would be assassinated; but that had not worked due to Tabini-aiji's preoccupation with the center of the aishidi'tat. But it accumulated a record.

So if Machigi fell—what effect would that have on Marid politics?

A sudden power vacuum, destabilizing the Taisigi Association, the whole south of the leadership of the Marid.

Who stood to profit from that?

The northernmost pair of Machigi's four neighbors, while the southern two would find their lives in danger.

A few days ago Machigi had been lord of the Marid, master of all his plans and schemes to widen his power, and now—he had just had to take protective measures inside his own staff and eliminate some of his historic ties. Bet on it. If those gunshots had not been mere window-dressing for the negotiator, Machigi had just, real-world, eliminated ties inside his staff, probably to the Dojisigi. Maybe to the Senji.

If that was so.

Had Machigi made that choice? Or had his bodyguard—being aware of Guild proceedings?

Thoughts jumped like lightning. The body went on to bow ceremoniously, acknowledging Machigi's challenge. "One confesses to being still largely uninformed, nandi. But one is at least pleased to have conveyed the dowager's favorable response. One can say—"

"We are *not* pleased!" Machigi snapped at him. "Convey *that* to her."

"Yes," Bren said simply. Yes was decidedly the safest answer. And it was an interesting response. Machigi was mad. So whether he was right or wrong about what he thought had happened, Machigi wasn't happy about what had happened.

And *that* said he was probably right, and Machigi had suddenly found himself fighting for his life.

Machigi turned his back and took a few strides toward the windows, looking—a gesture in itself, looking down on his city, his harbor, his private ocean. Anger was in the taut line of his shoulders. Nobody moved for the moment, and one had time to consider the vulnerability of that pose. Two fast moves on the part of the paidhi's guard, and Machigi would die and the head of his bodyguard would die—followed, of course, by the paidhi and his guard, and then by his guard upstairs.

Machigi outright dared him to try it. Wondered, perhaps, if that was the aishidi'tat's intention.

But getting rid of Machigi was, one surmised, not the *dowager's* intention. It might be Machigi's neighbors' intention. But he was sure it was not Ilisidi's.

He walked forward quietly, with a little flick of his fingers that told Banichi and Jago to stay where they were. He was increasingly sure of his reading of the situation now, and he came to stand beside Machigi, also gazing outward over the harbor, making himself part of Machigi's scene, equally vulnerable.

"This is a fair prospect, nandi. And your enemies are *not* in possession of it."

"My enemies," Machigi echoed him darkly, "number many more than my neighbors."

"You should not count the aiji-dowager among those enemies, nandi. She has taken quite a different view of your existence."

"Why should she do so? Where is *her* advantage in these dealings?"

Not a plain question—and one that challenged a human to make one ateva understand another. *Not* the least subtle atevi, either.

But Machigi was in a situation; and Machigi was asking. Machigi *wanted* to believe there was a way to get the upper hand.

"The aiji-dowager, nandi, has always maintained independence, even from her grandson. She is a traditionalist when it comes to the land, but *not* a traditionalist when it comes to an unprofitable feud." He spoke quietly, still looking outward, not intruding so much as a glance into Machigi's private agitation. "Being an Easterner, she has power and influence unaffected by the moods of the central district. She works outside the aishidi'tat, a position she has very carefully crafted over the years since the legislature saw fit *not* to make her aiji—and would never make her aiji. She has survived her husband, her son, and now sees her grandson in power, but she is no longer young, and you have offered her a chance that may not come again: a chance to settle the situation she had wanted to settle in the very beginning of the aishidi'tat. You will *be* aiji of the Marid, in this plan of hers."

He got Machigi's attention, a face-on stare; he noted that

movement in the tail of his vision. But he stared tranquilly out the window.

"Why?" Machigi asked. "Are you saying she wants to overthrow her grandson?"

"No." He wished he were surer of that statement.

"To start a war in the Marid?"

He answered calmly, he hoped not insolently, and still stared into the sunlight: "When has there *not* been bloodfeud within the Marid, nandi? If this situation exposes it—better to know your enemies. No. Your internal trouble is not even the lord of the Dojisigi. It is the Guild who fled here, Guild who urged you and the other lords of the Marid to back Murini."

"You say! Who said there *are* such persons?"

"Who died in your household today, nandi?"

"Insolent bastard!"

"Elements of the Guild were in the action that seated Murini in Shejidan. When he fell, and these people were driven out of the aishidi'tat, they brought with them their old attachments—some of them to the northern Kadagidi, some of them to other northern clans. They have found nests of refuge here, but one would by no means depend on their man'chi."

A long silence. A dangerous silence.

"This is, of course," Bren said, "a guess. But that you are alive is a testament to the skill of your bodyguard. Their man'chi to you one does not question."

"Insolent wretch. Who are *you* to judge?"

"You have asked me, nandi, to give you such service as I have given the aiji in Shejidan and the aiji-dowager. My advice. My observations, as directly, as bluntly, as honestly as I can frame them, lest there be any mistake. You were one that put Murini in power. It gave you one thing—distraction of the other clans to problems in the north. You reached for the West. You all but had it. And then Tabini-aiji overthrew Murini and took his office back. Worse, the Guild who had backed Murini came *here*, Guild whose man'chi is *not* to the Marid. Guild who have broken with the Guild in Shejidan. Tell me, nandi, where *their* man'chi will lie. Not with you. Not with any lord of the Marid. This is a problem to you. Here one can only guess, but you are alive, and your bodyguard, with you from *before* Murini, has kept you alive. Now the aiji-dowager, whose information is much more thorough than mine, has moved suddenly to keep you alive. You are valuable to her, nandi. Having been in your presence, one can say one can understand the aiji-dowager's reasoning."

"Three times insolent! You do not sit in judgment of me, paidhi!"

"Nor does one in any wise presume to do so. I merely observe that the aiji-dowager is no fool."

Silence. He didn't look at Machigi. He stood still, not to bend, and not to provoke the man further.

Machigi snapped: "Should we be impressed by her good opinion?"

"No, nandi. But you should not throw it away. Examine her reasons. You have asked me to speak for you and to use my offices. Ask your own sensibilities was it wise to admit these fugitive Guild back into the Marid. It was an honorable act, perhaps, but not to your benefit, surely. Murini is dead. To whom is their man'chi now? Is anyone certain it was ever to Murini?"

The silence resumed. Persisted a while. Then Machigi said, out of utter stillness, not a move, not a breath that slipped control: "My mother's brother died this morning."

God, who was Machigi referring to? Who in Machigi's clan had married in?

His mother. His mother's generation. Machigi himself was the son of Ardami, son of Sagimi—both Taisigi from way back.

But his mother—

His mother. Bren racked his brain to have it right. Mada, it was. Mada, a woman out of the far weaker Farai clan in Senji. They were not Dojisigi, the usual troublemakers—but allied to the Dojisigi, and they had for a hundred years been a thorn in Senji's side because of it.

The Farai were the same clan that had been sitting in *his* apartment in Shejidan and claiming they were heroes of the counterrevolution and Tabini's return to power.

Emblematic of which, they had camped in the paidhi-aiji's apartment, which they claimed by inheritance, clinging to their claim of heroic action on the aiji's behalf, talking peace while snuggling right next door to the aiji's own back wall.

"Farai," Bren said. It was all he dared say. Life and death trembled on a young man's temper.

Again that lengthy silence. Then Machigi said, quietly: "That is the *Tropic Sun* putting out into the bay, do you see?"

One did see, a middling-sized ship leaving a slight wake on the sun-reflecting harbor. "The freighter. Yes, nandi."

"That ship is bound north, to the railhead north of Najidami Bay, all the way around the south coast. Your plan would make all that traffic move by rail. That ship is not stout enough nor fast enough to venture the seas of your eastern trade. The dowager's plan would not make that shipowner happy."

"One could propose things that might do so. Trade with Separti Township."

"We trade there now."

"And the southern isle."

'We trade there now."

"But the southern isle would by then be receiving goods from the eastern ports. That ship would prosper, nandi."

"So, paidhi." Machigi turned, frowning, facing him. "You have brought papers. More of your promises?"

He had all but forgotten the folders he had tucked under his arm. He turned and gave a slight bow in courtesy. "Specifics of place and resources, aiji-ma."

The respectful, *personal* grant of loyalty. He tried it out now in cold blood, deliberately, consciously, a matter of politics. But it bothered him, having said it. He had never in all the world thought he would ever use that title to any but Tabini and Tabini's house.

He'd thought it wouldn't bother him. A human could lie about his loyalties. But the word damned near stuck in his throat.

And resounded off atevi nerves. It had to shock Banichi and Jago. It was downright humiliating for him, hurtful to do to them, and it necessarily dragged them into his declaration.

It resounded off Machigi's nerves, too, of whatever moral quality they were, now that Machigi had decided against killing the lot of them.

"Tea," Machigi said suddenly. That was an atevi social response to far, far too much emotion in the air. One needed to quiet down and restore a balance that had been, for the last half minute, careening too wildly to one side and another. *"Staff!"* Machigi snapped suddenly, which argued that they had been relatively isolated for the last while: staff had to be summoned from a comparative distance.

Worth noting. Machigi had let only his personal bodyguard in on this conference, so long as it was possible it could blow up into shooting, one supposed. Now that it had not, Machigi was apparently ready to talk in a different mode, in a more polite frame of mind.

"You need not be burdened with your documents," Machigi observed as doors opened and staff came in. "If you wish to deliver them to me, staff will take them. We shall read them later."

"Indeed, yes, aiji-ma." He slipped, deliberately, into the intimate-with-authority mode.

"You have specifics, you say?"

Bren gave an affirmative bow. "Early specifics. But I believe accurate ones."

"You work very quickly, nand' paidhi. Of course—there has been absolutely no confirmation from Najida."

"If we have any favorable wind, aiji-ma, best catch it and keep the ship moving in a good direction."

Machigi snapped his fingers and indicated the papers, which Bren handed to the servant who responded.

"Tea," Machigi said to the servants, "nadiin."

No softening -ji. No intimacy with any of his staff. That was downright shocking—or Machigi was in a hellish bad humor with staff. In Najida, even in Shejidan, staff would certainly take it that way, but Machigi gave no outward indication of it at the moment, which meant he covered his emotions very well when he wanted to. He mildly gestured toward the chair grouping near the tall windows, and they walked that way and sat down opposite one another, with the windows on Bren's right hand and on Machigi's left, to wait for tea.

The light cast a gloss on Machigi's dark face, and made the old scar more evident. The eyes were deep gold and deep-set, with that epicanthic fold some southerners had. It gave them a fierce, unsettlingly predatory look.

And Machigi surveyed him in silence, taking in human features in the same way, likely—since, excepting Barb, and excepting television and photographs, he had never seen one.

There was a lot to learn about each other, Bren thought, quietly folding and slipping his few notes into his inner coat pocket. A lot to learn on both sides. Machigi gave him reason to be comfortable, even complacent.

Here was a youth in near-absolute power. Perhaps in the way of youth, he was touchy about his prerogatives and a shade wary of intimacy, feeling a need to set staff at some distance, lest anyone presume, or lose their fear of him. Or there just *was* no attachment.

One had no information of any woman in the picture, either, nor even, now, any close relatives except the newly deceased uncle: Machigi was a survivor of bloody years in the Marid and several skirmishes with Tabini-aiji and the aiji-dowager.

He was alone. Angry. And alive.

While he himself had just made an emotional commitment to this man that left him entirely uneasy, as if the whole world had broken up in moving bits, and he didn't know what situation he was going to be in when—*when* he went back to Ilisidi.

And worse, ultimately he was going to have to go back to Tabini to explain his reasoning in offering this young trouble-maker the whole east coast of the continent, *and* a ticket to the space station.

Machigi didn't talk while they waited for the tea. He didn't. Their respective bodyguards had repositioned themselves. And the serving staff, after what seemed an interminable interval, came back with tea. Serving it took time. Drinking it took much more time.

He could not be comfortable in the situation. He could not even be comfortable with Banichi and Jago staring at his back wondering what in hell else a human was capable of doing, seeing what he had already done.

And he dared not show anything he felt.

Click! went Machigi's empty teacup onto the side table.

Bren set his down with a softer click and settled his mind to business.

"So, paidhi," Machigi said, "now that the aiji-dowager has made us a target of all the rest of the Marid—what is your advice?"

"That you take her offer, aiji-ma. One greatly doubts her offer has changed your enemies' plans from what they always were. One surmises you were aware when you made strong early moves to exert influence outside the Marid that you were going to disturb your neighbors. There is no evidence you consulted either of your northern neighbors in your moves on the west coast. The two southern clans will have acquiesced, since they follow your lead. One observes you offered young Baiji the hand of Tiajo-daja, a daughter of Badissuni's line over in the Dojisigin Marid. One has no idea whether Badissuni's house attempted to get a ride aboard your plan—you backed it. But one doubts you would have let that marriage go forward."

Machigi rested his elbow on the chair arm, chin on his fist, gold eyes focused entirely on his. "Go on. We are amused."

"They were too busy with their own problems to interfere

further in your moves to take the west coast. And Tabini-aiji's driving Murini out was more inconvenient to them than to you. Events kept your *Marid* enemies off balance. They fortified themselves against any retaliation from Shejidan; they plotted to get inside Tabini-aiji's defenses. My own arrival on the coast was not quite unrelated—your kinsmen the Farai had appropriated my residence in the Bujavid, giving me little choice but retreat to my estate. One hesitates to attribute to them the foresight to know I would go to the west coast as a result of their holding my apartment, but it is not impossible. I can assure you I had no orders from Shejidan in going to Najida, no advance knowledge at all regarding your dealings here. I walked into—dare I say, *your* operation at Kajiminda?— entirely by chance. I somehow doubt you expected, either, that Guild within that operation would attempt my life."

Machigi opened that fist, a brief, dismissive gesture. And smiled. The eyes did not.

"So," Bren said. "You did not know then, but do know now, that the aiji's son is at Najida. That was planned by no one, least of all his father or his great-grandmother. But it did heighten the impact of that attack. The successive attacks. It brought the aiji-dowager in. And it brought Geigi home from the space station. It exposed your operation, it brought Baiji down, and it brought the Edi into the conflict. One can imagine you did *not* authorize that attack."

"The attack was unauthorized," Machigi said. "And information was limited. Your people had the phones tapped from the moment *you* arrived on the peninsula."

"Indeed," Bren said. The wiretapping was news to him. "And might one suppose you did not authorize the attack on Najida?"

"Go on," Machigi said.

"The Guild operating in the vicinity of Kajiminda then flagrantly violated Guild policy and laid the bloody knife at your door. In their theory, neither the dowager nor the Guild would wait to ask questions."

"Go on," Machigi said again, increasingly darkly, and Bren kept going:

"The Farai are too small to swing the entire Marid by the tail. The Farai lord has kept the Senji lord at arm's length by courting the Dojisigi; and one strongly suspects it was the Dojisigi who set them at the same tactic inside the Bujavid, to gain information about Tabini-aiji's movements. You were to be eliminated, which would benefit the Dojisigi lord and the Senji. And it would be a race then to see whether the Farai tried actually to deal with Tabini-aiji and ally with your successor in the Taisigin Marid, thus getting the better of the Dojisigi *and* the Senji, or whether the Dojisigi would simply squash them overnight and *then* make a move to install their *own* candidate in the lordship in Tanaja. The fact the Dojisigi had offered a daughter to meddle in your plans for Baiji indicates they were already taking aim at you."

Machigi sat silent for a moment, then gave a silent, short laugh. "For a human, you present a reasonably accurate assessment."

"One has attempted to learn, aiji-ma. The plot against you leads only to the aishidi'tat doing all the work and the Farai, in their imagination, getting all the benefit. The Dojisigi then turn on them, or turn them on the Senji. Except for one thing—a Guild presence that is plotting its own course in the Marid. One has no exact knowlege to match the dowager's, one is quite sure. But one strongly suspects that there is an infelicitous *sixth* power in the Marid, and, on evidence I observe—they do not favor you. What was an ordinarily complicated piece of Marid politics now has taken a very alarming turn, and one begins to understand it is not the Dojisigi or the Senji at work. You have not cooperated with the Guild renegades. One believes the aiji-dowager has convinced the Guild you *are* a point of stability in this region. One is even moved to suspect the Guild in Shejidan launched its deliberation on outlawry as—between the two of us—a diversion."

That brought a sharp, angry glance.

"So. What *else* do you surmise?"

"That your own bodyguard is extraordinarily adept, or you would not now be alive."

Angrier yet. And not, necessarily, at him.

At persons closer to him. Intimates, of which this dangerous young man had very few.

"So. Are we to be flattered by the aiji-dowager's estimation that we have difficulties?"

"She has no pity for fools. She is convinced you have uncommon qualities as a leader, or I am quite confident there would be no offer, and I would not be here. She seems to believe that those qualities have alarmed your northern neighbors to the point of desperation."

"And of course she would never encourage that situation."

"Not, aiji-ma, *not* when the situation is entangled with the problem I have named."

"The dowager has a reputation, paidhi. She takes what she wants."

"Yet she has never taken so much as a village, aiji-ma. Territorially, she is not ambitious . . . not in her own district, where other lords view her as a good neighbor."

"She collects man'chi as some people collect minatures!"

Bren said with a little bow: "Indeed, she has drawn uncommonly diverse man'chi to her. But she does *not* as a rule offer alliances."

There was a reason the legislature had feared to make her aiji.

The fist was back under the chin, Machigi's favorite contemplative pose. The gold eyes were calculating, estimating *him*, since he was the only available target. Machigi said nothing for a moment.

But the muscles around the eyes held a little quirk of something that had not been there before. Intense concentration.

"You are different from my reports," Machigi said, "and difficult to read. One understands a human has no man'chi. Yet you *do* favor her side of the table."

"We have another quality," he said, "something akin. We *are* capable of loyalty. We are even capable of *dual* loyalty."

Quirk of the eyebrow. He'd said it with forethought—in utter honesty. Which Machigi probably had not expected but ought to recognize.

"Divided loyalties," Machigi said.

"Dual loyalties, aiji-ma. She knows it. I am advising you with *your* interests foremost at the moment."

Machigi gave a small disparaging laugh. "She has learned to wield your two-edged talents to her advantage, has she? How well do humans lie?"

"Some better than others," Bren said. "I have lived a long time on the continent, and everything I have done has a record. I have reserved truth when it served. I have *not* based a negotiation on a lie. Ever."

That was a smile. A small one, almost a laugh, and this one lighter than before. Machigi was either letting his emotions show now, or while talking about lying, he *was* lying and had turned very deliberately deceptive.

"We have broken with the Farai today," Machigi said. "My uncle moved too much to the Farai side of the balances: so my bodyguard informs me. We also understand divided loyalties, nand' paidhi. But you know that. Baji-naji, all things adjust. Balance matters. My uncle played both sides of the board. That *had* been his value."

"One very much takes the warning, aiji-ma."

"Well played, paidhi." The hand fell to the chair arm. "You have proposals for me, do you? Let us hear them. I will listen."

Machigi had dropped the mask, then, a little. And was not in a good mood today: was genuinely sorrowing after the uncle, it might be. Had quarreled with his aishid, it might be or taken a long look forward and backward.

One needed to keep it succinct and direct. "The documents

I have given you have names, aiji-ma, specifics of the eastern seacoast, small towns—several promising areas for a port, and in my estimation, the dowager's backing would carry weight. Local rail could be established, with negotiation: the Eastern lords are highly traditional, reluctant to see modernization go through their lands."

"Nothing to match mine."

"Yet villages will be reluctant to see economic advantage flow to their neighbors and not to them. Rail is a way to spread the benefit. When seen in that light—"

"You were an advocate for the railroad."

"Far less disruptive than roads, aiji-ma."

"You are building a railroad, paidhi, and we have not yet built a port."

"Or yet sailed a ship there, aiji-ma, true," Bren said with a shrug. "But I believe this can work."

"We build your town. Sooner or later Shejidan will push a rail connection all the way to the east coast—to take business from our ships."

"Ah, but, aiji-ma, they cannot gain right of way through eastern lands if the eastern lords object. And if these lords profit, you will have allies, because they have held themselves stubbornly independent of Shejidan. Ports grow into cities. And this port will have industry of its own, and fisheries, and it will thrive. The undeveloped land of the East one day will greatly resemble the view out that window."

"You dream, paidhi. The East is a rocky coast with treacherous currents and storms."

"Your ship captains will grow expert, and the orbiting station can warn you of weather with an accuracy unavailable to your ancestors."

Back went the chin onto the fist. "You dream, paidhi."

"The potential and the energy I see out that window is huge. You thrive, in relative isolation from outside ports, only with a limited trade to the north. Your industry and your inventiveness are evident. But the west coast is locked in a balance difficult to move, between Mospheiran interests across the strait and the sensitivity of the straits between. Let Shejidan manage that problem. You now have a far better offer on the table. Let your shippers hear of new ports, new markets, and they will race to get there. The Senji and the Dojisigi will doubt, at first. They will scoff. They will suspect you are up to something. And then they will be up in arms because advantage is coming to *you* and not them. And *that* is the point where your own force and leadership can bring the Marid under one clan, one authority."

An index finger lifted from beside the mouth. "The easier for the 'one clan, one authority' in *Shejidan* to snap up and swallow."

"Ah, but you will be an associate of the aiji-dowager. The East may be within the aishidi'tat, but the aishidi'tat is *not* within the East. The aiji-dowager hammered out that distinction to the displeasure of the Guilds in Shejidan. There is no Assassins' Guild there, except what surrounds her. There is limited rail there . . ."

"Which you mean to change."

"What is *not* imposed by Shejidan meets much more interest in the East. You will find you and the aiji-dowager, aiji-ma, have a great deal you could discuss."

Tap-tap-tap went the finger beside the mouth. And a frown gathered on the brow. "You are quick, paidhi. But are you accurate? Can you deliver these things?"

"One knows these resources and the situation, aiji-ma. And I have some influence of my own, at least that of my office."

"The white ribbon."

"I take my office seriously, aiji-ma. I am of no clan, of no region. I have displeased every lord I have dealt with at some point or another, but to the lasting displeasure of none that I have served."

"I shall personally read your proposals," Machigi said with

that same level stare. "I shall see for myself what you ask—and what you give. And then we shall estimate whether these proposals of yours will possibly appeal to me—or to the dowager."

"I ask no more than that, aiji-ma."

"You *cost* me, understand," Machigi said sharply. "You have already cost me certain assets that may not be easy to replace!"

"One understands that without needing the details. I have disrupted the peace here."

"Peace." A dour laugh. Machigi propelled himself out of the chair and looked down as Bren got up more slowly—painfully.

And stuck, half way, his back locked up.

Banichi moved. Machigi's guard moved. Jago moved, one step, her hand on her gun.

Bren held up a hand. Fast. "I can stand. I am perfectly well. A moment. Please."

He gave a shove at the chair arm with the other hand and straightened. He had to. He drew himself up to his full height— about to Machigi's shoulder—and got a breath. The situation among the bodyguards slowly relaxed.

"We *must* arrange, aiji-ma," Bren said, on a careful breath, "not to shoot each other."

Machigi laughed—laughed aloud, and a slight grin remained when he waved a casual stand-down to his guard, who moved back, not without misgiving glances at Jago, whose hand had not left her gun.

Bren declined to give any such signal. His bodyguard was at disadvantage already, and he opted not to interfere. He only said, "My profound apologies, aiji-ma."

"You are not to die," Machigi said, as if it were an order. "We offer the services of our physician. We insist. You shall not die under our roof!"

It was the last damned thing he wanted.

"I am far from dying," he said. "It is only a bruise, improving on its own."

"You ask me to rely on you," Machigi said. "Rely on me and

do as I say. Give me time to read these papers. Fro-ji." This to his guard. "Take the paidhi to nand' Juien. And give his body-guard latitude. One assumes they will wish to be with him."

Well, there was nothing for it, on that basis. He was far from happy to turn himself over to a physician to whom a human's physiology was uncharted territory. He didn't want to take any medications.

But he wasn't happy with his own body at the moment. Tano, the field medic in his aishid, *thought* nothing was broken, but it had hurt like hell while Tano had made his investigation. Damn, he thought. If he could just get a brief leave back to Najida—

But that wasn't going to happen. He cast an unhappy look at Banichi and Jago as he joined them on his way to the door, but they had their official faces on, and there was nothing to tell him what they thought of it, or of his shift of allegiances, or anything else that had happened in this interview.

"Perhaps Tano should come downstairs," he suggested.

Banichi said, as they exited to the audience hall, "He assuredly will, nandi."

8

They gathered downstairs, in a well-equipped clinic, crowding the little examination room. Nand' Juien was clearly a man of some professional standing and a few gray hairs. He listened and nodded while Tano, who had witnessed the event in question and who had a medical vocabulary, described the incident, the quality of the armor, his own observations of the injury, and the treatment.

One listened. One didn't know all the words that went back and forth, an entire vocabulary that Bren didn't have in any language, he strongly suspected. The physician approached him, respectful, cautious in feeling over his head and neck. "The discomfort is in my back," he said at one point, since the discussion had centered for quite a while on the fall, and the condition of his skull, whether or not there had been concussion—mild, Tano said—and on his upper shoulders, which were sore but not acutely painful.

From apprehension, the situation dwindled down to a lengthy technical discussion and then to a discussion of the similarities in human and atevi anatomy, involving a great deal of attention to his upper back.

The pain is in the ribs, Bren wanted to say. My shoulders are fine. But Tano was doing the talking, most of it in medical terms he didn't follow.

More discussion. And finally nand' Juien asked to take x-rays, and wanted him to go to the other room. That took more time and entailed shedding the coat and vest and shirt and lying on the table for a prolonged time while Tano talked to nand' Juien, then to Banichi and Jago. The talk was technical, but it seemed obvious. "No fracture," Bren heard, distinctly, and which yes, he was glad to know. So he wasn't broken. Just sore as hell.

The talk went on, the cold table eased his back, he was without the damned vest, and to his embarrassment, he began to lose threads, and his mind began to wander back to the interview with Lord Machigi and even to the papers, the proposals.

"Nandi." Nand' Juien touched his shoulder from behind, startling him, but Tano was there. He relaxed. The doctor said, "Exhale." And having his head between his hands, suddenly rotated it quickly one direction and the other. Joints popped in chain reaction all down his spine.

It startled him, and it hurt like hell, but it reached sore muscles all the way down between his shoulders.

Then the doctor wanted, yes, another x-ray.

Glowing in the dark occurred to him, but the brain was getting reports from his shoulders now, and from his middle back. The ribs hurt. But there was a faint tingling and a sense of relief. He was, he decided, in somewhat less pain. He contented himself with breathing, moving his shoulders just slightly, while nand' Juien and a new presence, his assistant, both talked to Tano.

No, this, this, and this medications would not be good, Tano said, and added that while the human metabolism was a little faster than one might expect, the dosage . . .

He couldn't hold that thread. For a moment he was just nowhere, and the doctor was saying something about the dose and that he would like to see him back in three days, once they had taped up the ribs.

Something about the bed being too soft . . .

Possibly it was. He didn't intend to meddle with Machigi's

furniture. He wanted his coat. He wondered if nand' Juien had somehow slipped him a sedative; and he didn't want that. They went on discussing the concussion he'd almost had.

He remembered he'd intercepted a chair arm on the way to the floor—had been blasted back into it. The chair moving out from under him had actually kept him from hitting his head any harder than he had, but it hadn't been a clean fall, that was sure.

He wanted to be up and have his head clear. Really clear. He had business to settle. He'd done something dire. He'd done something he couldn't undo . . . he'd put his bodyguard in a terrible position. They'd taken over an hour down here. Better part of two, for God's sake, and Banichi and Jago were carrying on as if everything was normal, and it wasn't.

And that did it. His stomach started into turmoil that wasn't going to settle until he had a chance to talk to his bodyguard. All his bodyguard, including Algini, whose involvement in things was a little chancier than the rest.

"I need to get up," he said under his breath. "Jago-ji. If you will."

"Is he permitted?" Jago asked Tano, and Tano came aside from the discussion and helped him sit up.

But it wasn't over. Nand' Juien and his assistant retaped his ribs, telling him when and how to breathe, then wrapped them about with a great deal of stretch bandage. That took another lengthy time.

It helped the pain of the ribs. But Tano could have done it. He wanted to go upstairs. He had begun to ask himself whether Algini was all right, left alone in the suite. Were they being stalled while something went on? He'd dismissed the bus. Was anything happening elsewhere that Machigi wanted a distraction to cover? Was Tano still in communication with Algini?

Did either have any idea what had gone on in his meeting with Machigi?

Nand' Juien prescribed alternate hot and cold compresses,

provided the wherewithal, handing a sizeable packet to Tano, and then said, turning to him,

"You have been a most interesting patient, nandi."

"One is grateful," he said with a little bow, and he accepted Banichi's and Jago's help getting down off the table. Jago handed him his shirt, and Banichi helped him put it on.

And the vest, before the coat. One was not at all surprised. Likely nand' Juien was not surprised either.

He buttoned the coat. He performed all the courtesies to nand' Juien and his staff. He gathered his bodyguard and escaped out the door and toward the stairs, with Machigi's guard in close attendance.

It was a long climb. He thought his brain was working up to speed. He'd all but collapsed downstairs—he still felt odd since that pop that had cascaded down his backbone. It was a damned, light-headed nightmare he'd gotten them into, and the situation with his aishid was beyond uncomfortable, all the way up the stairs and into their suite, where they had at least the illusion of privacy.

Banichi and Jago wore perfectly ordinary expressions as he glanced their way. Tano had evinced no disturbance when he had come down to the clinic. Algini acted in no wise upset when they arrived back in the sitting room.

And for about two breaths the light-headedness took away all rational faculties, for a moment of panic. He knew he had to level with them. All of them. His declaration to Machigi had dragged them into a damned difficult conflict of man'chi—that toward Tabini-aiji, in the case of Banichi and Jago and, God only knew—to the Assassins' Guild leadership, in the case of Tano and Algini. He was no longer sure. Everything had been neatly vertical while he served Tabini. His service to Ilisidi hadn't upset a thing: she was attached to Tabini. Algini's attachment to the Guild couldn't be an issue: the Guild served Tabini. It was all one happy package.

This declaration to Machigi, however, upset everything. And

they were still bugged, so he couldn't talk to them. He wanted them to know he *felt* loyalty to them and that he was doing what he had to do—but that wasn't the way things worked, in man'chi. Theirs was upward. He was the focus. And he'd just affected the way it was aimed, in everything. He saw worry in their faces. They gave him that, at least. They let him read them.

And he couldn't.

Maybe it was something he'd never felt with them: a sense of shame.

Did he wish he had done differently than he had done with Machigi? No. He didn't. He'd had to do what he had done. The same as he had *had* to trust Machigi's staff.

But hurt one of his bodyguard? He couldn't do that. And he had.

For the first time in all the time they'd been together, he didn't know what to do. What to say.

"Would you care for tea, Bren-ji?' Jago asked him, and he just froze, thinking, no. He couldn't. He couldn't just go back to life as normal. He didn't want it. But they had their listeners, constantly watching for signs of upset. Listeners who'd want to know what they did and said in the wake of the committment he'd given.

"Please," he said. Activity. Any normal activity. Something to keep the eavesdroppers guessing. And not even the bath with the water running was guaranteed to mask a conversation.

He headed for the table. For writing paper. He sat down there, a little dizzy, his thoughts trying to fog on him, and wrote.

Tano came and brought the tea. And a pill. "This should be safe, Bren-ji."

"Not yet," he said in a low voice, and wrote another sentence. A necessary sentence. He handed the paper to Tano first.

Machigi has called on me to operate as his mediator, he had written, *and I have declared man'chi to Machigi. Therefore I must give fair advantage to him and to the aiji-dowager. I feel pain, however, if I distress my aishid. I will not betray you. That I am compelled to say so with all evidence to the contrary is very painful to me. But that declaration is all I can give at this point. Please let the others read this, and let the last burn it.*

Tano read it and solemnly went over and gave it to Algini. Algini read it and passed it to Banichi, who passed it to Jago, who crumpled it in her fist and shot up a single Guild sign.

Five fingers. The aishid-lord unit. Banichi nodded, once. And Algini held up the same sign. Tano nodded, likewise once.

It had been a long time since something had hit him at that level. He wasn't going to do anything stupid like break down or offer expressions of human sentiment. He wasn't going to. He got up from his chair, bowed slightly, and said only: "One is grateful, nadiin-ji."

Jago tossed the note into the fire and made another Guild sign, a fast wipe of the thumb across the fingertips. Wipeout. It meant, situationally, half a dozen things, from annihilation to none at all. And she said, pleasantly, "Go to bed, Bren-ji. Stay there. Your aishid insists."

Get the brain to working. Hell with the painkillers, which he hadn't taken. He wanted to work.

But Jago opened the bedroom door and Banichi waved a hand toward it, Tano nudged his elbow, and the lot of them took him to the bedroom and took his coat and the vest, made him sit down and took off his boots, and there was nothing for it. With the support of the vest gone, he did feel exhaustion piling up.

Boots went into the closet. He gave up the rest of the clothes, and they tucked him into bed like a five-year-old and turned out the lights.

"It's not dark out, nadiin-ji," he said.

"So," Banichi said. "But it will be."

It was conspiracy. They left, except Jago, who leaned very close to his ear, set her hand on his bare shoulder, and whispered, "Man'chi stands, Bren-ji."

He was quite moved, but he had no time to enjoy that sensation because she tipped him backward into the covers and threw the blanket over him.

And walked out and shut the door behind her.

His aishid was out there discussing the problems he'd made them. He needed to get his wits about him.

But the bed was soft. He found it possible to relax. His aishid was still taking care of him.

Having said what he'd said, he had to deliver and just shut up and trust them. He was so used to thinking in huge territories, in planetary terms and centuries. His area of acute concern had gotten down to one set of rooms, four people, and himself. Five. And a finite number of hours.

Machigi had tested them. But Machigi had seen, and his guard had seen, with clearer sight than a human could, that that relationship stood.

If Machigi thought he'd fractured them, if Machigi'd imagined he'd panic or that there could be any distance between him and his bodyguard, Machigi was obliged to revise his expectations. Considering that Machigi's own aishid had stuck fast to him under pressure, that said maybe they had something unexpected in common.

He used that thought for a pillow. And his mind focused down to a single sharp point. Machigi and I have *that* in common. If we didn't, his aishid wouldn't have taken the action they did this morning.

9

It was a lot better, Cajeiri thought, to have Barb-daja back. Barb-daja took over watching nand' Toby, and that meant Cajeiri could go back to his own suite.

And first of all, he just wanted to go to bed early, in his own soft bed. It was embarrassing. There were so many things one *could* do, and he simply went to his suite with his aishid, well, with the two he *wanted*, and fell into bed and slept in his clothes and all.

But when he waked up, realized it was after dark, and walked into his sitting room to find out what time it was and if there was any supper at all, Veijico had come in. She was just sitting there alone at the table, with Antaro and Jegari across the room in chairs by the fireside.

He was a mess and caught at disadvantage, with his shirt and trousers wrinkled and his hair falling into his face.

"What time is it, nadiin?" he asked, looking at Antaro and Jegari.

"Midnight, nandi," Antaro said.

"Did you get any sleep?" he asked.

"Some, nandi," Jegari said, with a little move of his eyes toward their interloper, over at the table.

It was that bad, the feeling in the room.

Veijico had a right, one supposed, to come here, but *they* were not sleeping and letting her be here unsupervised, with, by now, the whole estate abed. They had all probably missed supper. And Jegari and Antaro had been at least as tired as he was.

He had slept right into dark and wasted all his chance to know what was going on in the house, was what.

"I shall have a bath," he said, never mind the hour, which meant Jegari, and only Jegari, would attend him.

And that served two purposes, only one of which was a quick, hot bath.

The other was getting Jegari alone and finding out when Veijico had come back and had she said anything.

"An hour ago, nandi." They shared the ample bathtub, both in water up to their chins, although Cajeiri had to sit up more and half-float, balanced on his heels. "We were not yet in bed. And she has apologized to you and to us."

"Apologized." That was certainly an improvement.

"She has been under the direction of nand' Bren's aishid," Jegari said with a little look under the brows. "She tasted their food for them. She stood guard at night. She cared for Barb-daja. She said they were very hard on her, but she agreed they were fair."

"Ha." That was good. But it was very sad about her brother, and he remembered her sitting alone at the table, only looking up when he had come into the room. "Has she any news of Lucasi?"

"No. Nand' Bren has people looking, but it is Taisigi that are doing the looking."

"That is by no means the best thing, Gari-ji!"

"No, it is not, nandi."

"Do you suppose they are even doing it?"

Jegari shrugged and made ripples. "One is sure they are looking, nandi, if they know he is in their territory, but how they will deal with him, one hardly knows. Except if Lord Bren says they are looking to recover him—one would think that was true."

"She must be worried."

"One would think she is very worried. This is more than her brother, nandi. This is her *partner* that is missing. Within the Guild—that is—very difficult."

"I shall speak to her," Cajeiri said. He did not look forward to it. It was serious, grown-up business. It was the sort of thing he preferred grown-ups to do. But Veijico had come back to him, to his rooms, so she still thought she was his.

So he supposed he had to do it. It was what mani would expect. And what mani would expect—well, that was just what he had to do.

So with Jegari's help he dressed and put himself in order, with a crisp ironed shirt and a fresh coat and trousers despite the late hour, and then he agreed with Jegari that Jegari would leave him alone. He had no private place to talk, just three rooms, so he found something for Jegari to do—going out to find out how nand' Toby was getting along and what was happening in the house, and maybe to get them supper. And in the meantime Antaro was to have her bath. So that would leave him only with Veijico for a guard.

That was a little scary, considering she had done things that put her on the wrong side not just of Cenedi and mani but of the Guild, and she had not been a reliable person. She was tall and strong and she was real Guild, and she could kill people faster than you could see it happen.

But Cenedi would not have let her come back into his rooms if she had not satisfied Cenedi and mani about her behavior. That gave him confidence. And he was absolutely sure Cenedi even if he was asleep was aware where she was.

So Jegari went out, Antaro went to the bath, and he went back into the sitting room where Veijico was.

Veijico stood up, properly and politely, finding herself the object of his attention. That, in itself, was an improvement. She looked very tired, and thinner, and just worn down.

"One is very sorry to hear your partner is still missing, nadi," he said.

A quiet little bow. "Thank you, nandi. One is gratified by your expression."

A textbook answer, mani would call it.

"Did you want to come back to us?" he asked.

"If nand' Bren had wished it, nandi, one would have stayed there. They needed me. But they sent me with Barb-daja. Now I am here. If you wish me to leave—"

"Are you sorry to be here, nadi?"

She bowed her head. "One regrets the difficulties, nandi."

"You left without calling the security office."

"We saw the kidnappers, nandi. We chased them to stop them." She bit her lip. Then said nothing at all.

But *he* knew he had called out to stop the kidnappers. And she did not offer that excuse to him.

That was way better behavior than he had seen.

"You followed my order," he said.

She gave a little nod, a bow, and said: "We ignored procedures, you being both a minor, forgive me, nandi, and a civilian. One is aware we did not exercise mature judgement."

"Did Banichi tell you that, nadi?"

"Algini-nadi did, nandi," she said. Algini was the grimmest of Lord Bren's bodyguard, and not the one Cajeiri would personally like to have reprimand him. He could imagine Algini, who said very little, might have said exactly those words and made every one of them sting.

He was sorry for her. But he did not forget that she had been rude to Jegari and Antaro, and if he said he was sorry, she might move back in and start running things again, and telling *him* how to behave, and ignoring all his orders except the one she absolutely should not have obeyed.

She obeyed orders, he thought uncomfortably, the same way he obeyed orders—he picked the ones he liked and managed not to be there in any official way to hear the others.

So off she and Lucasi had gone to be important and do the big thing, getting Barb-daja back, because they knew they had just made a huge mistake in putting Barb-daja and nand' Toby in danger.

He had less sympathy for her and her partner when he thought about that.

And about her attitude toward Jegari and Antaro.

And then suddenly, in the middle of remembering all the reasons he had been angry with her, it struck him what he was feeling, right in the middle of his stomach. He discovered the reason she made him nervous, and the *reason* he was just a little scared of her and never really believed she was going to do what he told her.

"You have no man'chi here," he said to her, right out in the open. "You were never *mine*, not from the time you came here. Maybe your man'chi is to my father, nadi, but it never was to me."

There was a lengthy silence after that, and Veijico did not look him in the eyes. She had clasped her hands behind her, and her head stayed a little bowed.

"*Is* your man'chi to my father?" he asked.

A lengthy silence, and she never looked up. She was thinking about that, he thought, or the answer was no, and she was not telling him what she was thinking.

So he did what mani did. He did not give her an answer. He waited.

And waited.

"Nandi," she said quietly, long after that silence had become uncomfortable. "One is only just realizing—"

He might get the rest of it if he he shut up and let her figure out her sentence. So he did, and she still was not looking at him.

"We thought we might be brought into your father's service," she said eventually. "But that proved not the case. We were left asi-man'chi." That was to say, on their own family man'chi to each other, no one else's. "We did not feel at ease here. We did not find a place."

"Because I am a child? Or because you do not really have man'chi to my father, either?"

"We began to have, to him," Veijico said in a low voice. "We thought we might. We wanted to, nandi. But he gave us away. And we tried. But we found none here. We had no idea—"

It was hard to wait. He was entirely upset with what she was saying. But she was getting the words to the surface, finally. And on mani's example, he just waited, no matter how uncomfortable it was or how long it took. And when she understood that was how it was, she began to answer him.

"We had no idea, nandi, what was wrong here. We did not find a place. We tried. But we—"

Another lengthy silence. He still let it continue.

Veijico cleared her throat. "Nandi, one has no idea of the man'chi in this entire household. We came here willing to join this household. But it seems to us—"

Third silence.

"It seems to us, nandi," Veijico said, looking up once, if briefly, "that *your* man'chi is not to your father the aiji but to the aiji-dowager. And to nand' Bren. And even to persons up on the station."

He took in his breath. *He* had no such idea. "I shall be aiji," he said angrily. "And I shall *have* no man'chi."

"But now you *do,* young lord. Or you seem to."

"Well, there is nothing wrong with it, nadi! Nor are you in authority over me! We are two months short of a felicitous year!"

"One is trying to explain, young lord. Not to offend you."

Second deep breath. "Do explain, then."

There was another long silence. And Veijico still stood looking generally elsewhere.

"We understood you would be a child," Veijico said. "And we were prepared for that. That you have a student regard for the aiji-dowager—is expected. But your regard for nand' Bren . . . We were not prepared for that, in coming here."

"Nand' Bren is a very important man! My father trusts him! Mani trusts him! And I trust him!"

"I have just spent time with nand' Bren and his aishid in Tanaja, nandi. I do not say I understand him, but one respects his patience and his consideration with one he need not have regarded. He has placed me very much in his debt. One understands, now, your estimation of his advice."

"So does my great-grandmother regard his advice," he retorted. But there, he had had an outburst of anger, and he had let her stray right off the track. And: never suggest the direction of your thoughts, mani had told him, and never suggest how to please you, if you want to know the truth from someone. So he said: "Finish what you were telling me."

The room went very quiet for several moments. "Just that—we were not prepared for this household, nandi."

She was getting away from him. He had let her get off the track, and she was not coming back to it.

"That is not all of it," he said. And he realized that she had never yet looked him quite in the eye. "Look at me. If you want to be here, do not lie to me."

More silence. But she did look at him—she had to look down at him—everybody did. But he folded his arms and stared right back up at her, with his father's look. He had practiced it.

"You are a remarkable boy," she said.

"I shall be aiji," he repeated. "And my bodyguard has to be *mine.*"

"That it must, nandi."

"So *can* you be?"

Again that glance to the side. She was going to dodge the question. And then she looked back, straight at him. "When we came here, when we came here, nandi, we found no connections. This household—is full of directions that made no sense. They are strong directions. There is nand' Bren. Lord Geigi. Your great-grandmother, not least. Cenedi. Banichi. They are not unified, though they cooperate. And we seemed most apt to fall under Cenedi's orders, but if we connected with house systems, your great-grandmother was in charge; and nand' Bren runs the household, with Banichi. And then there is Ramasonadi. And then the Edi, who are foreigners. And agreements that by all we can tell run counter to your father the aiji. Then nand' Toby is here, and *he* has connections to the Presidenta of Mospheira. All, all are very powerful interests, and one has no idea how they intersect. So we did not know what was happening or what orders we might get or what effect they might have. We tried to succeed for you. But we had no clear sense of whose orders we were following."

"Is that an excuse for ignoring me when I was going downstairs, or not knowing where I was?"

She did not look away this time. "It is not. One offers no excuse, nandi. We sensed you were annoyed with us, we sensed you wanted us to obey you; it was within the house, everything was safe—and we thought we would not lose you. Perhaps you wanted us to lose you. We did. And then we realized we had made a serious mistake, and we feared that you might have gone outside to shake us. It *was* our mistake, we knew we had fault in what happened, we tried to redeem it, and it only got worse."

He understood how *that* was. He had been in that situation far too often.

But she was an adult. Did adults get into that kind of mess?

And then it was as if a puzzle-piece clicked into place.

"You should have come back to *me. I* was out there on the porch. You should have come back to *me*. But you had no man'chi. Not to me. Not to my great-grandmother. Not even to my father! Had you?"

She did not flinch. "No. At that point, we were without man'chi. We had no idea what to do, then, but we were lost, and we had no clear sense what we were to do. One is grateful to the paidhi-aiji. To him. To his aishid. After everything that had happened . . . one felt, with his aishid—one felt at *home.*

Even in that place, one felt *safe*. One understands his quality. I know my estimation weighs nothing in this house. But I am sure now you are associated with one person whose direction is impeccable."

"Nand' Bren, you mean."

"Yes, nandi. Nand' Bren."

"But not my great-grandmother."

"One does not understand her, nandi. But one does not expect to understand a person of her quality. It is enough to understand that nand' Bren follows her."

"*He* cannot take you! I would be very surprised if he would, and you should not ask him!"

"No, nandi. One would by no means expect it. One is very junior to that aishid. We would have no place there. And we were assigned here, Lucasi and I, and one hopes—one hopes to find a place with your household, in spite of all we have done. One hopes Lucasi can find his way back. But if he does not—I would do all I can to find another partner, for the balance. If one were permitted."

She was upset. He was upset with her being upset, for different reasons. And mani told him never talk when he was upset.

So he did not. He walked away a few steps and looked back at greater distance.

"If you stay, you will not behave badly toward Antaro and Jegari."

"No, nandi. They have deserved your respect. I clearly have not."

"You will always be second to them. They have always been with me. They *are* in my man'chi, and they have never done anything I did not approve."

"One accepts that, nandi. I have skills, and I can teach them. I can bring them to Guild rank, nandi, in your service, and I will do that. I am older. At my best, I have mature judgment, which I would endeavor to use in your service, and I would do so wholeheartedly, if you will give me that chance. One asks.

One asks, knowing one has not performed well. One would be honored to form a team with Jegari and Antaro."

It was his decision. It was maybe the biggest decision he had ever had to make. And it was going to be even harder to undo if he was wrong.

"You will listen to Cenedi and Banichi, both, nadi, and you will *not* do another such thing as slip around my orders!"

"I entirely agree, nandi."

So. She had answered everything. He had run out of questions. "Then you will be here," he said. "Your baggage is still in the room." He started to walk out and leave her to whatever she had to do to move back in. But there was one thing he ought to say, that he wanted to say, and he stopped and gave a little nod of the head. "One hopes they find Lucasi safe, Vejiconadi. One very much hopes he will also come back."

"Nandi," she said faintly. "Thank you for your expression."

10

A whole night's sleep. Without nearly as much pain to wake him every time he tried to move.

Bren waked both with the astonished realization he was not in significant pain and the vague impression of hearing someone of his bodyguard stirring about. Which meant it was probably just before dawn.

A tentative wriggle of the shoulders and turn of the head produced one little residual crackle, but no lockup and no pain.

Odd. He hadn't known his back was exacerbating the ribs. But it had been. The shoulders could relax. So now the back could. And the chest almost could.

The whole business came of being blown down flat on his shoulders, Bren decided. The impact of the bullet from the front, the lump on the back of his skull—that cursed small gilded chair which had both broken his fall and gotten in the way of it—

And he was convinced now, even without the evidence of the x-rays, that he was only bent, not broken. It made him feel better, if only in morale. He'd taken worse falls in his misspent youth. He'd fallen down a ski slope no few times. He didn't bounce as well nowadays. But he was starting to get the better of this.

If he lived to get out of Tanaja.

That thought sent him toward the edge of the bed. He needed to get to work. People depended on him. His aishid did.

He hadn't quite made it upright when Jago came through the door, whisked it shut at her back, turned on the lights and whispered, with a worried expression:

"You must get ready, Bren-ji. *Lord Machigi* is here."

"*Here?*" He shoved himself to his feet. "What time is it? Jago-ji. Clothes. Please."

"It is still dark out," she said, and started for his closet, but Tano came in from the other door, and without a word Tano went straight to the closet and started pulling clothes out—shirt. Trousers. Jago diverted over to the dresser, and laid out linens.

Machigi. *Here.* In his rooms. Before sunrise.

That was not necessarily bad, but it was probably not good, either. Machigi would not be patient about whatever it was. And it was probably something he didn't want a lot of publicity for.

Either that, or Machigi had been up all night reading those papers and decided the human should share the misery.

He made a fast trip to the bathroom. Shaved. Slapped feeling into his face.

If he were atevi, he would have had to sit down on the bath bench to have his hair combed and queued. Tano did it in the bedroom while he was standing and tied the ribbon of his queue as carefully as he could, while Jago was helping him on with his shirt, not even protesting that he should wear the cursed vest. She just reached for the coat while he did the buttons himself.

Between the two of them, they had him dressed in record time—no tea, no time to get his wits in order, but at least his collar was straight. The half-buttoned coat somewhat hid the lack of a vest.

Banichi and Algini were, presumably, holding the fort in the sitting room. He walked in, where, indeed, Machigi was standing glumly by his fireside, with two bodyguards darkening the doorward side of the sitting room. Banichi and Algini were on the left.

"Aiji-ma," Bren said quietly, with a little bow.

"You have caused me trouble," Machigi said.

"One is distressed to hear so, aiji-ma. Please inform me."

Machigi swung around toward a chair and slouched down into it, leaning back and staring up at him like a predator at his prey.

"Throughout my administration we have had at least *courteous* relations with Senji Clan and the Dojisigi. Now we do not, and it is not on my timetable."

He could do one of two things. One was to plead he was innocent, and the other . . .

"If one has inadvertently shined a light on something already moving in the shadows, one would not count that a disservice, aiji-ma."

"Tell me you have nothing of *personal* bias! The matter of an apartment in the Bujavid, we are told, is well-known in the Marid."

"The Farai of Senji Clan have offended me, yes, aiji-ma. But an honest person does not advance a personal cause and paint it as advantageous to one's lord. I have never done so, nor do I now."

"*Brazen* fellow!"

He was directly challenged. He was insulted. His integrity was questioned. All of a sudden he was convinced there was nothing for it but go straight ahead with this no-nonsense young lord. He found his center, win or lose, all or nothing, for all of them. "I am often frank but never shameless, aiji-ma. I will own any action I have taken, personally, to your disadvantage. But I do *not* take responsibility for the underlying character of the Farai or for the unfortunate necessity yesterday for an action which I am certain your guard undertook advisedly— and not by *my* advice."

A short breath. That might have been a laugh. Or absolute frustration. "You walk into my city, you lodge under my roof, and in less than two days, you have destabilized a third of the Marid, paidhi. Is this how you usually work?"

"I would rather urge I have only been here two days, and your enemies have lost no time trying to bend *your* policies in *their* favor. One could have no doubt they are annoyed with me."

"As are *my* people, seeing one of your agents has attacked them!"

Bren lifted a careful brow. "One of my agents, aiji-ma?"

"That boy you allegedly lost."

"The lame one." God, as if he didn't know. Hell, what *had* Veijico's brother gotten into? More to the point—had he killed anybody? Shot up a Taisigi village?

"*That* one, yes, paidhi-aiji. How many agents do you *have* loose in our territories?"

"Only that one, that I know, aiji-ma."

"What are his orders?"

"To find his sister and Barb-daja, aiji-ma. He has evidently not heard they are back safely. If I could reach him, I would convey that news, but unfortunately neither he nor his sister left the house with Guild equipment."

"Stupid," Machigi said, "and inconvenient. Are we expected to *believe* this?"

"Something has happened beyond the incident you name, aiji-ma. Please inform me."

"You have issued no orders?"

"Unfortunately, no one is in contact with this young man, aiji-ma, not that I am aware, and not that my aishid is aware. He and his partner are young and inexperienced. At one point I had recovered the boy, but I let him off the bus before we entered your land. One hoped he would have the sense to contact senior Guild at Targai. May one inquire the nature of the provocation?"

"He has disrupted a delicate sitution."

Better and better. And dared one guess it had to do with Machigi's opening complaint this morning, relations with the Senji—who lay north of Targai and in a geographical line with the road they had taken in here "Unfortunate, aiji-ma."

"Who *is* this fool? *What are his orders*, nandi?"

"The boy, with his partner, was set to guard Tabini-aiji's son. He went out with his partner after Barb-daja, and he did report to me at Targai. He was injured, he was on another mission, once I was ordered here, and I put him off the bus before we crossed into your territory—hoping he would search discreetly and report back to Targai."

"Gods less fortunate, paidhi!" Down went Machigi's arm on the chair arm, and security twitched. Bren didn't. "The timing of this is all yours! You have stirred up a resting situation, antagonized the Senji and the Dojisigi, and given us a situation far more complex than a search for your missing staff!"

"One has no idea what this boy has done. Might one hear the offense?"

There was a moment of sullen silence. Then Machigi said, "He noisily discovered an outpost we have been attempting to ignore. He escaped. *Now* it becomes impossible officially to ignore its presence."

"Senji?" Bren asked. "The base from which operations have been conducted toward Najida?"

"Do not suppose yourself the sole object of offense, paidhi. Do not be so flattered."

"Senji. Operating in Taisigi territory. You are uncharacteristically patient with this situation, aiji-ma."

"And you are impertinent!"

"One merely seeks to understand, aiji-ma. You have observed this situation. You have done nothing against it. One is astonished."

"Do *not* be! You come in under the aiji-dowager's auspices, bearing a peace flag from the Guild, no less, and loosing a man from your expedition to sabotage an operation, asking *me* to use forbearance in apprehending him. Oh, I am *not* pleased, paidhi."

They were in danger. Serious danger. "One hardly has knowledge what operation this boy may have disrupted, aiji-ma, but there *was* no advance knowledge. You were in danger, and the aiji-dowager, *not* the Guild, intervened to offer an alliance. In point of fact, you *are* in a difficult situation or you would not have tolerated Senji intrusion onto your land. You have already moved against potential assassins. Your guard has successfully protected you this far, but they have been unable to rid you of a situation in your territory that has, one takes an unsupported guess, infiltrated your operations at Kajiminda and attempted to put you in the worst possible light. Whoever has done this is not your ally, and yet you have tolerated this presence in your land, observing but not moving to obliterate it. Is it that strong? I would think Senji, rebuked by your destruction of such a base, would simply pretend it had never existed . . . rather than go to war with you. War was *never* Senji's choice."

"Speak your mind, paidhi. We invite it. We *long* for plain argument."

"You know that the Guild that came back from Murini's regime is tending out of control."

"This theory of yours!"

"You assumed control lay in Senji or Dojisigi. But say it does not. Say control lies within the renegade Guild itself, and you are *not* contesting your accustomed rivals. Say it is not a Senji operation this boy has disturbed, and you have, since the events preceding my arrival, begun to suspect the nature of this base. It is no longer your *neighbors* you have to deal with, aiji-ma. Another enemy has targeted the Taisigin Marid, on a schedule hastened by my presence on the coast. And why? Because they can manage the leadership of the Senji and the Dojisigi. But you are far too intelligent, too active in administration, and too little inclined to take orders from anyone."

Machigi gazed at him, hard-faced but *not* out of control of his temper. "Go on, paidhi, and cease to flatter me. I am immune."

"It is, I think, fact, not flattery. Did the aiji-dowager approach your neighbors? No."

"Did she approach me, *uninfluenced* by the Guild in Shejidan? I think not, paidhi! Their deliberation was calculated to force us to negotiation. And the aiji-dowager, equal to her reputation for high-handed intervention in government, has stepped in."

Shocking thought. And entirely possible. He gave a little bow. "If your theory is true, aiji-ma, still, it is a better offer than that the Guild itself is giving you. *Their* offer would simply be a diversion—to prevent you cooperating with Guild from any other district."

"Oh, you are fast, to be so ignorant as you claim."

"One is conversant with your situation, aiji-ma, and what you propose as the dowager's motive is an interesting interpretation."

"Which makes every offer you have made us a lie!"

"Not a lie, aiji-ma. Not even empty. The task she set me was to come here, assess the situation, and make proposals to ensure your safety, since the aiji-dowager will *not* be made an instrument of anybody else's policy. You understand her reputation correctly. She will seek her own advantage. I am personally aware of the solution she proposed for the west coast and its troubles long before I was born, a solution the legislature declined. *I* have proposed it again in a configuration of alliances over which the legislature has no power, and which in my own opinion is likely to please her *and* serve you. More, I propose a context for that alliance that makes political and economic sense because I see a leader capable of carrying it out. Am I guilty of extravagance? Perhaps, but I have captured the aiji-dowager's interest in an outcome that will accomplish *everything* she originally proposed for a political solution and that will go a long way toward dealing with inequities between districts in the East, which I know has long been a concern of hers. Far from betraying your interests, aiji-ma, I have handed you a possibility unavailable to your predecessors and to your neighbors, and if the action of a random boy has disturbed a dangerous situation in your district, one offers personal regret, but it does *not* indicate a plot against you, not from the aiji-dowager's side. The situation is precarious because your enemies number more than your traditional rivals, and one fears there will be bloodshed, but not of the aiji-dowager's planning. Association with her is your *best* course."

Machigi's eyes flickered, following every point. "And your arrival on the west coast, paidhi, so swiftly followed by hers, was at *whose* instigation?"

"In truth," he said, "the Farai's. *They* possess my apartment. Lord Tatiseigi of the Atageini, who had lent me his apartment, decided to come to Shejidan for the legislative season, and for his convenience, *I* took a vacation on the coast. The aiji's son decided to pay me a visit, and in consequence, the aiji-dowager turned her plane about in midair and came to deal with her great-grandson. It was quite a ridiculous set of circumstances, entirely unrelated to anything now proposed."

"So it *was* an accident," Machigi said, a muscle jumping in his jaw.

"It was absolutely an accident, nothing plotted, nothing planned."

"This is likely a Guild question," Machigi said.

"If it is, aiji-ma, it is beyond my scope."

Machigi sat glowering, showing, in the rate of his breathing, agitation. Bren sat absolutely still, watching every tick, every cloud that scudded through those golden eyes, for a weather forecast.

And Machigi looked up, and past him, to the left corner of the room.

Where Algini stood.

Bren's heart leaped. He slowed his breathing. Tried to give no outward sign at all.

"The assassinations in the Township were excessive," Machigi muttered. "And your first hypothesis is correct: I did not approve. We are both, paidhi, within a chain of fortuity and accident."

So was he right? Right in the whole chain of logic? He fought to keep his own demeanor icy calm, but he feared he was readable. Machigi's face was grim, then showed a curious—of all things—amusement.

"You think you understand us. Yet you fear you do not."

"I apply such wisdom as I have to questions difficult to ask— and I am aware I may be mistaken."

"You are too well informed to be mistaken, paidhi." The fist arrived under Machigi's chin, a prop. "Well, my wise paidhi, let me inform you. This random boy has created a shooting incident between my watchers and something with which we have maintained an uneasy quiet. *We,* who have generally preserved the Taisigin Marid from the intrusion of this element, have now appeared directly to challenge it. The chain of fortuity and accident has added one more link. Suppose we take your word that this is *not* intended, and *not* a Guild operation. We have citizens at risk. We have the likelihood that what this boy has disturbed will be reinforced and that Senji in particular will take extreme measures to assure any conflict takes place in *our* territory—with the help of the Dojisigi."

It was not an incursion of thousands Machigi was talking about: it was a Guild-style operation, highly skilled individuals spreading out to remove key individuals, conduct sabotage of communications and resources. Most of all—to remove individuals. Machigi. His loyal guard. His staff. His unscheduled guest. And any lord backing Machigi.

Total collapse of the Taisigi authority and all their allied lords. A coup in the South.

"The Guild will by no means allow it."

The fist went down hard against the chair arm. "You say! You say your services are at my disposal."

"They are, aiji-ma."

"Then *what* do you propose?"

That took more than a heartbeat to assemble. And Machigi's patience with the situation was understandably on the wane.

"Access to a phone line."

"Let me advise you what your bodyguard will advise you. Phone lines between here and Shejidan run through *Senji* territory."

It was old thinking. And there were things neither the Messengers' Guild nor the Assassins' Guild in Shejidan had not made public.

"One can manage if you will give us access. Lord Geigi can reach the station."

"Ah. So now *Geigi* will become our ally. We are little encouraged to believe this."

"Aiji-ma. For me and for the aiji-dowager he will—"

"You say!" A second slam of the fist against the chair arm. "No, paidhi. We shall play this out for the audience *we* choose, under terms we choose. First of all, yes, call Tabini-aiji. Tell him we have a problem. Tell him loose the Guild. Then call his grandmother—and inform her what you have done."

Damn, Bren thought.

They had none of the resources they would have had even in Najida, and no access to the gear Geigi carried quietly about his person. And he was less moved to trust Machigi's motives than he had been yesterday.

He said, quietly, thinking—*stall. Consult with Algini. And: Damn it, his bodyguard has told him what Algini is. Possibly more than I know on that issue.* "One will do one's best, and no, aiji-ma, one does not set out to fail—but let me think on this. Grant me half an hour to arrange my information."

A hesitation. Then, to his vast relief: "Granted." And not to his relief: "But I shall stay here."

11

It was hard to get up and be bright in the morning, but when one had just scored a number of good marks with mani, one had to keep performing for a while or see the score dive below previous low levels. Cajeiri had learned that fact aboard the ship. Mani was suspicious of sudden changes.

And after doing an adult's job and getting Barb-daja back—well, he had not personally gotten Barb-daja back, but at least things had turned out well, involving being able to talk to her and translate for nand' Toby, so at least the glow of success settled on him—he figured he had to continue on good behavior.

For a start, he had to put on his better clothes for breakfast with mani. It was the first such breakfast he had attended in days, but he figured to invite himself, knowing the hour mani would be up.

So he dressed, with Jegari's help, and heard from Jegari that Veijico had been very polite to both him and his sister. She had expressed her hopes to fit in and just gone straight to bed last night, which was good, too.

If he could just stay awake this morning, and bring mani into a good mood . . .

But then came a knock at the bedroom door, which was a warning, and a moment later Antaro put her head in. "Nandi! The bus is coming back. They say Lord Geigi is aboard, but nand' Bren is still not! Veijico-nadi has gone out into the hall trying to find out."

Right at breakfast. And from Targai, over in Maschi territory and near the Marid. Cenedi had immediately sent the bus back to be near Tanaja, ready there if nand' Bren needed it in a hurry. But apparently it had turned right around again and brought back Lord Geigi instead.

So something this morning was not going well.

"We shall be at the door," Cajeiri said. That was where the news would be, that was certain, news about the situation that was surrounding Najida and threatening all of them; and Cajeiri did not intend to be left ignorant again.

It was not a simple matter, to call Tabini-aiji, personally, in the first place. From a phone in the heart of Tanaja, it took the local operator talking to security and then to the Bujavid operators in Shejidan, then operators talking to Tabini-aiji's major-domo and his bodyguards.

It involved also Tano and Jago coming out from the rear of the suite and taking station with Banichi and Algini, all of his guard now visible and engaged, and doing their part to verify for this and that person, yes, it was the paidhi-aiji himself, yes, he was calling from Tanaja, under Lord Machigi's auspices, and he wished to speak to the aiji personally.

And doubtless the delay in getting to Tabini both let Tabini have a cup of tea or two and let Tabini's office set up and trace the call to be sure it was coming from where it said it was . . . from all the persons apt to be listening in, it was a wonder if one side could hear the other.

Bet that Tabini's bodyguards would get every bit of information they could at the other end. They would also note every tap along the way, from here to Senji and God knew where— that went without saying.

But once they had Tabini's senior bodyguard on the line, Banichi talked to him personally, said several words of no sense whatsoever, and then handed the phone on to Bren.

During all of this Machigi sat and had tea—Tano's management—by the fireside.

Machigi had run out of tea by the time they got through to Tabini.

And Machigi sat listening while Bren took the phone, standing right next to him.

"Aiji-ma?"

"*Paidhi-aiji. One finds you, we hear, in uncommon circumstances.*"

"Aiji-ma, Lord Machigi has invoked the ancient rule of negotiation. At this moment one must inform you I represent him."

"*Has he, now?*" Tabini asked, and there was absolutely no need to warn Tabini every word was going to Machigi, in one way or another. "*Advise him we expect your return in due course, in good health.*"

"One is honored by your expression, aiji-ma. Lord Machigi has expressed interest in the gesture the aiji-dowager has made in sending me here."

"*We are aware of these gestures and her opinion.*"

That shortened the list of items he had to cover.

"Aiji-ma, there is a complication. May one explain further?"

"*Explain.*" Cold. Quite disturbingly cold. Tabini wanted information, but there was no ready belief on the other side. And conveying the situation—

"Understand that I have dismissed your force, which I brought here from Targai—"

"*We have had the report.*"

Probably an expert and detailed report—including one from Cenedi.

"There has developed, suddenly, a strong threat to Lord Machigi from within the Marid. You will surely know."

"*We would have an idea, indeed, nand' paidhi.*"

"Lord Machigi would be gratified by your recognition of negotiations now in progress, aiji-ma." A breath. "He is beside me as I speak. If you have any message for him, I will deliver it."

"Are you under duress, paidhi?"

"No. I am not, aiji-ma. I say again, I am willingly representing Lord Machigi."

A pause. *"Your safe return is a condition of the negotiations proceeding. You may tell him that."*

"Tabini-aiji says—"

"One has heard," Machigi said, frowning. The phone, though quiet, was amply loud enough, one guessed, for Machigi's hearing. Machigi snapped his fingers. "The problem."

"Lord Machigi says—"

"Let Guild talk to Guild."

That was an actual offer—that his bodyguard could talk to Tabini's. That was major. Bren looked at Machigi. And Machigi nodded, scarcely perceptibly.

"Lord Machigi agrees to that, aiji-ma."

"Good," Tabini said, and abruptly hung up.

Click.

"He has—"

"We are aware," Machigi said, grim-faced. A moment later he said, "Let Guild pursue it."

"Aiji-ma." With respect. Machigi had agreed to Tabini's proposition. Guild channels would exchange information, with coded assurances, and inform the lords on either side. "And you may be sure my bodyguard will talk to yours."

Machigi got up, headed for the door.

And stopped.

"I am posting a guard on this door," Machigi said. "They will be *my* servants, *my* guards closest to you."

Increased security—considering the situation? Or was it diminished trust?

"Aiji-ma." Bren gave a slight bow of appreciation. Machigi nodded shortly, gathered his guard, and left.

Bren gave a long, slow exhalation, then, as the door shut.

He hadn't had tea. He hadn't had breakfast. His stomach was upset—matching Machigi's, he was quite sure.

He glanced at his bodyguard. Their expressions—impassive until that door shut, he was sure—had relaxed into grim concern.

Algini threw a look at Banichi, Banichi looked at Algini and nodded.

Algini immediately went over to the table and got a pad of paper and a pen from among the neatly stacked writing supplies and maps. He sat down, rapidly wrote, the whole room focused on him, then laid down the pen, rose, and brought it to Bren's hand.

It said,

Nandi:

Machigi's bodyguard believes, consequent to the exposure of a renegade base last night, that a plot is now in operation to assassinate Lord Machigi. He is, with three elderly exceptions, the last of the Ardami bloodline. Two of them, my information states, are fools incapable of governing—but very apt to be figureheads.

Machigi himself once believed agents of the Dojisigin Marid had infiltrated his operation at Kajiminda, but his aishid informs us that view has shifted overnight. Machigi now concurs with his bodyguard that Tori of Dojisigi is no longer in control of his district, from a period long predating Murini's coup.

Predating. *Long* predating. Hell! What did *that* mean?

Guild sanctions and outlawry and the acceptance of the aiji's filing against him were all screening a Guild operation to invade Taisigi territory, neutralize or remove Machigi with his guard. Guild would then have taken out renegade targets in the district, and then would use Taisigi land as a base to take out their establishment in the Dojisigin and Senjin Mari, and elsewhere.

We provided a keyword in our transmission to Cenedi that reinstated Machigi's guard. They agree that Machigi did sup-

port Murini's rise to power—that position protected him after the Dojisigi had assassinated his predecessor. His bodyguard does not deny that. They maintain, however, that his entire aim was the west coast—which the renegades were content to allow—while they infiltrated that operaton.

When Murini went down, however, everything changed. The renegade Guild saw the Marid as their safest refuge—and Machigi as a problem, because his guard is not in their affiliation. The renegades could not control them, and Machigi, as you have seen, nandi, is not easily ordered.

Some of this we came in knowing. We were immediately approached by Machigi's bodyguard, who wish to have strong assurances of Machigi's survival if they come under central Guild direction.

Burn this note after the others have read it. These are Guild matters of extreme delicacy, predeliberation matters which I am not supposed to have revealed.

Good God, he thought, and passed the note to Banichi, who began to read it with an expressionless countenance.

It explained a lot. The renegades had penetrated the lower levels of Machigi's guard, but his personal guard were old-school, Taisigi, out of touch with the Guild but not of the breed that had gone to the renegades.

Renegade Guild were operating nearby. There might have been records. There might have been interrogations. One had no idea what had gone on in the night.

So Machigi had just been informed, perhaps, under what doors the threads were running. But he might *not* know just what deals with the devil his own bodyguard had been prepared to make to keep him alive.

Had Ilisidi known any of it? Some of it . . . likely.

Ask how long ago the central Guild had decided a Guildsman at a very high level should be guarding the aiji-dowager.

God, that was a cold thought. What *had* they brought back to the planet when they had arrived from space with Ilisidi's aishid, and with those of his, who had been on the station, absorbing information but incapable of reaching the planet.

The note had gone to Jago and last of all to Tano. Tano glanced over the note, then took the deadly piece of paper to the fireplace, where it quickly became ash.

Bren moved back the chair at the table, took pen and paper himself, and wrote, with his aishid gathered at his shoulders:

One understands.

One fears that Machigi himself will turn in the hand, if used as a weapon. Whatever his real intentions at the outset of our talks, have I offered him inducement enough to consider that his best prospect actually does lie in our direction? Yet if there is a chance of peace in the Marid, the dowager is correct: it lies in this isolated young man.

That also went into the fire. Banichi bent to take a piece of paper and wrote, standing beside him:

Machigi is dangerous in his intelligence and his determination, but his aishid has found in us their only chance of saving him. He stands to win or to lose everything. The question is whether his guard has made him understand that, and whether he sees with your vision.

Bren wrote, in reply:

I have to convince him.

There were sober looks, nods. That note in its turn became ash.

Then Algini took up pen and paper again, and wrote:

I can call on the Guild, using channels available through Machigi's guard, to protect Machigi, and to operate with immediate prejudice against Lord Tori of the Dojisigi. That will bring Tori's son Mujita to power. Loss of Tori will drive the Farai back to man'chi with the Senji and restore the former situation, if the lord of Senji survives this.

Operate with immediate prejudice. Assassinate. Within hours.

The *paidhi-aiji* didn't order assassinations. He tried to *stop* them.

Algini had confided in him, an extraordinary trust. Algini had exposed his own position, to get leverage on Machigi's guard.

All the Guild might be for hire, in a certain sense: its individual members took lifelong service with various lords and fought each other at need, limiting warfare as humankind had known it. But the Guild also took self-interested actions on its own, to preserve its power and even, one expected, occasionally to sway the course of atevi politics in a direction it liked better. It had been directly attacked. A section of its membership had peeled away in a major schism . . . half for the aishidi'tat, *for* the course of spacefaring advances Tabini-aiji and the paidhi-aiji had hammered out, and half dead-set against them.

Could the paidhi then say he had *no* responsibility for the fracture of the Guild—or for it now taking extreme action to deal with its problem?

Tori's whole line had been a problem—his father Badissuni had tried to overthrow the aishidi'tat, Tori had backed the coup that had temporarily unseated Tabini, and incidentally killed very many innocent people. Tori had assassinated Machigi's predecessor—and his father—and his brothers and sisters. Tori's hands were not clean, far from it.

There was nothing to say. Except . . .

He took the pen and added his own note of misgiving. *Tori's daughter Tiajo is a child.*

Algini wrote: *Tori alone will be the target. Better Mujita live to be a problem to his clan, until one of his advisors removes him. Tiajo is unproven, for good or for ill. But she will not be grateful.*

God, how did he get into this situation, bargaining for lives? And he hoped to hell his plea for a kid's survival didn't have a bloody cost later.

He took paper and wrote: *Are we dealing with an organization of these renegades? Is there a leader?*

He looked straight at Algini, and Algini just nodded.

He wrote: *Does Cenedi know this?*

Algini took the pen and wrote: *By now he does.*

Damn, he thought, certain that Algini had just bent Guild rules a second time. *Something* was going on between Algini and Tano and Machigi's bodyguard. God only knew if any information had gotten to Tabini's men before the bus left.

He didn't like their situation now—sitting in a target zone, with information coming to them mostly from Machigi's guard. He looked toward Banichi and Jago, longest with him, closest of his bodyguards, and had an idea they understood the situation to a depth he didn't, even yet.

Tano and Algini themselves would act for the Guild, when it came down to it—he was becoming convinced of it, and he didn't begrudge them that loyalty. Banichi and Jago, he was equally sure, would act for Tabini-aiji, who had sent them to him in the first place.

Tabini was ultimately where his allegiance still lay. He reached that personal conclusion. When all sums were totaled, despite his own attachment to the aiji-dowager, logic ultimately held him to Tabini's interests, and thus far he *thought* those interests remained congruent with the dowager's.

But hadn't Tabini warned him at the outset that his grandmother was a dangerous individual, a power to be reckoned with—and not always on his side? She knew at least some of what was going on—if not all—and played her own side of the chessboard, always, always with her loyalties in the East, and not necessarily congruent with the rest of the aishidi'tat.

Hadn't the dowager once made her own bid to rule and to shape the aishidi'tat according to her design?

And *he* was trying to save a young lord who could keep the Marid from falling apart in chaos. The Marid being in good order hadn't, historically, been an asset to the aishidi'tat.

Collective wisdom of the paidhiin before him had said, Don't interfere, when it came to atevi dealing with atevi.

What the hell else had he done in his whole career but interfere?

He'd become a Lord of the Aishidi'tat and advisor to three rulers. Four, if you counted Shawn Tyers; and five, if you counted Jase, up on the ship.

Maybe he should have said flat no when Ilisidi had ordered him here. Maybe that was where his judgment had failed.

No.

No second-guessing at this point. They were in the mess, things were in motion, and there was *no* way back from here, no way that he and his bodyguard could arrange. They had to survive and see to it Machigi survived.

For that, the question was: how good was Machigi's bodyguard?

And what could they do to keep either the Guild or the renegades from killing him?

He watched Tano burn the last note and stir the ashes.

The bus came in from the road with a cloud of dust and a rumble of tires on the portico cobbles, just narrowly making the turn of the drive: even Guild backed up, just in case. It was a wild arrival, and mani's guard was watching the bus with weapons in hand, even being assured by radio by Lord Geigi's own guard that it was Lord Geigi himself aboard.

Veijico had gotten out to the fore where she could see—she was tall enough, and so were Antaro and Jegari.

But Cajeiri was stuck behind a row of black-uniformed bodies, not supposed to be here, he was sure, the way the Guild was acting. So he tried to stay inside the threshold. He was behaving his best, so as not to be noticed and sent inside.

He had been in a good position until the black wall closed between him and the bus, just when the doors were opening, and that was just too frustrating. He ducked out for a fast look between Veijico and Antaro, and he saw, indeed, Lord Geigi's guard getting off and then Lord Geigi right behind them—it was amazing so fat a man could move so quickly, but Lord Geigi set his feet on the ground right behind his guard.

Immediately Lord Geigi had thanks for Cenedi, for the welcome, and then his eyes lit on Cajeiri.

Spotted. Cajeiri froze, expecting to be in trouble. But Geigi immediately moved from Cenedi to come and lay a hand on Cajeiri's shoulder—which he was entitled to do, because he was a lord and an adult and an intimate associate of Great-grandmother's.

"How is nand' Bren's brother, young gentleman? And has your great-grandmother spoken lately to her grandson?"

Lord Geigi lived among humans up on the station: his questions came fast and several at once, and maybe there was a reason Lord Geigi seized on him instead of Cenedi, who was immediately busy talking to Lord Geigi's bodyguard and who *had* noticed him; he was sure, now.

"Nand' Toby is well, nandi. Barb-daja is here, and mani talked to my father yesterday."

"But not today."

"Not today, nandi." Lord Geigi was propelling him and his bodyguard right back through the doors, on his way probably straight to see mani. Nand' Bren's majordomo, Ramaso, showed up, trying to be polite on behalf of the staff, but Geigi scarcely noticed the attention. He fired another set of questions:

"Has your great-grandmother spoken to nand' Bren himself, young lord? Has she any intelligence from the Guild? Has there been any trouble here?"

"She has, yes, she spoke to nand' Bren, nandi, yesterday, herself. One has no idea about the Guild. We just got up. Mani will be going to breakfast. And everything has been quiet here in the house."

"A condition which will not last, one is very certain. At *breakfast*, you say, young lord."

Lord Geigi notoriously had a great appetite, and he had been traveling from long before the sun was up. "Gari-ji!" Cajeiri said, glancing around, where Jegari was keeping up, along with Antaro and Veijico. "Run tell Cook that Lord Geigi will join mani and me in the dining room. And probably everybody on the bus will want breakfast. Tell him lots of eggs!"

"Excellent, excellent management, young gentleman." Geigi's hand had never left his shoulder, which was odd, but now Geigi squeezed it hard and let go, setting his own fast pace, leftward, toward the dining room hallway, giving no attention to his luggage, or settling in, or changing clothes from the trip, or anything of the sort. He was in that much of a hurry, and definitely had news that he had to get out either before or after breakfast. Lord Geigi might break all the rules, but mani never did.

Usually when it was a formal breakfast, Cajeiri would have his bodyguard go by turns and get breakfast in the backstairs instead of waiting to eat, but they all went into the dining room, and the three of them lined up in formal order in the dining room, while Lord Geigi's bodyguard had stayed with Cenedi.

They waited. One would lay a bet that a message had flown to mani, to advise her Lord Geigi would be at breakfast. It might change how she dressed. Cajeiri hoped with everything in him that mani would arrive as curious as he was and not tell him to go get his own breakfast so adults could talk.

Outside, the halls echoed to the sort of noise a lot of people made finding a place to be, and there was a lot of coming and going on the servants' stairs, just beyond the wall—usually one could not hear that at all, but the servants were in a great hurry.

Then it got quiet all of a sudden, so it was clear mani had left her room without any delay and was coming in this direction. The quiet went on, and outside, in the main hall, people would be stopping what they were doing and bowing.

Cajeiri stood up from table. Lord Geigi did. And his bodyguard came to attention. One heard the cane first: tap. Tap. Tap. Then mani came in, with only Nawari in attendance.

"We rejoice to see you safe, Geigi-ji." That was as informal as mani ever was. Nawari moved her chair for her and took the cane for a moment as mani sat down, then Nawari took his place along the wall. They were three at the table. Fortunate three, without Cenedi. Mani could *not* send him away.

"So speak, Geigi-ji, speak!" mani said, as servants arrived out of the back entry and quickly arranged the final table settings with very little fuss and then began to provide hot tea. "Tell us everything in order!"

That was how close an association mani had with nand' Geigi. Cajeiri made himself very quiet and hoped Cook would not break in with breakfast too soon.

"You will be aware, aiji-ma, that an order has come down from the Guild," Lord Geigi began.

"We are well aware," mani said, leaving Cajeiri frustrated and unable to ask what that order was.

"How much do you know, aiji-ma?"

"My grandson spoke to Bren-paidhi this morning. He has Filed against the entire Farai presence in Sheijidan. He is offering them three hours to exit without conflict. This is the sum of things in Shejidan."

"One is not surprised. The region is fast headed for extreme difficulties, aiji-ma, and Targai is being reinforced at this hour, to prevent any spillage of the conflict toward Najida. Your grandson will try to hold the trouble there."

"So the reinforcement has arrived," mani said.

"Some of your grandson's forces have arrived at Targai," Geigi said, "while four have insisted on providing security to me on the road here and intend to reinforce Najida. Reinforcements—"

"—Are moving up from Separti Township," mani said with a wave of her hand. "We are aware of it."

They were going to have a war?

But what about nand' Bren? Cajeiri wondered, biting his lip. What about everybody with him? What about Banichi and Jago and Tano and Algini?

But then Cook, doubtless proud of his efficiency, sent in the servants with the first course of breakfast.

And that meant there was no answer until after breakfast, and no sulking about it, either, or one would be sent from the table. Mani and Lord Geigi went on talking about the seasons over near Targai, and the two representatives from Targai who had come here with Geigi to make contact with the Edi—they were Parithi clan, a subclan of the Maschi.

Which was close to talking business at breakfast, except that everything else that was going on was very much too serious even to think about over food.

Cajeiri picked at his breakfast and had only one egg, and nobody noticed; so mani was upset, too, or she would have pushed another egg on him. Things were serious. Terribly serious.

She, however, said, at the end of breakfast: "Wari-ji, keep us apprised." Which meant tell her anything that had happened or was going to happen. And then: "Geigi-ji, attend me in my parlor."

Breakfast was over. Mani and Lord Geigi were going to talk in private.

But was she going to get nand' Bren out of the Marid?

Cajeiri wished he were big enough and his guard were old enough.

He said to Veijico, under his breath, when they left the dining hall and were headed to mani's apartment, to see if they would let him in for a felicitous third: "Jico-ji, go stand around security and learn things."

"Yes," Vejico said crisply and headed off at a tangent as they reached the hall.

Probably, given her partner was missing, the security station was where she very much wanted to be, to learn any detail she could.

And he had called her by the familiar, which he never had. She was adult, mostly. She was a weapon, the way Cenedi was, and in all that was going on, he was not going to turn loose any protection they had.

Especially a bodyguard who really knew how to use a gun.

The world was getting scary. That was the truth. And it was moving fast. And it wasn't a good morning. Not at all.

"Poisoning us," Bren said, faced with what was a truly attractive service, and with the servants still in the room, "is a process of inconveniently many steps, though conservative of the furniture. One believes we may just have breakfast this morning, nadiin-ji. One believes your lines of communication with the kitchen are either accurate, or they are not."

"Still," Jago said.

But Bren sat down, and Machigi's servants hastened to pour tea, the first time they had admitted the servants to serve a meal: Machigi said they were handpicked. It deserved, in Bren's estimation, acknowledgement of that fact. "Sit with me," he asked his own guard. "Provide me your company. We have done all we can do, or at least I have, nadiin-ji, and at this point I can only wait. If we are so far misreading things, there is no help for us."

Which was not altogether disingenuous, since it was a deliberate bravado and utter suspension of their discretion. At this point their best protection was Machigi's belief in their frankness, and too much quiet in the suite was an indication things were passing hand to hand—as they had.

It *was* a fine breakfast, probably Machigi's own ordinary menu, and with warnings from the servants: "The green dishes, nand' paidhi, are those your staff has listed as unpalatable to you."

"One is grateful," he said. So nice to have the poisons inventively labeled, in very lovely emerald green dishes that were probably from another, equally elegant, set. "Such a graceful solution to the difficulty. My compliments to the staff, and I shall recommend it to my own household."

"One will relay the sentiment, nandi," the senior servant answered.

It tasted as good as it smelled, a plethora of eggs and smoked fish—not originally to his taste, but over the years he had come to appreciate good preparations, and this was the best. The bread was hot and fresh from baking. The fruit jelly was delicious. He overdid a little, having lived mostly on tea and toast until now. Best take food when one could. A lot of it.

After breakfast, the hall was full of Machigi's guards, and God knew what was afoot elsewhere—phone calls and radio were flying hither and yon, mostly southward and shore to ship, one could imagine. Machigi had two allies, the southern clans and those ships that plied the harbor; and if he could rely on them, he would be advising them in whatever terms and codes he had at hand.

That was all Machigi's to do.

The paidhi was, in effect, down to a role more as hostage than as mediator, since their exterior protection was in Machigi's hands, and in the hands of his bodyguard—and in the fact that the Guild would exact a heavy price from whatever agency was proved to have assassinated the paidhi-aiji. It was not great comfort, that thought.

As for Guild policy in Shejidan, it had either gone a hundred eighty degrees about face, and Machigi's survival was the new policy, at Tabini's urging—or the Guild was taking its own course, and even Tabini might not know what would happen until it happened.

Lord Tori was not likely to see the sundown today.

Possibly he had given similar orders regarding Machigi.

The remaining worry regarded collateral damage. The Guild tried not to have that many. The renegades didn't give a damn, by the available evidence.

The next number of hours could determine not only who would rule the Marid but which direction the whole aishidi'tat might go. One hoped the central Guild stuck fast by its regula-

tions and took care about its targets, and did *not* overly desta-
bilize the Marid.

Not even mentioning the often forgotten fact that there
were aliens in the heavens whose perception of the stability
and therefore worth of negotiations with the atevi might also
hang in the balance. Ineffably frustrating—to know that was
the case and not to be able to make ground-bound atevi understand how very serious the situation was.

He did not want to die. He had a lot of things he had to do.
He had people who depended on him, not least of them the four
who shared the table with him.

So. Well.

It was a delicate process—convincing Machigi that there
was getting to be a level of trust on his side, so maybe Machigi's
level of trust of him could increase a shade.

And if not—the whole house of cards could collapse, and not
just in the Marid.

12

Mani and Lord Geigi were not discussing nand' Bren or the Marid, when Cajeiri brimmed over with the need to know what was happening. They sat discussing what had happened with the Parithi, two of whom had come on the bus, intending, Lord Geigi said, to stay current with what was going on here at Najida and over at Kajiminda because *they* were taking over Targai, with all its traditions and its antique treasures, just everything, all at once.

That was a new enough idea to catch at least the edge of Cajeiri's attention and to make him think about it. Clans were as old as the rocks and the trees, and clans just went on and on, and figured out some way to stay alive and in authority. Cajeiri had memorized lists and lists of clans by districts, and he could not remember any clan that had actually totally died out, well, except in the War of the Landing. If they went down, they were usually absorbed by a larger clan, like the Maladesi, who had used to have Najida before Lord Bren got it.

But Maschi clan, as ruled by its own house, had come that close to extinction. And Lord Geigi was not interested in staying on the planet and getting an heir. "Just ship my fool nephew to Malguri," was the way Lord Geigi put it, with shocking bluntness, "and let him do the only thing he can do for the bloodline, and be damned to him. Forgive me, aiji-ma, but the whole of Maschi clan is down to an old man, a fool, and a collection of ambitious hangers-on who were too damned close to my cousin to be trusted."

That was even more shocking. Cajeiri had never heard such language. Mani, however, just nodded and agreed to that idea, which shocked him even more. He was still thinking it over when Nawari brought in an old man of the Parithi, whose grandmother, Geigi explained, had been married once to a Maschi lord, so he *could* be Maschi in a side descent—nobody had ever been sure, and it was nearly a hundred fifty years ago anyway.

His name was Haidi, just Haidi, which was not a lordly kind of name, but he would be Haidiri if mani approved the idea.

"Haidiri," mani said, then, to the old man. "On our old associate's recommendation, and *his* recommendation is enough, you should find no difficulty with my grandson."

"Aiji-ma!" the old man said, bowing profoundly. And it was odd: a year ago it had been hard to tell when strangers were lying, but one came to be smarter about it, and this old man seemed to feel what he was saying.

Mani lost no time taking advantage of it, either. "At this moment, Maschi territory is the underbelly of the aishidi'tat, through which the association can uphold itself in strength or suffer a grievous wound. You will be in danger, nand' Haidiri, you and your house. You will be in great danger, and you will immediately require strong Guild protection. The Senji and the Taisigin Marid have viewed your district as theirs. You must disabuse them of that notion, and you will have associations from the North, the East, and the West willing to link with you, if you exhibit strong resolve."

"Aiji-ma, we have had the strongest representations of the danger. We understand our position, and we will appreciate any Guild protection that arrives."

"It is on its way, nandi," Nawari said. "And should, in fact, have arrived at about this hour."

The Guild could move in minutes, Cajeiri knew that. The

legislature might take months to make up its mind, but the Guild was faster.

A lot faster. Things were definitely going on. Not just there, but coming up from Separti, from the port there. And maybe from the train station—or the airport. It was scary.

And what about nand' Bren? he desperately wanted to ask, having run out of patience. Is Guild going to go to Tanaja and help him, too?

Then Nawari said something else, quietly, that totally changed the direction of the talk. "Aiji-ma, word from Cenedi. The Edi are coming up the hill. They are armed and in some great disturbance."

Tano went into the hall and came back again more than once, and there was again recourse to the written paper and the fireplace. Tano wrote:

We are maintaining an encouraging flow of information from the lord's staff. We have been advised of a delegation of merchants arriving in the building, who are a security concern both for us and for Lord Machigi. The household is under alert, but Machigi has agreed to meet personally with them.

We are also informed that members of Farai clan have been forcibly detained within the city, and that Senji and Dojisigi districts have both gone on alert, with personnel relocating to positions of greater security.

We are, thirdly, informed of the approach of sixteen out-lawed Guild members from the southern Marid bringing information and asking sanctuary in Taisigi territory. They are communicating with low-ranking members of Lord Machigi's staff and state they are breaking man'chi with their leadership. They ask registered Guild here to mediate an approach to the Guild, aiming at reinstatement. This question will be passed on to Guild headquarters in Shejidan.

Large numbers of Guild this morning arrived by plane and train in various places throughout the West, including Sarini province, which has alarmed the Marid in general, but particularly the northern clans.

Lord Geigi has left Targai and gone toward Najida. The rumor is that Lord Geigi is separating the lordship of Targai from Maschi clan and handing it to the Parithi subclan. Lord Machigi's staff asks for interpretation and clarification of this move.

Lord Machigi's staff wishes assurance that the action will not come here.

Bren wrote: *Regarding Lord Geigi, as before stated, Lord Geigi is anxious to return to space and, in agreement with Tabini-aiji, seeks to disentangle himself from terrestrial responsibilities. This move at Targai, while news, is consistent with that aim. Regarding Guild intentions and the sixteen who have surrendered, we have no knowledge of that matter.*

The first note went the rounds of everyone in the room and then went into the fire.

Tano went out into the hall again, this time with Algini, taking the second note.

And stayed gone a lengthy time.

It was not just the young men of the Edi who came up the hill, and they were not walking. They had come in the village truck, bristling with weapons. Cenedi reported it, and in that truck, the Grandmother of Najida had opted to come up the hill in person, intending to discuss serious business with mani and with Lord Geigi. Now.

Cajeiri wanted to go out to see, but if he went out of mani's sitting room, he might not get back in, and he knew nobody would let him outside.

So Cenedi went back out into the hall, and Cajeiri sat very quietly and waited. And jumped when there were several gunshots outside. Lord Geigi shifted in his seat as if he might get up.

Nawari headed for the door. But mani stamped her cane on the floor and said, sharply, "Do not let this escalate, Wari-ji! I shall see the Grandmother of the Edi!"

"Aiji-ma," Nawari protested. "These are not Guild. They have no discipline. One advises—"

Another stamp of the cane. "We shall see them."

Nawari was not happy about that. Cajeiri was not happy either and thought that where he was sitting was not safe if trouble broke out. He picked out a stout wooden table with drop leaves and thought that was maybe protection he could get to if he had to scramble for it. But if mani was going to meet with armed people, then he was certainly going to be here and help if he could. He had his slingshot. He had three good stones in his pocket, well, metal nuts he had gotten down in the basement hardware storage, and they were good. If anybody threatened mani, somebody else was going to get hurt.

Veijico, who had a gun, was still outside, on the duty he had set her. There was just Antaro and Jegari with him, besides two of mani's young men and two of Lord Geigi's bodyguard. "The table over there, nadiin-ji," Cajeiri said to his own bodyguard in a very low voice, "if there is shooting."

"Yes," Antaro said.

So they had their plan. And Nawari had gone out. The shouting had come into the hall, indecorous behavior in nand' Bren's house, and very rude of outsiders. He heard Nawari shout at someone to be quiet, and that was just unheard of.

There was a moment of quiet, then, and Nawari opened the door to admit the Grandmother of the Edi, who came grim-faced and bundled in her colored shawls. She was almost as wide as tall and walked wide-legged, arms folded, a scary old woman when she was mad. And she looked mad. Her escort came in, two of them, carrying hunting rifles, wild-haired from the ride in the open truck and dressed in hunter's jackets. The whole lot of them looked scary.

Well, so could Great-grandmother if she wanted to. But mani just leaned both hands on her cane in front of her, smiled, and nodded politely to the Grandmother of the Edi.

Servants came from their station at the back wall and brought a stout chair for the Grandmother, and she settled in, still with her scowl. What with her size and her fringed, flowered shawls and thick skirts, she fairly well filled the chair in one angry lump, with her two armed young men standing beside her.

Cenedi came in. And if things blew up, those young men had better think twice, facing mani's and Lord Geigi's Guild bodyguards at once. Even with rifles, those two had no chance, and neither did the Grandmother. Trust Cenedi to cover mani and Geigi's bodyguard to protect him—and if he had to dive for safety, there would be about six shots, none of them from the Grandmother's men.

"So what is your distress, Grandmother of the Edi?" mani asked pleasantly. "Be clear, even blunt, and we shall hear you."

"*Why* is the paidhi-aiji in Tanaja, Grandmother of the East? And *where* is our agreement?"

"If you have news other than the news we have consistently relayed to you, nandi, one would be interested to hear it."

"He *is* there, is he not? Negotiating with the lord who attacked your own great-grandson at Kajiminda and who assassinated *your* sister, Maschi lord!" This with a jut of her chin toward Lord Geigi. "You cannot forgive that!"

"One does not *forget* it, honored neighbor," Lord Geigi said. "One will never *forget* it. But rather than see more of your people die, rather than see the Dojisigi in the ascendant over the Marid tomorrow morning, I have shut the door on some reckonings and count them a private grievance."

"Your own sister, Maschi lord! *Shame!*"

Geigi frowned. Cajeiri had never seen Geigi frown that darkly, never imagined that pleasant, happy face could take on so dark an expression.

"At our request," mani said sharply, and *thump!* went the cane on the carpeted floor. "And for the good of the people, Maschi, Parithi, *and* Edi, we have asked the paidhi-aiji, though injured, to use all available leverage with a lord who, *yes!* has been troublesome to this district, and troublesome to my

grandson—but *not* as troublesome as his northern neighbors."
Up went the forefinger. "*On* which matter we have recent
news, Grandmother of the Edi, which contradicts some of the
things we have taken as fact, and the news is not good!"

The Edi lady looked as if she had met a strong wind; she
drew in a breath and folded her shawls closer about herself. "If
you have news more than ours, Ragi Grandmother, we will be
interested to hear."

"*Senji*, not Machigi, has been behind the corruption of the
Maschi lord in Targai, over a number of years. Lord Machigi
of the Taisigi moved to do the same with the *other* Maschi
lord, Baiji in Kajiminda. The Maschi lord Pairuti, in the hire of
the Senjin Marid, attempted to move his own allies into Kajiminda. But there they *all* ran onto the rocks, Grandmother of
the Edi, because a *clanless* agency has moved in on the Senjin
Marid and the Dojisigin Marid alike and poses a threat to all
the aishidi'tat and to the displaced peoples."

Mani paused there, to let the Grandmother of the Edi take
that in; and Cajeiri found himself confused, having no idea
what mani was talking about.

"The Assassins' Guild has fragmented," mani said next.
"The Guild who supported Murini, the force behind the Troubles in Murini's years, fled south when my grandson retook
the aijinate. And *they* have infiltrated the northern clans of
the Marid! We suspected it. The Guild has tracked these individuals as to location, but only recently, as late as today, it
has communicated its findings to us, and they present a very
disturbing picture. We can now state with some assurance that
the two northern clans of the Marid were heavily infiltrated
by these lawless elements. Taisigi clan, though not infiltrated
to the same extent, found its operations in Kajiminda taken
over by these persons. Its allies of the Southern Association,
the Sungeni and the Dausigi, have been troubled, but to a lesser
degree."

"What has this to do with us?"

"We are stating, Grandmother of the Edi, that the enemy is *not* who we assumed it to be. In fact, this enemy has attempted to bring down an attack on the Taisigi lord because he is their major obstacle. We do not maintain that he is innocent of offenses. But this renegade group, a splinter of the Guild, is bent on creating chaos in the south of the continent, and we cannot afford to pursue any grievance that takes out the Taisigin lord. He is the focus of their attacks. He is the stone in their path. So for the moment, he is *not* our objective."

"So we abandon our grievances? We do *not!*"

Thump! went the cane. "Grandmother of the Edi, we are your allies. We have gone to the aishidi'tat to right wrongs done you. We have called on the aishidi'tat to defend you. We have sent the paidhi-aiji into a hostile district as a personal favor to negotiate an end to Marid adventures in your district."

"Without consultation!"

Nobody talked to mani like that. Mani could snap her fingers and that would be the end of it. Cajeiri paid strict attention, in case he and his had to dive for that table.

"The information was classified," mani said, "and the opportunity to get the paidhi-aiji there without raising a general alarm throughout the Marid required decision within half an hour, Grandmother of the Edi. While one appreciates your willingness to consult, one could not consult without disseminating sensitive information across a broad area. Lord Geigi will inform you that we did not consult with him, either, though the message went to Lord Bren within his district."

"That is so, Grandmother of the Edi," Lord Geigi said. "All these things were done in support, not to the detriment, of the agreement between the Edi and the aishidi'tat. When one exists within the framework of the aishidi'tat, one has to accept that one's neighbors will move in their own defense, and likewise one has a right to expect they will move as energetically in one's own defense in return. It was, initially, your time to be defended. And now it is your time to defend."

The Grandmother of the Edi hitched her shawls tight about her and glowered, but she said, "We are here. Explain why we should abide this situation."

"Indeed you are here," mani said. "You are in this room, with arms and attendance. No outsider to our councils would have access here. You are *part* of this undertaking, Grandmother of the Edi. We confidently left to you the defense of Lord Geigi's estate at Kajiminda, while, reciprocally, Guild from my district *and* directly from my grandson have defended this peninsula and Najida village as well as this estate. We have at no time operated in indifference to the Edi people. You continue within our counsel, and we look to you to go on defending Kajiminda and the deeper peninsula as part of this operation—which is far from over!"

A second resettling of the shawls. "Then tell us, Grandmother of the East, what the paidhi-aiji is doing. What is he trading to the Taisigi?"

"He is seeking abandonment of any Marid ambitions in the West."

"That will never happen!" Another nervous rearrangement of the shawls. The Grandmother was not as furiously angry, but she was still agitated. "Machigi is our enemy, Grandmother of the Ragi. And he would destroy us without hesitation!"

"And we have made him an unexpected proposal. We are prepared to see him and his ships visit *our* coast, Grandmother of the Edi, far, far to the east, to give you peace. We have offered him trade—deep-sea trade—if he leaves you in peace."

"He will grow strong and fat," the Edi lady said, "and come take the West as well."

"This supposes you will have done *nothing* for your own strength in the meanwhile. We have not gone back on our offer of a lordship, a seat in the tashrid, a favored position on this coast, not to mention an alliance with us and an association with Lord Geigi of the Maschi."

"Add the Parithi," Geigi said, "who will sit between the

Senji and the west coast, presiding over the road that runs to the Taisigin Marid, in which arrangement they will expect the staunch support of the Edi people to keep that territory free of encroachment. We are establishing a strong buffer between your new lands and the Marid."

The Grandmother looked at Geigi and looked at mani, rearranged her shawls once again and took several deep breaths in the silence of the room. "And what arrangements is the paidhi-aiji making, Grandmother of the Ragi? Tell us that!"

"The paidhi-aiji, who has the insight of a lord of this region, and who also knows our resources in the East, has crafted a broad solution, which will divert Marid shipping from this coast and remove any reason for the Marid to covet a west coast port. We consider the paidhi's proposal, outrageous though it is, to have a great deal of benefit to all sides—except the northern Marid. It has apparently caught the strong interest of the Taisigi lord, whose position within the Marid right now is under attack by the renegades we have named. Of the five major clans of the Marid, he cannot trust two of them. He would be very wise to negotiate the offer on the table and divert himself from centuries of warfare to a settled agreement that will bring benefit to all sides."

There was a moment of silence. Another adjustment of the shawls, and now the Grandmother was thinking hard.

"He will attempt to trick us, Grandmother of the Ragi."

"Oh, one would be surprised if not, Grandmother of the Edi. And we are old, and we are wise, and we have seen a good many youngsters try one thing and another. Have we not?"

There was a lengthy silence.

"We have seen a good many things," the Grandmother said grimly. "And we will not be taken by surprise."

"We shall not, Grandmother of the Edi. And once he has gotten to like the taste of Eastern goods, he will have to keep his agreements to go on getting them."

"I shall inform my people," the Grandmother said. "We will

be watching. And if we are attacked, we will expect assistance from our allies."

"We shall assuredly provide it," mani said. "How encouraging to find us in agreement."

That, and a nod, was a dismissal. The Grandmother of the Edi got up, and Geigi got up, and escorted the lady personally to the hall, with her two young men. There followed a little renewed commotion out there, but not angry shouting. Cenedi left immediately, to get them all out the front door, Cajeiri was sure.

But there was still no loud shouting, and mani called for a cup of tea. The servants rearranged the chairs to what they had been, and they all sat and listened until the outside door opened and shut again.

That had been scary, Cajeiri thought.

But mani had gotten her way and the Grandmother of the Edi had backed down.

He noted that, too.

The day crept on toward evening with no further great to-do. Bren managed to do a little bending and stretching, trying not to overdo it.

And the surreptitious flow of messages went on. His bodyguard variously came and went.

He almost expected a dinner invitation from Machigi tonight, since things seemed to have settled. He didn't look forward to it. He'd much rather be sure things *were* settled; but it seemed in Machigi's character to push things and test the limits.

They had the three tall windows of the sitting room shuttered. The shutters were available inside, and his staff had employed them, making it just that much more difficult for snipers, in this room without a view of much of anything. He went close to one and reached to tip the slats up just to see whether it was dark out yet.

"Bren-ji," Jago said sternly.

He stopped with his fingers on the slats. He knew better. "One regrets," he said with a little bow, and resisted the impulse to pace the room.

He had not taken his watch with him on this trip. It was not part of an atevi gentleman's dress, and he had left it, along with his computer, in Najida. There was no clock in the room.

But it seemed to him that dinner was late. He was getting hungry, and he supposed by now the dinner invitation was not going to come, but he was surprised, in that instance, that supper had not arrived in their room. He hoped Machigi's servants were going to show up with a cart.

A stir in the hall gave him a certain hope of food.

Until he saw the attitude of his staff . . . grim and on alert.

He suddenly thought maybe he shouldn't be near the door. Maybe he shouldn't be in the room. He made a quiet move toward the door of his bedroom as whoever it was, and it sounded like several persons, came toward their door.

There was a pause, a few muttered syllables from his bodyguard, their attention all toward what was going on outside. Staff was talking to staff.

Suddenly Tano oriented toward him, while the other three stayed on strict alert, positioned so a shot incoming from the door wouldn't find them. Tano just quickly herded him into the bedroom, and without a word—which said that they didn't trust the monitoring—Tano snatched up his duffle, and set it on the bed.

Leaving?

He caught Tano's eye with a questioning look, and Tano gave him the sign for someone listening, and caution.

Not good. His gun was in the dresser. He went and slipped it into his pocket, brought his linens and put them in the duffle. Tano didn't object. Tano started hauling out clothes from the closet and packing, not with his usual neatness.

They were leaving and with luggage? It didn't sound like

an on-foot dash for the stairs and the back streets of Tanaja. It sounded as if they were going with transport of some sort. Which argued for official cooperation.

But—damn!

The outside door opened, in the other room. Tano didn't look surprised. He said two syllables that didn't make sense and then signaled Bren to come with him as he led the way back into the sitting room.

Machigi was there with his guard. It was Machigi's second trip to his room today, and it was clearly not to pass the time of day. Machigi was not looking at all happy.

"Aiji-ma," Bren said with a courteous nod.

"*Aiji-ma!* If I find you treacherous, paidhi, and a liar, expect not to live safely, not in Sarini, not in Shejidan itself. I will find you, or if I am dead, my successors will find you!"

"Kindly do me the honor of explaining the source of your displeasure, aiji-ma."

"The *source* of my displeasure! The incursion of Shejidan Guild into Dojisigi territory, and into the Senjin Marid! Now my guard advises me we are required—required!—to vacate and allow the Ragi Guild to set up operations in *my* premises! I am told to leave my people to the judgment of Guild from Shejidan. My guard says I should accept this and *trust* there will not be assassinations at the whim of Shejidan or the guest under my roof! Tell me why, nandi! Tell me why I should not shoot you with my own hand!"

"Nandi," Banichi said. "This region is temporarily under Guild regulation. Our Guild has moved to protect you, your council, your duly constituted institutions, and your citizens. *You* are officially and of this hour judged innocent. The lords of Dojisigi and Senji clans are outlawed."

That was stunning news. The Guild was suddenly cleaning house, and it was calling in every available member, on a priority above all other assignments.

Get its agents wholesale into the Marid?

Hell, yes. He figured it now. For over a year, the Guild had wanted this chance, wanted it badly, and lacked any way in to finesse the situation. And the renegades, in attempting to get Machigi out of their way, had tripped the legal switch— whether they wanted a confrontation or not.

"Our agreement is unaffected," Bren said. "The dowager, whether knowledgeable of this event or not, has offered her condition. From here, it is nearly certain you will meet it. You will be the most powerful lord of the Marid."

There was a space of silence. Machigi stared at him, jaw clenched.

"Who is it you represent *now*, paidhi?"

"You, still, aiji-ma. Until I am officially returned to the dowager or to Tabini-aiji. I had no more warning than you have had, I assure you. I doubt that Tabini-aiji was fully informed. My immediate concern, aiji-ma, is seeing you live to govern the Marid. And right now, I trust nothing outside this room."

Machigi stalked off a pace and looked at his own bodyguard.

"Our man'chi," the senior of that aishid said, "is what it has been. We have taken your orders, aiji-ma. We have stood outside our Guild. We have occupied a difficult position. We have seen these intruders trying to get in. We gave our warnings. We have tried to avoid this . . ."

"Warned me. You have, that." Machigi was scantly in control of his expressions. He was that overwrought, and one didn't move. One stood very still while a lord under seige argued with the bodyguard that was the reason he was alive. And there was a long, long silence, Machigi and the men he owed most for the situation.

"We have warned you," the bodyguard said. "Aiji-ma, we are not securely in control of the premises. Nor are they. We face a number of hours in which, if you remain visible, you will come under concentrated attack, perhaps beyond our collective abilities to hold back. You are placing us in an untenable situation, aiji-ma."

There was peculiar grammar in that *collective.* It used the felicitous unitary. It meant *as one.* It meant emotional sameness.

And Machigi stood there, a muscle working in his jaw and his eyes burning into the man he relied on for his life. Then: "What do you recommend, Tema-ji?"

Banichi gave a tap at his ear, an abrupt sign that disturbed Machigi's aishid. It meant: *who is listening?*

"Aiji-ma," the guard-senior said. "Just come. Now. All of us."

"Gods unfortunate," Machigi said. "Paidhi. Come!"

Bren looked at Banichi. Banichi made a slight nod and the rest of his aishid moved, fast, to the back rooms, while Banichi nodded again to the man named Tema.

Positions shifted, to control the door; and it was the lords' business to get in the center of that formation. Bren did. Machigi arrived beside him as Tano and Algini and Jago came back with, God, their luggage.

"One can part with the clothes, nadiin-ji," Bren said.

"An inconsequential weight, nandi," Tano said and set the bag on the floor by the table and swept the notes and notepad into it in an instant. Plus a packet of tea.

"At your direction," Machigi said to his aishid, and reached into his coat pocket and kept it there—not, one thought, for any inconsequential item—as his aishid opened the door.

Servants stood there, faces grim and worried.

"Get to quarters, nadiin-ji," Machigi said. "Stay there pending orders."

The servants moved back, falling behind. Instruction would send them to the back passages, the lower rooms, where, if their doors remained shut, no action would touch them—no legitimate action. One hoped the Guild arrived here first and with minimal incident.

And it was in no good frame of mind that Machigi and his guard led the way to those same back stairs, and down and down, past startled servants who plastered themselves to the walls and heard the same grim order: "Quarters, nadiin-ji, quarters. Leave off all duties."

It was a terrible situation. Servants devoted to the house would want to protect it—would do what the staff at Najida had done and protect the place, as best they could, moving fragile things. Their lord ordered otherwise.

And if their aishidi had contact with the Guild proper yet, there was no word of it.

Down and down the stairs. Bren struggled with the pace. Jago's hand arrived at his elbow, trusting him, but there if he should slip.

He was breathing hard by the time they reached a basement passage—basement, by the number of turns they had made—and headed down a bare stone corridor. Old, this passage. Electric wires were a dusty afterthought. And an iron door gave them passage into yet another tunnel.

Lungs ached for air. Ribs *hurt*. Bren reached a hand to the wall, and Jago's hand held him up from the other side.

In the dim light, Tema made a sign. Banichi returned another, something about transport, or leaving, Bren wasn't sure. But they kept moving, now with some shred of a concept where they were going.

Two turns more, another door, and they moved by flashlight, as that door shut with the resistence of age. Locked.

It was only dust in their way, dust, and a few pipes; and finally a stair upward, to yet another, modern door, with a keypad. Tema input a code, and the lock moved, and the door opened onto a short lighted hall. They might not even be in the same building. God knew. Bren didn't. He found himself dizzy, short of breath, not aware, when they stopped, that there was one more door to unlock, until he heard it click.

It opened on a concrete, utilitarian space with a smell of machines, and exhaust, and oil—garage. Transport. Their steps were quiet, but they disturbed a deeper silence as they went up a ramp. Four vans sat there, showing dim lights.

Outsiders, Bren thought, with a very atevi abhorrence of any help not from inside their operation. But they waited while one of Tema's men left cover, approached one van, talked to whoever was inside, and signaled a come-ahead.

They moved. The three other vehicles suddenly showed lights. And one didn't like the number of additional people involved. One didn't trust the situation. One didn't like it in the least . . .

Bren moved, however, with Jago, thinking with the scant supply of air he had, *God, we don't know the streets. We don't know where the hell we're going. Do we?*

They stopped at the first van. The side door opened, and they were supposed to get in with strangers . . .

"Rely on them," Tema said. "They will get you to Targai by a safe road. As safe as exists."

Three other vans, all leaving. Diversion. Confuse the enemy. Bren let Jago boost him up the step, to the seat inside. It was as far as he could get. The back door opened, and the rest of his bodyguard got in, Banichi moving forward to take the seat beside him.

And Machigi himself blocked the open side door.

"To Targai," Machigi said, "to Najida if you insist, paidhi. And one hopes sending *you* to safety is not the act of a fool."

"Aiji-ma, I *will* represent you to the aiji-dowager."

"*Survive*, paidhi. I give you that order."

"Do the same, aiji-ma."

Machigi gave a heave on the door and slammed it between them. The back door shut. The van started moving—one Taisigi driving, one more occupying the front seat, whether Guild or the garage's regular drivers one couldn't tell in the dark, with just the headlights and the reflected light off concrete to make them into silhouettes.

He was sweating, not alone from the haste getting here. This wasn't going to be a tame bus ride to Najida. In no sense. It wasn't just the schism in the Guild. It was the Marid itself. The paidhi-aiji was persona non grata with a lot of the Marid: he couldn't count the number of well-placed people in the region who'd like to see him dead . . . and the two handling the van were faceless, nameless, obedient to God knew what.

But they had no choice. Hunker down and hope the halls were never infiltrated—small chance. Machigi's orders might be to retreat to neutral position—but that wouldn't prevent the renegades from looking for hostages. He had to get clear before he blocked the solution—if there was to be a solution.

So did Machigi. Where he was going, whether any of three other vans loosed into the dark were Machigi's or whether he was going to some deep bunker to wait it out, there was no telling. The regular Guild would take the place, sooner or later, one hoped, with a minimum of damage, a minimum of bloodshed— the way things were supposed to proceed, with the Guild being the only armed force in the aishidi'tat.

But with a splinter of the Guild taking up position—God knew. God only knew. Lords didn't get in the middle of it. They had a responsibility to stay out of it, and let the Guild settle it, with the force of law. And to stand up and be assassinated, if it came to that, if one were taking the high ground. Lords had done that, to end an impasse. To protect a house. To protect a family. To save a dynasty.

That wasn't what would fall out here. The Guild was trying to get their hands on Machigi to keep him alive, but in the early hours there weren't enough of them, and innocents could get killed in the crossfire if Machigi tried to stay on, contrary to Guild planning. Get out, get out, get out was *all* they could do: he thought it with every thump of the tires on the drive—felt the sway as the van made the turn onto open street, and Jago moved to pull him aside on the seat, and get between him and the window. It hurt the ribs. Banichi helped from the other side, and the paidhi-aiji, Lord of the Heavens and half a dozen other titles, was obliged to kneel on the carpeted floor and hold onto the edges of the seats, keeping his valuable head lowest of anybody's.

Damn, he wanted his 20-year-old body back. His body from before his head had hit the damned chair in Pairuti's parlor would do at the moment. He never got dizzy like this. He hated it, hated the mess he was in, wished for once in a long career he'd told Ilisidi he wasn't going where she'd taken the notion he should go.

She was tired of him, maybe. Wanted to inherit a place on the west coast.

Wanted to make her grandson deal with the world her way.

He shouldn't have listened—

Thump. He swore the van had driven over a curb. And floored it. He lost his balance. But Banichi and Jago had him, and if either of the men in front proved traitor, there was fire-power enough in his company to make it suicide.

And by the fact nobody opened fire, the pair up front were doing all right, never mind the bump and the scrape of shrub-bery along the side.

They swerved onto pavement, headed uphill, fast.

"Situation," he asked. He didn't expect them to know more than he did.

But Banichi said quietly, "We are with Guild born to the district."

Born here, not Guild who had fled here. Taisigi-born. He had never in his life thought that would be comforting to hear.

The van cornered again, righthand turn, and sped up a paved road.

To Targai, Machigi had said.

Good. Good. Righthand and upland was a good direction.

His mind was racing. He couldn't see a damned thing but Jago's knees and Banichi's, and the back of the seat in front of him.

They turned, four more times, and the pitch was continually up. The whole of Tanaja sat in a stream-cut half bowl, fronting on the harbor, with the center of government midway up the hill. They were climbing, at every opportunity, headed for the heights where—God knew—he'd had a little chance to view the map—there was a road leading into the hills and off toward the main west road they'd used coming in.

They hit gravel, *not* the paved road they'd come in on, and that startled him. Bren propped his shoulder against Jago's seat, wrapped his arms around his ribs and kept his head down, telling himself if his bodyguard wasn't objecting they must be all right. He still had a concept where they were going, onto minor roads into the uplands, and that wasn't a bad notion: if trouble was coming, it might well come in from the northwest, or from pretty well due north, out of Senji district and across Maschi land. The whole district might light up if Geigi knew about it and called in help to stop it. They could run straight into a firefight.

Nobody said anything. They drove and drove, on bumpy, chancily maintained road.

Then a shot echoed. And something blew. The van swerved.

"Tire," the man in the front seat said, and the van was steering hard, swerving, with the shredded wreckage of a tire thumping in the front right wheelwell.

Damn, Bren thought, trying for calm.

A second shot broke the front side window. The van spun off violently to the side, bucking over rock and rough ground as the partner tried to steer. The van hit brush, broke through saplings, and the front end dropped with a brain-rattling jolt—that and the simultaneous impact with Banichi's arm and Jago's, before his chest and behind his head, so that he rebounded from one to the other. The back door opened, and Tano and Algini vacated the back seats, the hard way—the van was nose-down, and Banichi got his own door open and dived out.

Bren started to move. Jago prevented him. "Get down," she said.

Down. There wasn't much further to get down. But Jago was out of her seat, in the tilted floorboard, covering him with her own armored body.

"Nadiin," she asked, but there was silence from the front seats. "Bren-ji, are you hurt?"

"No," he said, as honestly as mattered to his ability to move. He had no questions. They were in a mess. The two in front weren't answering, and Jago got an arm between the seats, trying to ascertain their condition, while Bren stayed still and tried to breathe with her pressing on him.

"Both are dead," she said in a very quiet voice.

The same shot. Blind damned luck. And there was, around the van, except for the occasional ping of the cooling engine, no sound but their breathing.

"Come," she said. "This van is a target. Move carefully, Bren-ji. Can you get out Banichi's door without a sound?"

"One will do it, Jago-ji." He eased to the side, feet first, and felt his way into open night air. He paused, remembering his pale trousers and coat. "I shall be visible in the dark."

"Get below the brush. Get low, Bren-ji. Leave the luggage for now."

The rest of his bodyguard was out there somewhere, and, he would bet, given that side window shot, they had some notion of the trajectory. They were not sitting still, he'd lay money on that. But Jago was, if he didn't move. He wriggled out as quickly and quietly as he could, no matter the bruised ribs, and slid in under the brush, as compact as he could make himself, which hurt considerably.

Jago followed. She brought her rifle, tucked low, and took up guard over his position, above a streambed. A trickle of water flowed in it, among brush and rocks, a soft sound that overrode others in the night.

Absolute quiet for a time.

Then a thump and a skid on rock. Two sounds, somewhat upward on the slope. He felt Jago's hand on his shoulder. Someone ran.

Thump. A rock rattled down the slope. Something heavier fell.

Damn, Bren thought. He was in a cramped position. His leg was going to sleep. He wanted to move it. And daren't.

Then a faint, faint triple and stop green flash on Jago's wrist. Someone reporting. Thank God.

She didn't move for a moment. Then she patted his knee twice, which meant *Stay put*.

He did, as she eased out of the hiding place. He didn't hear her move. He did what she asked and stayed very, very still, as Jago reached into the van and hauled out one bag and the other.

Brush whispered. Bren stayed absolutely still. A shadow moved in and Jago didn't react. The shadow was Banichi-sized, and Bren managed quiet, small breaths.

Jago brought a bag. Banichi did. That was all. Jago came close and hissed, "Bren-ji. Come."

He didn't ask questions. He took careful hold of the prickly brush and hauled himself to his feet, trying to stay as involved with the brush as he could. He thought about his wardrobe. He didn't *have* a darker coat, damn his planning . . . he'd not brought one. And hell with it: if they were going cross-country, *he* was no help lugging that bag along, and his bodyguard had enough with their own gear. "Leave mine," he whispered. "I shall manage. My notes. Just get my notes, nadiin-ji."

Two other shadows materialized from around the end of the van, drawing his tense attention; but atevi vision was keener in the dark, and Banichi took no alarm, only passed the luggage to the shorter one—that would be Tano—and relayed the request.

Jago tugged, drew him away from the van. Banichi was right behind them.

How far to the border? Immaterial, he said to himself; borders meant less now than they usually did on the mainland.

Get to Targai if they could. If not Targai, then Najida or Kajiminda—any place where shots didn't crash through the walls. They hadn't even attempted to get the van out of its predicament. They just left it, committed to getting out on foot.

Maybe getting to a safe spot, where they could sit it out and wait for rescue.

He didn't argue. He didn't offer an opinion, whatever his bodyguard decided to do. If they were going to try to make it to Targai, he had to keep his discomfort quiet and try not to slow them down with personal problems.

13

They kept as much as possible to stony surfaces, in the higher areas of the hills, disturbing the ground as little as possible. "One is willing," Bren said, at a stop where he could find breath enough for coherency, "one is willing to go a little faster. I think I can, nadiin-ji. Or find me a place to dig in and wait for you. Then you go for reinforcement and come back."

"No, Bren-ji," Banichi said quietly. "Our best hope is to go, now."

They knew how the Guild was likeliest to proceed and what they could rely on; he didn't. He could do nothing about his clothing: he shone in the dark, he was certain of it. And they were going slower than he was, even when he tried to forge ahead.

And a request to shed the damned vest? They wouldn't hear of it.

A second shot like the last one, he thought glumly, and I'll be dead anyway. I couldn't stand it.

But two hours or so on, at the same steady pace, and he swore the whole of the Tasaigin Marid was uphill. They moved, and they stopped, and sometimes either Jago or Banichi left the rest and went on ahead, scouting during their rest time. Sometimes they would come back to report, or now and again the rest of them would just barely catch up, and then the one scouting would immediately be on ahead on another foray. Tano assigned himself to Bren, and Algini kept an eye to an occasional light-flash on his bracelet, that item of equipment like Jago's, that Bren had only once or twice seen them wear. He couldn't read it, no more than he could penetrate the verbal code that passed now and again, curt and infrequent; but green was good. Green was the good one. He'd observed that before.

Finally—Bren found himself increasingly scattered in his thinking, and mostly concentrating on not breaking his neck—his concentration lapsed. He managed to hook a dragging toe on a scrub root and took a stumble; he would have gone down a human-high edge, if not for Tano's arm.

He looked around to nod a thanks, and that movement did it: his head went light, his vision went iffy, and his knees went to water.

This is going to hurt, he thought calmly. He was standing on a rocky slope, or falling onto one, except Tano wrapped his arms around him and steadied him, and the fall didn't happen. Sky replaced itself with Tano's shadowed face.

"Bren-ji has to catch his breath," Tano said to his partner.

Bren-ji had to catch a good deal more than that. A functioning sense of balance would help. "Have to take the vest off," he said.

"Sugar," Algini said instead, and, Algini and Tano having all the baggage between them, got into one bag and came up with, of all things, a packeted soft drink.

Bren took it. It went down as sweet as fruit juice and hit his system like a hammer—stimulant, among other things, probably a dose of minerals. He thought for a moment he was going to be sick, then that his breathing couldn't possibly keep up with his heart rate, and then that it probably had helped him, once his body adjusted to it. He was not as dizzy, whether because of the stimulant or that he had had a little while to get his balance and catch his breath.

"I can walk," he said.

And they did.

An atevi border was soft for about half a day's walk, in a

vague overlap of property rights. But it got to be more the other side's territory the closer you got to the middle. He thought if they had more of that fruit drink, and he could keep hitting it, he could keep going until morning.

Maybe that could get them to a safer place.

Tano kept a hand at his elbow, carrying a rifle and the baggage on the other side, hardly balanced, he told himself. They hiked down an increasingly deep ravine for a considerable distance, with Algini going ahead of them to find the way and occasionally, very occasionally, when they were stopped for a second, showing that spark of green that meant either Banichi or Jago was all right out there.

Three or four rests later, and when his legs had ceased to report accurately what footing he was on, a shadow rose out of the brush ahead, and the fact Algini had not taken cover or opened fire on it informed him that that was probably either Banichi or Jago.

Good, he thought, and didn't try to ask questions. His bodyguard conferred together. Bren just half-sat against a rock and breathed for a while.

Jago came up to him then, and asked, "How are you faring, Bren-ji?"

She wanted, he told himself, no optimistic stupidity.

"Accurately, Jago-ji, one has availed oneself of drink from the baggage, and perhaps another one would be helpful. One is tiring, one has no idea where one is going, and one is a little light-headed. But one is doing fairly well—with Tano's help. Alone, I believe I would make progress, but far more slowly. I do think—if I rest too long, I shall get stiff."

She laid a hand on his arm, wanting to be sure he was focused, he thought. Human gestures of comfort were not likely when she was on duty. "We are one day, by foot, from the boundary, Bren-ji. We want to go until near dawn or until we find a defensible position. We are not yet in position to make contact with Guild forces. An attempt could attract unwelcome attention in numbers greater than we can deal with."

"Understood. We shall just keep going, then. Is there more of that drink?"

"Best wait, Bren-ji. It could make you sick."

"I shall make it, Jago-ji," he said.

"Yes," she said, thoroughly in Guild mode, and went back into the dark, leaving him to Tano and Algini. In a moment more, a trick of the eyes, she was gone.

He was glad they were not stopping and risking themselves because of him. Tano and Algini gathered up the baggage they were managing between them—maybe weapons, electronics, even explosives—given Tano's and Algini's special skills, the latter was not impossible. They had, he told himself, enough to deal with without hauling him uphill . . . and he had gotten a little second wind.

It didn't last beyond the next small valley and another climb. Near the top, he had to be pushed and pulled up the hill, by Tano, he supposed. In the ebbing of the boost from the juice, he was far too winded and dizzy to take account of who was ahead and who was behind him.

But he kept going once he hit the stony flat at the top, staggering a bit, until they encountered Banichi in the starlight. Jago, Banichi said, had gone somewhat ahead, and they should rest for the while.

That was good. Words were echoing in his ears. Details weren't coming clear. He needed to rest.

"We are coming into a difficult area," Banichi said, "and we are trying to find a way around it."

Going around. He thoroughly agreed with that notion. If there should be gunfire at the moment, he would not have the energy left to take cover.

He just sat down on a convenient rock. And then there *was* a gunshot, distant, echoing. Just one.

For the next few moments.

Then there were two. And one more.

Jago was all right. Jago had to be all right. If fire was still going on, she was fighting back. And she wouldn't be heading back to them, dragging a shooting match with her. If she was engaged with the problem, she'd settle it, and she wouldn't come back until she had.

Banichi stayed with them. Algini had the bracelet with the green flashes. Surely he would get some kind of signal soon.

They waited. And waited. The gunfire had given way to a great, deep silence. And Bren didn't ask questions to interrupt the stillness, because if Jago signaled she was in trouble, he was sure others had one try to catch that signal. That illusory green flash didn't come. He might have been sitting among a group of statues.

The rest were worried, too, he thought. They watched that bracelet and watched the hill around about them.

Three fast flashes. Then one.

Banichi gave two fast handsigns, got up, and melted into the dark.

More waiting.

God, he hated this. People were almost certainly dead out there—he hoped the casualties were all on the other side.

And the only favor he could do his bodyguard was not to ask questions and let them think.

The chill of the rock began to get into his backside and up from his feet. He was sweating under the coat, far too hot under the damned vest, and his feet in the light house boots were numb from cold. He still didn't move, except to shift his feet and make sure, if they had to get up in a hurry, that he could do it.

Then a couple more fast flashes came from Algini's device. A flurry of five or six, so fast he wasn't sure. Then three.

Algini didn't move. Tano shifted stance a little, then gave a fast handsign and moved off.

That left him and Algini, who stayed still, watching that blip of a lifeline.

They were in cover where they were. Algini shielded that tiny light with his hand, keeping its view to the two of them.

How long had Jago been gone? He didn't want to ask a question, which might distract Algini. But it seemed forever. His backside passed numbness, and the numbness of his feet was traveling up to his ankles. Not good if he had to move. Very, very quietly, and determined not to let the sore ribs glitch the move, he pushed himself to his feet.

Algini rose up immediately, seized his arm, and drew him back against the rocks.

Then Algini shot him a sign. Quiet. Atevi eyes might have made something out. He couldn't. He didn't want to ask. Staying still seemed to be the best course.

Algini left him then. That sign had probably given him Algini's best advice, but right now, one by one, his bodyguard had left him, and he was all alone in Taisigi territory—an unprecedented solitude. It was possible that things were, one by one, going massively wrong—in which case all he could do was burrow in, prepared to last days in concealment, and hope whatever was going on in Taisigi district ultimately favored Tabini.

It was possible, too, that he was not as alone as he thought. Guild could disappear with amazing effectiveness and still be on the job, in which case it was the paidhi's simple job to stay very still and tucked into the rocks, glowing in the dark as he inevitably did to atevi vision, and let Algini handle whatever came along.

A sound. A very, very faint sound seemed located off to his right. It wasn't the direction Algini had gone.

Stand still, he told himself. Stand very still. Atevi had trouble realizing how blind humans were in the dark. And he was blind, in this nook where Algini had put him. At least he didn't shine out across open spaces.

He hadn't thought of the gun in his pocket. Now he did, and with what he hoped was a natural motion, he eased his hand into that pocket.

"Kindly hold fire, Bren-ji."

He all but had a heart attack.

Tano was back. He hoped, instantly, for Banichi and Jago to follow.

But he didn't move. He saw Tano pass a shadowy sign to empty air, and Algini reappeared, answered in kind, then indicated a direction. Right.

Bren very carefully went that direction, around the side of the rock that had sheltered him. Tano overtook him, took a gentle hold on his arm, as much to signal him when to stop as to offer help. He kept walking, trying not to make a sound, and Tano said, in a very quiet whisper, "Jago is coming back. Banichi is holding position."

That was two things he knew, then, two very welcome pieces of news. They were heading in the direction of the gunshots. That was another thing he was sure of.

Tano suddenly had him stop and wait. He waited, absolutely still.

Then out of the dark beside the shoulder of the hill, Jago was back. "Opposition is momentarily cleared," Jago whispered. "Banichi is watching for any further movement. We have met one of Lord Machigi's problems."

The report was for his benefit. The Guild could communicate in many fewer words.

"There is an operations post on the height beyond the ridge," Jago whispered, breathing only slightly hard, and pointing up . "They may have picked up our signals. Sounds are dangerous."

His bodyguard at some point had picked up the other side's transmissions, Bren thought. And *Machigi's problems* . . .

The hostile base Machigi had talked about. It dominated routes in and out of Taisigi territory. It made terrible sense that their route, shaped by the land, had run them into it.

He didn't push his luck with more questions, but Tano said, "We are not surprised."

A veritable flood of information. Banichi was somewhere ahead mopping up. Solo, for God's sake. One hoped Banichi was all right and that the alarm switch hadn't been tripped up on the heights, to bring in reinforcements.

And where are the regular Guild forces? he wondered. If the Guild itself hadn't moved in to check an advance out of Senji clan, might they might be obligingly mopping up the Guild's local problem for them as they went? His bodyguard had been a while in space, but they had not rusted.

Damn, they had not.

But, twice damn, this wasn't their job. It wasn't even Machigi's bodyguards' job. They were supposed to be getting out of the way.

They were supposed to be getting back to safe territory.

But now *they* knew where the target was.

Was there any means to let the Guild know?

No safe way. Not in his way of thinking. He had a responsibility for whatever negotiations *followed* the Guild actions. He couldn't risk himself and his bodyguard taking on the Guild's job. They needed to get out of here. Fast.

Silence persisted in the land around them.

Jago had indicated they should stay put for a time, not, one suspected, to go wandering between Banichi and some objective, or bringing one very slow-moving, glow-in-the-dark human near the opposition.

But at least there were no more gunshots.

It got cold. Very cold. Bren blew on his hands to keep warm, glad of the vest, which at least kept his core warm.

Eventually Algini got up from where he had been sitting. Jago looked at him, then got up and motioned for them to get moving. She quickly moved off ahead of all of them, in utter silence.

Atevi could see in this murk. A human couldn't. To his eyes, there was no trail where Jago had gone. It was rocky, brushy country, and the night sky had grown overcast, so the dark in the dark places was deeper and played interesting tricks on human sight, especially when one was trying to hurry on rough ground.

Jago was, he thought, on a mission of some kind, and he didn't want to slow her down. Banichi was out there somewhere; Banichi might have signaled her, needing somebody to watch his back, and there was evidently some urgency about it.

The hills gave way to a flatter terrain, still at elevation. The Sarini uplands were part of the vast southern plateau, and now— Bren was sure it must be pushing dawn—they were well into that territory, the broad plains that constituted most of Sarini province. If that *was* where they were, it was a three-way border in the distance, where Taisigi land met Senji and both met Maschi clan and Sarini Province—a border that had lately been a permeable membrane, as agents of one Marid clan and the other had attempted to carve their way to the coast via Maschi holdings.

But there were wedges of land that had never known even the atevi concept of a road—breeding grounds, nature reserves left alone even during hunting season. It was a logical enough place for the renegade Guild to have established a base, a wedge of hills that would see only foot traffic, and that once in a hundred years. Setting up here might be illegal, immoral, and violating every concept of kabiu, but it *was* logical.

How other such bases might exist—if there was a plan behind what was going on.

That cell Tabini's agents had found and eliminated over inside Separti Township? They'd attributed that operation to the Taisigi.

Now he wasn't at all sure of that fact. Tabini's agents thought they'd gotten it all. He didn't entirely bet on that, either.

Their opposition had been clever. Nobody had suspected organization among the scattered elements who had run south. No one had—-except the Guild itself; and they hadn't been talking to the government.

Not to Tabini, not to the dowager, and not to him. He'd more than walked into the renegade's operation and exposed it—he began to think he'd walked into the Guild's long-term counter operation, and triggered it.

Well, hell, if the Guild had politely told its own membership what it was slowly doing, he'd have avoided the coast this spring.

And maybe more people would be dead. So he wasn't sorry for it.

He just wanted to get past this obstacle and into Maschi territory. Let the Guild handle it. That was all.

14

A sharp yell erupted in the dark, from somewhere in the apartment. Cajeiri flung the covers off and flung his feet over the edge of the bed.

Antaro, was his first thought: the cry had been female. He thought of diving under the bed or into the closet, but if there were intruders, that was too obvious a hiding place.

He heard voices, then, and Jegari and Antaro were talking outside, which was not the sort of thing one expected if they were dealing with intruders. But he was not hearing Veijico. So he thought it might be a fight, then.

So he had better get out there before it got worse. He grabbed his night robe, belted it on, and went out into the sitting room, blinking in the bright lights.

It was no invasion from the roof, and no fight among his bodyguard, either. It was Veijico, looking embarrassed, standing there in the hall in her underwear, and Antaro and Jegari, too—all of his bodyguard in their underwear, all of them with their hair unbraided and looking entirely unkempt. Veijico gave a miserable little bow in Cajeiri's direction.

"One apologizes, nandi, nadiin."

"Was it a nightmare?" Cajeiri asked. He had them now and again, although he had never waked the whole apartment, well, not since he was a baby.

"A nightmare, nandi," Veijico said shamefacedly. "One regrets. One regrets very much having inconvenienced the household."

She started to turn back toward the room she shared with Antaro. Cajeiri did not think he was going to get back to sleep. It felt close to daylight, anyway. "What time is it?" he asked.

Veijico politely stopped, and when Jegari said it was as late as he thought it was, Cajeiri ran a hand through his hair and decided on waking up.

"Well, one will hardly sleep after that," he said. He was sorry for Veijico. He supposed the bad dream was about her brother. And he knew he always wanted the lights on and people around him after he had had a bad dream. "I think we should have tea and toast," he said, "should we not, nadiin-ji?—Will you like some tea, nadi?"

"One is deeply embarrassed," Veijico said, "and would undertake not to disturb the house further."

"Tea," he said, insisting, and Antaro went off to her room to dress and probably to be the one to go after the tea. Cajeiri stifled a yawn. People were standing about in their underwear, a view which was interesting, from his standpoint, but he would see that from time to time all his life. When Guild moved in defense, they moved, whatever they were or were not wearing, and he was politely not supposed to notice it.

So he went back to his bedroom to dress, and before he was finished, Jegari, dressed but still barefoot, showed up to help him.

When he was done, he and Jegari came back out to the sitting room, where Veijico, in Guild uniform, was using a poker to stir up the sleeping fire. She put on three small sticks and poked the coals until it took fire.

She was deliberately not looking at anyone. Clearly she was still embarrassed.

"I have bad dreams sometimes," he said. "Sometimes I think people are shooting in the house. And then I wake up."

"It was like that, nandi," Veijico said, and still she did not look at him or at Antaro.

"Was it about the kidnappers?"

"If I were given permission—" Veijico looked at him, then, her back to the fire. "No, nandi. I shall not ask for permission. I would have to have Cenedi's support, and I know I would not get that."

"To go look for your brother?"

"It is not practical, nandi."

"Lord Machigi sent you and Barb-daja back. Everything will sort out, and Bren-nandi will get him to send Lucasi back, too."

"The Taisigi caught me, with Barb-daja. But Lucasi will not be caught like that. They will not find him. And he will go on looking for Barb-daja and for me. He will live off the land, and he will not come back until he succeeds or gets an order." A deep breath. "But if he shoots one of Machigi's people, nandi, it will be a risk to nand' Bren. And one very much hopes that does not happen."

So that was the dream. They had had disturbing news from the Marid all evening, reports of Guild movement here and there in an action Cenedi was not in charge of, and, what was truly unsettling, neither was his father. All yesterday they had known nand' Bren was talking to Machigi, trying to get him to deal with Great-grandmother, and Lord Machigi had directly promised to find Lucasi and get him home, but it was just what Veijico said: Lucasi would know none of what was going on. He would not want to be found, and if things blew up worse than they were, there was less and less chance of any good news about Lucasi. That was what Veijico was dreaming about.

"Do you want to go ask for news in the security room, nadi?"

"I am becoming a nuisance there, nandi, and I am not in good favor with Cenedi-nadi."

That was the ongoing problem. Veijico was still in trouble. He realized he had never quite told Cenedi he had taken her back, and how else was Cenedi going to know that, except she was staying in his suite?

"I shall speak to Cenedi," he said.

"One would be very grateful," Veijico said.

"I shall go talk to Nawari, meanwhile, nadi," Jegari said to her. "Nawari will tell me."

"One would be grateful," Veijico said again. But this time she looked at Jegari.

It was curious. Just in that, something shifted in the household. Cajeiri felt it. Adults had always said he would know things and he would feel things differently than his ties to humans. And he had thought they were just saying that to separate him from Gene and Artur and Irene, his *friends* on the ship.

But something shifted. Antaro came back into the room, and they were all together, and it felt different.

His father had unintentionally handed him a hard situation—trying to protect him by getting him a very young bodyguard that he would not try to shake off his track—not, maybe, reckoning how very hard it was going to be to work out man'chi with them and with Antaro and Jegari. Because mani was right. He had *not* felt his way through things. He was rowdy and disrespectful, and his ear had gotten very sore from mani's thwacks on it. She would say things like, "You have no grace," and "*Think*, boy. You were not born dim-witted." And grow very out of patience with him being slow when it came to guessing what he should and should not do.

Then she would say things like, "*Nand' Bren* can perceive these things. Why can you not use your head, young gentleman?" So he knew she was comparing him to nand' Bren. As if he were human. And things like, "You have to be among atevi. There are things you will *know* when you live among atevi."

Nonsense, he had thought. There was nothing wrong with him.

But all of a sudden he did feel something. Something like a puzzle piece clicking into order. It was like Gene and Artur on the ship: if somebody did something stupid, they could figure it out, and forgive it, and stick together anyway. And this way they had—had scared him. He had not understood it. But now that his aishid did it, just that little exchange between Jegari and Veijico, it all felt—better. Safer. Maybe it was Veijico needing them and them forgiving her. Maybe it was the precarious way things were; they had become an infelicity of four without Lucasi, but they did not make a felicity of three by shutting her out, and she more than knew that, he suspected she *felt* that—because *he* did.

So there was something to what mani had said. Things made sense suddenly. They were an infelicity that would not heal until they got Lucasi back. But they *chose* to be that, because they chose to take Veijico in; and she was suddenly different with them. Not alone, now. Antaro came back with toast and tea, and Jegari told her he was going out for a moment, and she should save him some.

So now Antaro had to figure it out. But he helped. He said, "Jegari has gone to find out if there is any news about Lucasi. He will be back. We should save his breakfast."

"Yes," Antaro said, and set up the teacups, four of them, and poured three, and served him one.

"Nadi," Veijico said quietly, taking hers, with a look at Antaro. And the room went on feeling better.

Jago had been back with them for at least a minute before Bren knew it. She was just there, saying nothing, but moving ahead of them, in the eye-tricking last of the night.

"Is Banichi moving ahead of us, Jago-ji?" Bren whispered when he caught up. It was a brief rest, in the dark, on the edge of dawn. "Why have we not met up with him?"

"We are having trouble getting around our inconvenience," Jago said, and indicated the rugged ground that rose on their left hand, across a ravine. They had traveled, they had climbed through difficult terrain, and they *still* were not out of the vicinity of their enemies?

"Is that the same place?" Bren surmised.

"Yes," Jago answered. "We are below it, but not away from

it. We are wary of surveillance, Bren-ji. We cannot dismantle it without betraying our presence. Banichi is mapping it. We are going to have to lie low for the day if this way does not work out. How are you faring?"

"I can do it," he said, impatient of the delay. And then he had to be honest. "If it doesn't involve a vertical climb. That—I can't."

"One hopes to avoid that."

So that was the story. They were increasingly exposed. There might be enemies waiting in ambush. The sun was coming up, and it was still night to human eyes—but to atevi vision?

They were getting into a region where there had been trouble, and it might have posted sentries. And the day was coming.

"I can go faster, at least," he said.

"Banichi is back," Algini said in a low voice, close at hand.

Where? he wondered, looking around like a fool. He saw nothing but rocks and brush.

But as they started moving, and just a little distance farther, a tall shadow appeared in their path, gave a handsign, and they all waited while Banichi and Jago exchanged a handful of words and signs.

Then Tano said, "Banichi has found the boy."

Lucasi? Good God. "Where?" he asked. And then thought of the enemy base. "God. Is he up *there?*"

"No," Tano said. "But ahead of us. We are going to where he is."

They'd made all possible racket in the district, including gunfire. The enemy had to be on high alert up there. Now they moved quietly, slipping down into a nook in the rock, behind vertical slabs, overgrown with brush, and down and up again, Banichi and Jago in the lead, and Banichi not stopping for a lengthy report.

They came to a split in the rock, a difficult passage over tumbled boulders, a nook deep in shadow.

He didn't see any sign of Lucasi there, not at first, and then he saw the direction of attention of the others and made out the faint outline of a figure sitting next to the scrub with one leg extended. That figure started to get up, but Banichi signed abruptly and it stayed put.

Bren came closer, finding, indeed, their missing young Guildsman, with a splinted leg and an attitude of utter exhaustion and dejection.

Tano, their team medic, dropped down on his haunches and asked, "Your condition, nadi?"

"Foot and ankle, Tano-nadi," came the faint answer.

"He was the one who started all this," Banichi said in the lowest of voices. "He came very near to being shot, but he spoke to me in time."

Jago had missed spotting the kid, when she had gone over the area. He had recognized Banichi in the dark. And he had somehow not gotten away from the original firefight, the one that had touched off the trouble. That was something.

"Can he walk?" Bren asked.

"He will slow us down," Banichi said. "He will have to keep up to our pace or hide and wait for help. We cannot risk *you*, Bren-ji. He knows that very clearly."

He didn't like the choice. He felt responsible for the boy.

But if the renegades succeeded in taking them, the aishidi'tat had a problem.

He went over to the boy and half-sat against a rock—if he knelt down to the boy's level, he thought, it would take his whole aishid to get *him* on his feet again. "One is glad to see you, nadi."

"Nandi," Lucasi said with a lowering of his head. "One understands the depth of trouble I have caused."

"Banichi has told you that your sister is safe, along with Barb-daja."

A nod. "Yes, nandi. One is deeply grateful."

"Banichi may have told you. You are in Taisigi district, and that post up there is not Taisigi. The Guild is moving on a nest of renegades of the Guild, from the years of the Troubles. And this will not be a safe place once they arrive. Can you possibly attempt to stay with us, or can you go to ground and stay there?"

"I wish to go with you, nandi."

"Make the safest decision, for your own sake, whether to try this or to go to ground. I wish very much to present you to your partner safe. But we cannot have you endanger this mission."

"I can do it," Lucasi said. "I can, nandi."

Bren walked back to Banichi. "I have told him the importance of our mission. He believes he can stay with us."

"I have my own orders for him," Banichi said, and he went over and said about two words, which Bren did not hear; but he saw the boy, who had risen to stand on one foot, nod emphatically. Twice.

They gathered up their gear then—or Banichi and Jago did. Tano and Algini were suddenly not in sight, and since Banichi and Jago started off, it didn't seem a good thing to ask too many questions.

Guarding their backtrail, Bren thought. They had to make speed and still avoid running into allies *or* enemies in the dark, and with dawn coming on.

Then he realized the boy was not with them. Banichi had, he thought, outright ordered the boy to stay put and wait for them to come back for him once they had this mess sorted out.

Which was as it was. Banichi was thinking about the mission, he had no question of that. About the mission and getting through this. He was glad if Banichi was doing what was necessary in spite of help from him.

He just hoped to hell Tano and Algini would get back to them soon.

They were about half an hour on, on a delicate climb downward, in the earliest of dawn, when all of a sudden the ground heaved and rocks fell, bounding hollowly down from the height.

Bren leaned back against a man-sized boulder and stared up

in startlement at the source of the explosion, a cloud billowing skyward above the ridge.

He didn't say anything. But that hadn't been any weapon he knew about.

It was, however, Tano and Algini's specialty.

And now that explosion and that cloud was a beacon for the neighborhood. It was going to upset any enemies in the area, who would probably run to see what had happened.

The renegades had certainly been stirred up from the hour Jago had fired the first shot. He had no doubt of that. But that towering cloud above the ridge was a magnet for an ambush. The other side would know it—and maybe blame Machigi's forces, which actually lay in the opposite direction. The combination of misdirections was not a bad thing—unless it brought action down on their heads.

Just hurry up and get back to us, he thought; and he hoped Tano and Algini didn't stay to do any more damage.

And he hoped to God the kid back there just kept his head down and melted into a hole in the rocks before their enemies came swarming out and around the area.

He—he just had to get down this slope, carefully, quickly. Safety was ahead of them, not behind. Banichi and Jago might have left the kid out of practicality, but they were held to the progress *he* could make, and the only thing he could do to help them was to watch where he put his feet and just do better, longer, farther than he thought he possibly, humanly, could.

He got down to flat rock. Banichi moved on, and he kept going, with Jago's help under his arm.

"Bren-ji," Jago said at one point, "go more slowly if you must!"

"For my sake or yours, Jago-ji?" he panted as he went. "If for mine, trust I can do this. I shall live, I assure you."

They went at the increased pace, Banichi in the lead, Jago close by him, being sure he didn't step into a hole, so he had one less thing to worry about. Staying upright. Moving. That was his job.

The sun was definitively up, now, removing the cover of darkness even to human eyes. Breathing and walking occupied all available intellect. And he was no longer sure he was using his best sense, but he pushed a bit harder, able to see, now. He made it to the top of a rise, wavered, with the far view of hills swimming ahead of him, then realized he was wobbling on the edge of a drop-off, and he caught himself one nanosecond before Jago snatched him against her and steered him to safer route, keeping him from descending the hill in a catastrophic slide.

"One is," *grateful*, he tried to say. But he hadn't the wind left. The whole world went fuzzy at that point. He might have been out on his feet, except Jago still had hold of his arm, and then had her arm around him.

"Here is not a good place, Bren-ji. Just a little farther. Then we shall rest an hour."

An hour. A whole hour sitting still. He wanted it so much.

But they couldn't afford that.

He had to tell them that. But he had to get where it was safe. He energized his legs and managed to keep going, sure, with what shred of intelligence he had left, that where Banichi was going, where Jago wanted him to go, was at least better cover, and a place where he could take just a little rest and get his wind back and then argue.

Maybe he could even take off the damned vest for a moment or two. It would be such a relief. God, he wanted to do that.

It was still another downhill, in among rocks, and past an overhanging shrub. Banichi waited at the bottom of a steep little slope, took his other arm and steered him to a little concealed nook and a flat rock he could sit on.

Then, silently, by the time Bren looked up, Banichi had left them. Jago was alone.

"Sorry," Bren said, trying to get his breath. "One is sorry, Jago-ji. Banichi is scouting?"

"As well we take a look ahead, Bren-ji. Use the time."

She offered him a drink from a small flask, plain water,

which they had in very short supply, he knew that. His mouth was dust-dry and he let a mouthful roll around and moisten his throat in little trickles. For not very much encouragement at all he would lie flat on the rock and stay there, but it would only hurt more, getting up, and the damned vest, once he was sitting down, at least helped hold him upright in some comfort.

"How are you, Bren-ji?" Jago asked him, sinking down on her haunches. She wanted an estimate, he said to himself, not stupid overstatement.

"I can walk," he said, "but my judgment is question—" More breath. New try. "Questionable."

She pressed her fingers against the side of his neck, where the pulse rate, he thought, was probably still rather high.

"Rest," she said. "I could give you a drug. But one advises not."

"If it keeps me going—"

"Better to rest. You may need it later."

"I need more time," he said, "in a gym, Jago-ji. I am going to do that . . . when we get back."

He won a slight smile from her, and with a little bow of her head: "I shall go up to a better vantage, Bren-ji. I shall not be leaving you."

"Tano and Algini," he said.

"They may overtake us here. The boy will probably be somewhat behind them."

So the boy was coming. Alone. God. He hadn't wanted that.

"Rest," Jago said, and stepped up onto the rock, and onto another, and left his field of vision.

At that point, it was his job just to sit there. And breathe. And let blood circulate back to parts of his brain he was sure were not functioning all that well. His feet hurt. Badly. He had burst a couple of stitches in the lightweight dress boots that were all he had with him, which was not a good situation. And he was lost. As lost as he had ever been in his life. He had absolutely no idea where they were, or even what direction they were going at the moment—west, he thought, and then wasn't sure, given the season and the latitude. He could judge where the sun would be, behind the rocks, but he couldn't see it from where he was sitting. It seemed they had not aimed due north-west, which would have taken them to Targai. But that could be an accident of where they had stopped, or the route they had to take, since they had wound around so many obstacles it had seemed they were going in circles.

They were still on the Southern Plateau, he was almost sure of that. They hadn't been descending that long. They wouldn't be descending northeast, toward the coast—that would only put them back in danger.

If they were ever out of it.

He was dizzy, still. Orientation in the world? He was doing damned well to orient himself upright.

He still thought that if he could just get rid of the vest, and its constriction, he could go faster. But Jago would shoot him herself if she came back and found him sitting there in his shirt sleeves.

So he sat. He sat with the spring chill of the rock working its way up his backside and the warmth of the sun and the heavy vest working its way down from his shoulders, for a reasonable meeting somewhere in the middle of him: his chest hurt and his backside was numb. He let his eyes shut, just drowsing up-right. Best he could do.

He wiggled his feet to be sure they still worked. He thought about Najida, and the bath that he was going to have when he got home, and his own bed. Breakfast.

Eggs and toast. Hot tea. He could do with that.

When he got there.

15

All the house was supposed to be at formal breakfast, after the one they had already had and shouldn't admit to. Cajeiri and Veijico and Antaro had been on the way, in the hall and headed for the dining room, all dressed and proper. A little toast and tea would not suffice for the whole morning, and Cajeiri had told his aishid to take turns going for a proper breakfast themselves. He was sure they had been awake long enough to be hungry all over again.

But Jegari, who had gone to the security room, intercepted them halfway down the hall, with a low-voiced, breathless, "Nandi, there is open *war* broken out in Taisigi district. Your great-grandmother and Cenedi-nadi and Lord Geigi are in conference, and breakfast is delayed. They have shut the doors to the dining room and nobody can get in."

Cajeri took that in for a few seconds, stopped right in mid-hallway, with servants witnessing.

War in Taisigi district.

Where nand' Bren was.

Where Lucasi also might be.

The shooting meant nand' Bren was going to have to get out of there. It was a situation far beyond argument and finesse.

"We shall go back to the suite," he said to them. "Come."

So they all did. Cajeiri sat down. Everybody did, by the fire. Veijico looked more than generally worried.

"Say," he said to Jegari. "What do you know, Gari-ji?"

"Nandi, a building was blown up in the outlying district of the Taisigi. No one knows by whom. It was a Taisigi hunting lodge. But nobody knows its current use.

"Second part of the report: Guild from Shejidan is moving in to take out the renegades in Dojisigi, in Senji, in Taisigi, all at the same time. Lord Machigi has disappeared. One of his closest advisors has been assassinated. One of his cousins has fled to the north, presumably seeking refuge with the Dojisigi. But nobody seems to know where Machigi is at all."

People were moving all over the place. It was chess with Great-grandmother. You had to remember who was where and watch out for pieces that jumped squares.

Only it was no chess game, and it was nothing as limited as a chessboard. It was scary, and nand' Bren was right in the middle of it.

"Here is what I know, besides," Jegari said. "There is some sort of trouble at Targai—one suspects the Senji have attacked. Your great-grandmother is discussing this in the dining room, with Cenedi-nadi and the rest, and Lord Geigi's bodyguard, and even Ramaso-nadi. Nawari told me it is likely that the same people were behind a lot of mischief in Kajiminda, and even Lord Geigi agrees. The Marid would stay at odds with your father, and that would keep the whole district of the Marid a safe refuge for the illicit operations. That was their plan. And it was not the Taisigi. It was almost certainly not the Taisigi. It was renegades. It was Guild who supported Murini."

Cajeiri drew a deep breath. He was getting a report. It was a real report, serious business that *he* actually knew something about. A lot of people had run south when his father had come back and taken the capital. And because they were in the Marid, which was not a lawful place anyway, nobody had much troubled about them being there.

"But they either went too far," Jegari said. "—Nawari said some could have been low-level tactical operatives given too broad an instruction, or they wanted to start a war. They wanted to take over Lord Machigi's western operation—and then when nand' Bren threw them out of Kajiminda, they decided to get Machigi assassinated, because they believed he was going to come down on them. That was when your great-grandmother sent nand' Bren to warn Machigi and make him an offer."

"She had Lord Machigi in a corner she could control," Veijico murmured, sounding impressed. "He was in trouble from both the renegades *and* the Guild."

A lot fell into place—scarily so, because everything these renegades had been doing could have worked, except mani was smart, once she was onto them. Just the fact that Machigi was talking to nand' Bren was going to scare the northern Marid and the renegades.

Cajeiri recalled all his study of maps. "Machigi's allies are the two smallest clans in the Marid."

"Yes," Veijico said. "And now the two largest may be in the hands of the renegades. The Guild thinks so. But the Guild is moving in."

And they were blowing up things over in Taisigi territory. The Taisigi were under attack.

He saw things, now. Banichi had told him once, on the ship—to make the enemy use the door you really want, lay down fire on all the others. It was the same thing mani had said to him.

"Mani is very smart," he said.

And then out of nowhere the worrisome thought came to him that if the legitimate Guild was all concentrating its fire on the Marid, then the only open door for their enemies was *here*. At Najida. Where an attack could threaten mani and try to get hostages, which was the *only* thing they could do.

He hoped mani was going to ask his father for a lot of help, fast, none of this waiting around. Mani would not like to do that, because she hated to admit there was anything she could not settle herself, but it really seemed to him it might be a good idea, very soon, because if all the fighting came their direction, Najida was wide open.

Was it the deliberately open door?

It was pretty stupid of his father to have left mani and him sitting in it, if it was.

Except his father and mother were having another baby.

He really did not like that thought. The stupid rebels had robbed him of his birthday party on the ship. He really, really looked forward to his ninth, which was very close now.

Dying and giving everything to the new baby was not at all what he intended to do. The renegades were very inconvenient.

"So the Senji and the Dojisigi are going to try to make the Guild come here," he said, "And they are not going to fight by Guild rules."

"One believes you are very right, nandi," Veijico said.

He was not as much scared as he was mad. The renegades were interfering with *him*, and they were hurting bystanders, and aiming at mani and nand' Bren, and everybody. And if his father was not already sending help here, then he was going to be very mad at his father, because his father was not stupid, and it meant bad things if his father failed to do that.

"My father will send help," he said firmly.

But then he had an even scarier thought, and he wished he were more confident his father could actually make the Assassins' Guild move where he wanted them to move, right now.

Jago stayed gone. Tano and Algini hadn't shown up. Banichi was off looking for a way out of here. It was a very lonely wait.

And it had gotten to that hour of the morning when the small life of the high plateau had just begun to stir into the sun's warmth. Bren watched a living-leaf crawl up the branch of a shrub, among last year's leaves that looked just like it. He heard a clicking that was a rockhopper greeting the day.

Then a movement scraped the rocks above him, and a booted foot and a plummeting body landed right by him.

Jago. Landing on her feet, as if it had not been that great a drop.

Time to move, then, was his first thought. They'd overtake Banichi, who'd be waiting for them.

"Tano and Algini are coming," she said and added, frowning: "They have the boy with them. Stay down, Bren-ji."

That wasn't as arranged. It wasn't what Banichi had told the boy to do.

He stayed where he was and waited, letting Jago guide the others in.

And sure enough, Tano and Algini came in from around the stony shoulder of the hill on the same track they had used. And just behind them was Lucasi. Lucasi was moving under his own power, limping, with a fairly substantial splint around the afflicted leg and leaving, one was certain, a clear trail behind him, even on the rocks.

Maybe it was pity that had made them bring Lucasi with them—but he didn't believe it. Tano might have a soft heart. Algini wasn't so inclined.

"Nandi." Tano arrived a little out of breath. "One apologizes. The place was being overrun. The boy knows too much."

Cancel any thought that things were going smoothly back there. Whatever they had blown up, the explosion had drawn in more trouble, and they'd diverted themselves back to pick up a liability who would spill a dangerous truth: that there was a high-value target wandering around out here, in convenient reach.

"One apologizes to you, nadiin-ji," Bren said. "We should have taken him with us in the first place."

"By no means," Algini said. "Nor will we slow you and Jago. The boy leaves a clear track. They will surely find us."

Lucasi looked mortified, head mostly down. "One asks," the boy said, "let me hold this place. One will *not* be a liabil—"

Algini gave him a single, hard shake, and didn't have to say a thing. Lucasi bit his lip and ducked his head.

"Jago-ji," Tano said. "Go. We are not now in the path of incursion, but we are much too close to it, and our trail is so obvious they will be cautious following it."

"Yes," Jago said, and, businesslike: "Bren-ji."

Move, that meant. Now. And Bren didn't object. Their best chance, under the circumstances, was his doing exactly what Lucasi was finally learning to do: shut up when Algini expressed an opinion and stick very close to whichever of them had him in charge at the moment.

What they *hadn't* said, doubtless out of politeness, was that Jago already had her hands full and didn't need two problems.

Jago headed out, and Bren followed.

And he was sure beyond any doubt that the area and the enemy had more to worry about in tracking Tano and Algini than Tano and Algini had in being tracked.

Things were beginning to stir around the house now that the conference was over. Mani and Lord Geigi and Cenedi had had their breakfast, so Jegari reported, which had turned out to be more of a lunch. But nobody was interested in talking to a boy.

So Cajeri, having thoughts of his own about what needed to be done, and with nobody listening to him except his aishid, said, "We shall go downstairs, nadiin-ji. We have business of our own."

He led the way straight down to the basement from the vacant dining hall, not caring whether or not the servants reported it, since both Cenedi and mani were too busy to bother with him. He had his excuse, besides: nand' Bren had told him to take care of nand' Toby, and by a slight stretch, he was still doing that.

He led his aishid straight to nand' Toby's door, and Antaro knocked.

Barb-daja answered the door. The smell of sandwiches and spiced tea wafted out. She and nand' Toby were having lunch in their room. That was a little disappointment.

But humans had different manners. He traded on that.

"Sorry," he said with a little bow. "Can we talk, nandi?"

"Come on in," nand' Toby said, past Barb-daja's shoulder. Nand' Toby was looking immensely better today, now that Barb-daja was back. He was still wrapped up in bandages, of course, and he was having breakfast with his shirt unbuttoned, but, then, nand' Toby was not on mani's orders, was he? Cajeiri edged into the room. Nand' Toby and Barb-daja had a little table with only two chairs, but there was the bed to sit on, and Barb-daja quietly relocated onto the edge of the mattress, collecting her tea and her plate, motioning for their guest to take her chair. "There's plenty, if you want, nandi," she said. And more doubtfully, as his aishid slipped quietly into the room to stand along the wall and he remained respectfully standing: "Or I'm sure we could send for more."

"We ate, nandi." They had, twice, actually. And using nand' Toby's name in the human way just was not right, and ship-speak *sir* was too general, besides hard to say. Cajeiri settled for a mix of ship-speak and Ragi.

"So what can we do for you?" nand' Toby asked.

"You can hear news, nandi."

"Tea, Barb," Toby said, and Barb picked up a spare cup from the little service—it was a seven-cup set—and poured.

Cajeiri sat down and took the teacup with a proper little nod/bow-in-place. Nand' Toby offered that atevi courtesy, too, being polite and proper, so one had to take at least three sips before saying anything. Mani had thwacked that into his skull.

And he ought to wait. It was terribly rude to discuss serious things over somebody's food. And in proper manners he needed to wait until they were through with their lunch.

Humans did not observe such customs, however. Even adults thought it was perfectly fine to talk business over food. At least that was true on the ship. He cautiously began to break mani's rules.

"Mani and Lord Geigi and Cenedi-nadi have talked. A message came. The Guild is attacking enemies in the Marid."

"A message from Bren?" nand' Toby asked.

"Not from nand' Bren, no, nandi. I think it came from the Guild to Cenedi."

"I think," Barb-daja said, "I'm *sure* Bren was doing all right with Machigi."

"This isn't going to make the man happy, Barb!"

He had been talking in ship-speak, and nand' Toby and Barb-daja spoke in Mosphei', which they used on the Island, but it was close enough they all understood each other.

"Bren's going to be all right," Barb-daja said. "Machigi wouldn't dare do anything if the Guild is moving in. He'd be a fool. If the dowager wants to talk to him and Bren is talking, then Machigi is safe if anybody is. He'd be crazy to make a move like that."

And everybody said Barb-daja was not a serious person and was always doing and saying wrong things because she was a little stupid, but she had been with nand' Bren, she had seen the situation in Machigi's court, and at that moment Cajeiri really, really was grateful she could explain that.

"The Guild will guard him," he said. "I think so. Yes. And his aishid is with him. They won't let anything happen to him. I think." Here was the hard thing to explain. "When we came down from the ship, Murini ran. The Guild with him ran. All to the Marid."

"Murini's bodyguard, you mean."

"Lots. Lots of Guild. In Dojisigi. In Senji. The Guild in Shejidan is fighting them."

"Them." Nand' Toby looked confused.

"The Guild in Shejidan says they did the bad stuff in Kajiminda. Not Machigi. They try to kill Machigi."

"So the Guild in Shejidan is going after the ones in the Marid?"

"Yes." He was relieved. "They can't get Bren. The bad guys.

But they can come here. Mani won't talk to me. I don't know what they're doing. But I think they come here. The Murini Guild."

"You're saying the bad guys are going to attack here."

"Yes! They want to catch us. We're not safe in the house. Mani won't talk to me. I don't know if she called my father. But the Guild in Shejidan maybe sent everybody to the Marid. So my father doesn't have a lot of people, maybe. I don't know if he can help."

Toby looked at him soberly and finally had a sip of tea.

"Can we get nand' Cenedi to give us guns?" Toby asked.

"You ask him. We get guns. We set booby traps in the halls, too. All sorts of things."

"Where'd you learn that?" Toby asked him. "Booby traps?"

"On the ship. We used to make them. Safe ones. We can make bad ones."

"I'll bet you can." Toby downed the rest of his tea in two large gulps. "We're going upstairs, Barb. Help me get dressed. We need to talk with Cenedi. Cajeiri."

"Nandi."

"Come with me. You're going to translate."

The boot seam was giving way, a stitch at a time. That was a damned nuisance, and grit and bits of dry weed found their way in. But stopping to deal with it was impossible. Bren picked out a bush, a rock, any objective on the way ahead, and getting there, picked out another one, trying not to slow Jago down and not to cripple himself by stupidity. He planned his transitions from high ground to low, never gathering too much speed, never risking his balance. He had one contribution to make to Jago's efforts, and that was a mobility exceeding Lucasi's and, he hoped, enough common sense to go with it.

So he did his best. Whether they were walking into something and where Banichi was at the moment—he left that to Jago, whose senses and skills were on the alert. Tano and Algini were lagging behind them with Lucasi and hadn't shown up in the last brief rest.

Jago suddenly held up a cautioning hand. He froze right where he was—not an advantageous spot, but at least a tenable one, in the shadow of a tall upright rock and next to a growth of scrub.

She melted backward and indicated he should get deeper into cover.

He did that, set his back against springy brush and put his hand into the pocket with the gun, just in case.

She was leaving him for a while, she signed to him. He couldn't go where she was going or do what she was going to do.

But if Jago couldn't handle it, he was sure it couldn't be handled. He just needed to stay absolutely still, remembering the acuteness of atevi hearing. She was apparently going hunting.

He settled to stay where he was. His best contribution was to rest and catch his breath, in the theory they were likely to have to move and maybe move for a long distance and fast.

In the best of situations, they'd nearly caught up to Banichi, and she was going to move up on him with the appropriate moves or signals, so Banichi wouldn't, God help them, shoot them both by accident.

In the worst—they were running into trouble, and Jago was going to have to handle it.

He mopped his face with the back of his cuff, never mind the chill in the air. He wanted to sit down, but that involved moving, and not moving in the least was just safer. He had a rock and a springy bit of brush to lean on, he had his legs braced, and he was not in pain, which was all he asked, at the moment. He was sure she'd be back in a few minutes.

He didn't know how far they were from that nebulous transition that humans would call the three-way border, the district between Taisigi land and Maschi territory, and likewise between the Marid and Sarini Province. "Border" might be a lovely distinction for a human brain that didn't like shades of gray, but the people who'd like to kill them wouldn't be at all fussy about where they were when they ran into each other, and they wouldn't be safe until they'd gone far enough to have a substantial enough contingent of allied Guild forces between them and everybody who wanted them dead.

It wasn't mani nor even Cenedi they found, going up the stairs; it was Lord Geigi, with household servants carrying baggage, and headed for the stairs.

"Is the enemy coming, nandi?" Cajeiri asked.

"Not imminently, young gentleman," Lord Geigi said. "Staff will be moving furniture. A precaution."

"Is mani calling my father?"

"One is certain your father is aware of our difficulty, young gentleman."

It was an adult trying to keep him from worrying. Which always meant there was something to worry about.

"Is mani calling my father, nandi?"

Geigi had intended to go on down the stairs. They were impolitely in the way. Lord Geigi said, "It is being taken care of, young gentleman."

Nand' Toby said, in Mosphei', "What's the problem?"

Geigi understood ship-speak. And he looked at nand' Toby, looking out of breath and bothered.

"Communications," Lord Geigi said in ship-speak. "We have transmitted a general alert to the station. Phones are not . . ." It was a ship-speak word Cajeiri did not know. It was not fair.

"What?" he asked. "Reli-ble."

"Reliable," Lord Geigi said in Ragi. "Neither phone nor radio is secure at this point. The enemy is preparing something." And Lord Geigi said it again, in fluent ship-speak, adding: "I've alerted the station, nandi. They will be contacting Mospheira *and* Shejidan, and at that point, what they will do is up to them. The Edi, on the other hand, have contacted the Gan, and that is—" Another big word.

"Nandi," Cajeiri said, frustrated. "What will the Gan do?"

"They will come, young lord. They will arrive in the middle of things, armed and with no connection to Guild authority. One has asked the Grandmother of the Edi to fortify Kajiminda, and if the Gan then arrive in the midst of this, one can only hope not to have complete confusion." He changed to ship-speak, addressing nand' Toby and Barb-daja. "Guild action does not tend to be long, nandiin. We must hold Najida for the next number of hours, perhaps three days, before help will . . ." More words, involving Shejidan. Cajeiri drew a quick breath and got a question in.

"My father has nobody to send, nandi?"

The question drew a strange frown, a calculation, maybe, and a hesitation in answering. "Your father will have received our message, young gentleman. One has every confidence he will act—or that he *has* acted would not surprise me in the least. If you would assist, young gentleman, persuade your great-grandmother to move downstairs. *That* would be to the good."

"But what is my father doing, nandi?"

"One has no idea at all, young lord," Lord Geigi said, and said in ship-speak: "We expect attack. Cenedi hasn't been able to get new information from the Guild. We can send messages out, but no one is talking to us, and we only dare say what we don't mind the enemy hearing. At this point we simply get ready." And back to Ragi: "Persuade your great-grandmother to move downstairs, young sir. *That* would be a service."

Nobody was going to listen. Mani was clearly in a bad mood. And the enemy had tapped the phone lines.

"Can we get guns?" nand' Toby asked.

"Nawari, in the security office, nandi," Lord Geigi said. "He's arming any staff who knows how to use one."

Time passed. More than half an hour. An hour. Bren watched the shadow creep across a small knob of rock, and pass it entirely, and eventually start to decline off the rock entirely.

He heard nothing. Saw nothing move but a small creature digging roots, out beyond the rocks. He had been still enough that that shy creature felt safe to come out. His feet had gone to sleep.

The shadow crept off the rock entirely and traversed the brown dust of the ground.

He'd stood and waited as long as he could. He moved very carefully so as not to rustle the branches he'd been leaning on and sank down to one knee, and finally down to sit as far back in the rocks as he could manage.

He still refused to worry at this point. If Jago had gotten into a situation, he only hoped she would rely on him absolutely to do what she had told him to do. The last thing he wanted was for her to risk herself and Banichi because they expected him to be a fool.

And, he told himself, Tano and Algini would be arriving here, sooner or later. He hadn't heard any explosions besides the one back at the ridge. But that didn't mean that pair was through dealing with the opposition, and it didn't mean that anything had happened to them. It was entirely possible they would show up and just move him along toward Jago, relying on the signals they occasionally passed to one another. The second last thing he wanted was to be rambling around out in the countryside, either to draw enemies to himself or to get himself shot by his own bodyguard.

He didn't know whether there was any specific Guild code for "I've left the paidhi in a cul de sac and I hope he stays there," but he wouldn't be surprised to know that his bodyguard had a code for pretty much that idea.

The one thing he was sure of was that he truly had no business even taking a look outside his hiding place, no matter what. A human just couldn't easily judge what an atevi could hear or what one could see in near darkness. Twilight and high noon were the two times when the differences most mattered— advantage went to the human in blinding glare but to the ateva in near darkness. And he very much hoped somebody showed up before dark.

He grew hungry over the afternoon. He grew very thirsty. He didn't carry a canteen, which he regretted. And Jago, who had had that foresight, hadn't left it with him, so she planned to get back before he was in dire straits, at least.

Which he was not yet, only uncomfortable and with far too much time to think of things that could go wrong.

The best thing he could do to alleviate the discomfort and get ready to move when Jago got back was rest and sleep. He had his pistol, the only excess weight his staff let him carry. He had taken it out and laid it across his lap as he sat, but it was far, far better not to fire it and bring down the entire countryside—not to mention making his bodyguard scramble to get back to him and possibly risk their necks doing it.

So he had the rock to lean on. It was cold, here in the shadow, but the damned vest, besides keeping him upright, kept him warm, give or take his hands and feet.

He tucked his hands under his arms and shut his eyes.

Actual sleep eluded him except by fitful moments, but very slowly, very slowly, he noted the shadow creep across onto another rock and climb it, until the whole nook was in twilight. It grew decidedly colder. His backside was long since numb. His legs and his arms were getting there.

He was careful shifting position. But he had to, several times, to prevent his legs going to sleep. It was, thank God, not damp dirt, but it was chill. So was the rock, give or take the thin, springy brush he had for a cushion at his back.

It had been an anxious day. A few of the servants were armed, even if Cenedi still refused to let Antaro and Jegari carry guns; and some of the young servants were out at more distant posts, watching the roads. It was a scary feeling, and an empty feeling, as the house at Najida went on defensive alert.

Mani still refused to go downstairs. By late afternoon, vari-

ous Edi and two of the Guild that had come in with the bus
came in for mysterious meetings with mani and Cenedi. Cajeiri
could get no reports about what they were saying, but he was
sure it had to do with Guild moving somewhere: it had that
kind of hush about it.

So there were at least some reinforcements, he told himself. He hoped there were a lot of them, but nobody had said
anything about that where his bodyguard could overhear it—
informing nand' Toby of what he knew and getting nand' Toby
armed had had one unintended side effect: Cenedi had found
out that information was leaking out, and Cenedi had not been
happy.

So now nothing leaked, not even from Nawari and not even
to Antaro.

And nobody had time for supper, either. Cook made pizza
for most of the staff and a country dish for mani and Cenedi and
for Lord Geigi and him, too.

Cajeiri could smell the pizza. He had far rather have that.
But saying so would upset the cook, and mani would call it
rude. Pickled eggs and spiced fish were not too bad. He ate with
mani in her upstairs sitting room, and so did Lord Geigi, who
had second helpings. So did nand' Toby and Barb-daja, who had
been talking to mani and to Cenedi and nand' Geigi—well, they
had been answering what Cajeiri translated, a lot of it about
Tanaja and what Barb-daja had seen. Cajeiri had been translat-
ing back and forth; but everything stopped long enough for supper. Cajeiri was glad of the break because his brain hurt, and
eating was a little while he did not have to be thinking of words
that had gotten away from him.

Nand' Toby and Barb-daja got pizza right in the same room,
which was just unfair, but they were specially privileged because they were allergic to the pickle spice, so mani said.

Mani, especially since the last report from Nawari, had been
upset about something before supper. There was a long list
of things she could justifiably be upset about. Her bodyguard

picked it up: they moved especially fast when they came into the room—even during supper, which was how urgent things were getting to be; and they delivered their reports in concise order, largely to Cenedi, who still gave no hint whether the reinforcements they thought might come were coming here or not.

So supper had gone very fast, for one of mani's suppers, just the one dish and tea, quickly disposed of.

And immediately after there was more serious talk, mani with Cenedi and Lord Geigi, while Cajeiri translated as much as he could get into his head, for nand' Tobi and Barb-daja.

Mani's guard, stationed on the roof and at various places nobody mentioned, had all the roads under watch. The Edi were watching the overland roads and trails.

And nand' Geigi had left orders at Targai when he quit the area, telling the little Parithi clan not even to try to resist any invasion, but to stay under cover as much as possible and even to abandon the house if they had to. Parithi had no Guild of its own there to defend them, and in Geigi's opinion and everybody else's, they were not a priority for Shejidan to move anybody in to help them.

Meanwhile, the men who had come in from Tanaja on the bus had vanished again, telling nobody what they were up to.

Cajeiri tried to communicate all the detail. He had not used his ship-speak this much in most of a year. Mosphei' had a different accent and put in pieces ship-speak left out, so he kept having to correct himself. And when nand' Toby had something to say, he had to ask nand' Toby several times to get things straight, and then find a time to break into what mani and Lord Geigi were saying to get it across, whispering.

Nand' Toby had been working for the Presidenta of Mospheira all during the Troubles, and he understood just how everything was laid out along the whole west coast, and who was where, and who was allied, and who was trouble. So that at least made explaining mani's answers easier in the other direction.

The one fact he gathered from mani and Cenedi was what they had already found out, that the Guild was acting on its own in the Marid. Guild who had man'chi only to the Guild were running things at the moment, and Cenedi was not reliably informed, the way Cenedi put it.

Cenedi was angry about that, Cajeiri thought, but even as high as Cenedi's rank was, not to mention mani's, there seemed to be nothing he could do to get the Guild to obey and get people to Najida. Going into the Marid and, as Toby put it, knocking heads, was probably a good idea on the Guild's part. But mani had rushed into action, a situation neither she nor Cenedi liked, because this second power, this other outlawed Guild, had tried to get Guild action focused on Machigi . . . which mani believed meant they were going to kill him.

Now here they sat.

And Cajeiri thought his father in Shejidan was probably doing just what mani was doing: sitting. And it was probably what even the Presidenta over on Mospheira was doing: getting his people into protective positions until it was clear exactly where the Guild was operating and what they were doing, and sitting in his office asking sharp questions and listening to reports. It was all these powerful people could do—because the Guild, which had always taken orders, was obstinately not taking orders or giving out information.

And it was not just the Maschi and the Edi and the Marid involved. Mani in fact had told nand' Geigi that when the Edi had appealed to the Gan for help, the lord of Dur had found out; and everybody speculated that Dur, of all their allies, might do something—being far enough from the renegade's territory that he was not directly in danger. Cajeiri was excited and encouraged to hear that; Dur was one of his father's staunchest allies, and particularly the young lord of that district, who was incredibly brave and reckless and had an airplane. A yellow one.

Dur had boats. And planes. And if they came down, things would be a lot better.

But in either case, the bad news was that the help from the north was going to take time getting here.

And now the Guildsmen who had come in on the bus had disappeared, and Cenedi would not talk about it or answer mani's questions, which probably meant Cenedi knew where they were.

Probably, Cajeiri thought, they had headed back into Targai district, which definitely had trouble; or maybe they had gone down into Separti Township or over to Kajiminda to give Guild help to the Edi who were protecting it. It still all added up to the fact that they might be on their own for a while, and what was blowing up larger and larger in the Marid was like a storm coming up way too fast. There just was not time, now, Cenedi said, to expect any help. They were going to have to get through the night, and possibly a few days longer than that, on their own.

Meanwhile, mani's bodyguard *was* putting booby traps in place. A lot of them. Really interesting ones. Cajeiri had wanted to see in detail what they were, but nobody would let him.

So they were getting ready, with mani's young men posted on the roof and elsewhere as they had been.

Nand' Toby said, too, that if they wanted, he could phone the Presidenta of Mospheira and get help, and Geigi said that the station would provide intelligence to Shejidan.

"We shall just keep behind our walls, nadiin-ji," she said, in that tone of voice that ended argument. "We shall defend ourselves."

"I don't understand why," Cajeiri said to nand' Toby and Barb-daja, "but mani says no."

Then Cenedi's chin lifted, and he sent an attentive look into nowhere, as if he were hearing something from that earpiece he had.

He said, quietly, "Aiji-ma, nandiin, there is movement out of Senji, bypassing Targai. It has reached the airport. It will likely come this way."

The airport. That was *close.* That was just about an hour away. Whatever was going to happen had started.

It was difficult to be bored to tears while being terrified, but given a whole day hiding in a hole in the rocks, it was possible, Bren decided. He shifted position to keep his legs from going to sleep, but his backside was beyond numb.

It had gotten dark. Darker than dark. Clouds had moved in, and there was not even starlight to help. And the strain of listening for hours had taken its toll on mental acuteness.

He wasn't listening as well as he had. He actually grew increasingly sleepy and dull-witted with exhaustion, and he leaned his head back and shut his eyes, just reassuring himself with the faint night sounds—telling himself that if those creatures were stirring, nobody was near.

He came closer to sleep. Felt the slight movement of a breeze . . .

A very light breeze. The waft of a white, sheer curtain. The smell of flowers. The shadow of the lattice.

The garden apartment. That was where he had joined up with Banichi and Jago, a different world ago.

It was the night he'd started carrying an illegal gun in the first place. If he let this dream continue, in the next moment he'd see a shadow beyond that lattice. A gun would go off.

He'd begun another life, that night, on the chain of events that had led him to Ilisidi.

And a close association with Tabini, who'd taken him target shooting up at Taiben, in days when he'd been far more innocent.

Best not sleep. Keep awake. Keep alert. He'd be embarrassed when Jago got back and scared hell out of him.

Had to move. His leg had a cramp.

Damn, he wished he'd hear from Jago. Or Banichi. Or somebody.

Was that the breeze stirring the grass?

God. The other night sounds had stopped. He just realized that.

His heart rate picked up. Calm, Banichi had told him. A rapid heartbeat never improved one's aim. Think of the problem, not the emotional context. And Jago had advised him that it was generally wiser to watch an approaching enemy from cover and find out the number involved before doing anything, including running.

He couldn't stand sitting in a hole and waiting, however. He wanted to get up onto his feet. But he had to manage that without scuffing a foot or moving a pebble. Which meant deciding it was going to hurt his chest and that he was going to lever himself straight up anyway, without minding the pain.

He could do it.

He'd damned well *better* do it.

He did. Control the breathing, Banichi would say. Keep balanced, Jago would say.

He tried. Poking his head out of his little nook just wasn't bright. As best he could judge, he was in deep shadow.

And there was, please God, the chance it was Jago coming back. He couldn't just fire blindly at whatever came.

He eased the safety off the pistol, however. He looked at the ground, judged the slight difference of shadow and deeper shadow that his human eyes could barely make out, and decided it was best just to stay absolutely still and hope. He wasn't the one to take on trouble, and his bodyguard didn't need his warning.

Whoever it was, he had the impression they were moving on or near the track he and Jago had laid down.

The sound was coming toward his rocky nook, in all this emptiness. In grass, there was no help for it: there was the vestige of a trail . . . just not much likelihood of anybody happening onto it by total chance.

Closer. God, he didn't want to have to shoot. If some stranger came in here, setting that pistol off would echo like doom, from one end of these hills to the other, and would bring all sorts of trouble he couldn't outrun.

But no choice, he thought, hearing a step in the grass outside.

"Bren-ji," a whisper said.

It wasn't Jago. It was Tano or Algini, one or the other, and he felt the blood drain from his head. "Here," he whispered back, and a shadow slipped in between the rocks.

Algini, he decided, feeling the aftermath of the adrenaline rush.

"Jago's been gone all day," he whispered.

"Yes," Algini said. "We have contact."

God, that was a relief.

"Banichi?"

"No," Algini said, and relief plunged right back into worry.

But there was no chance to ask extensive questions. Algini moved, and he went too, out into the clear. "Tano?" he whispered, outside.

"He is coming," Algini said, and Bren tucked the gun into his pocket and went with Algini, moving as quietly as he could, in Algini's footprints, or as close as a human stride could make it.

He was quickly out of breath, his mouth was parched, and blisters made walking painful; Algini had to slow down, and finally to rest, hunkered down next to a line of brush.

"Tano will catch up with us," Algini said.

"Banichi?"

"Possibly switched off," Algini said. "Possibly out of range."

Jago might know. Wherever she was. Bren found himself chilling in the wind and tried not to shiver. Algini was never a fount of sympathy: his mind worked otherwise, on facts and necessities, and one decided it was far better to let Algini think and listen and not to be nattering away with questions to which Algini had no answer. Whatever had happened, had already happened, and at this point they were headed, he hoped, as directly as possible toward Targai, where they could reach

Geigi and, if they were lucky, signal the bus to come get them. They were on flatter ground . . . which could mean they had reached deep into the uplands and maybe were approaching one of the few roads that ran through Maschi lands.

"Water, if you will, nadi," was his one request of Algini. Algini passed him a small flask, and he held the water in his mouth a long time on each small swallow. It was stale, but it was the best thing in hours. He started to hand the flask back.

Algini made an abrupt move of his hand, then held up two fingers.

Tano, and company. They were going to meet and probably part again after conferring and laying plans.

Then Algini, uncharacteristically, volunteered information. "We have now lost Jago's contact, nandi."

His heart sank. There was still nothing they could do about it. "Yes," he said, acknowledging he had heard. Nothing more. He looked at the ground and tried not to think what could have gone wrong. Jago would go to help Banichi only if she were sure Tano and Algini were going to find him.

So they had found him. What else was going on out there in the dark at the moment, he had no idea, and he was convinced Algini would tell him if he knew anything more.

They waited.

16

Great-grandmother would *not*, she still said, take refuge in the basement . . .

"Are we to sit in a hole in the ground along with that coward and malefactor Baiji! We will *not*, nadi!"

Cajeiri never recalled Great-grandmother addressing Cenedi so rudely. It was late, people needed to settle to bed, particularly nand' Toby, who was not that well; but that was not happening, not while mani held out abovestairs.

Cenedi replied, jaw set, "Aiji-ma, I will carry you downstairs myself if you will not go. Then I will stay there with you to be sure you stay, when your guard needs my presence. Live or die, they will have to get along without me, because *you* clearly need me more."

Cajeiri never recalled Cenedi answering back to mani, either. He found his mouth open, and shut it, and his bodyguard, there to witness along with Lord Geigi, was likely dismayed.

"What's the matter?" nand' Toby asked.

It was not a good time to be talking. Cajeiri didn't say a thing.

Then Lord Geigi said, offering a gentlemanly hand, "Aiji-ma, let us go down together for a light snack and leave our bodyguards less worry, shall we? We shall have Cook provide us cakes and tea, and we shall have my radio, and we shall keep well apprised of the situation on the grounds. Kindly do come, aiji-ma, and keep me company. Otherwise this waiting may be very tedious."

Mani's temper was up, for certain, but Lord Geigi bravely persisted.

"Sidi-ji," he said. "Do join me. You know what they say about lords who ignore their bodyguards."

"Gods unfortunate, when did *you* become *mine?*" she muttered, and sharply: "Great-grandson!"

"Mani!" Cajeiri said instantly.

"You will come with us. And bring our guests down."

Finally! "Yes, mani!" Any other answer was apt to get a thwack with her cane, and not a slight one. "Please come downstairs, too," he said to nand' Toby and Barb-daja. "Get some sleep."

"How close is the enemy?" Toby wanted to know. "I can shoot, understand. I'm a better shot than my brother."

"This is Guild business," Cajeiri said. "It's going to be bad up here. Mani says come down right now, and I'll bet she knows something. So we have to go with her. Or she won't go." He looked at his bodyguard. "Taro-ji, Gari-ji, I don't think you should be up here. Jico-ji—do whatever you decide to do."

"I am Guild," Veijico said quietly. "I shall be upstairs, nandi."

It was also possible to be bored while worried sick, and there was nothing to do but sit and stew about the situation.

"Is there any reason they would switch off, Gini-ji?" Bren asked, desperately, finally, in their long sitting still. "Do you think they are still all right?"

Algini took a while answering. The Guild held certain information very close, and it was not likely at all that Algini would divulge method, only conclusion.

"When Guild goes against Guild," Algini said, "yes. One might switch off."

It was his dearest hope Jago and Banichi had done exactly that.

It had to pass for good news. Banichi and Jago were a force

of two. The number of renegade Guild in the district was certainly far higher than that, even if they might have slightly reduced the odds tonight. They knew the direction Banichi and Jago had taken, at least generally, and prolonged silence and absence could tell them that there was something ahead of them they didn't want to meet.

That would put that problem out into the far edge of Machigi's territory, or right in the near edge of Geigi's, neither being good news for their situation.

He began to wonder if that was the case. And once Tano caught up, they might decide that, instead of going north and trying to cross into Maschi territory as quickly as possible, they might veer off to the northwest and try to reach Najida directly. He wasn't completely in favor of that. It would be farther. A hellish lot farther. He wasn't sure how much he had left in him; and he most of all wanted to get back to Najida and in reach of a phone.

But if Tano and Algini said that was the best thing to do, he was going to have to find it in himself to do it.

If he could shed the damned vest . . .

But they weren't going to let him do that.

Algini knocked his knee with the back of his hand, a signal to pay attention. Something was going on, but Algini hadn't moved, otherwise, and just waited. And waited. "I have shut down my locator," Algini said. "But Tano will find us."

Tano was close. But there was a chance the enemy was close, too.

Moments passed.

"They are here," Algini said, in a night no different to Bren's eyes and ears than the last hour. "Come, Bren-ji."

Tano and Lucasi. He got up. Algini took a grip under his arm on the way down the slight rise, for which he was grateful, and from out of a very little cover of brush, there were, indeed, Tano and Lucasi, the latter under his own power with, apparently, a stick he was using as a cane.

"We are all going dark now," Algini said to him in a low whisper. "We have to make time toward Maschi territory."

Still going north, then. Going for the major road. Or close to it. "Yes," Bren said, and he just kept up as they started off, holding the thought in his mind that Banichi and Jago might have done the same, and they all might be heading toward some mutually agreed goal, to make a rendezvous.

He walked, at least doing no worse than Lucasi, who was walking with an improvised crutch and with his ankle now professionally splinted clear to the knee. They were a hell of a group, he thought, two of them doing well to be walking at all and not going as fast as Tano and Algini could wish. Bren had one sip more of water and kept going, trying not to breathe like a steam engine on a grade and trying to keep his feet out of holes, of which there were a great many, given the rocky, graveled ground. Tano and Algini were lugging heavy packs, and they made no fuss about it, just kept going doggedly at what was undoubtedly a slower pace than they would like to set.

They were now out of cover. One really, truly didn't like this.

There was, however, a rock ridge running in the far distance. They seemed to be going toward that.

There would be cover there. He liked that better. He decided there were a finite number of steps between here and there and he *could* do it. Lucasi, who had not said a word, was likely telling himself the same thing. Once they got there, they could surely rest for a bit.

Try not to pant. That was noisy. He couldn't help it. He just had to hurry. The kid was in the same shape. And toward the last, Tano and Algini each took one of them by an arm and just kept them moving.

They reached the shadow. And went into it, and down to a split in the rocks.

There was a downslope about three times a human's height, down to a dirt road.

And there Tano stopped him and let him sink down and lean against a rock just slightly too high to sit on. It was enough. He tried to collect his breath and his wits.

Algini left his bag and slipped away, out of sight. Not one more of them, Bren said to himself, regretting that departure.

But Tano didn't talk, the boy didn't talk, and that set the rules he was sure Tano and Algini had laid down. He didn't talk. He just sat and waited.

And waited.

And still waited.

Tano checked the time, doubtless himself wondering how long it had been.

And then there was a faint, distant sound. Even human ears heard it. A vehicle was coming from somewhere to the north. The road ran more or less north and south.

Somebody was coming.

The sound kept up. The boy's head was up. There was no doubt Tano heard it, and he stood there attentive to the night and their surroundings.

Trouble, Bren thought. As if they didn't have enough. But Algini would lie low out there. Algini might be able to see it.

He listened to the sound for several minutes. It was coming closer.

And then it changed pitch, then started up again. Shifted gears, maybe. Maybe a climb. Definitely coming this way.

"Come," Tano said, and led the way behind the rocks.

Apparently they were moving to deeper cover, along the same line Algini had taken. Letting the vehicle pass them.

It was definitely getting closer.

Tano led the way around the end of the ridge, onto the exposed slope, and there was a van coming fast, running with no headlights, and here they were, out in the open on the slope.

Then it ticked into his thinking that they were going toward that van, and doing so recklessly. Tano seized him by one arm and took hold of Lucasi by the other, on his bad side, and took them down the slope, just about the time the van reached that point on the road.

It braked. Flung open a side door. Algini ducked out, beckoning them on, and Bren threw everything he had into it—damned near fell on his face, if not for Tano, coming down the last of the slope.

Two were driving. He caught the silver glint on the uniform, the profile against the faint, faint light from outside.

"Is it Jago? Banichi?"

"Bren-ji," Jago said from the front seat as Tano seized Bren a second time by the arm and edged as far over as he could to give room to him and Lucasi—and two armored bodies between them and the walls of the van. "One regrets the long silence, Bren-ji," Banichi said. "We are reasonably well."

Algini shut the door and dropped into the back seat. "Targai is too risky a run," Banichi said, throwing the van into reverse, backing around. "We are heading straight west, for Najida."

"One will by no means argue with that," Bren said, feeling all the exertion of the last number of hours. He felt absolutely drained of strength, not least from sheer relief. "Is the van from Targai?"

"No," Jago said. "It is probably from Senji district."

"We have a little difficulty about fuel," Banichi said. "But we are headed for a station."

"Apai?" Algini asked.

"Yes," Banichi said. It was a name which meant absolutely nothing to Bren. But his bodyguard knew. His bodyguard kept abreast of things that never occurred to the paidhi-aiji to wonder about and checked maps he had not, while he was deciding the fate of the east coast, thought to look at. But his aishid might have, while those atlases were on the sitting-room table. And there was fuel at a place called Apai, which was probably a crossroads in the back country. That would mean market roads, or a farm, or hunting station . . . more such details his bodyguard studied and that he hadn't even thought of when they'd diverted themselves into Taisigi territory.

It was even possible his guard had studied these things before they had ever left Najida, in case of the unanticipated. He had never even thought to wonder.

Their enemies could have studied those things too, about Najida, about the territory they were in.

Their enemies were now missing a van. And probably several occupants. The windshield was badly cracked. There could be blood on the seat he was sitting on; but at this point he couldn't care about it. He rested his head on the seat back and just breathed and took in the fact he had all his bodyguard back, their voices, matter-of-fact about their desperate business, reassuring him that, at least for the next hour, nothing was within his power to fix but it might be within theirs. He had no complaints.

Unless—

"Have we the ability to contact Najida, nadiin-ji?"

"Safest not to do so, Bren-ji," Jago said, half turning in her seat. "We are dark at the moment and move best that way. Our opponents use the same systems, and they know each other, likely, only by what zone they occupy. Our best hope of getting out of here is to be misidentified."

"Understood," he said, and he shut up, content to let his bodyguard make their own decisions without his meddling. But, damn, he wanted to make that call.

He put a hand to his chest, site of the most forceful reminder not to meddle in Guild business. It could have killed him. It all could have ended right there, leaving more than his affairs in a hell of a mess. His bodyguard hadn't called him a fool. But he had, every time he made an injudicious move. Every time he risked things larger than himself.

The bruise was better now than it had been, or he didn't think he could have made it across country. He was sweaty, he was dirty, he was miserable, his hands and feet were still half frozen, he was sure he had deep blisters on his right foot, the sole had come loose on the left boot, and he had definitely picked up a bit of gravel in the failing boot to add to his misery, but the greatest immediate discomfort was the vest itself. It had to stay on, that was all, and the feet—he was sitting down now on a padded seat, out of the wind and no longer freezing, but his feet were cold.

Riding, however, was bliss. They weren't safe by a long shot. There was a long way to go. A scary long way to go.

But going to Najida—that was where he needed to be.

That was the place he wanted most to protect, personally, emotionally. He was only upset about leaving Geigi at Targai in what could be a very dangerous situation.

Whatever was going on over at Targai, however—and an incursion from Senji was high on the list of possibilities, as well as action from the renegade Guild—there was a good chance Geigi's bodyguard had already gotten Geigi out of it, the same as his was doing for him, the same that Machigi's had done for their lord. Ordinary citizens were off limits as targets. If the lord wasn't there, the Guild was supposed to cease operations. Which protected civilian lives, civilian property, and historic premises. That was the way it was *supposed* to work.

But they were up against people who mined public roads. Who kidnapped children. The whole district was getting to be no place for high-value targets, no guarantee for the ordinary citizen.

It was why the Guild had to win this one. The Guild had committed everything, broken with precedent, outlawed half the Marid and pulled in every asset they could lay hands on to stop this lot and restore the regulations that had always stood.

He had to trust it. Had to wish the Guild luck. Most of all, he had to rely on present company to keep him alive and be prepared to run for it, and run hard.

And he hoped to hell they didn't, in this stolen van, draw fire from their own side.

＊　　＊　　＊

There was occasional shooting outside, up above. It came and it went, and it was long after dark outside.

Mani and nand' Geigi sat in a basement room having tea and discussing old times. Nand' Toby and Barb-daja had gone to their basement room to get some rest. Cajeiri sat in the corner of mani's room, teaching Jegari and Antaro chess.

And he had just made a bad move, because he had been thinking about what was going on upstairs instead of where his district lord was sitting relative to the magistrate.

Antaro made the correct move. He lost a district.

"Good," he said confidently, as if he had been testing her.

Louder gunfire. A heavy boom that shook the walls.

"That's out on the road," Jegari muttered, looking up.

"I hope it was them and not us."

"Hssst!" mani said, objecting to the turn of conversation. The cane thumped sharply. "Bad enough we are confined down here with the spare linens and the brooms. Shall we also endure pointless speculation?"

"One is extravagantly sorry, mani," Cajeiri said, half-rising, with a little bow, and sat back down. He knew better than to chatter when Great-grandmother was upset and out of sorts. Great-grandmother truly hated fidgeting. And probably her back hurt. They had gotten pillows for her chair, and Great-grandmother, on principle, refused to fidget with them.

They went back to their chess game. "One apologizes, nandi," Jegari said under his breath.

"One is not concerned, nadi-ji," he murmured, and advanced a village lord.

Great-grandmother and Geigi continued talking quietly, about anything but what was going on outside.

The rifle fire up above became more frequent, and it sounded scarily closer.

17

The fueling station turned out to be a farming village. "One requests you get to the floor, Bren-ji," Banichi said. "We are going right down the street as if we belong here."

Getting down onto the floor was not a comfortable act, but Bren managed it, braced against the bench seat, familiar situation. Tano and Algini got down, too, along with Lucasi, in the theory, he knew well enough, that if enemy fire took out Banichi and Jago, it wouldn't get all of them at once.

Little chance the villagers themselves would fire at them. Word would have gone out by radio that there was a Guild action proceeding, and it was against all common sense for a civilian to interfere in a Guild action. It was a law that kept civilians alive and kept their property undamaged. It limited return actions and *more* Filings. And for what these villagers ought to know, the law applied. If the Guild wanted to confiscate the local fuel supply, the village magistrate would complain to his lord, notably Machigi or Geigi, depending on which side of the border he felt they were on, or would apply to both, and request compensation. The lord who presided would supply the fuel for their farm machinery and then send the fuel charges to the Filing party, a modest claim that was incredibly bad form to dispute and fairly bad form to pad, though it happened.

So the village was not their worry: the village would just phone Tanaja and advise them of a problem. The villagers personally had nothing to defend, no worry about action coming at them except stray bullets or somebody deciding to interdict the enemy's fuel supply by draining the tank, the stealthy option, or blowing it up, the attention-getting one, and entailing a much larger lawsuit once the dust settled.

In any case, if things went as usual, the villagers would always get their justice. And Guild in the field would not have to worry about some desperate and innocent amateur with a gun.

They stopped, Bren judged, somewhat apart from the pumps. Algini scrambled up and out the side door, which wasn't usual—their explosives expert looked at the pump before they pulled up to it.

Which brought really uncomfortable thoughts. There were all sorts of nasty tricks that never should be used where civilians might stumble into them. And he worried about them until Algini thumped quietly on the fender, had them move up, and unscrewed the cap.

No booby trap. No explosives, no shots fired. Fuel was flowing. They could get out of here. They were within lands where law still applied.

Algini came back to the door while the fuel was running and put his head in. "We may get a full tank, Nichi-ji, but by no means certainly so. The last of it may be foul, and I hesitate to put it in. Local maintenance seems slipshod."

"We should not risk it," Banichi said. "Cut it off short."

"Yes," Algini agreed.

The local fuel delivery hadn't been made; they were evidently on the short end of the month, a bit of bad luck, pure chance. Baji-naji.

Bren rested his forehead against his hands, on the floor. They might end up hiking the last bit to Najida. He didn't look forward to that in the least. But he'd do it without objection. Getting safely out of Taisigi territory was absolutely paramount. If they could cut over to the airport or the train station—but those were likely targets.

Damn the luck that had moved the Shejidan Guild onto the offensive before they got clear.

But it was not luck. It was a reaction to the dowager's move. He had no doubt about it. And Ilisidi was probably having a quiet fit about the situation. And planning next actions.

Which the paidhi-aiji hoped to God wouldn't involve sending him immediately back to Tanaja to mop up and settle what the Guild had upended, but he was relatively sure either she would or Tabini would. He had that to look forward to.

One bath, a good supper. A day to rest up. *Then* he'd go. Once the shooting stopped.

If Machigi was still in charge.

Likely Machigi was on a boat somewhere—maybe headed out to Sungeni territory, in the Isles, allies he could rely on.

The nozzle was withdrawn; the fuel cap went back on. Thump. "How much do we have?" Jago asked, and Banichi answered: "Three quarters. Our next source is the airport, if we go that direction."

"Dangerous," Tano said.

"We have one choice," Banichi said, as Algini joined them and shut the door. "There is the hunting lodge."

A small silence. That evidently was not a popular choice.

"We could divert toward the township south road," Jago said. "Time taken, but safer. There is that fuel stop midway."

"One can walk if need be," Bren said, from his position on the floor. "If we have to, nadiin-ji, I shall do it. Or one can take cover and wait."

"We shall attempt the airport, Bren-ji," Banichi said as he put them in gear. The dialogue was truncated, dropping courtesies, the Guild in mid-operation. "From these roads, there should be an indirect approach."

For now. Depending on what they met. If they could once reach the airport road, it was a straight shot to Najida.

From Lucasi, throughout, there had been not a sound, nor any now, as Banichi restarted the engine. The young man, lying on the floor opposite Bren, was the picture of exhaustion, head pillowed on his arm. He actually slept while the van sped through the village and onto rougher road.

There was something to be said for being horizontal, even on a dirty floor mat. Bren stayed put, and Tano stretched out on the seat, doing much the same above him, eyes shut; Banichi was driving as fast as the roads allowed. In places grass had grown up and whipped the undercarriage—lying with his ear near the floorboards, Bren was well-aware of the ground under them. In places they scattered gravel, and once they drove through water. A road on the continent and especially near an uneasy border region, was an approximation of a driveable route, not a guarantee. In disputed territory, particularly, nobody did road maintenance.

It suited their purposes, so long as the wheels and tires held out.

But his bodyguard were still discussing the route and a branch in the road ahead. He caught the edge of it, which involved passive reception of some signal and the possibility of encountering legitimate Guild at the airport. Or the enemy. Legitimate Guild would, the consensus was, move on the airport and the train station. They would take those as a priority.

"But," Tano said, "we cannot produce the right codes for either side."

That was a problem, Bren thought, beginning to grasp the nature of the debate. He had been halfway to sleep like Lucasi, but now he slowly levered himself up to a sitting position in the aisle, against the seat.

"Perhaps, nadiin-ji," he said, resting an arm on the seat edge, and speaking above the engine noise, "perhaps *I* should be the password. My voice is reasonably distinctive on the continent, is it not?"

"Far too great a risk, Bren-ji," Tano said.

"As great a risk if we are all shot at because we have the wrong codes?" he said.

"That is a point," Tano said.

There was silence from the front seats.

"It is, however, illegal for you to use Guild communications," Algini said, from the other side. "We are almost certainly within a Declared zone."

Rules. Regulations. It happened to be what the fighting was about. Guild communications were Guild communications.

He couldn't say it wasn't important. "Then *you* tell them. The Guild would hesitate. Our enemies would not. They would come after us. That would sort it out."

Banichi said, "We do not have fuel enough or speed enough to outrun a pursuit."

Silence from the front seat.

"The hunting station," Tano said then. "There will surely be some local communications. As well as fuel."

"Dead-reckoning to Najida low on fuel is not my preference, either," Banichi said, and suddenly turned the wheel, waking Lucasi, who sat up in alarm and grabbed at the seat back ahead of him to save himself from sliding under Banchi's seat. "The middle road. There is no connection here to there but a hunting plain. We are about to start some game, nadiin-ji."

If our suspension holds up, Bren thought, holding on to the seat. If our steering holds out.

"Where are we going?" Lucasi asked faintly, getting to his knees and up to the seat.

"There is a hunting station," Tano said, "and another road. The place may be shut down for the season. It *may* be in hostile hands."

Comforting thought. Bren had the most confused notion of which direction they were going, but it seemed to be generally away from Najida—not due south, which would have backtracked, but southwest.

There had been a road on the Taisigi side of the border. There was some sort of road that led down through the hunting ranges. He wasn't even sure it continued to the border. If it did cross the border, it would do so nearest Kajiminda.

Except—

"The renegades staged their operations against Kajiminda from somewhere, did they not, nadiin-ji?"

"There is that possibility," Tano said.

"We shall need to find out," Algini said.

The shooting had died down for a while. Cenedi came downstairs to inquire how mani was getting along and to report that there had been contact with intruders but no casualties on their side, except one villager who had reported in for medical treatment for a cut from a rock chip.

Mani and Geigi had both slept, and Cajeiri had, too, at least a little nap before Cenedi came in. Now it felt like breakfast time, and Cajeiri's stomach was empty.

"Well, well," nand' Geigi said, when he mentioned it, "do not wake Cook at this hour, but is there anything in the kitchen?"

"There are sandwiches and tea, nandi," Cenedi reported, in the dining room. "Shall I have staff bring it down?"

"Staff has enough to do," mani said. "If we are quiet, let these young rascals bring us a tray."

Something to do. In great relief Cajeiri instantly got to his feet, and so did Antaro and Jegari.

Mani snapped, "Not *you*, young gentleman."

"But three of us can bring enough down for everybody, mani."

"Then no diversions. Go straight to the dining room and straight back. No nonsense! Do you hear?"

"*Yes,* mani-ma!"

One lost no more time for fear Great-grandmother could change her mind. Cajeiri headed for the door with Cenedi, and Jegari and Antaro came right behind him.

It was down the hall and up the servant stairs. Cenedi took the door to the dining room hall, but they kept going the back way to the kitchens and on through to the dining room, where it was spectacularly true: There were stacks of sandwiches, and an urn of hot water for tea, and and tea sets and carrying-trays. They piled up good helpings on three trays, filled a big teapot that had seven cups and then took the route out into the hall, because the kitchen, with its ovens and cabinets, was a cramped space to be carrying big trays through.

There was a sudden strange sound, far off from the house, hard to figure.

It seemed to be an engine, a powerful one. And all of a sudden there was shooting from off the roof.

Cajeiri stopped. Antaro and Jegari stopped. They were in a hallway right in the heart of the house, with thick walls between them and any trouble, and Cajeiri delayed to look around the corner to the main hall, to find out what was happening—thinking maybe it was his father's men coming in and that that was covering fire he heard.

The vehicle was coming right to the front door, right under the portico. And the shooting was still going on. Somebody was trying to reach them, Cajeiri thought. Trouble outside was trying to stop them.

Then an explosion banged through the main hall, like thunder breaking, and a wind came with it, and things were breaking and splintering, and the wind threw him sideways, with trays and hot tea and sandwiches spilling everywhere. Cajeiri hit flat on his back and hit his head, and before he could get up, he heard shooting going on in the main hall, just a few feet away.

Then shooting came back from the garden hall, near the bath, and there they all were in the middle of the dining room hallway, and his head really hurt.

"Nandi!" Jegari scrambled over to him through puddles of tea and started helping him up, dragging him to his feet. Antaro grabbed his other arm.

The tea, Cajeiri thought foolishly. They had broken one of nand' Bren's teapots and most of the cups. He was on his knees in the hall, and his ears were still ringing so it was hard to get his knees under him.

"Enemies," Antaro said, pulling at him, "in the house."

Cajeiri struggled up and had no chance even to catch his balance. Antaro and Jegari dragged him through the door back into the dining room.

They had no guns. Cenedi and all mani's guard and Lord Geigi's and even Veijico were up here, involved in the fighting. They could not have enemies coming downstairs and finding mani and Lord Geigi with no protection.

"Downstairs," he said, out of breath, his head pounding. He had never been so scared in his life. He was ahead of his guard, blind headache and all, on his way to the kitchen stairs and down them.

But when they got to the foot of the stairs, there was fat Baiji, barefoot, in a night robe, running toward them in panic, from the end of the downstairs hall.

"Stop!" Cajeiri yelled, and just then gunfire broke out in the hall, just around the bend, out of their sight. "Get him!" he yelled at Jegari and Antaro, as Baiji tried to break past them and get up the stairs. They grabbed him and threw him on the hall floor at to the foot of the stairs, Baiji howling and protesting at the top of his lungs.

The fight had spilled into the downstairs, from the garden hall stairs, from around the bent end of the hall. Mani's guard never would have let Baiji loose, and Baiji was too stupid to get loose on his own, which meant something had happened to one of mani's young men, on guard down there.

And mani and Lord Geigi were in danger if the fight came around the corner and headed this way.

Shots rang out from that direction.

"Come on," Cajeiri said. It was not far to mani's door, and they could get there. They could protect mani from inside until Cenedi could get down here.

"Move!" Antaro told Baiji, dragging him along. Baiji was shouting curses at them, protesting he was not to be handled. Jegari got his other arm, and he started howling in pain. Cajeiri did not look back. He ran straight for mani's door and tried to open it.

They had it locked. Of course. And when he looked back, he saw Veijico down by the bend of the hall, with a gun. "Get in a room!" Veijico shouted, running toward them.

"Mani!" he shouted, pounding on the door. "Let us in! Let us in!"

Lord Geigi opened it, and they started to go in, all but Veijico. She stood against the wall, her pistol aimed back toward the bend of the hall.

"Lock it after you!" Veijico said, and they were still trying to get in, but Baiji tried to resist in the doorway and blocked them. Lord Geigi took a fistful of Baiji's coat and spun him into the room with a fearful crash of furniture. Baiji went stumbling backward over two chairs and up against a table before he hit the floor.

Geigi shut the door. Veijico was still out there.

"Get over here," Mani said to them sharply, from where she sat. "They may fire through the door. Here is better protected."

They all did what mani said, except Baiji, who huddled on the floor in the corner whimpering about assassins.

"Have you decided now, fool, who is trying to keep you alive?" Geigi snapped at him from across the room, and Baiji, on hands and knees in his corner, launched into a new theme, how he had never meant any harm and had been scared by the Taisigi and had been all alone, considering his uncle Geigi was in space and he had not been certain if the aiji was going to be able to stay in power . . .

"Silence!" mani snapped, "or *I* shall have you shot!"

Baiji swallowed the rest of it, looking as if he were going to choke.

And all of a sudden there was shooting in the hall right outside.

Veijico, Cajeiri thought in distress. Veijico was all alone out there, and the shooting stopped, and there were footsteps in the hall.

Then somebody tried *their* door.

And none of them had a gun.

There was nothing they could do. Just—

He took the slingshot out of his pocket. He had his several choice bits of metal.

Fire came through the door, and the lock blew in. The door flew open, banging backward, and a foreign Guildsman with a rifle swung it straight toward them.

Cajeiri fired the hardest draw he had ever done, and the man fell backward into the door, slamming it back. Two other men were coming behind him, and Cajeiri loaded another shot just as gunfire broke out, and the men turned around, firing rifles back down the hall.

The nearer of them lurched into the room, and all of a sudden the inward-opening door slammed back into the man from Baiji's corner. Jegari flung himself past Cajeiri, Antaro trying for the other man, who turned, swinging his rifle toward her. Cajeiri fired.

His last stone hit the man and made the rifle jerk as Antaro tried to shove it out of line.

But all of a sudden a shot from outside hit the man, and hit the door behind him, and there was blood everywhere. Veijico heaved herself into view on the hall floor outside, grabbed the doorframe with a bloody hand, and pulled herself halfway up as footsteps rushed closer.

"Nandiin!" somebody yelled, and uniformed Guild showed up in the doorway, helping Veijico, standing over the three attackers. It was Cenedi and mani's bodyguard, and they held the hall out there, and they were all safe.

Cajeiri started shivering. He didn't intend to. But he was out of ammunition; and everybody was all right, and he just wanted to sit down.

Mani did sit down, her cane braced before her. *"Well,"* she said.

Baiji crept out from behind the door on his hands and knees.

"Do not attempt to run," Lord Geigi said to him, "or they will have no patience."

"How is Veijico?" Cajeiri managed to ask as, Jegari and Antaro having disentangled themselves, mani's young men dragged the attackers out. He tried not to let anybody see he was shaking all over. "Cenedi-nadi, how is Veijico?"

"And how are *you*, Great-grandson?" mani asked sharply, from his left.

"We broke the tea set," was the first idiotic thing that came out of his mouth. He had never sounded so stupid, and his voice did shake.

And there was still gunfire going on somewhere above, but distant.

"They used a grenade at the front door," Cenedi said. Cenedi was bleeding all down his left arm, red dripping from his fingers, but he had a rifle in his right hand. "It blew out both ends of the hall, nandiin, regrettably. They used a truck to get under the portico, blew the door, and then got in through the front. Our people stationed on the roof got in through the back to stop them, but some of the intruders got down the garden hall stairs and let Baiji loose, doubtless while looking for higher-value targets. One apologizes profoundly for letting that happen."

"We will have to apologize to the paidhi, when we get him back," mani said dryly. "One supposes the house is now open to the winds, and we are sitting in an unfortified sieve, while my lazy grandson has still not managed to get *his* forces out of the airport."

"That would be correct, nandi," Cenedi said. "They are still pinned down." Cenedi then added wryly: "We do, however, have the enemy securely pent up between us."

Mani laughed. Actually laughed.

Cajeiri was amazed. Shocked. He just stood there shivering. And Cenedi's men dragged out the man he had hit with the slingshot, who had not moved at all.

"Nadiin-ji," he said, as Antaro and Jegari edged close to him. "See how Veijico is. Help her. We *have* help coming."

His father's men were trying to come in. Cenedi said so. But they were stuck. And there was no front door any more, and there were still enemies.

The whole place smelled like gunpowder. And there was cold air blowing through the halls, taking that smell everywhere.

At one moment Bren was sure they had driven off the edge of a ditch and in the next, the van, hitting the full compression of its shocks, and grinding something on its undercarriage, bounced. Bren, sitting on the floor, held on.

Then, surprising him, they leveled out onto a defined, mowed road, gathering speed.

They were clearly not conserving fuel now. But they were making time. Lucasi had gotten up on the seat again at Tano's order, without a word. It was one more armored body between the paidhi and trouble, but Lucasi didn't object.

The floor was not, however, a good vantage point, and after they had run on gravel for a while, on an unexpectedly well-maintained road, Bren got onto his knees and carefully levered himself up onto the seat, with Tano's help.

He still couldn't see anything but grass and a little trace of previous wheel ruts beyond the foglights and what might be a few sprinkles of rain on the windshield. He sat still, not asking pointless questions, composing what he could say if they did get him a civilian phone. It probably, he thought, it didn't matter that much what he *did* say: the reaction his voice got was going to get them protection or it was going to bring every enemy on the west coast howling in pursuit.

He didn't know what they were going toward, but he hoped for luck—baji-naji, when it got down to it, blind luck to hold out just a little longer. There was less of value out here in a hunting preserve to encourage hordes of enemies to set up roadblocks. There was scant reason for the occupants of a hunting station to expect an armed invasion.

But there was no reason for an ordinary hunting-range road to have been well maintained, either.

And a hunting station probably constituted the most heavily armed, resourceful sort of citizen populace they were likely to meet, well, give or take the Edi.

That meant *he* might have to get out, talk to the locals, risk another shot to the torso or worse—he could hardly contemplate it without flinching—and look like the degree of authority that private citizens had no business shooting at. Even if the locals viewed him as trouble, or an outright enemy, they would most likely just want him to get out of their district as fast as possible and not have him draw fire or damage their property.

He felt his collar lace and straightened it, straightened out his cuffs, which were a disgrace—he had to pick grass seeds out of the lacework.

The road climbed, then descended. There was a little flickering of lightning out the south side of the van.

"There," Jago said, and Bren saw nothing . . . which by no means surprised him.

"Let us out, Nichi-ji," Algini said, and the van immediately slowed.

The sound of one lonely engine out here might catch someone's attention. And he knew what Algini and Tano were doing, even before Banichi slowed to a stop and those two got out.

They were exhausted. All of them were exhausted. They sat a time with the engine pinging in the chill night air, waiting.

Look it over, figure what they were dealing with. Signal. One of them had to go off passive recept if they were going to do that. That was a risk.

So was driving blindly into an enemy outpost.

It was a long wait. Jago slept, catnapping. Lucasi slept. Bren tried to and succeeded intermittently. At his third or fourth waking, Jago was awake, and Banichi was catching a little sleep, his arms folded on the steering wheel.

Tano and Algini were out there somewhere on a cold, increasingly rainy night, looking the situation over.

"Ah," Jago said suddenly and nudged Banichi. "A come-ahead," she said.

Banichi just started the engine and drove, not breakneck but at a fair clip, with the fog lights on.

It was about a kilometer farther on that the lights picked out a distant set of log buildings at the edge of a stand of trees. An open-sided equipment shed: There was the tractor and mower; a small open-bed truck, and a fuel tank. *That* was what they were looking for. A few buildings, one the typical barracks for the seasonal commercial operation of the center, one the manager's residence, one larger building—a processing center, again, for use in its season.

Banichi pulled into the center of the cluster and parked near the porch of what looked like the manager's residence.

Jago opened her door and stepped out. Bren clutched his gun in his pocket and watched as Jago went up the steps.

"Attention the house!" Jago called out as he rapped on the door. "Assassins' Guild, on other business!"

No shot came. That was encouraging.

A machine growled out of the dark. Bren's heart jumped. But it was a generator cutting on. Floodlights slowly brightened. A light came on inside the house.

The door opened. A man wearing only trousers came out into the cold and spoke to Jago, quietly. Bren couldn't make it out. The man's stance looked anxious. But unless he knew someone, an angry ex-wife or business partner, had Filed Intent on him, a citizen should have nothing to fear from legitimate Guild.

Lucasi waked, sat up, looked around him. And asked no questions.

Jago walked back toward the van, down the short steps. Then another figure, in Guild black, showed beside the house.

"Banichi," Bren said in alarm.

"Tano," Banichi said calmly, and as Jago walked up to the van, he rolled his window down.

"There is a radio in the office," she said. "We have agreed not to drain the tank. The manager has a wife and children, one an infant."

"Let me go out, nadi," Bren said quietly and got up, no one hindering him this time. Lucasi opened the side door, and Bren climbed down as the man came down off the low porch.

"The paidhi-aiji," the man said.

It was hard to be mistaken in that point of identification. Bren gave a little nod.

"At the moment, nadi," Bren said, "I am on official business. Is your man'chi to Lord Machigi?"

"Yes, nandi."

A second nod. "Have you had news from Tanaja?"

Hesitation. An answering nod.

"Would you be so good as to inform us, nadi?"

"One hears there is a Guild action in Tanaja," the man said. "There are five of us here, two children. This is our livelihood, nandi."

Bren bowed. "My aishid operates under strictest Guild rules, nadi. Be assured you will have compensation. We need fuel. Is there a key for the office? We need the radio."

"We have no keys here. The door is unlocked."

Tano had come into view. Algini hadn't. Tano stood by him, rifle at rest, while Jago went up onto the other porch and carefully opened the door.

The inside light came on and brightened. Bren gave a courteous bow to the manager, then went over to the other porch, all the while feeling extremely exposed in the floodlights that bathed the yard.

He went in. Jago flipped switches and initiated their call to Najida estate.

It took a bit. "Stand by," she said, then handed Bren the microphone and the headset, which Bren held to one ear.

"This is Bren-paidhi," he said. "Who is speaking?"

"*Nandi?*" came the answer.

"Is this Nawari?"

"*Yes. We are under attack, nandi. So is the airport.*"

Just a little uncharacteristically rattled, for Nawari. It was a good thing, he thought, that Banichi hadn't taken them down the main road past the airport. But he couldn't ask questions that might betray Najida's situation.

"We are about to enter into Sarini province."

"*Nandi, one begs you observe caution!*"

"How is Kajiminda faring, nadi?"

"*Kajiminda has not come under attack, nandi. Najida and the airport are both under assault.*"

"Call Shejidan," he said. "Advise them I am on the border and on my way toward Najida."

"*Yes, nandi.*"

He nodded to Jago. Jago flipped off the power, rifle in the crook of her other arm, and led the way out, where Tano waited.

The manager still stood on the porch, shirtless in the cold wind.

"Nadi," Jago said to him. "If anyone asks you where we went, do not hesitate to tell them we are headed toward Kajiminda. And tell them we *told* you to tell them."

"Nadi." The man looked as puzzled as he should look, as Banichi manuevered the van around the corner to the fuel pump and Tano moved to do the fueling.

Bren boarded the van quickly once it stopped by the fuel tank, getting his pale conspicuous civilian self out of view. Lucasi welcomed him in with a pistol in hand, and Tano took the van's fuel cap off. In a moment, fuel started flowing, the van sinking under the weight.

God, Bren thought, with a prickling up and down his spine. Let us get out of here. Soon.

Algini had to be out there. The man on the porch had to figure there might be more of them.

Jago got into the front seat, arranging her rifle between the seats as she did so. "That man on the porch claims he is Taisigi. He has served Guild traffic coming through here, to and from Kajiminda. He assumed they were from Tanaja and kept the road mowed."

Could a Senji accent pass? Maybe. Could Machigi have hedged the truth in a major way? That was always a question.

Just as there might or might not really be children in that house. The same way Algini was off in the little woods, there could just as easily be a partner with a rifle aimed at them at this very moment from that front window and more trying to get out the back door. They could start a small war here if someone took a signal wrong.

It seemed forever until fueling stopped and the fuel cap went on. Lucasi climbed back in by the side door. Tano climbed aboard and left the side door open.

Banichi started the engine and backed them around as Tano worked his way past Bren to take a rear seat.

Algini? Bren wondered. They were still moving. It was not a surprise, however, when near the trees that bordered the road, they slowed for the turn, and an armed shadow appeared in that open doorway, climbed aboard, and shut the door, breathing a little heavily.

Algini made his way to the rear and sat down. "Cold," was all he said.

They were leaving behind them a functional generator and a radio, not to mention fuel. And if that was a local Guild operation, the man had everything he needed to make them serious trouble.

Except for Jago's instruction: I want you to tell them . . .

The man had gotten news by radio. Likely, the moment he had seen a human step out of the van, he had known all the names but Lucasi's. He'd know that they were from Shejidan's Guild, and Tabini-aiji, *and* Cenedi and the aiji-dowager. With him shining in the floodlight, they were far from incognito.

If the man was local and honest, he might be of the same mind-set as Machigi's aishid, worried about their own lord's situation, upset about news of a Guild action in Tanaja. But—

God, this man must have been at least in some wise a forward observer on what had gone on at Kajiminda. He had to have occupied an uneasy post if he had seen more and more suspicious sorts heading that direction. He might have sent back reports to Machigi, which might have gotten no farther than Machigi's bodyguard, reports that had made Machigi's bodyguard fear for his life and try to keep the situation quiet—assuming the best about the man who'd at least made a strong move to protect them and get them out of Tanaja.

At least they'd gotten fuel. They'd gotten a message out so at least their own side—and every enemy within a hundred kilometers—knew they were out here. Their allies were warned now not to shoot them by mistake, and if their enemies diverted themselves away from current objectives—Najida and the airport—to chase after them, that could upset drawn battle lines. If there was an airport attack ongoing, then somebody was stuck in the airport, and it wasn't likely the renegades.

Tabini's forces were most likely. Tabini would move to protect his grandmother, his son, and Lord Geigi, all of whom had helpfully stationed themselves in a war zone.

It would be very nice if Tabini had force enough to spare and could come get them out of this pickle. But he had no desire to divert them from their main job, which would be to get reinforcements over to Najida. That was earnestly to be desired.

The tires spat gravel as Banichi turned them out onto the road again, and by what Bren could figure, they were heading due west. The border could not be that far away by now, if they were not already in it. They were on a line to intercept the Kajiminda road, and from there—

From there either head to Kajiminda, or turn left to Separti Township, not a safe place, or turn right and head for Najida, hoping for the best.

He didn't want to draw an attack down on Kajiminda, which had been safe, thus far. More, he didn't trust that short, flat, wide-open road to Geigi's estate. He didn't know why: the feeling bordered on superstition. He had a bad feeling about it—less so about heading for Najida.

They needed to move fast.

Because if trouble turned away from the airport and headed for them overland, he'd really like to be close to some sort of shelter.

It was nand' Bren who had just called, and he was not in Tanaja, he was most of the way home. Cenedi had brought that news downstairs. Nobody could mistake his voice, Cenedi said. And when mani heard it, mani actually laughed, though shortly. "Clever fellow," was what mani said about it. "Are we surprised? We are not."

But, Cajeiri thought, but what can we do to help him? There were enemies all over, and nand' Bren was going to try to get through? They should help him.

"So what will we do, mani? Shall we go after him?"

"One is quite certain the paidhi will have good advice with him, young gentleman," Cenedi said. "When he gets near enough, we may; but in the meanwhile we can only attract attention toward him and open yet another action. That would not help."

It was not the answer he wanted. But at least Cenedi had stopped to listen to him.

And nand' Bren was smart. And he had Banichi and Jago with him, and Tano and Algini, who were no one to ignore, either. They would not let him do anything risky.

It was a scary situation. There was a lot of hammering going on upstairs, and some staff had made a dangerous run out to the garage to get boards, which now were going up to reinforce the front doors and the broken window. They were not going to be open to the breeze for much longer. Baiji was locked up in his room again. Cajeiri had no idea where they had taken the three intruders or whether the one man was dead. And nand' Siegi had transfused a lot of blood into Veijico, who was down the hall along with two of mani's guards who had been shot and one of the household staff, a girl who had been near the front door. She had been hit by a piece of shrapnel. She was only fifteen, and everybody had been very upset about that.

Veijico was doing all right, Antaro said. But Cajeiri would feel better only when he saw her for himself—and mani had told him firmly to stay out of the physician's way while he was working; and then when Antaro said nand' Siegi was through, mani had said he should stay out of the halls and not be running about until they had repaired the doors.

So he was trapped in mani's room, under mani's direct supervision, and he had to do what he was told.

He was at least where he could protect Jegari and Antaro as well as himself and mani. That situation he agreed with. He had complained they should have a gun, but Nawari had stationed two of mani's young men in the hall, and they had guns enough, mani said.

Mani had actually said he had done the right thing. She very rarely paid compliments, so he was very proud of her saying so. Lord Geigi said the same. And except for a very few casualties, they had come through the attack fairly well, except nand' Bren's beautiful stained-glass window: Cenedi said that was gone.

It should have been exciting. But with people hurt and nand' Bren out there trying to get home, it was just scary.

Staff had brought them breakfast, because he had scattered the last breakfast all over the upstairs hall.

But his stomach was too upset to enjoy it.

Nand' Bren could not possibly make it here in the way he indicated he was going to do. But, he thought, with a tasteless bite of toast, nand' Bren could be very clever, and maybe what he had told them he was going to do was not at all what he was going to do.

He dared not ask, however. Credit with mani went only so far. He just sat and ate tasteless toast, so tired his eyes were trying to shut.

But every time they did, he saw the man pushing his way into mani's room, and he saw the man turning to look at him and aiming the rifle. Over and over and over.

He was not going to sleep, no matter he had been up all the night and was shivering he was so exhausted.

Not on *that* kind of dream.

The sky lightened under a spatter of rain, and the van's right-hand windshield wiper wasn't working but halfway. The road passed near a small forest as the rim of the sun came up under the cloud. Morning light cast long shadows, picking out every clump of grass and lump of dirt, while rain fell down as a fine mist.

Banichi slowed the van to a stop, said something to Jago, and got out.

Break for necessities in a relatively secure place, Bren thought. Tano got up and opened the door, and Algini got out, and then Lucasi followed, and Bren did.

It was more than that, however. Banichi and Algini talked for a moment, Tano added himself to the conversation, and then Jago did, a close conference in which Lucasi hung back, sensing himself not included, perhaps, until Banichi said, "Guildsman."

Lucasi limped forward with some speed and quietly joined the conference.

That left Bren, the civilian, leaning against a young tree, resting, and with the distinct impression there was some discussion going on that Banichi didn't think he would necessarily approve of.

Like leaving him behind again. He saw that coming. But it

made a certain sense. If it contributed to their safety, he would hide in whatever hole he had to and just wait.

None of them had had any significant sleep except Lucasi. Banichi had been driving nonstop, refusing Jago's offer to take the wheel, and by now he had to be exhausted.

And now they proposed to go do something desperate and didn't think he needed to be part of the planning—as if he could penetrate the code or get more than a handful of the signs they were using even if he were standing over there in the middle of it. There were things they needed to say in Guild context, with meanings an outsider wasn't going to grasp without a half hour of explanation, and even so—probably wouldn't like. He was increasingly sure he was not going to like the outcome.

There were nods. "Yes," Jago said, and Tano, and then Lucasi nodded, too, so Lucasi was in on it.

Bren waited, glumly. And it was Banichi who came to him.

"Beyond this point," Banichi said, "there will be difficulty, Bren-ji. The van is far too noisy, far too obvious a target to bring straight down the Kajiminda road. We would do better to leave it, get a rescue party organized from Kajiminda—not taking for granted it is still in allied hands—and you cannot keep our pace, either getting there or getting out, if need be."

"You want me to stay here," he said.

"You will have Lucasi," Banichi said, "and he will be armed and equipped with a locator. He is young. He will, however, suffice for a simple mission. We expect the Edi will have camped around Kajiminda, that this is a force the renegades have not wanted to take on, adding one more enemy to their difficulties—and that they have remained unengaged. But equipped. The difficulty is that they will be looking for Guild and not expecting us to be on their doorstep. We are going to have to get through and make a careful approach. If we can, we can get back here, bring you to Kajiminda, and then make a little noise."

"To draw the renegade attack away from Najida. To bring the renegades under Edi fire."

Banichi nodded. "Your own excellent notion, Bren-ji, some-what reworked. Considering your recent negotiations with Machigi, you directly threaten them, perhaps more, to their perception, than the aiji-dowager. Be patient and stay hidden. The van would be more comfortable a place for you to wait, but we advise you put as much distance between yourself and the road as you can. The trees in the other direction are an obvious line of retreat and an obvious ambush for anyone who sees the van as bait. We intend that they be cautious and slow in their investigation should they come here. Lucasi has instructions. You may listen to his advisements—up to a point."

"Yes," he said. "Just—" One could argue that it might be safest of all for them *all* to retreat into the wild and stay there until the Guild finished its business in this district. But that didn't help their allies. He'd offered an idea, sleep-deprived and exhausted; and they, likewise on no sleep, had taken it. Which worried him. "Be careful, Nichi-ji. I want you back. I want you all back. One is quite adamant on that point."

Banichi said: "We always are careful, Bren-ji. Rely on us."

And then Banichi left him, headed into the trees. Jago, de-parting, gave him one backward glance. Algini didn't—just picked up their gear. Only Tano, at the last moment, came back and gave him his canteen, then went off to catch up with Al-gini, the lot of them making, one suspected, a cautiously obvi-ous trail.

Banichi had parked the van, however, on a small dome of sandstone, and it was clearly up to them to get out of here with-out laying down obvious tracks in the other direction.

Bren looked in Lucasi's direction. "We should go, nadi."

"One will try not to leave marks," Lucasi said. "But kindly walk atop my track, nandi." Lucasi settled his makeshift crutch and limped off around the van, passing over an area where there was a muddle of footsteps in a patch of dirt that overlapped the sheet of buried rock atop which the van was parked.

He understood the game clearly enough. Walk on the rock,

leave no track, while Banichi and the rest laid down just enough trail to be followed—and believed—by experts.

The one they laid down had to be far, far harder to find; he understood that. Lucasi was walking without his stick, hobbling along, probably in considerable pain, on what rapidly became a climb toward the rocky heights, the rugged upthrust of the plateau, on the edge of the coastal lands. On that steep climb, Lucasi stopped now and again and plotted his path; he finally found a place where the occasional rock became a lower, flatter spot and where a straggle of brush grew from the underside of low, body-sized shelves of rock.

Lucasi sat down, immediately bent over and struggling with pain. Bren sat down. They had climbed well out of view of the road—either road, since the Kajiminda to Separti road crossed that same patch of woods to the south.

He wished they had the strength to keep going just a little higher.

But they had to stay findable, didn't they, by their own side? Lucasi's face was running with sweat. He didn't speak, he didn't complain.

Hadn't he sworn never to interfere with his bodyguard or get in their way? This whole stratagem had started with his idea. Granted, four very astute bodyguards had accepted the notion, but it still had his fingerprints on it, and he'd sworn, while being picked up off the floor at Targai, never, ever to interfere with his bodyguard again.

That vow hadn't lasted long, had it?

He sat. He had a tiny sip of water and offered some to Lucasi, who silently accepted it and nodded thanks, handing the canteen back.

This wasn't the brash young man who'd repeatedly caused them trouble. Lucasi was quiet and very sober, his eyes, once he'd caught his breath, scanning the area constantly, his ears doubtless on the alert. Which of his aishid had personally gotten to the young man he wasn't sure, but someone had—

maybe Banichi, possibly Algini. But it had evidently made an impression.

And now the kid had an assignment from them, the biggest assignment they could possibly hand the boy—namely *him*—and he didn't plan to make it harder for the young man. He sat still and silent, not to distract him, trusting atevi hearing to pick up anything moving out there, any sound of a motor, or any gunfire.

All he personally heard was the wind, whispering in the brush. The gray, scattered clouds intermittently shed a little rain, spots that grew thick on the stone, then slowly evaporated.

Lucasi turned his head sharply, as good as a screaming alarm. The young man lifted his hand slightly and quietly got to his feet.

Bren stood up.

Come, Lucasi signaled, and Bren followed him, treading as carefully over gravel, taking care not to scuff the stone or break a weed stem. They kept going for what felt like half an hour or so before Lucasi found another stopping point and offered him a place to sit down.

"What did you hear, nadi?" Bren whispered as faintly as he could.

"Trucks, nandi," Lucasi said. "Three or so. Coming toward us from the north."

From the direction of the intersection near Najida, and generally toward Kajiminda. It could be their enemy reacting to that call he'd made from the hunting station. He hadn't heard a thing. But he didn't doubt Lucasi had heard it.

They sat in utter silence for about a quarter of an hour.

Then he did hear something, a heavy boom. That also came from the north.

Something bad was happening over in the direction of Najida. And they sat here listening to it as if it were some distant weather report.

"Can you tell where Banichi and the others are?" he whispered.

"One is not supposed to discuss the equipment, nandi."

The kid was following the rules. Any of his own aishid would have just answered the question.

But the kid, he noted, had one of those locator bracelets— whose, he wasn't sure; but he didn't think the boy had had one before. And the answer probably was that they were operating with the locators' send function switched off, as they had done all along. He could surmise that when things were safe, or if they wanted to lay a trap, they would switch on; and whether there was any special equipment that could pick one up if it was switched off, he hadn't a clue. One didn't know if all Guild locators worked the same way or how sophisticated was the information they could pass. It was a complex code, individual to the group. He knew that much about it. And Lucasi not being part of his aishid, it was well possible that Lucasi couldn't interpret their signals and that the only reason he had that bracelet was to pick up any signal out there.

But something was going on with those booms and thumps and that sound of trucks moving. Somebody was active out there and not being stealthy about it. It could be Edi, even. Or somebody hot on the attack, or desperate in flight.

Banichi and the rest had had time enough to be into trouble by now if they had tripped any alarm.

They'd need to be sure, first off, that it *was* the Edi in control of Kajiminda.

And then they had to convince a force of Edi hunters and fishermen and farmers that this particular set of black uniforms was on *their* side.

Meanwhile, if those passing trucks took the north branch of the road, where it intersected, they were going to find the abandoned van and realize somebody was out and about in the landscape.

God, he didn't like this. He wished now they'd opted to head down to Separti Township and hoped to pick up reinforcements from the Guild Tabini had stationed there . . . but that might be a pipe dream. Anybody Tabini had stationed anywhere might have shifted position under direct Guild orders—not Guild serving as bodyguards but Guild forces that Tabini-aiji might ordinarily use.

So Separti wasn't a sure thing, either. Nothing was.

Boom.

He didn't jump. But his heart did.

"Are you supposed to listen to my suggestions, nadi?" he whispered to his young guard. "But not to be led into anything stupid?"

"Yes, nandi, that is the instruction. But your aishid did not at all say stupid."

"One is gratified. But one instructs you, nadi, that you explain to me what we are doing sitting here and what my aishid is doing. It would be useful in deciding what I would suggest."

The kid looked confused, caught between general orders, Guild teaching, and specific orders.

"Nandi, one is simply instructed to keep you as far away from the enemy as possible. One has a general route to follow that circles somewhat; and one hopes we are on it, so your bodyguard can find us at need. But we are under no circumstances to go back to the van, and we are not to go across the road into the woods, and we are not to make any noise at all."

"And what are *they* doing, meanwhile? Did they explain that, nadi?"

"They are taking Kajiminda, nandi."

Taking Kajiminda. If it were only that simple. Which meant the kid didn't know any more than he did.

Boom. Again, toward the north. The train station, maybe; maybe Najida itself.

God, what was going on?

18

It was increasingly noisy up there. And something serious was going on. Mani was cross because she had been trying to take a nap, so had nand' Geigi, and the booms and thumps, which had been only occasional, now just went on and on.

"The Guild," Mani complained, "is not usually so inconveniently loud." She adjusted a shawl, folded her arms, and tried to go back to sleep. Nand' Geigi did, his chin sinking on his chest.

Cajeiri just sat, aching from want of sleep, and played chess with Jegari and tried to make the time pass faster. His concentration suffered. He was distracted, trying to picture the land out there and locate the booms. The east-west road to Kajiminda and the north-south road to the train station and the airport crossed just east of the house and a little uphill. And there was a huge open field opposite the house that ran on up the hill to where the crossroads were, and uphill after that, on and on, he supposed. He wished he had paid better attention in that direction when they had driven in from the train station.

And for a while the shooting had sounded as though half of it was coming from directly across the road opposite the house, but lately there was a lot more of it and it seemed to be coming from the intersection farther away, or maybe farther east than that. Echoes made it hard to tell.

But nobody up on the roof was shooting right now. Which he supposed meant the fight had moved off.

He would have liked to ask mani or nand' Geigi, but they were pretending to sleep again.

And he was afraid to talk too loudly. If he annoyed mani, he might have to stop the chess game and just sit and think about what could go wrong. And he did not want to sleep, or have dreams, right now.

So he whispered to Antaro and Jegari: "One wonders what is going on, nadiin-ji. Slip upstairs and find out."

"I shall," Antaro said, and left very quietly.

"The fighting is up on the hill by the crossroads, nandi," Jegari said in a whisper. "One is far from sure, but one might hope some of your father's force has gotten here from the airport. One cannot believe any of our own people would have left the grounds, even if they were successful in driving the attackers off. There are too few of us."

"Can Cenedi tell who it is?"

"Easily," Jegari said, then: "Under some circumstances." And then he added, "But I am not supposed to tell you that, nandi."

That was irritating. He wished *he* could go apprentice with the Guild. He really wished it right now. Right now his father was sitting in Shejidan signing papers and making phone calls and could not personally come to rescue him and mani. His father had sent the people at the airport. And being able to send people had something to recommend it. If people would do what you told them. But it was not the same as getting into a plane and going there.

Antaro came back downstairs in a hurry and entered without knocking.

"There are allies on the hill!" she said. "One is not sure whether they are from the Guild or directed from your father, nandi. But one understands they are not Edi and they are not the renegades."

"About time," mani said, arching a brow. "Deliver your news, nadi. What is going on up there?"

"Cenedi-nadi is coming downstairs himself, aiji-ma," An-

taro said with a bow, and in fact there was the sound of someone on the stairs. "But by what I know, aiji-ma—""

It was a good thing that she went on to answer. Cajeiri had
held his breath, knowing mani's mood.

"Our allies, of whatever sort, have gotten out of the airport,"
Antaro said, a little out of breath, "and they are attacking the
renegades up at the crossroads, and the renegades cannot come
closer because there are Edi on the hill across the road from us
and our own defenses on the roof."

She said that much to satisfy mani before a knock at the
door announced a presence, and Cenedi himself came into the
room, not, however, looking that much happier.

"Aiji-ma. The siege at the airport is broken. Your grandson's
forces are in possession of the airport, and the enemy is attempting to cover their retreat to the south. But we fear they
are going toward the paidhi's position."

That was terrible news.

"Where is the paidhi at the moment?" mani asked. "What
is he doing?"

"He has taken the Esig road out of Taisigi territory toward
Kajiminda, but he has not gotten there. Nand' Geigi, what do
you know of that terrain?"

"The Esig road," Lord Geigi said, "would be a route our enemies could use back into Taisigi territory—if they try to fall
back from the intersection."

"Can they reach it overland?" Cenedi asked. "The maps indicate no track within that section, and rugged land."

"It is, nadi. It is very rugged land, with hardly even game
trails. It would make far better sense for nand' Bren to go to
Kajiminda. Certainly not to attempt to come here."

"Yet they have not arrived at Kajiminda. Phone lines are cut.
We have radioed the Edi to be aware of allied forces in the area.
We dare not be more specific."

And that was where nand' Bren was supposed to be? Cajeiri
wondered. But he was lost somewhere?

If they were stuck somewhere, there was that thick woods that ran down all the way to Kajiminda's walls. He remembered that very well. One could not see an ambush in that woods.

"But," Cajeiri said, risking all manner of displeasure, he knew it, but he could stand it no longer. "But can the Edi look for him, nadi?"

"Likeliest," Cenedi continued without even looking at him, only at mani. "Likeliest the enemy is aware your grandson's forces have landed at Separti. They have given up holding off his force at the airport, and they are holding the intersection while a number of them make a direct run to intercept nand' Bren, to take him as a bargaining piece. That would set your grandson's interests against the Guild leadership's interests. That is, one fears, their immediate objective. That and controlling access to the Esig road itself."

"So one assumes they will open a second position at the Esig intersection, near Kajiminda," mani said. "And they will trickle back from the Najida intersection and fold up into Taisigi territory. As if my grandson's forces would not cross that border."

"Just so, aiji-ma. They have become aware of the second force at Separti, and they know Guild forces are in Tanaja. But if they can find nand' Bren and take him hostage, then they will pressure your grandson to negotiate with the Guild. That is what we fear they will try to do."

"Get past them," mani said with a wave of her hand. "Can we not spare a unit? While they are blowing up the grass on the hill, can we not get a unit cross country to reinforce the paidhi's guard and move him into Kajiminda?"

Please, Cajeiri wanted to say, but mani did not favor that word. He looked at Cenedi, wishing hard.

And Cenedi said: "We shall try it, aiji-ma."

"Do so!" A sharp wave of mani's hand. "Let us do something useful! The Guild can stay out of our way until we have recovered the paidhi-aiji. They chose to press things. They might have waited!"

"Send my guard, too, Cenedi-nadi," Geigi said.

"Nandi," Cenedi said, to both, apparently, and left without another word.

But there was no guarantee it would work. Mani was angry. Lord Geigi looked worried. Those were his closest associates nand' Geigi had just sent to get past the enemy; and Great-grandmother was sending men, too. It was dangerous. It was terribly dangerous to try to slip behind the enemy, and the field that ran up to the ridge overland was just tall grass and brush: it did not offer very much cover.

"One most fears," Lord Geigi said somberly, "that nand' Bren is stalled, trying to get to Kajiminda."

"If our Edi allies do not mistake him for the enemy," mani muttered. "One understands the Guild's distrust of civilian assistance."

"But," Cajeiri began, dangerously getting mani's sudden full attention.

"Who *is* nand' Bren?" mani asked. "And why do you have this angry tone with us? You seem quite distressed, Great-grandson."

Who was nand' Bren? That made no sense at all. Nand' Bren was nand' Bren. Nand' Bren was his favorite association.

But he suddenly, and with a sense of panic, understood exactly what mani was asking him.

"Nand' Bren is *mine,*" he countered angrily, "and everyone has treated him very badly. No one cares now if I am offended. But they *will* someday."

"Threats, do we hear? One would have thought nand' Bren belonged to your father, young gentleman. But he has been mine. And currently he says he belongs to Lord Machigi. He has a very fickle charm."

"Well, but he is *ours,* and *you* sent him to Lord Machigi, and now he is out there with our enemies, and we are upset, mani! We are upset with this!"

"Never assume, Great-grandson," mani said, holding up a

forefinger, "never assume that your enemy has done what they have strongly forecast doing. One imagines the enemy would be quite satisfied if all sorts of forces went running over to re-inforce nand' Bren. Then they would move in this direction and try to take *us* as hostages, not to mention nand' Toby and Barb-daja. That is their purpose here, or they could have stayed in the Marid and tried to fight off the Guild from within their strong places. This is a risk for them. This is a desperate risk, and they will spare nothing and stick at nothing. This is life and death, and *finally* we have gotten them to commit forces in an exposed position."

He understood, then. He thought he did. Great-grandmother was *happy* the enemy was here. She was happy there was fight-ing going on, because she thought they were doing exactly what she wanted them to do.

He was thinking that when he heard a strange buzzing and roaring sound go right over them, and then go off to the south.

He jumped to his feet. He would never forget that sound. He looked up as if he could see it right through the floor and the roof above.

"That," he said, excited, but not knowing quite what *that* plane was doing here, "*that* was an airplane, mani-ma!"

There was sure as hell something big and noisy going on over to the north, and Bren's best guess put it somewhere close to Najida, which didn't help his state of mind in the least.

All he could do was sit on a cold rock under a hot sun and have a sip of water from the canteen Tano had given him, and share it with Lucasi, who looked grimly off to the north.

The two of them were stuck, was what, and Lucasi was the worse off, having a splinted ankle that was swelling against its bandages. Bren had the misery of the vest and the bandages about his ribs, not to mention a wider and wider split in his boot, which picked up the occasional piece of gravel along the side of the sole. But blisters were a worse misery; he didn't want

to take either boot off to find out what couldn't be helped . . .
he feared if he took either boot off for a few minutes, he might
not be able to get it back on.

The bruising and the bandages about his ribs that had been
misery a day or so ago had begun to diminish. The sore spots
he had from nonstop wearing of the damned vest had begun to
be an issue, but at least he was breathing with less pain. He
climbed. He had done that.

Which didn't mean he was running any foot races if a problem showed up.

And he kept hoping that Lucasi's occasional check of the
locator bracelet would get a signal from the rest of them.

It hadn't. And didn't.

And then something caught Lucasi's attention. He looked
northwest, and kept looking.

"Do you hear something, nadi?" Bren asked him.

"A motor, nandi. Several more of them coming down the
road."

The road was a distance off. They couldn't see it from where
they were sitting, which also meant someone down on the road
couldn't see them up here.

"Coming from the north, nadi?"

"Yes, nandi." Lucasi looked a little doubtful. "Can you not
hear it?"

"Human hearing is less keen," he said. "So is our sight after
sunset. You are my ears, day and night, nadi. What do you
hear?"

"One would guess several heavy vehicles, nandi," Lucasi
said in a very low voice, and all the while they could hear intermittent booming and thumping from the north. "One would
say a force of some strength is moving."

That was good news and bad.

And after a glance toward the west, and with a second worried look: "Forgive my lack of experience, nandi, but one fears
worse trouble than trucks. There may also be a general and

much quieter movement overland if they are too many for the transport available and if they have chosen to scout out a retreat. We need to find a place to lie very low."

"But Banichi and the others must still be able to find us, nadi."

"One will try to assure that they can do so, nandi." Lucasi set his hands against the ground, a three-point stance, and hurled himself to his feet, dragging his crutch with him—the benefit of a young body in good shape. Bren made a slower, more pained try, and Lucasi gave him a hand and a gentle pull to help him up. "One will try to work back—"

Lucasi stopped suddenly, looking to the north and aloft.

Bren began to hear, faintly, both the heavy growl of engines to the west and an engine far more high-pitched, faster moving, up above.

"Small plane," Bren said, and followed Lucasi, still carefully, footprint for footprint, in a quest for a hiding place, a grassy low spot, anything that might conceal them from aerial observation. Lucasi was heading for a clump of berry bushes, thorny, but the only cover there was close; and by now the plane was close and maybe following the road for navigation. Its elevation would lay out the entire dome of rock like a map.

All of a sudden the pitch of the sound shifted. It was coming at them. Bren looked up and saw it.

"Nandi!" Lucasi urged him, and came back for him.

It was yellow, bright yellow, that little plane. And Bren knew that plane, that noisy little engine, and the pilot, right down to the white sun-blaze on the nose. He raised a hand and waved as the plane roared by.

"Nandi!"

"That is Dur, nadi!" he said, his spirits soaring, as that plane flew on a departing diagonal toward Kajiminda, waggling its wings and swooping low as if to taunt the convoy on the road. But it was not for the convoy, that signal, that wild risk of ground fire. "He has seen us! Dur has come in! He cannot land for us, but what he sees, he will report to Najida."

"Then one is glad, nandi!" Hope was all but a stranger to Lucasi's face these last few days. But his look wandered from confusion to a glimmering of understanding. "He will get us help, from Najida or from the airport."

"I think he will try to guide them, nadi. I do. One has no idea how long it will take, or who will be in a position to come here, but he may be able to spot the situation at Kajiminda and report that, too. He is no amateur observer. He may not understand the whole situation, but he will be accurate. And he can land that plane in amazing places!"

"Then I must get you to cover, nandi," Lucasi said. "He was clever about his path, but one is anxious all the same. Let us go down the slope a little. The brush is not enough."

They moved along a distance, then, as Lucasi pointed out a likely spot, Bren ended up helping Lucasi on the steep, bare stretch of rock, and below that descent there was indeed the kind of thing Bren had been hoping for, a flat space of scrub and eroded dirt, and a shattered sandwich of upthrust pale sandstone that offered shelter from most sides.

Better. A lot better. He only worried now about his bodyguard being able to find him: but if the plane got to Najida and Najida called Kajiminda, that was no problem.

All they had to do now was to avoid attracting unwanted attention until his bodyguard was able to pick him and Lucasi up and get them safely within a defensive perimeter.

And a moment when their enemies might be in retreat right down the Kajiminda road was not the time for them to go looking for him. His aishid would trust him to use good sense. He should stop worrying.

But he couldn't.

The whole house was in an uproar. The new barricade at the front door was being taken down, admitting a gust of cold wind up and down the halls, because the young lord from Dur was trying to land right on the road near the village, and the Edi on guard on the hill were shooting at him. The guards on the roof reported it, and the moment they had a gap in the barricade, Ramaso sent one of the young men running out to talk to the Edi.

More, Great-grandmother insisted on coming upstairs. "One is extremely weary of sitting in a box," mani said, and they all agreed with that, but *not* with mani risking herself, coming upstairs when people were shooting.

But no, if young Dur was landing his plane right on the road, and if young Dur was trying to land to confer, mani would not meet him sitting in a basement, no, absolutely not, it would not do.

So Lord Geigi and mani headed upstairs to mani's sitting room, and Cajeiri followed.

It was upsetting—mani being stubborn, and the Edi shooting at their ally. Cajeiri, for his part, was having trouble even putting on a clean coat, he was so tired. His own bed was only a step away as servants helped him dress, and he wanted just to sit on it—it was the first time he had been back in his own rooms since the shooting had started; but he had to stand up to be helped with the coat, and he had to hurry or miss something, and he was so incredibly tired; and so, he knew, were Jegari and Antaro.

But there was so much going on that he could hardly bear it. When he gathered up Jegari and Antaro and went out into the hall again, the barricade was down and sunlight was coming in the front, and whoever was supposed to go talk to the Edi must have gone; but the plane was still circling: he could hear it in the distance. He so wanted to see it again—he remembered the yellow plane as one of the most wonderful machines he had ever seen, as good as the starship in the heavens, and he was furious that the Edi were trying to shoot it.

Servants were out and about, too, and Ramaso was by the open doorway, giving orders. He went to the security station, but nobody was getting in there, and Cenedi was in the way.

He stayed and he listened, and Cenedi was giving orders—they were talking to the Edi and talking to the young lord from Dur, actually in the plane, and very hard to understand.

But then he heard Dur agree to something, and he thought that probably the plane was coming back. He went to the area of the door, and listened, and listened. The portico beyond the gap where the barrier had been was busy with mani's young men, who were setting up another barricade, dragging panels into place.

"You should not go out there, young gentleman," one of the servants said.

It was better than Cenedi noticing him. He drew Antaro and Jegari with him, back out of the immediate vicinity of the door, which everybody was so anxious about.

He was so tired and frustrated he sank down against the out-of-the-way part of the wall, where they had put some of the boards from the barrier. He watched out for nails, and sank down on his heels, and rested his head on his arms, and just—

—drifted off, still waiting for the young lord of Dur.

The convoy or whatever it was had long since ground past them, though Lucasi said he could hear it to the south of them and thought it might have stopped. It was possible they had reached the abandoned van and had a little delay figuring out whether it was rigged with explosives.

It might *be* rigged, for what Bren knew. Tano and Algini could do that very quickly, and he couldn't remember if they had come near the van while they were discussing what to do.

But they heard no explosion.

And it was highly possible that their enemy, failing to be blown up, was trying to figure out now where they had gone.

They might follow his bodyguard to Kajiminda, which would bring the enemy under Edi fire and complicate Banichi's situation trying to get into Kajiminda.

Or they might decide right away that the track toward the

woods was a decoy and go casting about for where they were, figuring a high-level hostage might save their situation.

Lucasi checked the locator at irregular intervals, just a fast look.

He did pick up something.

"It is not our associates," Lucasi said. "We could be picking up Najida."

"What about the enemy, back where we left the van? Can you tell direction?"

"One is not authorized to say."

Damned Guild regulations, Bren thought.

And then Lucasi added, looking worried: "It may be our enemies, trying to draw a response, figuring we could take them for our allies. I must admit, nandi, that I am not an expert with this."

At least Lucasi was not overestimating his abilities. That was actually comforting.

But the signal apparently stopped.

There had been the plane. Allies knew where they were. Or would know. Things could start to move . . . which itself could be a point of danger.

The sun had passed zenith. The temperature was a curious mix of cold rock, where they were sitting, and a potential for sunburn, where heat beat down from overhead. They hoarded their water, shared it very, very cautiously, and kept absolutely still.

There had been no repeat loop by the airplane. It was likely on the ground somewhere, either at the airport or at Najida, if not headed back to Shejidan airport, hours away, or down to Separti, or, God knew, some convenient patch of grass where Dur could report to somebody who could do something about the situation. One could hope things were going on, and that plans were being laid in detail—

Plans that involved the whole west coast and peace or continued war, not to mention lives saved or lost.

And here he sat, holding a good many of the keys to the situation in his head, and he wasn't in shape to do anything. Lucasi had wilderness skills and a weapon, but he couldn't walk far. So they were stuck on this damned hilltop. Plans could have gone to hell. The situation was changing, with that plane involved. One *hoped* his bodyguard had seen it, and had seen the convoy, and had drawn conclusions . . . but if they changed plans, they couldn't advise him, either, without advertising their presence.

He thought wildly of just taking out on his own and hiking to Najida, hiding in ditches and behind rocks, getting there any way he could, then getting on the phone there and raising hell with Shejidan until he could get them to send his bodyguard some help over at Kajiminda. If he were Lucasi's age and had two good feet . . .

But he wasn't. And the kid wasn't in shape for it, either.

He thought of a lot of things, none that were practical, and most of which were rash in the extreme, and he knew, sensibly speaking, that a stray, pale human in run-down boots and a pale dress coat wandering through the lines of fire was just not going to end well.

But, damn it! There were a lot of entrenched opinions out there about to bump into each other and in need of the paidhi to knock heads together . . . Edi mistrust, Ragi mistrust, Marid mistrust, several clans who didn't like each other, the Guild itself fragmented, and the Marid under attack. People were going to get killed, people he intensely cared about were in the middle of it, and he needed a damned phone.

Which—he swept a careful hand back over his hair, trying not to look any more disreputable than he already did, unshaven and dusty as he was—would ironically make a cell phone a very handy thing, except such a call could be intercepted, and he would bring the whole damned renegade force down on him and Lucasi.

So what good was that? What the damned Guild locator couldn't do, it couldn't do either. His ideas were running up against two facts: he wasn't in shape to run for it, and going against his agreement with his bodyguard was far too risky. Getting shot by the Edi was no better than getting shot by the renegades.

Lucasi leaned close and indicated direction with a move of his hand. "Someone is coming, nandi."

From the south. From the direction his people should come—but from the direction the heavy firing had come earlier.

He drew a deep breath. And Lucasi flicked the button on the locator he wore.

Green light flickered twice and went out.

Lucasi cut it off fast and looked at it as if it had been a bomb.

"Get to deep cover, nandi. Quickly!"

"What did it say, nadi?

"That was the wrong signal, nandi. We are in serious trouble. Go. *Quickly.*" Lucasi lurched to his feet and seized Bren's arm, pulling him along, but it was a question who was helping whom . . . a damned sad situation, Bren thought incongruously, and with it came the hope the next shot he took didn't land in the same spot.

Upon which, in between protecting his balance and Lucasi's and trying to prevent them both from breaking their necks, he tried to think what to do, how to work their way out of this.

If he had to fall into hostile hands, the best thing was to stay alive, and keep the kid alive, and try to work his way out of it with words—a far better defense than a gun in his hand. The damage he could do Tabini—he could, Banichi's word, *finesse* that. That was his job. Get him to a leader he could talk to, he could find *some* chink in the opposition's armor, *something* to bargain with.

Brains. And a plan. A plan only happened if he had a situation in front of him.

He wasn't doing damned well with Banichi's kind of work.

They skidded, leaving a track. It was a wonder both of them made it to the bottom of the sandstone shelf in one piece, but they hadn't been quiet about it. He caught Lucasi by the sleeve to keep him from pitching over, while Lucasi, with his bad ankle, was trying to balance the heavy gun in the crook of one arm, having unslung it from his back, and manage his makeshift cane with the other; it was not an outstandingly successful combination.

"Please do not attempt to shoot anyone even if you get a target," Bren said. "It will only get us killed, nadi. I can talk to them."

"This is my fault," Lucasi said. Both of them were panting for breath, and bits of rock crumbled under their feet and slid downslope, rattling all the way. "Hide, nandi, and I shall lead them off."

"You shall do nothing of the kind, nadi!"

"Forgive me, but Guild cannot accept civilian orders in a combat situation . . ."

"This is not a combat situation unless—" His foot skidded on the sandstone dome. He recovered, and Lucasi rescued him from pitching over in the other direction. "—unless I say it is, nadi!"

"One begs understanding, nandi. Banichi left me in charge of your safety."

"*Banichi* could have taken a rifle to the halls in Tanaja, and he refrained, because there are other answers in this world than Guild policy, nadi! At this moment I am at the end of my patience with Guild policy, when it would be perfectly possible—" Another difficult sideways step. "—to settle this directly with the lords involved—" Slip. "—without blowing things up."

"The lord of the Dojisigi only *thinks* he is using the Guild who have taken residence with him . . ."

"The paidhi-aiji, however, is better-served, better-protected, and less a fool than the lord of the Dojisigi, who is probably *deceased*, nadi. I tell you that you are not to fire that rifle!"

"But," Lucasi said.

"This is an order, nadi! If you fire, we shall both be dead, instantly. If I have my way, I can at least gain us a day. *Obey my order!*"

"Yes, nandi." A desperate maneuver for balance as they hit level ground. "But best hide and not be in such a position in the first place."

"Just—" Bren half-turned to assist Lucasi, and caught movement at the top of the ridge.

Three uniformed Guild appeared at the top, an instant before one of them yelled,

"Halt!"

"Obey them," Bren said, and held up empty hands. "Put down the rifle, nadi. Let me deal with them."

There seemed to be four of them. Their enemies came down the sandstone slope in better order than the two of them had just done, and Lucasi held his rifle aimed at the ground.

"Nadiin," Bren said, keeping his hands in sight. "My bodyguard is under my orders, so you may rest easy; and I trust you know—"

He didn't know what had hit him. He went sideways, and fire sprayed the sandstone and came back. The whole world flashed black and red, and he was lying on the ground under Lucasi's weight with an automatic rifle going off just over his head.

"Get to cover, nandi!" Lucasi yelled, over another three-shot burst, and got his weight off him. *"Go!"*

"Nadi," he protested, outraged, but there seemed nothing for it. There was a lump of rock half a body length away, and he rolled downslope to get there, tangled in the damned long dress coat and trying to get all of him into cover. Lucasi aimed another burst up the hill, on which there was one man down and no sign of the others. In the next second, Lucasi came rolling downhill into the same inadequate shelter. Lucasi, being considerably larger, needed more of the rock, which Bren tried to give him.

There was a moment of no-sound, which made Bren think he had gone deaf; but he heard Lucasi moving around. He heard the scrape of a rock under his knee.

"Nadi," he began, exasperated.

"He would have fired," Lucasi said. "Forgive me, nandi, but he moved to fire."

And did the civilian second-guess Guild instincts? If it had been Banichi, he never would have questioned the judgement. It wasn't Banichi, by a long shot. And he had lied to that dead man about having control of the situation. Clearly. He was upset about that.

But the fact was, they were alive and under cover. He didn't know how they were going to get out of this nook, and he didn't know how many rounds Lucasi had left. He could hope maybe the pair who had fled back up over the hill were waiting for reinforcements, but he had the unhappy suspicion they were just working around to a better vantage, to come at them from behind their rock.

"He would have fired," Lucasi said again.

"One believes you, nadi."

"One regrets shoving you so hard."

"Since I am alive, I by no means take offense. You have actually done very well, nadi."

It was a young face, struggling with distress and imminent failure. And they were in one hell of a mess.

"I have a gun," Bren said. "One rather expects they will come around the hill and up. Might one suggest you bring the rifle to bear on that situation, and I will watch for anyone to come over the hill, at a range that will give me time to miss at least once."

"Yes," Lucasi said, and shifted about to do exactly that, while Bren took the pistol from his pocket and tried to still his racing pulse. He had, unfortunately, their precision weapon, and he was long out of practice.

They waited. There was a sound at one point, a thump, the

shift of a light rock from somewhere over the hill. And then a rock sailed over the crest and rolled down the sandstone dome.

Do them both credit, neither of them was fool enough to fire at it. They sat pat.

They waited.

Then after a considerable time, a second sound, from their right. The rock they were hiding behind obscured the source of it.

"They are coming downhill," Bren said.

"I have a signal!" Lucasi whispered, suddenly twisting about to show him the blinking green light. "Nandi, *our* signal. Your bodyguard is out there."

From the certainty of disaster to a different kind of fear. They'd made enough racket and had enough guns going off to alert the surrounding countryside. His bodyguard knew he was in trouble and had surely gone from a stealthy approach to a desperate haste, maneuvering to take the opposition out.

But how many were there on the other side? Were they the advance guard of the whole damned force that had been banging and thumping away over at Najida? There could be a hundred or more in that convoy.

"What is my bodyguard doing?" he asked in the faintest whisper.

"They are coming in," Lucasi said. "Nandi, do not fire."

God, somebody with a correct code was moving up on their position. He took his finger deliberately off the trigger and curled it around the guard, for fear he might squeeze the trigger in sheer terror; but he wasn't letting his finger stray far from it, either.

Then he heard the best sound in the world.

"Bren-ji?" Jago's voice.

"Yes," he said to the empty air. "Yes. Kindly get under cover, Jago-ji. One believes trouble has gone downslope to get around us."

A little sound, the whisper of a leather-clad body moving,

and with scarcely a piece of grit disturbed on the rock, a lithe, large shadow came around the rock and settled between them.

Bren just leaned back against the rock in relief. "Is everyone all right, Jago-ji?"

"Yes," she said. "But this is a moderately difficult situation you have here, Bren-ji. We believe there are nine to thirteen of the opposition, perhaps more, scattered about."

He carefully put the safety back on the gun and inserted it into his pocket on the second try.

"Are you injured?" Jago asked him.

"Perfectly fine," he said. God, he was *not* going to shake like a leaf. He reminded himself they were a long way from out of this, which kept up a moderate draw on spare adrenalin. "Lucasi has kept me in one piece."

"Credit to him," Jago muttered, keeping her head down. "Algini has gone downslope to reconnoiter and see if he can give us names."

"Did you reach the Edi, Jago-ji?"

"No. They are shooting at everything that moves, and Tano caught a richochet."

"Is he all right?"

"Minor, but nuisanceful in operations. We suspected that the situation over at the airport had changed, and we became concerned for your immediate safety."

"You saw the plane."

"We did see it. Dur, one believes. We have no knowledge where he is based."

"He saw us. He will have reported our position, Jago-ji. If we can hold out, if the airport has opened up—"

"The convoy clearly saw the plane, too. They immediately attempted to penetrate the Edi perimeter. That set the Edi firing at every movement. We were making no progress there. And we were concerned—" Jago shoved another clip into her pistol. "—that you might be in trouble from the shift of positions. We knew they would not come west of the road. That left the east as a safe route for them, and *you* in considerable difficulty. We thought we should hurry about it."

"One is very grateful," he began to say, and then heard shots from downslope. He utterly lost his train of thought, thinking of Algini, and Tano, who would be with him.

"Where is Banichi?" he asked.

Jago gave a nod vaguely upslope. "Up there."

Bren did begin to shiver, just slightly, and stopped it by resting his arm on his knee. He was, he found, chilled to the bone and dry as dust. He still had a little water in the canteen, but if they were pinned here any length of time . . . it was no time to be profligate with that resource.

A click of rock on rock upslope drew his attention. He looked around on reflex, but the rock cut off his view of anything but Jago, who had looked upslope, and Lucasi, who had flattened himself atop his rifle and tried to get a look up above.

"Banichi," Jago said, and about that time there was a hurried movement on the slope, and Banichi added himself to their group.

"Bren-ji," Banichi said, settling in, and threw a hand signal to Jago and Lucasi. "We need to move around this rock, Bren-ji. Our opposition is maneuvering from the other direction, and there are a number of them. This position will not suffice."

Not out of the soup yet, that was clear.

"Yes," Bren said, and he pushed himself toward his feet with a hand on the rock, trying to stay bent over. Jago took his elbow and steered him around the rock and down to a new position.

"I am going back upslope, Bren-ji," Banichi said. "Keep your head down."

They were in tight quarters. Bren found himself sandwiched between Jago and Lucasi and the rock. But it might give Jago a better vantage on what was coming.

Jago said something in Guild slang; Lucasi said, "Two clips."

"Banichi," Jago said, and something else.

"Yes," Lucasi said.

Which left the civilian completely underinformed, but there was enough bad news to occupy his mind. He kept waiting for gunshots, and then Lucasi called attention to another blip on his locator.

"Tano and Algini are setting up," Jago said, Bren was sure, for his sake. She was watching her own wristband. And it flashed.

"There is—" Lucasi began to say.

Gunfire broke out downslope, and it went on.

"They will be moving," Jago said calmly, and when Bren drew the pistol from his pocket, Jago said, "That will be little help to us, Bren-ji. Stay under cover."

She had her rifle ready, a heavy pistol laid carefully by her foot; Lucasi set up flat on his belly, this time with his rifle aimed down slope.

Jago said something to him again, and he said, "Yes," and inched a little closer.

"Cover me while I reload," she said. "Save your shots, nadi, unless you have a definite target."

"Yes," Lucasi said.

The gunfire downslope went on, with momentary pauses. Then a shot came from behind them and over their heads.

"Ready," Jago said, aiming downslope.

Bren pressed himself close into the rock, trying to give Jago and Lucasi as much room as possible. She fired a burst, a second, and a third.

Fourth and fifth, then. Fire came back and knocked chips off the rock and the sandstone slope beyond them.

Damn, Bren thought. Lucasi fired. Jago reloaded, quick, accurate movements; and fire came over their heads from Banichi's position.

"Save your shots," Jago repeated to Lucasi, with iron patience, "unless you see targets."

"Yes," he said. "One apologizes, nadi."

Jago put herself back in position and waited, grim-faced.

It was quiet for a moment. Lucasi's locator flashed.

"Locator," Bren said, figuring that neither of them had attention to spare for it; and Jago took a look, then pushed a button on her own several times.

"Watch downslope," Jago admonished Lucasi.

"Yes," he said.

Tano and Algini might be in trouble down there, Bren thought; and then Jago said, "The dowager's guard."

"Here?" Bren asked, one sharp question, and then all hell broke loose on the slope, shots going off and echoing off the heights, and Banichi was shooting over their heads.

Lucasi let off a shot, simultaneously with Jago's.

"I claim the next, nadi," Jago said. "You are down to three shots. Reserve them."

"Yes," Lucasi said, and wriggled back a little.

Another burst of fire from below. Bren just tried to make himself part of the rock. He had his hand in his pocket, holding his pistol. He had remembered to take the safety off.

Then amid it all, a flurry of light from Jago's bracelet, three times repeated.

Jago cast a look upslope, braced her rifle against her body, and tapped one button three times.

Three flashes came back, and Jago pressed the audio plug in her ear.

"Lord Machigi's guard," Jago said, "is entering the vicinity."

Good God, Bren thought, feeling a cold chill. "On what side?"

She held up a cautioning finger, listening.

"They likely do not expect to find us at close range with them. Depending on their objective—which may be, opportunistically, Kajiminda—our presence here may startle them. We have no word indicating Lord Machigi's whereabouts." A moment more of silence. "Banichi believes they are presently on the road we used. On our track."

The silence from downslope persisted—until a single shot from below added one more quandary to the debate.

What in hell were Machigi's forces doing—if not chasing them? They had a damned war going on in their district, and Machigi decided to make a grab for Kajiminda? Damn him!

Or could a coup have put somebody else in charge of Machigi's guard?

"Can you contact him, Jago-ji?" Damn the rules on Guild communication. "Tell his guard to stand off. We have enough going on here!"

"Banichi has the communications."

Twice damn it.

"Can you signal him to contact them?" he asked. "Tell them to stand off."

"Yes," she said, and relayed something in verbal code, and nodded.

"Nawari signals presence," she said with a deep and relieved sigh.

That was the dowager's guard.

And early. They had been on their way before Dur had shown up. Thank God.

The area was quiet, now. They were hearing nothing from the enemy.

But they had one shiny new problem.

Machigi.

And he'd promised to represent the man.

Where did *that* come in?

They could hike back to the van and deal with Machigi. They could hike to Kajiminda and have the Edi—

God. The Edi.

The Edi were holding Kajiminda. Machigi was on a road in a direct line with the spur to Kajiminda, with a likelihood of going there.

Do what? Go back to the van? Hope Machigi didn't open fire—*hope* that he could get Machigi to turn around and keep away from Kajiminda. Hope that it was even Machigi in charge of that lot of Taisigi—if they were Taisigi?

He didn't know if he could walk that far. The blisters had gotten bad. He wanted to take the damned boots off, but he knew the rocks and dry weeds would finish the job. He wanted to shed the damned vest, but this was certainly no place and no situation in which to do it.

Damn, he thought, weary and hurting. Just damn.

Things were going rapidly to hell.

Jago, however, had remained in active communication with Banichi. She took a look downslope and then urged them to move out.

Down. Into the open.

God, he thought. They were going to get shot. He levered himself up, however, and did it, with Lucasi holding his left arm and limping on the slope, and Jago holding Lucasi on the other side. It was a long, long descent toward the rocks that had sheltered their attackers. One lay dead there. A bloody trail led off to the east.

Something moved, a dark figure from around that corner that scared hell out of him. Algini had joined them, and Jago had immediately taken position by a towering rock, rifle aimed upslope.

Someone was coming down. But Jago just held her position. Banichi, Bren thought, and he was right. Banichi arrived as Jago turned her back to the rock and let him past—Banichi carrying a heavy lot of gear with him.

"Bren-ji," Banichi said pleasantly, as if they had met in the house. And then, utterly businesslike: "Nawari has sent for the bus. He will intercept it for us and hold it. But we have our other difficulty. Which direction, Bren-ji?"

A ride. Instead of a walk. But the question remained.

And not a question. Not with the whole west coast settlement in jeopardy.

"Both the Edi and Machigi know that bus," he said. "With it, we stand a chance, nadiin-ji, of getting their attention."

"And others'," Tano said grimly.

"Dare we contact Machigi's forces? Do you know if Machigi is actually with them."

"We have spoken to Tema," Banichi said.

Machigi's senior bodyguard. Then that question at least had an encouraging answer. Or at least a surer direction.

"Is there any clue," he asked, "what they want?"

"We have asked," Banichi said, "and they have—"

A distant rattle of small-arms fire came from beyond the rocks. To the south.

Machigi's position.

Dammit.

"What do they want?" Bren reprised the question.

"They say, to test the proposed treaty."

Right into an Edi district. With gunfire breaking out.

"A renegade convoy went that direction," Bren said. "Can you call them, Banichi? Can you find out who is firing?"

Banichi opened the bag he had brought with him and rapidly plugged his short-range communications into the larger unit.

He made the call. Or tried to. No response. Then something did get through. Banichi gave back a set of code words.

"They are engaged with the renegades," Banichi said. "But report a second direction of fire, indiscriminate."

The Edi. God. "They should not come farther west," Bren said. "Tell them to hold where they are."

Damn!

And they had to stop it.

There was racket outside. Cajeiri thought it was the yellow plane landing.

But it was not the plane. And he was not sitting in the hall any more. He was lying on the couch in in Great-grandmother's sitting-room, and Antaro and Jegari were standing nearby.

And the young lord of Dur, very impressive-looking in his brown leather coat, which Cajeiri so wanted—was standing on the other side of the room talking to Great-grandmother and Cenedi.

The plane had landed, and the young lord of Dur was here, and here he was, waking up on mani's couch looking stupid.

He got up, fast.

"Is my ribbon tied?" he whispered to his bodyguard, since he had been lying on it.

"Yes, nandi," Jegari said.

He knew his coat was wrinkled. He tried to put it to rights. Antaro and Jegari helped him, and he went very quietly over to where the young lord was talking to mani.

Mani was, however, in a cheerful mood.

"We shall retire for a while," mani said, "since my great-grandson has now come back to the living. Cenedi, you are to go off duty for a while. That is an order. Lord Geigi is abed and has not roused. Dur is surely exhausted."

"It has been a long day, aiji-ma," the young lord said. "But a good day. Excellent news."

"Nandi," Cajeiri said with a little bow. "Mani-ma. News?"

A gentle thump of the cane, which rarely left Great-grandmother's hands. "We have just dispatched the bus up from the village—where it has sat out this nuisanceful day. Nawari has called for it. He is in contact with nand' Bren's guard. There is another inconvenient circumstance reported, but we demand sleep before we deal with it."

"The bus is going to pick up nand' Bren!"

"That it is, young gentleman," Cenedi said. "But say nothing yet to nand' Toby. We do not have him back."

"May one ask?" he began, feeling wobbly on his feet. "May one ask, mani-ma—?"

"We do not yet have him back," mani repeated. "Do not trouble nand' Toby with what we cannot answer. But Nawari has called for the bus. He is in contact with the paidhi's guard. Go find your bed, young gentleman. It is not over. Sleep when you can."

"Mani," he said, bowed, and managed to walk decorously to the door and let Antaro open it for him.

He walked outside. So did the young lord from Dur, who politely bowed. And one had to apologize. One was embarrrassed, and distracted with worry, and full of questions nobody would answer.

"Nandi," he said to young Dur, remembering the yellow plane, and his father, and other scary circumstances. "One was waiting to see you."

"One understands so, nandi. One will be extremely honored to renew the acquaintance at leisure. Nandi."

Young Dur was clearly on another mission. And in a hurry. With a second bow, he headed down the hall toward the doors.

Everybody knew everything, and he just stood there feeling foolish and upset. "Nadiin," he said to Antaro and Jegari.

"Dur-nandi spotted nand' Bren," Antaro said, "and his aishid has just gotten to him. Nawari has not gotten there yet, but he has called for the bus; and your father's men are landing at the airport right now—we shall have help very soon, nandi."

That was good news. That was a great relief, on that matter.

"But the Taisigi followed nand' Bren," Jegari said. "And they are about to run right into the Edi. And the lord of Dur's plane is on his way, and some of the Gan people are with him. They are coming in at the airport, as soon as they are clear to land; and young Dur is just now on his way to the airport to explain the situation with the Edi when his father gets here—hoping the Gan people with his father can keep the Edi from attacking the Taisigi."

He was too tired. Things all jumbled up together. "So what is anybody going to do?" he said. "How can mani go to bed?"

"One doubts she actually will, nandi. One suspects she and Cenedi are going to be on the phone with your father."

"And tell him he should *do* something?" He was in favor of that. "We shall go to the security station." He could hardly walk, he was so tired. But walk he did.

And the first thing he heard was something about the bus.

They had just changed its orders. His father's men had intercepted it at the intersection, and they were sending it to the airport instead.

The security station contacted Cenedi. While they stood listening, Cenedi ordered the village to send the truck out; but that was evidently at Kajiminda.

They stood there very quietly, trying to be inconspicuous.

Then Cenedi showed up, not happy, no; so something was going to happen. Fast.

It was as fast as a human could walk, in deteriorating boots, with blisters, and the effects of bruised ribs, but Bren put on the best effort he had in him, wading through tall grass and forcing a path past obstinate, reaching brush. Guild leathers shed the burrs and stickery seeds. His clothes did not. He had a collection of them, of every available species.

He had had a drink of water, at least, from the canteen. Lucasi, with cracked lips, declined to share it, which won points with Jago: Jago shared her canteen with Lucasi, to the last, and that meant they were now entirely out of water . . . but in prospect of it once they intersected with the road, once they met up with the bus . . . they would be all right.

Fire was intermittent in the far distance. There seemed to be no separation of direction. It could be their angle on the situation. It could be that forces had closed on each other. They did not stay now for information.

Close call on a hidden hole; watch his damned feet, was what he most needed to do right now, and he'd been wit-wandering. Pay attention. Business at hand. He had to make it to the road, had to—

They had one locator going now, Jago's. He saw it blip occasionally. Damnable situation. The Guild jealously guarded its equipment, its communications, in particular. But the one contingency it hadn't reckoned with was a schism in its own ranks, equipment compromised all up and down. Nawari was risking his neck using the thing; Jago was on passive reception, he thought; but still only one of their units was on at all, for whatever reason. They had just that one assurance . . . and the promise of the bus, once they got to the road.

Until Banichi, carrying the communications long-distance unit slung from his shoulder, suddenly reached for his com and listened while he walked.

Then stopped, said something in code, and stood there listening for a very brief moment before he issued another string of code and shut down.

"The aiji's men have diverted the bus."

"Tell them that poses a problem," he said.

"One has said so," Banichi said. "And Nawari objected to the move. But the aiji's men have pulled rank."

Higher-ranking problem. God. An order from the dowager? A direct threat to her or to Cajeiri that they were not talking about, even on Guild channels?

They were stuck. They were damned well stuck without transport. Just the van, parked back on the road in the middle of the trouble.

And the shooting was still going on back there, faint in the distance.

"Damn," he said, and thought. "Can we get Najida?"

"One will try to arrange something," Banichi said, and made the call, in a string of code. They stood there, on the slant of a grassy hill, stalled, while Banichi talked in code. Guild business. Guild communications.

Damn, Bren said to himself. Damn. Damn.

"Nadi. This is the senior of the paidhi-aiji's aishid. One requests a person in authority on an urgent matter."

Banichi clicked off, exhaled, then indicated downslope. "We should keep going, Bren-ji. Nawari has contacted Kajiminda, trying to get them to send word to persons in the field. Meanwhile, he is calling Najida to ask for the village truck."

It was going to take time. But it was hope.

Bren just started walking. So did they all. Lucasi struggled hindmost, doing his best. Tano was lagging a bit, in God knew how much pain. Algini was carrying Tano's gear, and Jago had Lucasi's rifle.

A few blisters? Damned well nothing. If someone had the foresight, they might bring water. Maybe a medical kit, but they had that.

The truck. It wasn't going to be bulletproof. It wasn't going to have any aura of authority. But it had wheels. Wheels were better than—

Damn! Hole. He'd wrenched his ankle, not sprained it. Banichi seized his arm and kept him steady.

"One could carry you, Bren-ji."

"Only if I slow you down," he said, panting for breath but still going. "One can walk, Nichi-ji."

Damn, he said to himself. Damn. Damn.

And the firing was still going on, with, suddenly, a loud thump. Something had blown up.

He kept walking, kept walking. One hill was like another, and he trusted Banichi and Jago knew where they were going. They kept him between them, occasionally half-dragged him over a gap, which hurt the ribs, but it kept them going.

Finally, finally they had to half carry him down a steep slope, and Lucasi slipped and skidded a fair distance down the gravel before Algini overtook him, hauled him to his feet and got him moving, then climbed halfway back again to steer Tano down the same steep face.

But beyond the rocks, beyond a ridge of scrub, a moving column of dust in the distance marked a vehicle coming down an unseen road.

They forged ahead, around a thorn thicket, up a little gravely, rock-centered rise, and then—

Then they saw the Najida truck coming at all the speed it could muster.

It was too good, too fraught with possibilities for things going wrong, and Bren made a desperate effort to hurry. He made it down last the gravelly slope with help from Banichi and Jago and waited by the pebbled roadside, where dusty grass struggled to survive, edge of a sparse meadow on the flat far side of the road.

The feet hurt. God, they hurt.

But the truck came on and rumbled to a stop. It was a flatbed with removable sides, and, thank God, the sides were in their sockets.

And Nawari was there with two of his unit, and Lord Geigi's bodyguards—all of them. The driver was one of Nawari's men—whoever had gotten the truck to Nawari was not with them. It was all Guild, all in dusty black leather and armed, a formidable force on the Guild scale of things.

"One is glad to see you, Wari-ji," Bren said, "one is very glad. This is no safe venture. We have to get to the crossroads, next after the Kajiminda road—" His voice cracked. Banichi took over and gave orders with more precision, he was sure, and Jago pulled him around to the other door of the truck.

"Tano should ride in the cab," he said. "One can manage back there."

"Hush, Bren-ji," Jago said, opened the door, and shoved him inside. "Is there water, nadi?" she asked the driver.

"A can in the back," the answer came, and Bren thought to himself, *Just hurry*. But he could hear everybody climbing aboard behind, and then Jago came back immediately with somebody's canteen and gave it to him.

He didn't argue. He drank two good gulps and a third, and was going to pass it back, but she was gone, climbing aboard, as the driver took off the brake.

The truck rolled forward, accelerated.

Bren had another sip of water and wiped his mouth. His hand came away smeared and gritty, and he rubbed his face. No razor. Stubble he never let show. His clothes had taken on the color of the landscape and were stuck together with burrs here and there . . . he presented no sane-looking figure, he was sure. He had another, more conservative drink, dehydrated, lips cracked, sunburned, he could feel it, and too rattled, now that he sat on a padded seat with a canteen in his hand, to manage a coherent thought or lay any sort of plan for how he was going to approach the situation ahead.

Najida truck. The Edi at least knew the truck.

The Taisigi didn't.

"We shall go to the Edi side," he told the driver, one of the dowager's men. And asked, "How were things at the house?"

"Holding, nandi," was all the man could tell him.

19

The driver asked for all the speed the old truck could muster, raising dust from the graveled area and traveling brushy meadow road at the risk of its suspension. Bren had no way to communicate with his bodyguard. They were back there laying their own plans; he had no idea what those plans were or whether they were able to communicate with Najida and with Machigi.

He grew light-headed from sheer exhaustion. He was braced bolt upright in his seat by the cursed vest, without which he would not be coming home at all, and he could feel the foot in the split boot swelling. His body wanted just to shut down for a few hours, and he couldn't afford that. He had to be mentally sharp. Had to talk to the Edi, for starters, and there was no guarantee the Edi had any sort of unified command.

God, he had to get his wits about him.

Fuel was going to hold out. They had enough. That was a positive.

But the brain was going.

Parts scattered when he tried to analyze them, irretrievable.

But out the windows, the land looked familiar. He began to know when they were nearing the Kajiminda intersection by the shape of a solitary evergreen, the grass, and the pale color of the stone. They were getting near. The gunfire—he couldn't hear. The truck rattled and thumped.

The intersection came in view, where trees were in greater

evidence, a small woods in the distance, which here covered both sides of the road.

And now the driver was talking to someone on short-range.

Then gunfire was audible, even over the racket of the truck. The driver made the turn on a track through the woods and suddenly blew the horn. Repeatedly. It scared the hell out of him—he wasn't expecting that. But it wasn't the kind of move enemies would make, blowing the horn like fury while blazing down the middle of the road.

People came out of the woods onto the road ahead of them, carrying rifles pointed aloft, not aiming at them, thank God. The driver pulled up short of them, and Bren opened his door.

Banichi was faster, reaching him before he had to jump to the ground; and Jago was right there.

So were Lord Geigi's men. They came up even with the door, and one of them shouted out in another language—the Edi language, Bren realized suddenly. It must be. The attitude changed, visible surprise. And he walked out near them.

"Nadiin, neighbors! Cease fire! Cease fire! We have news!"

He was unmistakable on the mainland. He traded on that. He was their neighbor. And Lord Geigi's men spoke the language. That was beyond an asset. It shocked the four Edi and got the rifles aimed at the ground. It got them face to face in a far calmer mode.

Talk was hot and heavy for a moment between the Edi and Lord Geigi's bodyguard. Bren heard his own title referenced, and the dowager. And Lord Geigi.

There was objection, and Machigi's name figured in it, angrily.

Geigi's men answered, in strong terms.

"Neighbors," Bren said. "Neighbors, listen to me. There is more than one forces involved. One is a renegade Guild force, one you see here, and there is, yes, Machigi, who is here to stop the renegade Guild."

"Who are these renegades?" they wanted to know.

"Murini's men." He had a succinct answer for that one, that ought to tell them everything. "They have committed crimes. They have laid the bloody knife at Machigi's door, but of recent offenses, he is not guilty. At the dowager's request, he is attacking them, with Guild regulars at his command."

"He is in our territory!"

"He is killing *your* enemies. He is killing the people who bombed the road and kidnapped one of your children, nadiin-ji! Let the Grandmother of the Edi and the Grandmother of the Ragi solve it. This business has too many sides. Let the Grandmothers have the say! You have to stop shooting!"

"We will not let him on our land!" one shouted.

Geigi's men said something in the Edi language, then, that involved the Grandmother, and heated words went back and forth, not one of which he could understand.

The guns here stayed still, but the firing beyond the curve of the road, farther into the encroaching woods, was still going on, echoing off the rocky heights to the left.

"Nandi," Geigi's Guild senior said then, in a low voice, "go. They will not be persuaded. Get back to the truck."

"Bren-ji," Banichi said, meaning business.

Damn, he thought. His bodyguard wanted him out of here. Geigi's did. He took a step toward the men, hit a sore angle with his foot and limped inelegantly.

It hurt, damn it. Several things did.

Not least, the prospect of seeing the whole situation gone to hell. "Neighbors," he shouted in Ragi, and pointed toward the road. "Off in that direction you have the sort of Guild who has done you immeasurable harm over two hundred years, the same element who backed Murini, the same element who fled Tabini-aiji, ran into the Marid and encouraged the Senji and the Dojisigi to actions against you. At their backs, beyond that woods, you have one Marid lord who is as angry with them as you are and who, if you stop shooting for an hour, will obligingly push these renegades right into your laps, after which time you can open fire to your hearts' content. If you want to settle with your *real* enemies, listen to your neighbor, who has talked with the lord of the Taisigi and gotten his cooperation. You have heard the facts from me, you have heard them from Lord Geigi's guard, and you four do not have the authority to decide life or death for the Edi people! Go as fast as you can and tell the elders in charge *exactly* what I said, and we will hold this road for you. Tell the elders come back here and defend *this* place, and let the Guild with Lord Machigi drive your enemies this way, do you understand me? Does this make sense to you? And then you will kindly oblige me by *not* shooting the Taisigi, while your elders and the aiji-dowager work out an agreement that will save your land! Do you hear me?"

There was a small space of silence. One said something in his own language, but it sounded like a question; and Lord Geigi's men answered in that language in no milder tone, something involving Najida, Kajiminda, and the paidhi-aiji. Then they shouted an order, and the young men took off running, back into the woods, guns and all.

God, it was all he had in him. He was spent. He wanted to sit down right where he was.

"Bren-ji," Banichi said, laying a hand on his shoulder. "You have done what you could do. At this point *you* are the person the renegades would most like to lay hands on. More to the point, the word is going out that you are here. The Edi are not a disciplined force. Some may fall back. Some may panic. We shall hold this place, up on the heights. Can you drive the truck?"

"I shall not," he said. "Not leaving you here, no."

"The renegades have failed to get past Machigi," Banichi said. "They have the Edi between them and Kajiminda and somewhat between them and Separti Township. And then there is this road, back they way they arrived. The Edi will not take orders in any organized way, and if they start to take losses and panic, we are too few to hold what comes behind them."

"I can make them listen."

"You have no experience of this situation, Bren-ji. Your bodyguard advises you abandon this area, and fall back. If we have to, we will draw back to Kajiminda."

"Afoot?" he shot back. "No, nadiin-ji. If you have to leave here, you will need a little speed, will you not?"

Banichi looked exasperated.

"Tell Machigi I am here," he said. "Tell Machigi to push them if we can't organize the Edi to do it. The Edi will shoot what shows up first, am I right?"

"We can hold that," Banichi said, with a wave of his hand toward the rocky side of the road, and went to instruct the driver. The truck started up, pulled over near the rocks, and backed in, positioning itself for a run for Kajiminda. Everybody aboard the truckbed began getting off.

Bren found a small outlier of those rocks, next to a stand of brush, and sat down with a wince from the damned vest. His bodyguard was off giving directions. Geigi's men positioned themselves off in the brushy outskirts of the woods, Nawari and his crew off in the rocks near the truck.

He just sat, and he wished he had the canteen he'd left in the truck, but he was not inclined to walk after it.

He was done, utterly done. He rested his head on his hands and was so dizzy he thought he might fall asleep where he sat. Three forces were going to collide and start shooting, and he could just sit here on his rock, undisturbed, unnoticed. That would be good. Just no one to notice him for at least an hour. He could sleep.

But the fire kept up, sporadic, even lazy. God, how long could they keep at it without running out of ammunition? They'd get down to throwing rocks at each other. Damned fools.

He came very close to sleep.

Then a whistle sounded in the woods, and a voice, calling out in accented Ragi, told him something had changed.

He started to get up. It wasn't graceful. He grabbed hold of the brush one-handed and hauled himself up to a wide-legged brace before he got his balance.

A group of Edi, five in number, in hunting camoflage, came down the road, calling out and stopping where one of their side had planted three stacked rocks.

Good idea, those rocks. They got attention. And Geigi's men went to them and talked to them, and guns were in safe carry when they came in, properly quiet and respectful.

Bren started in their direction, but Geigi's men waved them off again, a little back up the road.

Sit there, that was. And talk to anybody coming in. A welcoming committee. It was amazingly genteel.

One only hoped they got their information straight—a whispering game, one to the next. But it was what they could do.

He was on his feet. He limped over across the road to the truck, opened the door and got the canteen.

Jago came around the end of the truck. "Best you stay with the truck, Bren-ji. We are organizing."

"Yes," he said. "One will, Jago-ji." He hoped Banichi wasn't mad at him. He couldn't even figure out whether he deserved it. If they were going to get killed, he really didn't want anybody mad at him.

He climbed up to the seat of the truck and sat down, closing the door mostly, and very quietly, and had a small drink of water.

He was too damned tired, he thought, to be properly scared. He was scared in a numb sort of way that was not much different from acute terror. But he was here, and he had to be here. Worst was knowing he'd done everything he could do.

It got very still for a while. He heard Tano talking to someone, he thought, on com. Maybe talking to Machigi's people. Maybe there was a code for *Watch out for our allies once you get close to them. Please just shoot at uniforms.*

That wasn't too comforting, either.

His bodyguard and Geigi's and the dowager's were scattered out. Lucasi and Tano were still on the truck, which argued that

Banichi had taken his plan for a fast retreat, those being the two that weren't able to sprint for it, but he wished people were a little closer to the truck.

More of the Edi showed up. Once, through the driver's rolled-down window, he heard a scattering of whistles and began to think, they *can* communicate. They *are* communicating.

That was hopeful. That was hopeful in a major way. But he wasn't hearing the firing nearly as often now.

Something was going on. There were just the whistles.

The Edi were moving.

Moving back.

Then a distant fire opened up.

That—that might be Machigi.

And one couldn't damned well hear. One couldn't get a direction on it. Bren opened the door, slid down to the step-down and held on to the door, getting down. He didn't want to distract anybody.

He just wanted—

"Bren-ji!" Tano said from the rear of the truck. He turned around, saw Tano leaning on the sidewall of the truck, pointing off to the northwest. Lucasi struggled to the same vantage with a thump that rocked the truck, as gunfire rattled steadily in the distance.

"What is it?" he asked.

Tano pressed the com to his ear, talking to someone. "The bus!" Lucasi cried. "The bus is on the road, nandi!"

He still saw nothing. But he trusted atevi hearing. He stood holding on to the truck door, hoping the engine block was some shield against anything coming his direction.

They had the bus, they lost the bus—somebody outranked them and took it from them. And now it came back.

Without a damned word.

"Bren-ji," Tano said. "Tabini-aiji is coming."

God. He wouldn't. An absolute cold chill went through him. Tabini. Risk *himself*. Risk *everything*.

And if Tabini came charging in here with the Edi *and* Machigi *and* the renegades going at each other and none of the latter respecting the aishidi'tat, he didn't lay bets on which side would attack whom.

"Tano." He made his way to the side of the truck so he could look up at both of them, the resources he had. "Tell Tabini-aiji the situation. Inform him. One doesn't care who hears at this point. It is not the time for him to come in unaware."

"Yes," Tano said, and: "We have code we can use, nandi."

God, God, God. He could hear the engine now. And the gunfire was still going on out there.

If Tabini came here to repudiate the deal with Machigi, everything could collapse. If Tabini came here thinking he was going to deal with the Edi, he needed to know where Machigi was. It was a damned mess, was what it was.

He needed to haul his own aishid out of this and let them explain. Right now it was just Tano. He thought about hitting the truck horn; but they might think he was in jeopardy and risk themselves trying to get back.

But atevi hearing. They were going, any minute now, to hear the bus. *He* could. They were going to know. There was only one motor in all Sarini Province that sounded like that.

He stood beside the truck and listened to Tano say words that made no sense, and all the while the situation was getting closer on both sides, and gunfire and heavier rounds were going off, the latter shaking the earth. Inside the bus, it was so damned soundproofed it was unlikely anybody heard it; but he couldn't judge. It was getting hot here, getting closer to their position, and from his vantage he didn't know how many of the Edi had gotten back here and how many were lagging back firing at the renegades or at Machigi. The whistles had stopped. The gunfire was steady.

"Do the others know?"

Tano gave him a troubled look. And then said, "Yes, nandi. One has called them. They are coming back."

Back. Where in hell were they? Doing what?

He heard the whistles again from off in the woods. And gunfire. *And* the bus. He limped back to the side of the truck, to the front fender, where he had something of a vantage.

More whistles, increasing in complexity. The forest across the road was alive with it. And of all people they could reach with communications, the Edi were not on the list.

Damn, he thought. And heard an alarming burst of gunfire, and saw movement in the trees.

He was not in a good position. A shot kicked up the sand out in the road, and then a volley answered it. He retreated to the side of the truck and saw Lucasi leaning on the roof of the cab, with a rifle, and Tano, one-handed, similarly bracing himself with his sidearm.

He took out his own gun. Thumbed the safety off. More than his aishid had heard the bus. The opposition must be hearing it. So, depending on distance, might Machigi.

The bus had taken the turn. It was coming up the road now, raising a column of dust above the trees.

A column suddenly interrupted.

"Nandi," Tano said. "Guild is deploying. They instruct us to hold position."

Hold position. There was no damned way they could move, except to run the truck straight through the Edi.

Who likewise knew that motor. The bus refueled and garaged in Najida village. They'd think it came from Najida estate. They'd hear it as allies moving in. They'd expect Guild under Cenedi's orders.

Close. Close enough to let them use common sense. He heard the engine rev up again. It was coming.

"Nandi," Tano said again. "Banichi has warned Machigi."

Tano's partner and Banichi and Jago were out there using short-range to reach Machigi—spotting for them, it might well be. Doing a little damage of their own if they got the chance. It made sense. But he wanted them out of there. They were, like him, like Tano, running on empty. They didn't have it in them to move as fast as they needed, think as sharply as they needed. He wanted them back, dammit, before something happened . . .

The bus came around the bend of the snaking road, full tilt, and applied the brakes. He stood staring at it as it sat there, huge, red and black ,and shiny under a coating of dust. He couldn't see through the window tint. But they'd see him.

Then a voice like doom thundered out: "This is a Guild operation. Guild forces are dispersed in the area. All civilians, cease fire and fall back behind this point, for your own safety. This is a Guild operation under the auspices of Tabini-aiji, under the law of the aishidi'tat. Cease fire and fall back to this position."

Nobody in the woods could fail to hear that. He hadn't known the bus had a loudspeaker. He'd bought it already made from Shejidan, he'd ordered it in by rail, he'd traveled on it. He knew it had tinted windows, a refrigerator, and every passenger comfort. But he hadn't known the driver had a loudspeaker. That was a surprise.

The strength just started to go out of him. The Guild wanted the damned fight? The Guild could have it. Just—if Tabini was going to take action against Machigi, he had to protest it. He'd agreed to represent Machigi. He had to go do it.

He headed for the bus as the doors opened. He heard a racket behind him—Tano, getting down from the truckbed, his ears told him; but his eyes were for the bus door and the uniformed Guildsmen coming out of it. Tabini's personal guard, those men.

Tabini came next, in immaculate black brocade, black lace at the cuffs—that pale gold stare that could convince a man he was a damned fool to argue.

He gave his own back, not about to start with any apology for what he'd done. He stopped at the requisite distance and gave a short, correct bow. "Nand' aiji. One is grateful. One is also obliged to request your forces use caution. Machigi-aiji has engaged the Guild's enemies. One also—" He ran out of air, grew downright dizzy, damn the restriction of the vest. "—has Guild deployed in support of Machigi."

Tabini said, expressionless, "And what outcome does Lord Machigi want?"

"He wants to ally with the aiji-dowager under the terms she has presented him. These terms are—" Another breath. He was aware of Tano at his back and another presence, which had limped there. Somehow Lucasi had gotten down from the truck and come with Tano. Now he heard another. He was not sure which one, but he did not breach etiquette to turn and look. "These terms are that he take firm governance of the Marid as a whole. By the Guild action, he will hold that position. He will ally with the aiji-dowager in a trade agreement. He will shift his routes eastward. He will expect the Edi people—to become neighbors within the aishidi'tat. Under your governance. That is his position. The Marid—will be a member state—of the aishidi'tat . . ." Someone else had arrived at his back. Two sets of footsteps. They were all there. He got a breath. He was getting there. "One asks—one asks support—from your office."

"We want you back," Tabini said grimly. "And we have you, paidhi-aiji. You have delivered his position. Now, by the same antiquated custom, you represent *us*. And we want your uncompromised opinion. What do *you* think we should do about Machigi?"

"One found him—intelligent. A strong leader. Sensible." His heartbeat had been going strong. Now it began to get out of hand. "You should deal with him. He has problems in his district. Poverty. Traditions. The aiji-dowager—" He was going to need to sit down. He got a breath. Remembered he was standing there like a fool with a very illegal pistol in hand, dealing with Tabini, whose guard was hair-triggered. He wanted to put it back into his pocket, but any move with it could have Tabini's guard reacting. He gave a little bow, having completely lost his train of thought. "Deal with him, aiji-ma. His paths go several ways from here. Be careful with him. Treat him well. I want to put this gun away, aiji-ma. I need to put the safety on."

"Help him," Tabini said sharply, and immediately Jago was on his right, taking the gun, and Banichi on his left with his hand inside his elbow.

"Get him on the bus," Tabini said.

"I have not been injured," Bren objected. "One is just a little dizzy, aiji-ma. One will do quite well—" They paid him no heed at all and took him toward the bus door. "Is the aiji-dowager safe?" he asked.

"My scheming grandmother is perfectly well," Tabini said. "Get aboard. Sit down. Nadi, get the paidhi a drink."

Alcohol would not do well at all. He did not intend to drink it. But Banichi and Jago put him into a seat, and then Algini helped Lucasi up the steps: Tano made it under his own power, but barely.

"We shall leave the Najida truck to transport the Edi wounded," he heard Banichi say, and Tabini came back aboard, and the door shut definitively.

"We need to contact the Taisigi," he said to Jago, who had sat down beside him in a largely empty bus.

"That will be done, Bren-ji," she said, and just then the drink arrived, orange, which he wanted more than anything; he tasted it carefully, and found no hint of alcohol. So he sipped it, a hit of sugar, moisture, and a relief to his throat. It was almost beyond him to hold it. But the plush seat had a drink holder. And a cushion for his head. He was filthy, head to foot. His hands left muddy marks on the sweating glass.

"Everybody needs orange," he said. "Tell them that."

"That can be arranged." Tabini leaned on the seat, as the bus started up. "Quite the storm you raised, paidhi. You try to drown my son, you invade the Marid—when you come back to Shejidan, kindly manage things more quietly."

"One is grateful," he said in an unsteady voice, "one is exceedingly grateful for your understanding, aiji-ma."

"Ha!" Tabini said, slapped the seat back, and walked up to take hold of the upright pole beside the driver, while his bodyguard moved back into the seats. The bus pulled up beside the truck, backed around.

"The equipment," Tano said. "The paidhi's—"

Notes were in the baggage, Bren thought.

"Hold the bus a moment, aiji-ma," Algini said, and went back down the steps toward the truck. A handful of Edi stood in view of the open door. They said nothing, just leaned on their rifles and watched.

A moment or two more and Algini brought the baggage onto the bus and left it on the bus steps.

More fruit juice arrived. Algini took one and sat down next to Tano.

Bren heaved a sigh. Thought about unfastening the coat and the damned vest, but it was beyond filthy, and he was, and he told himself if he just didn't move for the length of time it took to get to Kajiminda or Najida or wherever they were going, he would be fine.

He drank another sip. Two. And set the drink back in the holder and let his eyes shut. Jago was beside him. Banichi and the kid were aboard, Banichi talking to the senior of Tabini's bodyguard, somewhere back there; Algini and Tano were in the seat opposite, and they were going somewhere safer, aboard a powerful huge bus that had left a sizeable force of Guild in Tabini's personal service.

He'd done as much as he could do. He rested his head against the backrest and shut his eyes, which began a short, confusing slide toward sleep.

Safe, he said to himself. Whatever happened. Safe. He'd gotten his people out. That was what he knew for certain.

20

Mani and Father were shouting at each other. That was not unusual.

It did make it a good time for one to be out of range. And Cajeiri did not want to go back to his rooms, where he would hear nothing at all, and he was not supposed to be downstairs in the area where nand' Siegi was operating on Tano.

He had been down there when Lucasi came down to see Veijico, but he had decided that it was better to stay outside and not interfere. Veijico was happy, and Lucasi was happy; in fact, there was happiness just all over the house, for most everybody. The staff had gotten nand' Bren back, and they were running like mad trying to prepare Lord Geigi's rooms for Father to stay the night. Lord Geigi was in the security station relaying messages to his bodyguard, who were still off where the fighting had been—they were waiting for the bus to come back and get them.

He and nand' Toby and Barb-daja had all been outside when the bus had come in the first time, with Father and his guard, and nand' Bren and Banichi and Jago and all; and nand' Bren had walked off the bus on his own, limping just a little and incredibly dirty. Nand' Bren had bowed a hello to him—to *him*, right after his father had passed, and he had bowed back and asked nand' Bren if he was well, which had been a stupid question.

"I have someone to see you," nand' Bren had said, and Algini had just started to help Lucasi down from the bus.

"Nandi," Lucasi had called him, and had bowed very contritely, and had not even asked questions.

"Your sister will be very happy," he had said.

And meanwhile nand' Bren hugged Toby and even hugged Barb-daja, which did not surprise anybody who had been much around humans. And Barb-daja had made a fuss, and Toby had said Bren looked like hell, but he knew nand' Toby meant it kindly.

Besides, it was fairly true. Nand' Bren was a mess. And he limped on, with his bodyguard, and with nand' Toby and all, and mani had met Father in the hall, and then nand' Bren.

"Pish, pish," she had said, waving him away. "Your guard will debrief. Go. Go, paidhi. Well done! Extremely well done!"

"Aiji-ma," nand' Bren said, with a bow. "Thank you."

"Pish! Thank *us?* It seems rather the other way about, does it not? Ignore the damage, paidhi-ji. We shall see it set to rights. Shall we not, Grandson?"

That, to Father. Who was already scowling and probably thinking of things to say. Probably mani had been thinking of things to say for several hours, too. Cajeiri would not go into that room for anything.

Lucasi had gone straight downstairs to see Veijico, and he had gone down to talk to both of them, but nand' Siegi had nabbed Lucasi after he had no more than told his sister he was there. Nand' Sieigi had said he was a hazard to health and to go bathe, and he was going to take x-rays once he had gotten through with Tano. And nand' Siegi had taken Tano right in hand, but Tano said he did not think it was that serious; he thought Algini had gotten all the pieces of the shrapnel out.

So Tano was getting x-rays.

So all the pieces were falling into place, with all the excitement over, and he was glad about it. He was tired of being scared. He wanted to have his aishid, and to get some sleep in his own bed, and not to have his father lecturing him about coming here and causing trouble.

Besides, he had not caused the trouble. The trouble had *been* here. He had just helped turn it up.

Lord Geigi was at the security station getting the news from his aishid, who were still out where nand' Bren had been; and so was Nawari and several of mani's guard. They said they had the Edi all on one side and the Taisigi separated from them by a number of real Guild, and that Machigi was going to go back to a hunting station just across the border and stay there running his government. Meanwhile, Lord Machigi was going to write a letter to Lord Geigi and ask Lord Geigi to settle agreements with him.

Geigi's nephew Baiji was not going to be any happier. He was still locked in nand' Bren's basement.

But Geigi said he would look forward to the letter, and he told his aishid to tell Machigi's aishid, which was how things were done.

It was going to be different if Lord Machigi turned out to make an agreement with mani and with Lord Geigi *and* with his father, because the Marid had been at war with the aishidi'tat over and over, and Machigi had sponsored Murini, or at least been somewhere involved in what happened.

He was not sure his father would forget that. *He* was going to have trouble forgetting it. But if mani thought Lord Machigi could be useful, and if Lord Machigi had come in to stop the renegades, who were, after all, Murini's supporters in the Guild, and if *his* aishid had been working with the regular Guild all along, the way they seemed to have done, then there was a lot more to find out about Lord Machigi—who, after all, was the only lord in the northern Marid who was still alive. Lord Machigi was not stupid. So he could be a good ally or a bad enemy.

That was something more to remember.

"Are you going to forgive Lord Machigi, nandi?" he asked Lord Geigi.

Lord Geigi looked down at him. "One will be very interested

to see this letter," he said. "Such serious questions, young gentleman."

"But you will forgive him," he said, because it occurred to him he knew a lot about Lord Geigi, "because you are mani's closest ally. But you have known nand' Bren longer."

"One has, indeed," Lord Geigi said, and laughed as if he had thought of some funny secret. "One owes him. One owes him, and one owes your great-grandmother *and* your father, who made such a judgment of *me*, in years gone by. Old adversaries, finding they have interests in common, can make agreements, young lord."

"You were never an enemy."

"Oh, if I had stayed married to my Marid wife, who knows. I could have had a Dojisigi son. All in intrigue against the Taisigi. One wonders if Lord Machigi has any inkling of it. Perhaps one should broach the matter."

One was confused. One was lost again in the tangles of adult politics.

"But you are nand' Bren's ally."

"That I am, young gentleman. And yours."

He was not sure Lord Geigi was not teasing him, talking to him as if he was a child. But then he thought, no, he means it.

He gave a very serious bow, thinking about his father and the new baby and suddenly thinking it was not the baby that threatened him. It was his connections, his mother's quarreling family and uncle Tatiseigi, that made him important in the central regions; and he had mani to the east, and she might even get the Marid for an ally. And Dur was a connection, too, at least the young lord was.

But Lord Geigi was the space station. And the West. And the Edi.

He decided to take it very seriously and bowed quite properly. "I shall remember that, nandi. And you may count on me, someday when it matters. Remember it."

"I shall, young lord," Lord Geigi said. "I shall, indeed."

*   *   *

There was no salvaging the clothes, least of all the bullet-frayed vest, which had gone mud colored and sweat stained; they had gone off with his valets, and Bren had strictly instructed them not even to attempt to resurrect them. He sat in the depth of the bath, up to his chin in hot water, which had stung the blisters and the cuts and scrapes, but he ignored that. He had Toby opposite him and another guest of the house, the gallant young lord of Dur, who was quite pleased to be invited along. An off-schedule snack had arrived—Cook was feeding anyone who was interested, and his aishid, he was sure, was beyond interested. He couldn't eat but a few bites; he had a little tea, a little fruit juice, and made slow work of half an atevi-scale sandwich, while Toby put down a whole one and young Dur had two.

Toby had a broken rib along with the other damage—the latter in waterproof bandage. "We're twins," Toby declared, a bad joke. "But thank God they had you wear that vest."

"If they hadn't I wouldn't be here," he said, and changed to Ragi for young Dur's benefit. "My brother says we match."

Dur politely laughed. "One is very glad you wore the vest," he said, the identical remark.

"My bodyguard is going to insist, one fears. One at least hopes for one made to my size."

"One hopes for days in which one need not take such precautions," young Dur said.

"Have you phoned your father? One is extremely grateful he has troubled himself, and one would not wish him to make undue haste."

"One has, indeed, nand' paidhi. But he has a dinner invitation, and he looks forward to it. The Gan leaders, likewise."

"Dur's father," Bren translated, for Toby, "is still coming. Dinner with the aiji and the aiji-dowager and Lord Geigi. The kitchen is probably beside itself. The Gan. And the Edi. We're going to have to put up tables in the garden, if there's anything left of it."

"It's a little messy out there."

"We'll manage," he said. He was vastly content.

Dinner—he wasn't sure he could stay awake through. He'd try. Having a tableful of Ragi trying to maintain decorum with a tableful of Edi and Gan folk intent on having a discussion—and a visiting northern lord—was going to be interesting. A good thing Machigi had taken the prudent course and pulled back to the hunting station, where he was not going to be part of the immediate negotiations. Machigi had his own mess to clean up. Interesting if he could manage it.

He had his notes. From that bag Algini had swept up off the truck.

And Machigi wanted him back.

Tabini did.

Ilisidi did.

It was a good thing to be wanted.

Even in mutually incompatible directions.

He had another sip of orangelle. Still without alcohol. No painkiller, not yet. He wanted his brain in good order when he sat down at the table, wherever they found to put it.

He wasn't going to be able to move in the morning. That was guaranteed.

But tonight—given a nap in his own bed in the meanwhile—he'd manage.